Murder 101

Faye Kellerman is the author of twenty-eight novels, including twenty *New York Times* bestselling mysteries that feature the husband-and-wife team of Peter Decker and Rina Lazarus. She has also penned two bestselling short novels with her husband, *New York Times* bestselling author Jonathan Kellerman and recently teamed up with her daughter Aliza to cowrite a young adult novel, *Prism*. She lives with her husband in Los Angeles, California, and Santa Fe, New Mexico.

D0324423

Also by Faye Kellerman

With Jonathan Kellerman

With Aliza Kellerman

FAYE KELLERMAN

Murder 101

HARPER

Harper
An imprint of HarperCollins*Publishers*
77–85 Fulham Palace Road,
Hammersmith, London W6 8JB

www.harpercollins.co.uk

This paperback edition 2014
1

First published in the USA in 2014 by
William Morrow, an imprint of HarperCollins*Publishers*

A catalogue record for this book
is available from the British Library

ISBN: 978 0 00 757989 1

Set in Meridien by Palimpsest Book Production Limited,
Falkirk, Stirlingshire

Printed and bound in Spain by CPI, Barcelona

To Jonathan
And to Lila, Oscar, Eva, and Judah

CHAPTER ONE

As he inspected the final work, holding it up to a bare bulb, he was blinded by the array of brilliant hues in every color of the rainbow. The opalescent glass was lovely, but it was the handblown clear glass in the emerald greens, the ruby reds, and the sapphire blues that gave the piece its pop, casting tinted rays of spectacular light onto his walls and furniture.

The stained glass was first-rate: the execution of the piece . . . not so much. The caning between the shards was sloppy and the little painting that was on the glass was one step above Art 101. Not that anyone would notice the difference between the genuine and its imposter in its current dark and dank location. Certainly the moronic caretakers weren't a problem. And in this case, making the switch was a walk in the park because the work could be concealed in a briefcase. His toolbox was bigger and bulkier. But he'd done it before. He could do it again.

Sometimes he didn't even know why he bothered with the small stuff. Maybe just to keep his brain alive because this little bit of intrigue was nothing compared to his future plans. But to pull off something that big took time and he was fine with that. He'd wait patiently.

The bells were tolling two in the morning: it was time. First, with a makeup sponge, he painted his face brown. Next, he called Angeline on a throwaway cell and told her to wait outside, that he'd be over in five. Carefully, he swathed the piece in bubble wrap and then slid it into his leather briefcase. His tools were already in the car.

He checked his watch again. Then he slipped on his black gloves and covered his head and face with a black ski cap. Next came the black scarf around his neck: good camouflage but also necessary in the cold. A last-minute check in the mirror and what he saw looked perfect. He was nothing more than an inky shadow floating through the night.

Just the way he wanted it.

Be careful what you wish for.

After three decades of police work as a detective lieutenant in Los Angeles, Peter Decker had always imagined a quieter existence in his sixties, something in between retirement and an eighty-hour workweek that had been his former life. He knew that with his active mind and his penchant for restlessness that he wasn't ready to hang up his shield just yet. In his brain, the ideal job was something with a regular schedule with nights and weekends off.

The good news was he now had a manageable desk job, fielding calls that centered on senior citizens with chest pains, missing pets, and controlling drunken teenagers following Saturday night binges. In the last six months, the closest he had come to real crimes were the calls concerning several house break-ins where the burglars pilfered electronics—cell phones, laptops, and tablets. None of the thefts were surprising because Greenbury was a town that swelled with students in September and then cleared them out by June.

The Five Colleges of Upstate New York was a consortium of liberal arts schools, each with its own identity. One specialized in math and science, another in business and econ. A third was a girls' school and the fourth focused on fine arts, theater, and languages. The fifth college—Duxbury—was ranked as an elite academy founded in 1859 a few years before the Civil War. The sprawling campuses made up of brick and stone buildings sat on hundreds of acres of dense, bucolic landscape: parks, natural springs, and open forest. It was a world unto itself with its own police force. That made Decker's job as a cop and detective even more limited.

There were very few issues of town and gown because Greenbury's population consisted of retirees and working-class families. They owned most of the independent stores and restaurants that fueled the town's economy. The students, by and large, were from swanky homes and were pretty well behaved even if they often partied at all hours of the night.

The Old Town of Greenbury was a typical college burg with streets named Harvard, Yale, and Princeton. There were blocks of franchise stores: Outsider Sportswear, Yogurtville, Rentaday Car Service, Quikburger. It had a triplex movie theater, a half-dozen cheap dress boutiques, several nail salons, bike rentals, a health food store, and lots and lots and lots of bars, grills, and restaurants. Every popular cuisine was represented, including a kosher eat-in or take-out storefront café that Rina frequented almost daily.

Decker thought about his wife.

If anyone would have adjustment problems, he thought

3

it would be Rina. Instead, she had adapted far quicker than he had. Immediately she threw herself into the local Hillel that serviced all five colleges. She offered to host Friday night dinners in her house for any student who was interested. When too many students became interested, the dinners were moved to a catering hall at the Hillel. The meals were prepared by the local students, but Rina was there almost every Thursday and Friday pitching in with the cooking and baking. When that still didn't fill up her time, she volunteered her services as a Chumash teacher if Hillel would provide a room. She posted a sign-up sheet. She expected five kids if she was lucky.

She got seven.

Word got around and a month later, she had eighteen kids. They asked her if she was willing to teach a class in elementary Hebrew. She agreed. Most of the times, her evenings were busier than his. Decker hated to admit it but he was bored. It was bad enough that his days were stultifying but then the captain, Mike Radar, asked him to pair up with the *kid* and take him into the field, and the days became even longer and even more stultifying.

Tyler McAdams, aged twenty-six and Harvard educated, was five ten, one fifty, with hazel eyes and dark brown hair that was expertly cut. His aquiline features included a Roman nose. He wasn't slight, but he wasn't muscular, either. He looked like what he was—an Ivy League kid from a wealthy family. His clothes were expensive, his overcoat was cashmere, and he rotated gold watches on his wrist with the days of the week.

Within a very short period of time, McAdams had managed to alienate everyone in the department with his endless carping that he was smarter, better looking, and better educated than anyone around. There was truth in his complaints—he was smart and good-looking—but his constant whining diminished any of his discernible assets. McAdams claimed that he had originally taken up the job because he was curious about police work even though he had been accepted to Harvard Law. He decided to defer the acceptance for a few years, figuring the job would give him a leg up from any of the other wonks and dorks.

Or so was his story.

Decker didn't press him; he wasn't interested.

McAdams's hiring had been nepotism. His father was a major contributor to Duxbury College. The dean had called in a favor from the mayor, Logan Brettly, who, in turn, called in a favor from Radar. McAdams had no experience in law enforcement, but he didn't need it because nothing much happened that required extensive know-how.

So Decker agreed to let the kid ride with him, listening to him bitch and moan. This time he was complaining about their next visit on the roster: a senior with chest pains. The fire department was having its monthly drill so the call came into the police. Patrol could have handled it, but Decker volunteered his services. He didn't mention the call to McAdams, but as he was leaving the kid jumped up and grabbed his fancy schmancy coat to come with. He always did that. Maybe it was because Decker let McAdams bend his ear.

Lucy Jamison was eighty-six, a pale and thin widow. When Decker offered to take her to the hospital, she demurred. She was feeling better. Decker fetched her a glass of water, making sure that she drank it all. Wintertime was deceptive and seniors easily became dehydrated because of the dryness indoors and outdoors.

The old woman talked about her life as a young girl in Michigan. She showed Decker and Tyler pictures of her children, her grandchildren, her great-grandchildren. Decker turned the heat from 80 to 74. When she said she was fine, Decker left his card. She opened the front door and waved good-bye as the two of them walked back to the car, their boots crunching the snow.

Heading back to the station, Decker cranked up the heat as McAdams rubbed his hands under the warm air of the car's heater. The kid was wearing a coat and gloves, but his head was bare. Not that he needed a hat. It was in the midthirties with a full sun and an iridescent blue sky, the scent of pines and burning wood wafting through the town. White-covered hills undulated in the distance. The Hudson wasn't too far away but the area was miles from the nearest coastline, something that Decker had yet to get used to.

"How'd you do this for thirty years, Old Man?" Tyler asked him.

Decker hated when the kid called him Old Man. He wasn't young but he wasn't ready for the glue factory, either. He still had a head of thick, gray hair, a full mustache with traces of its former red color, and a mind that was quick and perceptive. So instead of answering the rhetorical question, he said, "That was the third chest pain case in a month. You really need to learn CPR."

"I'm not putting my mouth on that old crone. Her breath was rank."

"Acetone," Decker said. "Diabetes that's not very well controlled."

"Whatever," McAdams said. "Anyway, if it was between you and me performing CPR, you'd do it anyway."

"That's not the point. It's a skill you should have. Everyone expects a cop to know CPR just like everyone expects a cop to know how to shoot a gun."

"We don't carry guns."

"We don't carry them, but we have them if we need them. You do know how to shoot a gun . . . or did they let you slide with that one as well?"

6

"If we're playing one-upmanship, you're going to lose."

"You have youth and education on your side. I have real experience. That must be worth a few brownie points."

"No one uses the term brownie points anymore and no need to be snide, especially because I'm out here in the trenches with you."

"Trenches?"

"Stop pulling rank. I have seniority." McAdams looked out the side window. "I'm not putting you down, Decker, but if I were actually insane enough to want to do this as a *career*, I'd probably be upper brass in NYPD within . . . say, four to six years?"

"You think so?"

"I know so. It's not about experience or passing tests or paying your dues. It's all about how to work the system, which is something I excel at. I learn exactly what I need to get the job done. Stuffing my brain with useless knowledge is inefficient. Like learning CPR. We get called out, I know you're going to handle it. You or Rolters or Mann or Milkweed—"

"Nickweed."

"Whatever. We get called out and CPR needs to be done, I'm not the go-to guy. Why should I waste my time learning something that I'll never do?"

"Because it is possible that we won't be around and then you'll look like a jackass. If I were your superior, I'd insist on it."

"But you're not. And since I'm not asking for your opinion or advice, I suggest you stop wasting your breath. Need I remind you that a guy your age doesn't have that much left."

Decker stifled a smile. He was riling up the kid on purpose and enjoying it. "You have a short fuse. You should work on that as well."

"Remind me why I volunteered to ride with you."

"Let me guess," Decker said. "I think you're one of those dudes hoping to glean something from my vast repertoire of police work. I think you're figuring that just maybe I'll tell you something truly original and fascinating and then you can write a novel about it. Or better yet, a screenplay. I can see you living in Hollywood. You'd fit in nicely."

"You're being condescending. That's fine. It must be hard to be the junior partner and intellectually inferior to someone as young as I am."

"Nah, I'm used to that. You've never met my kids."

"But you don't work with your kids, do you?"

"Nope. I don't. And I really don't work with you, McAdams. We just kind of ride around together. Not much in the way of meaningful conversation going on."

"You want to talk Proust, I'm in."

"Sure, talk to me about Proust. I like madeleines. My wife bakes them sometimes."

"He was boring and I hate philosophy. It's very mathematical and that's never been my strong suit. I mean I got a 720 on the SAT but that's about average for Harvard." When Decker said nothing, the kid squirmed and said, "So what was your favorite case as a detective?"

"No go, Harvard. You're just going to have to use your own experience for movie material, although God help us both if we ever caught a real case. Not a plain homicide . . . a whodunit."

"A whodunit? That's what you call homicides?"

"Not all homicides, just whodunits. Do you have even the slightest idea how to begin an investigation?"

"Just from TV . . . is it that different?"

"You are joking, right?" When McAdams went quiet, Decker felt a little bad. Why was he even bothering? The kid remained blissfully silent for the rest of the ride back, sulking and moping around until he clocked out at five.

If he wasn't such a twit, Decker might have felt sorry for him. The kid didn't fit in at work: he really didn't fit in anywhere. He wasn't a student anymore and he was too young for the average resident living in Greenbury. So where did that leave his social life? Had he shown any genuine curiosity about police work, Decker would have invited him over for dinner. But Decker wasn't in the charity business. You reap what you sow and that's a fact.

Living in a small town had its perks, particularly when selling real estate in L.A. and buying in Greenbury. He and Rina had walked away with a nice nest egg in their pockets. Their new house on Minnow Lane was built at the turn of the twentieth century, bungalow style with three bedrooms, two and a half baths, and a wood-burning fireplace with erratic radiator heating. The selling point was the previous owner's remodel. He had opened up the ceiling and exposed the beams. It was not only aesthetically pleasing, it allowed Decker and his six-four frame to move about the house without bumping into door headers. The yard was now brown and lifeless but they had bought the house in the fall when autumn leaves were ablaze with color and the weather had been brisk and beautiful. Spring was going to be a true spring, not an L.A. spring with fog and smog.

The house had only a one-car garage where Decker parked the Porsche, leaving Rina's old Volvo in the driveway. Every morning, Decker cleared the windshield and moved the car to the street so he could get out. It was the least he could do for schlepping her to pursue his dream.

The advantage of the new location was driving distance

to their four biological children—two were hers, one was his, and one was shared—as well as their foster son, Gabe Whitman, who was busy touring as a classical pianist. Two of the five were married so there were spouses and grandchildren in the mix. Decker's daughter, Cindy, who had been a GTA detective in L.A., was working patrol in Philadelphia. But it was just a matter of time before she was promoted back up to being a gumshoe.

The house was warm with wafting cooking aromas, immediately putting Decker in a good mood. Inside the compact but modernized kitchen, Rina was working, her hair tucked into a knitted tam that she wore for religious reasons. She was garbed in a thin blue cotton sweater and a knee-length denim skirt, stirring a soup for tomorrow night's Shabbat dinner. She was using a big cauldron, which meant guests.

"How many are we expecting?" Decker kissed her cheek.

Rina kissed him back on the lips. "Six to eight. But lunch will be just the two of us, so don't fret."

"I like company."

"Liar. But you're a good sport. Go change. Dinner will be ready in about ten minutes."

Decker sat on a chair at the breakfast bar. "I'd rather talk to you and get some pleasant company for a change."

"The kid is still getting on your nerves."

"He gets on everyone's nerves."

"Why don't you invite him over for tomor—"

"No."

"Take the high road, Peter."

"I'm taking no road. He's nasty and condescending. It's bad enough that I have to deal with him at work. Why should I let him ruin my weekend or, even worse, inflict him on you? He'd only wind up needling me for being observant, narrow-minded, and provincial."

10

"Or maybe he'd see another side of you."

"If I invited him over, it would only feed his delusions that he really is my superior."

"The kid might be a snot, but I guarantee you he knows who the real cop is. He probably feels like an imposter."

"He is an imposter."

"Give him a chance."

"He won't accept the invitation from me."

"So maybe he'll accept it from me." Rina picked up the phone. "What's his cell?"

After Decker gave her the number, she punched it in and waited. "Hi. I'm looking for Tyler McAdams?"

Over the line, the kid said, "You called my cell so you found me. Who is this?"

Decker heard his response and mouthed, *I told you so*.

Rina blithely continued. "This is Rina Decker. My husband and I wanted to invite you over for dinner tomorrow night." There was a long pause over the line. She went on. "I don't know if Peter told you but we're Jewish and we're observant. I'm having six to eight students here from the colleges and I thought they might be interested in what people do postgraduation, even if it's a temporary job."

McAdams still didn't speak. Finally, he said, "Uh, thank you."

"You're welcome. If it's an inconvenient time, we'll take a rain check. We usually have people over Friday night, so it's open-ended. But I'd love to meet you. I always check out my husband's partners."

"No, you don't," Decker whispered.

She gave him a playful slap. "Please come."

"Sure . . . great. What time?"

Decker was making a face. Rina wagged her finger. "Six-thirty. It's pretty informal. And I'm a great cook."

11

"Sounds like a win-win situation because I like to eat. Thank you."

"You're welcome. We look forward to seeing you. Bye." She hung up. "Done."

"It's not enough that he's a leech at work. Once he's tasted your food, I'll never get him off my back."

Rina took the casserole out of the oven. "Lots of people have ridden on your back and you're none the worse for wear. You've got a strong set of shoulders. One more kid certainly won't break your spine."

CHAPTER TWO

The kid was on time, which would have been fine except that the students were on Jewish Standard Time. Rina answered the door and proceeded to charm while Decker elected to sulk. It seemed like a lifetime until the other guests arrived. The group—four guys and two girls— brought flowers and wine, leaving the empty-handed McAdams feeling a little sheepish. "I thought this was informal. I would have brought something."

Decker said, "Don't worry about it."

"I'm not *worried*, but I just don't want to look like a clod."

"If only you could remedy that with a bottle of wine." Decker smiled and put his arm around the kid as he led him to the table. "C'mon, Harvard. Just relax." Introductions were made all around. Decker whispered, "There are a couple of ritual blessings we need to make. The first one is over the wine—"

"I know what Kiddush is," McAdams said. "There are one or two Jews in the Ivies. I had a Jewish girlfriend at one point."

"What happened?"

"She's not my girlfriend anymore, that's what happened."

"She dumped you." When McAdams shot him a dirty look, Decker said, "It happens." He seated himself at the head of the table.

Rina said, "Tyler, why don't you sit here between Adam and Jennifer. Both of them are interested in law and I know you've gotten into Harvard Law."

"Adam and McAdams," Decker said. "Already sounds like a law firm."

Rina smiled. "It does." She placed the other four students at the table and then Decker made Kiddush. There once was a time where he stumbled over the Hebrew words. But after twenty-five years of embracing her culture and his genetics, he recited the blessing fluently. After drinking wine, the group washed their hands and said the ritual blessing, and then Decker made the HaMotzi, the prayer over the bread.

Finally, the meal could begin in earnest: soup, salad, rib roast, lentils with red peppers and onions, green beans with hazelnuts, and mixed berry cobbler for dessert. It was enough to break the zippers and pop buttons on any waistline. There was lively conversation between the students and Rina as they discussed the *parashat hashavua*: the weekly chapter of bible. The kids were intelligent and opinionated. McAdams, on the other hand, was quiet. Like a lot of secular, upper-crust kids of his generation, he was probably scripture impaired. But he was polite and spoke when he was spoken to.

By nine o'clock, things were starting to wrap up and that's when Decker's landline rang. Rina and he exchanged glances. Decker's father had died a year ago, but his mother was still alive and in her nineties. Rina's parents were both in their nineties. Whenever they got a phone call on Shabbat, it was a reason to worry. Decker held up his finger and went to the answering machine, which identified phone numbers. "It's local."

"Thank God," Rina said. "Probably a robocall."

The voice kicked in. It was Mike Radar and Decker picked up the phone. "It's Decker. What's up, Captain?" He listened intently over the phone. "When? . . . Okay . . . okay." He checked his watch. "Does he know when the lock was broken? No idea? All right, I'll look into it. Do you know how far it is from my house? . . . no, I'll handle it. Just tell me how to get there on foot . . . no, I don't mind walking if it's not too far. A mile away is no problem, Mike . . . no, really, you stay put. I just ate the equivalent of half a cow and it would be good for me to get a little exercise. Unless it's something more, I'll call you on Sunday."

Decker hung up the phone. "There was a break-in at the local cemetery and the watchman is all up in arms. The other detectives are ice fishing in Canada for the weekend so the captain wondered if I wouldn't mind handling it."

Rina feigned mock outrage. "You mean your colleagues didn't invite you with them?"

Decker grinned. "Actually, I made the cut, but I declined. Maybe next time."

McAdams said, "I would have gone. Nobody asked me."

"They probably thought your blue blood couldn't handle the cold." Decker sighed inwardly. He had to make the offer to look like a good guy. "Come if you want."

"Of course, I'll come."

"Take the car. I'll meet you there in about a half hour."

"I'll walk with you, Old Man."

"Harvard, it's really cold outside. I'm doing it for religious reasons. No reason for you to suffer."

"I'm not gonna let you outmacho me."

15

"Suit yourself. Let me grab a few things and we'll be on our way."

"I'll get your jacket, Tyler," Rina said.

"Thanks." McAdams jammed his hands into his pants pockets. His eyes were darting back and forth and he walked in itty-bitty circles. When Rina brought over his outerwear, he bundled up and then forced a smile. "Thank you for dinner. It was delicious."

"You're welcome."

"Do you want some package warmers for your feet and hands?" Decker asked. "I'm taking some with me. No sense getting frostbite."

"Yeah, sure."

Decker gave a wave and he and the kid were off. The night was moonless with thousands of stars sprinkling the dark sky like salt on black velvet. Without the cloud cover, the temperature had dropped to the teens. No wind . . . just cold air and the mist of warm breath wafting through darkness.

McAdams said, "Thanks for dinner."

"You're welcome. It was my wife's idea."

"Yeah, I intuited that. She is a good cook. She's also lovely . . . I mean personality."

"She's lovely all the way around. I'm very lucky."

McAdams said, "You have a large family. I counted like seven different people my age in the various pictures."

"Five kids, two spouses, twin grandsons, and a granddaughter."

"Wow." A pause. "I take it the black guy is a son-in-law? Or maybe you were married before."

"I was married before, but not to Koby's mother. He's married to my elder daughter, Cindy, who's a cop in Philadelphia. Koby is in medical school at the University of Pennsylvania. They have twin boys. The older two white

16

boys are my stepsons. The girls are my biological daughters and the youngest kid is our foster son who's been with us for the last four years. He is a classical pianist who just graduated from Juilliard."

"Impressive. What do the other kids do?"

"Sam and his wife are both doctors. They have Lily. They live in Brooklyn. Jacob—the one who looks like Rina—just finished his Ph.D. in public policy. He's still . . ." Decker laughed. "He's still finding himself. My other daughter, Hannah, is in a Ph.D. program at the Ferkauf School of Psychology in New York."

"Not bad . . . but no Crimson."

"Yeah, you Harvard guys think that there's only one school in the world."

"No, we do accept Princeton or Yale. But that's about it."

Decker smiled. "What about yourself, McAdams?"

"What do you mean?"

"Parents, brothers, sisters, city of birth? For as much as you yap when we're driving, I don't know anything about you."

"Nothing much to tell. I grew up in the city. By the city, that means Manhattan. My parents divorced when I was ten, and both of them were remarried by the time I was fourteen. A couple of half sibs, a couple of stepsibs, all of them younger and none of them as smart as I am. I don't have much of a relationship with any of them."

Talking about family was obviously painful for him so Decker didn't ask any more questions. They walked the next ten minutes in silence until the local graveyard came into view. That was another thing about small towns. Cemeteries were right in your face, not like L.A. where they're situated in no-man's-land off the freeway. This one was several blocks of upright headstones with a secluded,

17

gated portion for the mausoleums: domed structures with fluted columns. Since the captain had mentioned something being broken into, it had to be one of the crypts.

Decker said, "Do you want a hand or foot warmer package? My feet are ice at this point."

"Yeah, sure."

After handing him the packets, Decker took a couple for himself, broke them in half, and dropped them into his snow boots. "Ah . . . better. I'm not really cold—after eating that much meat you can't be cold—but my hands and feet get numb."

"Why did you insist on walking? Surely there's some religious dispensation that allows you to drive the car when working."

"Yeah, I could have taken the car. Probably would have been smarter. What can I say, McAdams? Without a Harvard B.A., I guess I'm just handicapped."

The watchman was a dead ringer for Ichabod Crane with a long face and extended skeletal frame and sunken eyes unsuitable for daylight. Any minute, Decker expected to see the headless horseman. His given name was Isaiah Pellman and his family had been living in Greenbury for two hundred years. The history was given by way of introduction to his good character. There were a lot of loquacious people in Greenbury as well as a lot of odd ducks. Eccentrics were everywhere in the world, but they were more noticeable in smaller populations.

They were chatting while standing between rows of headstones. Pellman said, "I check the Bergman crypt all the time, so I was really surprised when this happened."

Decker pulled out a notebook. "What specifically happened?"

"My key doesn't work the lock: that's what happened."

"Okay . . . so the lock wasn't broken off?"

"No, it was broken off and exchanged for a different lock."

"And your key always worked the lock before?"

"Yes, sir, it did."

"Are you sure the lock just didn't freeze?"

"I'm sure. First thing I did was heat it and oil it. The key goes in, but the tumblers don't move. Everything worked perfectly four days ago. I called up the family and explained the situation a few hours ago. They told me to cut the lock and make sure everything inside is okay. But I told them I was gonna call the police. So I called the police. And now you're up to date."

"Who does the crypt belong to again? Bergman?"

"Ye-ah. They're all buried inside—Moses and Ruth and their three children, Leon, Helen, and Harold along with their spouses—Gladys, Earl, and Mary. Ken Sobel's the one I deal with. He's a grandson from Helen Bergman, who became a Sobel when she married Earl. Ken's older cousin, Jack Sobel, was buried here around six months ago. He was seventy-three."

The man knew his local history. "How old is the crypt?"

"Erected in 1895."

"And the family visited the crypt for a funeral about six months ago?"

"Ye-ah. Then Ken Sobel came back in the fall. Ken's in his late sixties. He comes down four times a year as regular as clockwork. And he always makes sure the lock's on tight."

"So he has a key."

"He does. Others as well but they don't come down."

"Could Ken have changed the lock?"

"No, sir, I asked when my key wouldn't work. And he said no, he didn't change the lock. And he's the one who's in charge. He told me to break the lock and make sure everything's okay inside. So that's when I called you—the police."

"Anything of value inside the crypt?"

"No. Unless the bodies were buried with jewelry."

Decker said, "Jewish custom is not to bury bodies with anything material."

"So there you have it!" Pellman exclaimed.

"Indeed," Decker said although he really wasn't sure what Pellman was talking about. "Has this ever happened before? That your key didn't work the lock?"

"No, sir, not on my watch."

During the interview, McAdams's toe was constantly tapping. Finally, he said, "Why don't we just go and see what's going on? If everything looks fine, we can all go home." He looked at Pellman. "Well, not you, but I'm not getting paid to freeze my ass off."

Decker was annoyed, not just at the kid's rudeness, but at the disruption of the interview. He always collected as much information as possible before he witnessed the crime scene . . . if there even was a crime scene. "Mr. Pellman, do you have anything else you want to tell me before we look around?"

"No." The man was stunned. "Should I be telling you something?"

"It wasn't a trick question," McAdams said. "No is a perfectly acceptable answer."

"Take your time, Mr. Pellman," Decker said.

"No, nothing else."

"Okay. Thanks." Decker folded his notebook. "Do you have a pair of bolt cutters?"

"I do." He shuffled his feet and didn't move.

"Could you get them for me?"

"Uh, sure. I don't know if they're strong enough to cut the lock."

"Only one way to find out."

Pellman said, "I guess you're right about that." Slowly he headed toward a shed that sat about two hundred yards away.

"Queer old guy but then again they're all odd over here."

Decker turned to the kid. "Don't interrupt when I'm interviewing. It distracts me."

"Just trying to move things along."

"Tyler, this is probably nothing, so it's no big deal. But if you have a chance to investigate a real crime, you can't rush it along. You'll miss things. You've got to slow down."

Before McAdams could respond, Pellman came back with the bolt cutters and handed them to Decker. "You want to see the crypt and the lock?"

"That would be helpful."

Slowly Pellman took them over to the Bergman crypt, an enormous rectangular stone vault with a dome ceiling. Each of the four outside walls hosted a leaded glass window that would have lit up the interior had it been daylight. Five stone steps led down to a padlocked concrete door. No foul odors seemed to emanate from the ground, but it was so cold that everything was frozen solid including dead matter. Decker looked at the bolt cutters and looked at the thin shank of the padlock, something that teens would use on their school lockers. With a little muscle, he should be able to make a clean cut through the U-shaped metal.

Decker said, "Can I try your key just to make sure?"

"Sure."

Decker inserted the Schlage into the key slot. He could move it a millimeter to the left and right. The insides didn't appear to be frozen, just that the key didn't work the lock. He handed it back to Pellman. Then he handed the cutters to McAdams. "Go ahead, Harvard."

21

"Me?"

"Yeah, take a whack at it."

McAdams threw dagger eyes, but he secured the blades of the cutter around the U-shaped metal. "Okay." He took a deep breath. "Okay." He pressed down hard and the lock slipped under the blades. McAdams swore.

"If you don't get it on three, I'll do it," Decker told him.

"Chill, Old Man. I'll get it, I'll get it."

Number three was the charm. The kid used all his muscle, the blades cut through the shank, and the lock snapped off. When McAdams started to go in, Decker held him back.

"How about if we pick up the lock from the floor and stow it in the paper evidence bag. Just perhaps there is a crime scene involved and maybe the lock has a fingerprint. And as luck would have it, I just happen to have a few bags in my pocket." Decker handed him a small paper bag. "Or would you prefer that I pick it up, boss?"

McAdams swore, but he bent down and picked it up with his gloved hand.

Decker said, "Place it in the bag. Then you write your name, the date, the time, and the location."

McAdams did as he was told then gave the bag back to Decker. "Only because your wife fed me."

"And fed you well." Decker took out a flashlight and a magnifying glass. He peered through the lens and studied the door. "No pry marks." He pushed the door open and swept the beam across the crypt. There were a number of horizontal marble headstones in the ground, but no bodies that weren't six feet under. Decker counted the marble tombstones. At current, the crypt was hosting ten graves with room for more. Decker handed McAdams an extra flashlight. "In case you didn't bring one. Keep it." He turned to Pellman. "Could I borrow your light? It's stronger than mine."

"You betcha." The watchman handed him his battery pack.

"Thanks." Decker crossed over the threshold and stepped inside. The temperature wasn't as cold as he thought it would be. Thick walls kept out the sunlight and heat but they also kept out the extreme cold. Decker swept the beam around to get the lay of the land.

The space was as big as his current living room, around two hundred square feet, and beautifully adorned. There was carved molding on the ceiling, and jeweled stripes of iridescent colored glass tiles were inset into the walls. Each gravestone was marked by the inhabitant inside—name, beloved husband/wife father/mother, grandfather/grandmother/date of birth/date of death. Nothing unusual except that the headstones of the matriarch and the patriarch were inset with tile work—two different pastoral scenes elegantly laid out in tiny pieces of glass mosaic. He squatted down to study the artwork. McAdams kneeled next to him. Decker whispered, "Doesn't matter now, but for the record, don't kneel. It might mess up something. You want as little contact with the ground as possible."

McAdams squatted. "Not only am I a solid chunk of ice, I'm gonna be sore."

Decker ignored him. "Nice tile work, no?"

"It's okay . . . actually more than okay. It's done well."

"Somebody put money into these headstones." Decker stood up and inched the light up and across the walls until he reached the windows. They stood about ten feet above the floor. Hanging just under the dome in the upper four windows were stained-glass panels. Decker didn't notice them when he first came in because it was dark. He illuminated each panel with his flashlight, letting the beam rest on each for a minute or so before moving onto the

23

next one. They probably sparkled beautifully in the daylight.

"It's the four seasons." Decker turned to McAdams. "See, that one's winter, that's spring, and summer and autumn." He regarded the kid. "I think they were custom made." He turned to Pellman. "Have those stained-glass windows always been inside the crypt?"

"For as long as I've been here and even before."

Decker turned to the kid. "What do you think?"

McAdams shone his light on the four panels. "My mother has some Tiffany lamps. I'm not saying they are Tiffany, but it looks like good quality."

"Agreed," Decker said.

"You do know that the company made stained-glass windows for religious purposes."

"Go on."

"Just that the studio made a lot of devotional items for churches and synagogues. Do you know Manhattan at all?"

"Not too well."

"There's a famous synagogue on Fifth Avenue that has an original Tiffany. As does the Portuguese synagogue on the west side."

"Courtesy of your ex-Jewish girlfriend?"

"You have a honed mind, Old Man. The studio also made windows for wealthy people's mausoleums. So if they were real, I wouldn't be surprised."

"Could you tell if those are Tiffany or not?"

"Not at this distance. You could look for a signature, but that can be forged. It happened all the time. Mostly you tell by quality."

Decker turned to Pellman. "Do you have a ladder?"

"Not on me, but I can get you a ladder."

"Thank you. That would help."

24

"Be right back."

After he left, McAdams said, "Why in the world are you climbing up there? Are you that bored with the job?"

"Harvard, it always helps to get up close and personal. I'll do the climbing, you just hold the ladder." The two men didn't speak. McAdams was fidgety. Decker said, "You okay?"

"Kinda creepy in here."

"Yeah, cemeteries are a little spooky." Decker paused. "Not this place, though. Someone took the time to make it pretty."

Pellman came back with the ladder. "Here you go."

Decker handed him his big, bulky battery pack flashlight and took his smaller light. He started climbing toward the windows. "Guys, shine the lights on the window, okay? I want to see them up close."

The two men focused the light on the "autumn" stained-glass window. It was about fourteen by twenty inches in size and was hanging from two chains that were hooked into the ceiling.

"Is there a signature?" McAdams shouted.

"What kind of signature should I look for?"

"Tiffany Studios . . . something like that."

Decker was face-to-face with the artwork. He shone his light through the colored glass. He wasn't an expert, but it looked pretty good to his eye. It took him a few seconds to find the signature: *Tiffany Studio. New York.*

"Do you think it's real?" McAdams asked from below.

"No idea."

McAdams said, "There must be someone in one of the colleges who could authenticate it."

"Good thinking." Decker continued to study the work: each cut piece of glass, each thread of metal that held the glass into place. All the metal, including the frame, was

25

dark bronze in color but with a hint of dark green peeking through. He knew from watching those antique shows that the patina—the way the metal aged over time—was important in authentication and to his eye, the metal work between the glass pieces and frame had plenty of patina. So did the chain from which the panels hung.

All the links had plenty of patina except for the two metal loops soldered to the frame and attached to the hanging chains. Those two loops were darker than the frame and looked flat when compared to the rest of the metal. Decker saw a raised chip of what he thought was a metal shard poking up, but when he touched it, dark paint flicked off and fell onto the back of his hand. Carefully, he climbed down the ladder and folded it up. "Uh, with the family's permission, I'd like to get an art expert down here to look at all four windows."

McAdams said, "Why? What did you find?"

"I'm not sure, but I'd like someone to take a closer look."

Pellman shuffled his feet. "I suppose I can call up the family." He hemmed. "Maybe it would sound better if it came from the police."

"I'd be happy to call them up and tell them my thoughts." Even in the dark shadows, Decker could tell that Pellman was relieved. The watchman gave Decker Ken Sobel's telephone number. "Do you have something to secure the door with?"

"No, not on me."

"I don't suppose there's a hardware store open at this time of night?"

Pellman said, "Just call up Glenn Dutch. I'm sure he has something around his house. If not, he'll open the store for you."

McAdams said, "Dutch's Hardware is on Gable Street."

"Do you have the number?" Decker asked Pellman.

"I don't have it, but Roy might have it. Roy's a friend of Glenn's and I have Roy's number."

"Could you get Glenn's number from Roy, then?"

"Surely, I can." He checked his contact list on his phone. "I must have it at home . . . Roy's number. I'll call up my wife and she can get me Roy's number who can get you Glenn's number." Pellman walked a few feet away to make his calls.

McAdams said, "You want to tell me what you found or are you going to make me play twenty questions?"

Decker said, "I found paint."

"Paint?"

"Paint flicked off on one of the loops soldered onto the frame. It was painted to make the solder joints look old. And, come to think of it, whoever put those loops on the frames did a sloppy job of soldering. Now it could have been a recent repair. I'm just saying it wasn't in keeping with the original work."

McAdams said, "What did the glass look like? The individual pieces, I mean."

"The glass was beautiful . . . really iridescent."

"Did you find any cracks?"

Decker regarded him in the shadows. "Interesting you should ask. I remember thinking that the glass was in really good shape. Why?"

"This may not be true for window panels, but my mom always said that the lamps have been around for a while. It's nearly impossible to find something in pristine shape—without any cracks—that hasn't been forged."

"Good to know," Decker said. "On the other hand, the panels have been hanging in the same place for over a hundred years untouched." A pause. "On the third hand, the works are hanging in a noncontrolled environment.

27

With all the weather fluctuations, you might expect a few cracks. On the fourth hand, I only looked at one panel so maybe the others have cracks in the glass."

"So that's the way you do it. You just keep talking to yourself until you hit on something."

"Sure, I talk to myself if no one else is around. When I was head of the detectives' division, I used to talk to my other detectives. We'd bounce stuff off one another and we were right more than we were wrong."

"You know, I am standing right here, freezing my ass off. You could bounce shit off me."

"McAdams, I've been trying to bounce shit off you for the last six months and all I've had to show for it was a face full of crap. S'right. I know I'm a terrific detective. If you want to learn, I'll be happy to share what I know. And if there's something that I don't know but you do know, well, that's fine with me also. A great detective starts by being a great listener."

CHAPTER THREE

With the Bergman crypt once again secured by a padlock courtesy of Glenn Dutch's Hardware, they left the crypt at 11:30. It was late to be making calls, but if it had been Decker's crypt, he would have wanted to know right away. He handed a slip of paper to McAdams. "This is Ken Sobel's number—the one who was up here most recently and seems to be in charge. You can do the honors."

"Me?"

"You're my superior."

"So I'm assigning you to the task of making the call."

"It's my Sabbath. Can you do me the favor?"

"It's late."

"I know. But I still think we should call him."

"Why?"

"Because it's the proper procedure. Pellman has already told him that there was something wrong with the lock. He's probably waiting to hear from him." A pause. "Look, if you don't feel comfortable—"

"Don't be ridiculous." McAdams took out his phone. "I'll do it."

But he didn't do it. Decker said, "Start by introducing yourself."

"I know how to handle this, okay." Decker didn't answer and McAdams regarded his phone. "How much should I tell him? I mean, what if he ripped the panels off himself? Aren't we giving him a heads-up that we're suspicious?"

"Let's just stick to what we know, okay."

"We don't know anything for certain so why are we even calling him?"

"We're calling him to let him know that everything looks fine, but we'd like for completeness sake to have him authenticate the panels. But you've got to lead into that conversation. First tell him that everything looks okay. Then compliment the panels, then ask if they're real Tiffany—"

"I get it!" Abruptly, McAdams shoved the phone into Decker's hand. "You've obviously got some script in your head. Just do it and get it over with, okay. I'm freezing . . . beyond freezing. I'm numb everywhere."

"I'll make the call but could you at least punch in the numbers for me?"

"I don't think I can move my fingers."

"Give it to me."

"I'm kidding, Old Man."

Decker said, "Put it on speaker so I won't have to repeat the conversation." McAdams was sulky—his pride was wounded—but he did as told. Decker waited for the line to connect. The two of them were walking back to the house in a cold that had turned positively polar. He usually paced while talking on the phone. At least this time, his movement had a purpose.

After he heard the hello, he said, "This is Peter Decker from the Greenbury Police Department, I'm sorry to call so late, but I'm looking for Ken Sobel."

The voice on the other end was alert. "This is Ken Sobel. What took you so long? What's going on up there?"

"We broke the lock on the crypt, sir. From what I could see, everything appears in order."

"Phew! Good to know. It would be really ghoulish if someone had broken into the mausoleum and did some mischief. So why didn't Isaiah Pellman's key work?"

"We don't know. Could someone else in the family have changed the lock?"

"Not to my knowledge. I'm usually the only one who bothers to go up there . . . except for the funeral six months ago. I was up there about four months ago and everything was in perfect order."

"Who else besides you has a key?"

"My sister . . . some of my other cousins."

"Mr. Pellman checked the lock about four days ago and it worked. So if anyone had changed the lock, it had to have been in the last few days."

"I assure you that none of my relatives have been up in the last few days."

"Okay. I do have a question or two if you don't mind my asking."

"I'm here."

"There are four beautiful stained-glass panels inside the crypt. The scenes look like the four seasons. I even got on a ladder and looked at the autumn panel. I found a Tiffany signature. Are they real Tiffany?"

There was a pause on the other end. "Why do you ask?"

"I'm a suspicious guy, which is a good thing for a detective. When I first talked to Isaiah Pellman, it sounded to me that someone broke the original lock on purpose. And then I saw those panels. If they're real Tiffany, they're worth stealing."

"But you said everything looks in order."

"It does."

"So I'm confused."

"Are the panels Tiffany?"

"Yes, and they do represent the four seasons. My grandmother commissioned them at the turn of the century."

"Okay. It might be a good idea to send someone up here and have them authenticated. Or my partner suggested that maybe someone from one of the colleges could authenticate them with your permission, of course."

"That's ridiculous. Of course, they're real!"

"I'm sure they were at one point."

"What?" A long pause. "You think someone broke in and replaced the panels with forgeries?"

"Mr. Sobel, I'm certainly no art expert. But I did climb up on a ladder to get an up-close look. That's how I found the Tiffany signature. And I only looked at the autumn panel, sir, so I don't know about the others. But on that panel, someone had painted the two soldered loops on the lead frame that secures the two chains that hang from the ceiling. The loops were painted dark brown to match the patina. The paint flaked off on my hand. Did you do a repair on that work?"

"No, I did not! And it would be absurd to think that Tiffany Studios would paint something to make it look like old patina. Because when they did it, it wasn't old. Furthermore, the glass is held in place by copper channels, not lead. It was a very expensive way of doing stained glass. Tiffany invented it as far as I know. So when it was new, it would have been shiny."

"Tell him about the perfect glass," McAdams whispered.

Decker nodded. "Also the stained glass in the panel was in perfect shape. My partner says that with authentic Tiffany, it's more usual than not to find a crack or two somewhere."

"I don't fucking believe this!" Sobel said. Decker heard a female voice in the background. Sobel was talking to it in an angry muffled voice. "Someone may have ripped off our Tiffany panels . . . yes, in the crypt!" Back to Decker. "Are you sure about this?"

"Not at all. It's up to you on how you want to proceed."

Sobel was still muttering curse words under his breath. "I'll bring someone down . . . I can't do it tomorrow. Is the crypt secured?"

"Yes, we put a new padlock on it."

"I'll see if my appraiser—better known as my son-in-law—can come down with me on Sunday. His place is closed so he'll do me the favor for gratis. Well, not quite gratis. I've spent a fortune at his gallery . . . figure it benefits my grandchildren. Does Sunday work for you?"

"Sunday would be fine. I'll give you my phone number and my partner's phone number." After he gave Sobel the digits, Decker said, "Feel free to call either one of us. In the meantime, I'll make sure that the watchmen check the crypt lock during their work hours."

"What did you say your name was again?"

"Peter Decker."

"Are you new? I don't know you."

"I came on the force about six months ago. Before that, I worked for LAPD."

"LAPD." A pause. "Have you ever worked an art case before or should I send in an expert in the field?"

"I was a lieutenant when I left LAPD. I ran a squad room of detectives so I'm familiar with every kind of crime imaginable, including art theft and forgery. But you can hire your own person as long as we communicate. I don't have turf issues especially with something so specialized. You're in Manhattan?"

"Yes."

"So there are probably a lot of specialists in your parts. How about if we take it one step at a time?"

"I suppose that makes sense. What was your specialty?"

"As a lieutenant, I mostly supervised my detectives. I only worked the field if it was a very big and puzzling case. Before I was promoted, I was a homicide cop for twenty years."

"Homicide! Let's hope there's no need for that!"

Decker smiled. "I agree."

Sobel thanked him for calling and hung up. Decker gave the phone back to McAdams. They walked the rest of the way in silence. When they got to the house, Decker said, "Can't say it was a hoot, but you showed some professionalism coming out with me in the cold."

"Yeah, tell that to my frozen feet . . . and my frozen ears. I should have taken the car. If I come down with frostbite, I'm taking disability."

Decker eyed him. "You know, McAdams, police forces are paramilitary organizations. Rule number one: no one wants to hear your bitching so suck it up. No guarantee they'll like you any better, but when you don't talk, you can't get on people's nerves. Do you want to come on Sunday? If you've got other plans, I can handle this alone. It might even be easier if I handle it alone. But it's up to you."

"I'll be there. What time?"

"He didn't tell me."

"So we have to wait by the phone twiddling our thumbs?"

"Remember what I said about sucking it up five seconds ago?"

McAdams sighed. Then he said, "Do you think the panels were stolen?"

34

"Ah . . . a work-related question. Good. I think it's a distinct possibility."

"So we have an art theft . . . and if Pellman said his key worked just a couple of days ago, it's a recent art theft."

Decker held up his hands. "Voilà!"

McAdams smiled. "I'll see you on Sunday. Thank your wife for me."

"This should be evident, but I never assume anything. You don't talk about this to anyone. You should never talk about work, period."

"No problem there, Old Man. I don't have anyone to talk to."

It seemed like ages since Rina had to wait up for him to come home. In fact, it had only been months since Peter had retired and they had moved to Greenbury. She was fine with the move, but she suspected that Decker was less than thrilled. He didn't talk about it and she hadn't asked, but perhaps a taste of his old life would be a perfect lead-in.

When he walked through the door, Peter looked cold but not at all tired. His nose and cheeks were bright red. Rina got up from the couch and made two cups of tea in the kitchen using the hot water urn that she always set up before the Sabbath. When she returned, he was hanging up his jacket and scarf. He took off his gloves and hat. "Man, it's good to get out of the cold."

Rina set the hot tea on the coffee table. She was wearing thin pajamas. The radiator was spewing out puffs of hot air. "I finally understand saunas. You get hot, then cold, then the hot doesn't feel so hot." She fanned her face. "I'm ready to camp outside. I'm dying. Of course, it could be the M word."

35

"Open a window."

"I do. Then I get cold. No winning the war on hormones."

Decker picked up his tea and sipped. "You look as young as the day I met you."

"And you're a smooth talker. You also have a gleam in your eye. Or is that an ice crystal? What's the case, darling?"

"It wasn't much but at least it was more than grabbing a cat from a tree."

"Want to talk about it?"

"I just told the kid not to talk about his cases with anyone."

"I'm your wife. I have Fifth Amendment privileges."

Decker smiled. "It's nothing much. Could be an art theft of Tiffany panels. There are glass panels still up there but we don't know if they're the originals. They may be forgeries. The owner is coming up with an expert on Sunday to authenticate them."

"I suppose the next question is, who would steal them? Who'd even know about them?"

"Excellent. Can you be my partner instead of the kid?"

"How's the kid?"

"Obnoxious as usual." Decker took another sip of tea. "Tonight, I did see a glimmer of curiosity."

"Ah . . . maybe all he needed was a little real police work. He did go to Harvard."

"His brain is not the problem. He needs a personality transplant."

"He seemed polite enough when he was here. Anyway, it's good to see you grumpy. That means you're happy. Do you know anything about Tiffany?"

"Not much. What about you?"

"I think he used to have a studio upstate. I think it

was dismantled, though." Decker was quiet. Rina said, "What?"

"I think there's a museum in Orlando . . . what's it called? See that's why we shouldn't be talking about business on Shabbat. Now I can't look it up and it's killing me."

"It's a Tiffany museum?"

"It has a bunch of Tiffany windows. I was there when I visited my uncle years ago . . . it's an American art museum . . . it'll come to me." Decker finished his tea. "Is stained-glass Tiffany the same Tiffany that owns the stores?"

"I think it was a father and son. The son did the stained glass."

"Louis Comfort Tiffany."

"Yeah, right. Good for you."

"So the jewelry guy was the father?"

"Yes, and I think Tiffany jewelry went corporate a long time ago."

"I'll look it all up after Shabbos." Decker moved closer to his wife. "Right now, let's just enjoy being together."

"Ooh, I like it when you're doing real police work. It makes you romantic."

Decker was taken aback. "Have I been a slacker in the romance department?"

"You're always romantic, Peter. But you've seemed to be at loose ends since we got here."

He took a breath and let it out. "It's been an adjustment. At times, I'm a little bored. That's pretty natural after working with LAPD for all those years. But I don't want to go back. I think I just miss the rush of a real case. That first blush of excitement. And even though this art thing is probably nothing, it gave me a little jolt. I'm fine.

Honestly. It's all just part of the process of adaptation, I think. Of aging . . . of getting old."

"You are not old."

"Not according to the kid. He calls me Old Man."

"You're not old." Rina kissed him again. "Besides, there's old . . ." Another kiss. "And then there's vintage."

CHAPTER FOUR

The cemetery seemed quaint, much less foreboding in the daylight with old headstones carved with names like Whitestone, Potter, MacDoogal, and Hawthorne. The Bergman mausoleum seemed like a dowager, too grand for the neighborhood, but since it had been there for years, Decker supposed that it was now just part of the scenery. It was chilly but not cold, brisk but not blustery. The sun was immersed in a sea of deep blue.

The man who emerged from the Mercedes was in his late sixties, white haired but with a lively step. He was around six feet and had a ski-tanned face, milky blue eyes, and a prominent chin. He was dressed in a cable-knit sweater and jeans, loafers but no socks. In tow was a younger, shorter man with brown eyes and curly brown hair. He was wearing a black suit, white shirt, and a red bow tie. On his feet were black Oxfords over black socks.

"Ken Sobel." He pointed to the younger man. "This is Maxwell Stewart, owner of the famed Stewart and Harrison gallery. If you deal with him, you'd better have your game face on. The man is a shark."

"Call me Max." He appeared around forty. "Don't pay attention to Ken. I never do."

"Peter Decker. Thanks for coming down."

Sobel said, "Are you a police officer or a police detective or . . ."

"I'm whatever the department needs. This is my partner, Detective Tyler McAdams."

More handshakes. Then Sobel turned to Isaiah Pellman who was trying to disappear in nonexistent shadows. "What the hell happened, Isaiah?"

"Just like I told you, sir. The key didn't work."

"When was the last time you tried it?" Sobel asked.

"Last Tuesday. It worked fine."

"So what happened?"

"I don't know, sir."

Decker said, "Let me give you a recap of where McAdams and I came in and why I asked you to come down."

Sobel said, "I know why you asked me down. You told me that over the phone."

Stewart said, "Let the man finish."

"Be brief," Sobel said. "I've got a dinner engagement and it's a three-hour drive."

"It's ten in the morning, Ken."

"You know how brutal traffic can be."

Decker gave a quick summary of the events of Friday night while McAdams rocked on his feet, no doubt feeling superfluous. At the end, Decker turned to McAdams and said, "Anything you'd like to add?"

"Not a whit."

Decker turned to Pellman. "We're going to need that ladder again. Mr. Stewart will need to look at the panels up close."

Stewart said, "You want me to climb up a ladder?"

40

Sobel said, "It's not that hard, Max. One foot over the other."

"I'm wearing leather-soled shoes." He turned to his father-in-law. "If I break my leg, you explain it to Natalie."

"I'll catch you if you fall."

"I'd take them down for you," Decker said, "but I don't want to screw anything up."

"It's fine." Max was clearly peeved. "If I had known I had to climb up, I would have worn sneakers. I really do think the old man likes to see me sweat."

"Been there, done that," McAdams muttered.

"That's enough out of you, Harvard," Decker said.

Stewart said, "You went to Harvard?"

"Graduated two years ago."

"What house?"

"Cabot. And you?"

"Lowell."

The two men started playing name game despite a decade of life between them. If McAdams was good for anything, it was building rapport with the Ivy League elite with second homes in the smaller towns along the Hudson. But that did nothing to endear him to the regular working stiffs of the town.

Pellman came back with a ladder and his flashlight. He descended the five steps into the crypt and unlocked the door. Everyone crowded inside. Decker turned on Pellman's flashlight although there was plenty of sunshine coming through the windows along with bursts of iridescence coming from the stained glass.

Stewart looked upward. "Could you shine the light on that one?" Decker illuminated the autumn panel. Max said, "I can already tell that it's a reproduction. Good glass, lousy work."

Sobel swore under his breath. "Are you sure?"

"Yes."

"How can you tell?"

"Ken, how can you tell when it's time to dump stocks? It's my business."

He waved off his son-in-law and then started pacing. "Goddamnit, how did this happen?"

"What about the others?" McAdams asked Stewart. "What do you think?"

Sobel suddenly remembered there were three more panels to evaluate. "Yeah, what about the others, Max?"

"Could I have the light?" Stewart asked.

"Sure." Decker handed him the battery pack.

The dealer studied each panel, and then he said, "Okay. To my eye, summer is also a fake. The other two . . . I'm going to have to climb up and take a closer look."

Sobel continued to swear and mutter to himself as Decker and McAdams balanced the ladder against the wall, going as close as they could to the window containing winter. Stewart shook his head then scaled the risers. When he was eye level with the panel, Decker stepped up two risers and passed him the battery pack. Stewart studied the work for a long time. "This is real."

"Thank God for small favors," Sobel mumbled.

Carefully, Max climbed down and went over to the spring panel. "Legit." Stewart climbed down again and dusted off his pants. "Two and two, Ken."

"Goddamnit! What the hell is someone going to do with two panels in a set of four?"

Decker said, "I take it that the panels are valuable on their own."

"Of course," Max said. "But as a set, the value goes up exponentially."

Decker said, "You should take the real panels out of the crypt and put them in a more secure place."

42

"My thoughts exactly," Stewart said.

"How involved is it to remove them?"

"Not too hard normally. The chains just hook into the loops in the frame but it looks like the links were tightened around the loop, which isn't the original design. It would help to have two people up there. One to detach the panel from the frame and another one to hold the tools."

Sobel was still swearing. McAdams turned to Pellman. "Do you have another ladder?"

"Let me check." He came back with a shorter ladder. "This is all I had."

"That'll work." Decker turned to Stewart. "Shall we?"

"Let's."

It took less than an hour to remove all four panels, another hour to remove the chains and the ceiling pieces. At straight-up twelve, the two original panels and chains were bubble wrapped and then blanket wrapped and sat in the backseat of the Mercedes. The two forgeries would be entered as evidence of a crime. Sobel jangled his keys as he turned to Decker. "Now what?"

"I'm going to need the names of everyone who has a key to the crypt or even knows that the panels exist."

"That's a long list," Sobel said. "A long, long list."

Stewart leaned over to McAdams's ear and whispered something. When McAdams smiled, Sobel said, "Can you tell me what could be even remotely funny?"

"Just two Harvard guys shooting the shit, Ken."

"Well, shoot the shit some other time, okay." Sobel was irritated. "I don't even know where to begin."

"Start with your relatives," Decker said. "Any of them have money problems?"

"That would be my sister-in-law," Stewart said.

"Cut it out, Max," Sobel told him. "She doesn't have money problems."

"My brother-in-law is a good guy. Why he married Melanie is the family mystery. Well, I know why he married her. She's beautiful. But she's also unpleasant and a shopaholic. And don't look at me that way, Ken. They're going to ask their questions anyway, right?"

"Right," McAdams said.

Sobel was angry. "I guarantee you that none of our relatives stole the panels."

"I'm sure you're right, Mr. Sobel," Decker said. "But I have to start somewhere. Anyone innocent won't mind talking to me."

"Sure, talk to Melanie, talk to whoever you want, I don't care." Sobel turned to his son-in-law. "You don't really think that Melanie stole the panels."

Stewart put his arm around his father-in-law. "Honestly, no. That would be a new low even for her."

"Make us a list and we'll take it from there," Decker said. "Also, what about locally? Anyone in town know about the panels?"

"Just Pellman here and the other watchmen."

"We put all the mausoleum keys in a lockbox, Mr. Sobel."

"That doesn't mean one of you didn't use it." When the caretaker blanched, Sobel said, "I'm not accusing you, Isaiah. Just saying out loud what the police are thinking."

McAdams snapped his fingers. "What about anyone at the colleges? Maybe an art professor knew about them from your parents' time? Littleton has been around for a while and back in my dad's time, it was noted for bringing in local experts on regional painters and craftsmen from the area. Tiffany's studio wasn't all that far from here."

The boy had a brain. Decker said, "That's a good thought."

"I never had any dealing with the colleges," Sobel said.

"We can find out," Decker said. "Would you know if the panels had ever been loaned out to a museum exhibition or recorded in a book on Tiffany?"

"Or any other art glass book?" McAdams asked.

"I don't know," Sobel grumped. "You don't know how depressing this is for me."

Stewart put his arm around his father-in-law's shoulders. "The good news is we know the panels weren't destroyed, Ken. They were taken by someone who wanted them because he knew what they were. And the panels can't be sold in a reputable auction house, because there's no provenance of ownership. So if the thief is going to sell them, he'd have to use the black market. We'll find them. If not, you've got insurance."

"I don't want insurance. I want the works." The man teared up. "They were my grandparents' legacy. My grandmother commissioned them from Tiffany Studios."

"I know." Max kissed his cheek. "At least, we salvaged two of them. And if we need to do a facsimile of the others, I've got artisans who are just as talented as those at Tiffany Studios although almost anyone could do much better than those pieces of dreck."

Sobel nodded. "Thanks for coming down, Max."

"Oh please, Ken. You know I'd be insulted if you asked anyone else." Stewart looked at Decker and McAdams. "We'll get that list for you. I'm sure we won't think of everyone, but as names pop up, we'll send them off to you."

"Thanks," Decker said. "And I don't care how long it is. A long list isn't as big a problem as no list at all."

Sobel nodded and slid into the driver's seat. Stewart sat in the backseat, with an arm placed skillfully over his glass charges. They drove off in a wisp of exhaust, tooled up for the long ride back to civilization.

Pellman said, "I'm gonna put the ladders away."

"That's fine," Decker said. "Thanks for all your help."

"Do you think that Mr. Sobel suspects me?"

"No, he's just upset." Decker patted his shoulder. "We'll talk to you later."

The men walked back to the car. McAdams put the key into the ignition, turned on the motor, and headed back to the station house less than five minutes away. "What now? I'm sure you have many ideas bouncing around in that predementia brain of yours."

"A few. I'd love to hear what you're thinking."

"Age before beauty."

Decker said, "This is the drill. We bounce ideas off each other. I say something, you say something. There is no right or wrong. So it's okay to say stupid things."

"That's never been my problem, Old Man."

Decker smiled. "No thief would go through all that rigmarole to keep the panels for himself. He had a fence or he was hired for a buyer. If it was a buyer, he probably wants all four panels before he shells out money. I'm sure our thief is going to return and try to steal the other panels. So that means surveillance."

"You mean like monitor cameras on the crypt's door?"

"No, I mean like a guy sitting in a hidden place waiting from the thief to return and arresting him."

"It's an open area. Where could we park a car so it wouldn't be noticed?"

"He's going to come at night so that gives us some cover," Decker said.

"We're going to sit here all night, every night until we catch a thief that may or may not show up, take one look at the lone car, and hightail it out of here?"

The kid had a point. "Maybe we could do it with cameras linked up to a surveillance van parked elsewhere. Or I'm only a mile away. I could actually just do this from home."

"And where do you propose we'd find the technology in rural little Greenbury?"

"You're the techno guy. You tell me."

McAdams frowned. "I suppose we can stick a camera in a strategic place and link it up to a tablet or smartphone, Eagle Eye or some system like that."

"That would work for me. We could rotate the watches of the laptop at night between the five of us detectives."

McAdams said, "Do you really think the thief would return to the crypt knowing that the cops are onto him?"

"Why would he think we're onto him?"

"What if the thief saw all the commotion that went on this afternoon?"

"Did you spot anyone nosing around?"

"Not really, but I wasn't looking. What about you?"

"I checked around several times. I didn't notice anyone watching."

"Maybe no one was watching us on the streets. But I'm betting that a few of the neighbors pulled back their curtains to see what was going on."

"Yeah, you're probably right about that. And that leads me to another thought. If we start asking questions locally, eventually the local paper will find out. So will everyone else, including the thief—if he's local. This is a very small town."

"So I repeat. What's next?"

"Not doing surveillance would be negligent. Let's do something before the case blows wide open. Could you help me hook up a camera?"

"Who's gonna pay for this?"

"I'll ask Mike. It's something that's handy to have."

"And if Mike says no?"

"I'll pay. These things aren't that expensive even for an old retiree like myself. Of course, if some rich kid with gold watches wants to pitch in, I won't object."

Despite himself, McAdams smiled. "Maybe that can be arranged." He pulled into the station's parking lot. "Okay. Happy hunting. And what do I do while you're out there making suspect lists and checking them twice? Practice shooting jelly beans out my nose?"

"Can you really do that?" McAdams rolled his eyes and Decker said, "Think about it, McAdams. You tell me. What useful things could you do?"

"Quit this job and do something that will exploit my many talents?"

"Does that include law school?"

A pause. "Eventually."

"How about if you look up past crimes of cemetery theft? If nothing shows up nearby, branch out using Greenbury as the center of the circle. Lots of fancy mausoleums in the area. I'm sure this has happened before."

McAdams sighed. "Fine."

"Too exhausting for you, Harvard?"

"I just think it's stupid."

"Why's that?"

"Because we both think it's a professional theft, especially because the original panels were replaced with forgeries. The probability of finding those stolen panels is very low. It's a lot of effort for very little or no outcome."

Decker shook his head. "Man, you really are in the wrong field. What the hell were you thinking when you signed up?"

McAdams gave the question some serious thought. "My main motivation for taking this job was pissing on my father's expectations. He is really into my going to Harvard Law. Stalling a couple of years is making him nervous and that makes me happy."

"So here's the deal." Decker put his hand on the kid's shoulder. "I can handle this all by my lonesome. So if you want to just fart around, I'm okay with that. No one will have to know. You tell me, Tyler. What do you want to do—if anything?"

"I know I'm acting like a dick." McAdams rubbed his forehead. "I am a dick. I don't like being a dick, but I don't know how not to be a dick. I guess being a dick is better than being a tool. Although I guess I'm kind of a tool, too." He looked up at Decker. "Some people just don't have winning ways."

"Do you know how many different and difficult personalities I've had to work with over the years?" When McAdams didn't answer, Decker said, "Yes, you're a little obnoxious, but nothing I haven't seen before. Besides, I don't care about personalities. I just care about getting the job done and I need to organize my time. In or out?"

"If it would be useful to you, I will look up art thefts on the Internet."

"It would save me time so, yes, it would be useful. And while you're on the computer, find out what you can about Tiffany and, specifically, those panels. See if they were ever mentioned in any book or loaned to a museum for a traveling exhibition."

"I'm not sure I can do all that with just a laptop."

"It's called research. You never wrote a term paper in college?"

"I had all of Widener at my disposal."

"There are five colleges about a mile away that are highly regarded. I know they have libraries."

49

"You know if I start doing that, word might get around that I'm researching Tiffany and grave robberies."

"I'm not too concerned about that, Harvard. You're town, they're gown. Never the twain shall meet."

CHAPTER FIVE

Wan and out of breath, he forced himself to walk calmly down the hallway, knocking on her door instead of banging. As soon as Angeline answered, she took one look at him and asked what was wrong. He came in and gently shut the door. Then he began to pace: hard to do in her tiny one-bedroom apartment.

"*What?*" she asked. "Tell me!"

Panic in her voice. He managed to get it out. "They're onto us. They know about your forgeries."

Angeline felt her heart race. "*My* forgeries? *Our* forgeries, okay."

"Whatever."

"Not whatever. This is a partnership." She rubbed her forehead. "Oh my God, are you sure?"

"Yes." More pacing. "That fucking lock. I knew it was too cold to go out. I knew that there was a chance that the metal would freeze and the key would break off."

"So why did you go out?"

"I figured it was so cold that no one else would be out and I could work without being bothered." He knocked his fist against his head. "Shit! I'm so damn stupid! Wasting

51

all this energy and time and risk for something so in-significant. Serves me right for being greedy!"

Yes, he was greedy, but her main concern was calming him down. His voice was getting louder and louder. She put her finger to his lips and spoke in low tones. "It's like one in the afternoon. Let's sit down and maybe we can work out a plan."

"That's it! No more. I can't take the chance any longer. Not when such big things are at stake."

Angeline tried to take his hand but he pulled it away. She said, "Sit down and let's talk."

Eventually he plopped down on her futon. She sat down next to him, putting her hand on his knee, hoping to make him feel a little bit more relaxed. "Are you sure they know about us?"

"Positive."

"Your client told you this?"

"No, he doesn't know anything about this, thank God for that. I just saw them today at the graveyard at the Bergman mausoleum around an hour ago. I saw the dumbfuck watchman talking to Ken Sobel and his son or son-in-law. It's not good, Angeline. We have to stop."

Not as dumbfuck as you thought. "I guess if you change out the locks and the watchman does his job, discovery was a possible outcome."

"I was going to replace it back with the original. It took me a while to get the fragment out. I couldn't exactly take it to a locksmith."

"That's true." Angeline took a deep breath and let it out. "When you say they're onto us . . . do you mean *us* . . . or the *forgeries*?"

He looked up. "The family knows about the forgeries . . . I'm not positive about us." A pause. "I'm sure they

52

don't know about us. If they did know, we wouldn't be having this conversation."

"So there you go." Angeline felt calmer.

"They can link me to the forgeries if they know my client. But I don't see how that would be possible. You don't even know my client. Unless . . ."

"What?" He always did that. Calm her down to make her nervous again. "Unless what?"

"You have the stained glass that was used in the forgeries. So . . . we need to get rid of the glass."

"Right." She smiled. "You're thinking more clearly than I am."

"And we should do that immediately."

"Okay. So why don't you grab a beer from the fridge and catch your breath and let me pack up my leftover crap. You think about where we should hide the stuff until things cool down."

"I'm not going to hide it. I'll dump it when I go back up north."

"No way. It's top-quality glass and I still have over a thousand dollars' worth of material. I'm not throwing it away."

"It's not wise to hang on to it, Angeline."

"Just . . . chill." She got up and looked at him. Slim, dark, sultry, brilliant, a little bad boy, a little evil and a great fuck. "Think about a plausible story so if the cops pay me a visit, I don't sound like a moron."

"Why would they visit you?"

"Because they'll probably talk to everyone in Littleton— me, my friends, my professors. We're an art college remember?"

"The cops don't touch the colleges, Angeline. Upstate owns this town."

He was right about that. Whenever student shit spilled

into Greenbury, the colleges called up the police and cleaned up the mess so mommy and daddy were none the wiser. "True, but just in case, we should plan something."

He was still in a very dark place but not nearly as panicked as he was a few minutes ago. As she started packing up the glass, he stood up and grabbed a beer from her minifridge. "If you think that there is any chance that the cops will talk to you and will somehow magically find out that you've done stained glass way back when, let's get you some new glass altogether. So when they ask if they can have a sample of your glass, you can say sure."

"Great idea!" She walked over and threw her arms around his neck. "Now you're thinking."

He gently extricated himself from her grip. "I'll go check the Dumpster for empty boxes."

It took him a few minutes to find two big empty boxes. Since the apartment building housed a lot of students, the Dumpsters were always filled with discarded cartons from college kids ordering useless shit. She took the boxes and began the tedious job of wrapping up sheets of glass, one by one by one.

He watched her as she worked, sipping his beer, thinking about how his client had specified paying once he had *all* four panels . . . which of course was no longer an option. Angeline's artistic ability was fine when the panels were twelve feet off the ground. But it wasn't good enough to fool a trained eye. He'd have to find a way to get to the original panels—impossible now—or find a craftsperson good enough to convince a dealer that the works were genuine. And if he commissioned any noteworthy artist to copy the window, he'd have to pay for all four of the panels, because any reputable glass person would ask him why he'd only want two of the four seasons. That would cost big time and in the end, it probably wasn't worth it.

When the big one went down, all the other jobs would seem like pocket change. He just needed to hold on and hold out. He wondered if he should tell his contact about the change of plans.

When she finally finished up packing, she stood up and brushed off her jeans. "You can take it out to the car, but be careful. It's breakable and heavy."

He hoisted the boxes and she followed him outside, watching him stow away the prettiest glass she had ever worked with. It just broke her heart. She felt her eyes moisten.

He closed the trunk and turned to her. "Don't worry, beautiful." He kissed her lips. "It'll be okay."

"I'm just pissed." Her voice was soft. "I actually loved copying those windows. I was really good at it."

Does the word delusional mean anything? He said, "I'll hide the glass somewhere safe. I won't even tell you about it. If you're questioned by the cops, you can honestly be in the dark. When things cool off, you can get your glass back. You're graduating in June anyway. You'll leave this dump and no one will be the wiser."

"I can't wait. I am so sick of small-town living. I can't wait to go back to a real city." Angeline kissed him passionately. "I want to be with you."

"I want to be with you, too. But we have to be patient." Once inside, he whispered, "You know I'm just as vulnerable as you are, Angeline. I still have the two original panels."

She was flabbergasted. "You do? I thought you already sold them."

"The client didn't want to pay me in installments. The truth is I think he has an overseas buyer who will only pay for all four works. So he didn't want the responsibility of having any until we had all four to give him."

55

"Where are they?"

"Need-to-know basis, Angeline. Especially now."

She was aware that he had several places to hide the stuff because he had given her keys—just in case. One bin she had even rented out for him. But as far as she knew, it was empty. But maybe not.

Need-to-know basis.

"Yeah, I guess you're right," she told him.

He kissed her again. "You know you are my girl."

"I sure hope so." She broke away and sat on the futon, the cogs in her brain beginning to turn the wheels. She had spent almost all the money he had given her on her latest handbag. "Can't we just sell the two panels we have?"

"We can't do anything right now."

"I know that. But maybe later."

"Let's not get ahead of ourselves. Right now we're in the weeds. First we have to get ourselves out of this mess and then we can move on. In the meantime, we just shut up and deny."

"But, like, can't we use the panels as leverage? Either your client buys them or we'll get rid of them as we see fit."

He glared at her. "Are you being deliberately thick-headed? We can't touch the Tiffanies. They are stolen, Angeline! The police know they're stolen! Have patience and then when we're thinking more clearly, the solution will be evident."

She nodded. "I guess you're right. The panels aren't going anywhere. I suppose somewhere down the line, we should be able to make a little money out of this."

"Exactly." He could feel his mojo coming back "I've been doing this for a while, babe. Long before you came into the picture."

"Yadda, yadda, yadda."

He smiled. "You want to fuck before I go?"

She hadn't penciled in fucking. She still had a paper to finish up and she was going to meet a couple of friends later in the day and get shitfaced at Morse McKinley: the best parties, the nicest RAs and the most lax on booze. She looked at her watch. She supposed there was enough time to rip off a quick one. She shrugged, sat on her twin mattress, and began to undress.

Within twenty-four hours, a preliminary list from Ken Sobel had come through the station-house's fax machine. Since most of the extended Bergman/Sobel family lived in Manhattan, Decker began to make preparations for an overnight into the city. That meant gearing up not only for the three-hour drive, but also packing a few gifts since he and Rina would be visiting the kids.

Rina's oldest son, Sam, his wife, Rachel, and their baby daughter lived in a rented tiny one bedroom in Brooklyn. They could have rented a bigger place but the kids wanted to save up to buy something after they were done with their training. Jacob, Rina's second son, had moved from Baltimore to Williamsburg where the kid, now in his thirties, was as comfortable with the Chasidim as he was with the hipsters. He and a college friend rented a modest two-bedroom flat that was party central. Hannah, Peter and Rina's daughter, lived a few blocks away from Sam, sharing a place with three roommates. Decker's oldest daughter, Cindy and her husband, Koby, lived in Philadelphia. There was absolutely no room to stay unless they wanted to share the nursery with the twins and sleep on an air mattress on the floor.

The days of roughing it were long gone. Decker was willing to stay at a hotel in Queens or some other borough that was cheaper than Manhattan. But this week they got lucky. Their foster son, Gabriel Whitman, owned a roomy two-bedroom condo bought by his father's money, which was about the only thing that his dad had to offer besides good genetics. The place included a big living room with a piano, two bathrooms, and a refrigerator that was actually in the kitchen. It sat two blocks away from Juilliard right near Columbus Circle. At the moment, he was touring so he was more than thrilled to lend his digs to the Deckers. Not only was it quiet and spacious, Gabe was compulsive so it was cleaner than most five-star hotels.

Once the car's trunk and backseat were packed with luggage and bags, Decker and Rina took off at four A.M. Monday in bitter darkness, hoping to beat Manhattan traffic. Rina had a cooler filled with fruit, cheeses, and Danishes and two thermoses filled with coffee. After the heat kicked in, Rina was comfortable enough to remove her gloves and hat and bulky jacket.

She saw sweat coming off Peter's brow. "Do you want me to help you off with your jacket?'

"No, I've always wanted a portable sauna."

"A simple 'Thank you, darling. That would be lovely' is sufficient." She helped him pull his arms out and removed his parka and threw it on the backseat. "Coffee?"

"Will it burn my lip if I drink it while I drive?"

"I'll test the waters." She poured the coffee into a Styrofoam cup. "Something between lukewarm and hot."

"Bring it on."

She gave him the coffee and put on one of Gabe's CDs. "If you get tired, I'll be happy to drive. You've got work to do. I don't."

"I'm fine. I like to drive."

"Great." Five minutes passed without a word exchanged. Rina finally pushed her seat back and closed her eyes. Just as she was drifting off, she heard Peter talking to her. "Come again?"

"Sorry. Go back to sleep."

"I'd love to talk instead of sleep, but I know you use your time in the car to think."

"Not much to think about. Just got a bunch of people to interview."

"You want to talk about it with me?"

"Why not? You're a captive audience." Decker told her what he learned. When he was done, Rina said, "Interesting. Do you suspect someone in the family?"

"Can't say until I interview them. But the extended family is very large and then there's the daughter-in-law with a spending problem. The crime was calculated. We'll just have to see how it shakes out."

"Anything I can help you with?"

"No, just enjoy the kids and grandchildren."

He grew quiet and so did she.

Decker said, "The expert that Ken Sobel brought in— who also happens to be his son-in-law—has an art glass gallery in Manhattan. I looked up the website. That place has more Tiffany lamps than most museums."

"Are you thinking that he stole the windows and is using the gallery to fence them?"

"Maybe, but the gallery has pieces way more valuable than the panels. And it's been in the same two families for fifty years—Harrison and Stewart, two brothers-in-law."

"There's always room for more profit."

"True and that's why I'd like to interview Max Stewart away from his father-in-law, especially since he's the one who mentioned the spendthrift sister-in-law. It's always interesting when someone points the finger at someone else. Plus he knows the Tiffany market."

"Makes total sense."

Decker paused. "If I brought my wife with me, it would make the visit seem less like an interrogation and more like a fact-finding mission."

Rina was surprised but tried not to show it. "Sure, I'll come if you want."

"The truth is that I don't have the same kind of manpower that I did in L.A. It's just me and McAdams and you know way more than he does about detective work."

"I do?"

"I've been bouncing things off you for years. You've helped me way more than you probably realize."

Rina smiled warmly. "I've very touched." She nudged his shoulder. "So where do we begin?"

Decker grinned. "Did I just unleash something?"

"You did."

"Look, I don't want you to *do* anything. Just look around while I talk to him. And . . . if he has employees who feel like showing you around, maybe you can feel them out."

"Not a problem."

"I mean, don't go around *asking* questions—"

"Peter, I know the difference between being a curious person and a detective. You're the latter, I'm the former. I'm just keeping you company. No harm in that."

"Actually, it might be fun for you. The gallery also sells jewelry, without a doubt beyond my price range."

She was still glowing from the compliment Peter had given her. "I don't need diamonds. I don't need anything. I'm totally happy with what I have."

"I like to buy you things."

"Flowers are always in fashion."

"How about orchids?"

"Orchids are lovely."

Decker sighed. "Maybe one day the orchids will come with a trip to Hawaii."

"Maybe," Rina said. "In the meantime, we can always do a little hula all by our lonesome."

CHAPTER SIX

Williamsburg still teemed with black hats, but now the area was divided between the Chasids with their Borsalinos and the fur-trimmed shtreimels versus the hipsters wearing fedoras, derbies, newsboys, and porkpies. Both groups wore full beards, and even the dress wasn't that dissimilar. There were synagogues, kosher marts, and religious bookstores and dress shops. But the neighborhood also boasted hip bars and restaurants. Even the kosher crowd was getting into the act with establishments serving more exotic things like oxtail soup and grilled chicken hearts.

Sammy Lazarus, and his wife, Rachel, lived a few blocks away from the action in a tiny apartment with their sixteen-month-old daughter, Lily. She was Rina's first blood grandchild and the Deckers' first granddaughter. The little girl had a mop of curly blond hair, bright blue eyes, and a perpetual sunny disposition. As soon as they walked into the living room, Lily began running around in circles, flapping her hands in sheer joy. "Yay, yay, Nana, Boppa, Nana, Boppa, yay, yay, Nana Boppa, yay."

Decker hadn't had a greeting like that since: well, his memory didn't go back that far. But it was nice to be wanted. Rachel invited them in with her wide, white smile. Over her clothes, she wore a butterfly print apron that was dusted with flour and her blond curls were pulled back into a "messy" bun. She gave both of them a big hug. "Someone is very excited." The toddler was running amok. "Can I get you guys something?"

"I'm fine." Rina gave Rachel a kiss on her cheek then tried to corral Lily. "Well, hello, gorgeous. Does Nana get a kiss?"

The toddler stopped in her tracks, backed up, and planted a wet one on Rina's lips. Rina picked her up and smothered her cheek with kisses. "Who does Nana love?"

"Lily." It came out "Weewee." She reached out her hands to Decker. "Boppa."

Decker took her from Rina and tossed her in the air until the child was spasmodic with laughter. When his arms felt as if they were falling off, Decker lowered her to the floor. "How about a break, Miss El?" But she was already running in circles again.

"It's been too cold to go to the park. I think she's a little cooped up. The sun's out. Maybe I'll try to take her today."

"I'll take her if you're busy," Rina offered.

"If you wouldn't mind, that would be helpful." Rachel had taken the time to set up a little spread on their dinette table. She spotted Decker looking at it. "Just a little nibble in case you were hungry."

"Thanks, honey. I'll take some coffee." Rina looked at her watch. It was a little after nine and too early to go out in the cold. Lily had brought out her box of blocks, meaning that they had other vistas to conquer before the park. Rina sat down on the floor, opened the lid, and dumped out the box. "How about if I make a tower and you can knock it down."

The little girl responded with something approximating

"knock it down." Decker made a cup of coffee for Rina and one for himself. Then he took a minichocolate Danish and popped it in his mouth. He turned to Rachel. "How's the residency coming along?"

"One more year." She paused. "I love my profession but sometimes it's hard seeing sick children, especially now that I have Lily." Her eyes watered and she quickly blinked. "How's your new job?"

"It's slower paced, but it's better than retirement."

"Do you miss the LAPD?"

"Not when I'm only three hours away from all the people I love. Moving was a great decision." He hoped he had sounded convincing. The truth? It was hard to regroup. "Today I'm actually here for work. Nothing crucial so we decided to mix it with a little pleasure."

"That's great. We're always so happy to see you. What kind of work are you doing here?"

"Mostly talking to some people. Actually, I've got to be in Manhattan at ten. How long do you think it would take me to get to Columbus Circle?"

"Around a half hour more or less," Rachel said. "What are you looking into if I can ask?"

"An art theft."

"Sounds very intriguing."

"Most intriguing thing I've done in six months." He looked at Lily and Rina.

Rachel said, "I don't know which one is having more fun."

"My vote's with Rina."

"It's so nice having both of you on the East Coast. Sammy is so happy." Again, Rachel teared up. "So we're all going out for dinner tonight?"

"That's the plan."

"It's ten of us, right?"

"Gabe is out of town and his girlfriend's working, so it's only eight."

"That's right. You're staying at Gabe's apartment."

"We are."

"Can we come, too?" Rachel smiled. "I'm kidding . . . sort of. Sometimes this place is very small. I'll make the rez for dinner. How long are two you staying in the city?"

"Just overnight. Then we're off to Philadelphia."

"Give my love to Cindy and Koby. Wow, the twins must be, like, four?"

"Almost four and finally out of diapers, which is good. They're so tall and big that Cindy was running out of disposable options."

"Maybe the next time we can all get together."

Decker said, "That would be great although I'm not sure I could handle all that energy in one room."

Rina spoke up from the floor. "This comment is from a man who has handled hundreds of homicides?"

"My cases involved a different type of energy. Besides, not one homicide victim has ever given me lip." He fished out his car keys. "I'll pick you up in about two, three hours?"

"That should be perfect. Lily will be napping by then anyway." Rina looked at Rachel for confirmation.

The young woman shrugged. "In a perfect world, that would be a yes."

It took a half hour to reach the apartment building and then another fifteen minutes to find a parking space. When Decker finally nabbed a spot, it was eight blocks away from the Sobels' address and required him to back the car into a snowdrift that exploded onto his rear bumper. His blood must have thickened. It was cold but not nearly as cold as up north. He didn't even bother with gloves. Decker

66

had gotten used to the fresh snow crunching under his boots, slow going but pristine. The Manhattan sidewalks were awash in a thin, salty sludge that was often slippery. The current skies were dove gray and while not gloomy, there wasn't a hint of sunshine anywhere.

Melanie and Rick Sobel resided in a complex between Broadway and Amsterdam. The lobby was small and spare with a black, granite floor and mahogany-paneled walls. A doorman let him in. Another uniformed man who sat behind a desk rang up the Sobel unit. Once given permission to enter, Decker rode the elevator to floor 24 out of 40.

He stepped out of the lift and into an anteroom with two doors. The one on his left was closed, but the one on his right was wide open. He knocked anyway and a female voice told him to come inside. He closed the door behind him and waited in an entry hall. From his vantage point, he could peek into a white space that defined the living room. Beyond the floor-to-ceiling windows were rooftops and then Central Park, which, in wintertime, was a quilt of snow and brown. On sunny days, the space would be flooded with light and heat. Unfortunately it was steely outside and the cold had seeped through the glass.

Melanie showed up a minute later, dressed in a white tank top and a white short skirt. She held out her hand to shake Decker's, and then she rubbed her arms. "It's freezing in here."

"It's a little frosty."

"I've been holed up in the back. It's boiling back there. Absolutely no temperature regulation in the apartment. The boiler doesn't do anything for the living room and it turns the den into a steam bath. I've complained and complained, but I think that's just the nature of prewar apartments. They just didn't have the HVAC. Let's go into

67

the den. I can always open a window if it gets too hot."
She turned and Decker followed.

It was a magnificent walnut-paneled room adorned with
carved beams and crown molding. The bookshelves were
filled with more knickknacks than books: lots of framed
pictures along with lots of models of exotic cars—Ferraris,
Maseratis, Bugattis, Porsches, Mercedes, a Delahaye, a
Voisin, a Pierce Arrow, and a dozen other makes he didn't
recognize. The furniture was heavy wood and the seating
was leather. And, as Melanie predicted, it was warm.
Within minutes, Decker was dabbing his forehead. He
removed his parka.

"Can I take that from you?" Without waiting for an
answer, Melanie called out to Katrina. A uniformed maid
came in, took Decker's coat, and left. Then Melanie cranked
open a window and immediately Decker felt a welcome
shot of cold air. She pointed to a couch and both of them
sat down.

"Are you warm or cold?"

Decker nodded. "I'm comfortable, thank you."

"Then you're a first. No one is comfortable in this place.
I would have loved to be able to regulate the temperature,
but Rick refused to even consider anything postwar. He
had to have his prewar co-op. I admit in general the resale
is better—unless you're at 15 CPW or something—but
c'mon, how many more sweltering nights do I have to
put up with just to have bragging rights?"

She bent down to pick up something imaginary on the
floor and gave him a full view of her cleavage. She was
wearing sandals on her feet. Her face was skin stretched
over pronounced cheeks, a big forehead, and a sizable
chin. She had artificial lips that were puffed out like a
sausage. Her complexion was just short of leathery: probably from hours in a tanning bed.

"I don't know how I can possibly help you. I don't even know why you're here. Actually, I do know why you're here. Max sicced you on me, didn't he?"

"Your father-in-law gave me a list of people who knew about the Tiffany panels. You're on the list."

"Am I the first person you've talked to?"

"Third."

"Who were the two before me?"

"Max and Ken."

"And I repeat, Max sicced you on me, right? He can't stand me. The feeling is mutual."

"What don't you like about Max?"

"Other than his arrogance, his pompousness, and his bullying, he's fine."

Decker took out a notebook and began to take notes. His wont was to sink into the back of the couch. Instead, he chose to be professional, precariously perched on the cushion's edge, feeling about as balanced as a Cezanne painting. Weird that he should be thinking in art metaphors. "This is the deal, Mrs. Sobel."

"Melanie, please. Mrs. Sobel is my mother-in-law."

"Okay, Melanie, let me explain the logic. Detectives always work from the inside out—"

"Yeah, yeah, it's always the husband who knocks off the wife."

"I wasn't thinking about guilt although you're making a good point. I was thinking those closest to the victims of the crime usually know the most. I started with Ken, now I'm interviewing his children."

"But there are a zillion people who know about the panels. My father-in-law has two brothers. My husband has cousins. Why start with Ken?"

"First of all, I've got your entire family on my list. I started with Ken because he was my first contact. And he

69

seems to be the leader of the family." Decker waited for her to respond. When she didn't, he said, "I'm just going down in order. Your husband is working and you were kind enough to let me talk to you at ten in the morning. So here I am."

She threw up her arms. "I've got nothing to hide. Ask away."

"I'm going to ask some pretty obvious questions, so bear with me. Did you know that the crypt had original Tiffany pieces?"

"Of course. Everyone in the family knows. And probably a lot of people not in the family. Ken is not the model of discretion. And if you're looking for someone to grill, I would suggest you talk to Max again. It's like the one thing he wants that he can't get hold of. I wouldn't put anything past him."

Decker tried to keep his face flat. "Really?" She didn't answer. He said, "I went online and looked at the Stewart and Harrison gallery inventory. The place has things far more valuable than the windows." She still didn't answer. "Does Max have any vices I should know about?"

"If you call greed a vice, then yes. With Max, it's always about having more, more, more. And he accuses *me* of being a spendthrift."

"He's a spendthrift?" No response. "Is he in hock?"

Melanie blushed. "I wouldn't know about that. I mean he has all this jewelry but do you think his wife ever gets to wear anything . . . well, maybe she wears it, but she certainly doesn't *own* it. I suppose she can *borrow* it if she wants." She looked at Decker. "The point is that everything that Max and his family own is in that store. I mean he and my sister-in-law own this tiny, tiny duplex where they couldn't even entertain a gnat. C'mon already. Just sell a couple of lamps and get something decent. Not

70

something where the kitchen has a view of an air shaft. See what I'm getting at?"

"Not exactly." Decker looked up. "Maybe you should explain it to me."

"The gallery belongs to Max's father and his uncle, Joe. Max is nothing more than a glorified salesman. I think it eats at his kishkas."

"So he doesn't own anything in the gallery? Is that what you're saying?"

"I don't know what he owns or what he doesn't own. All I'm saying is he always wants more."

"So you're thinking that maybe he stole the windows so he could resell them and get some of his own money?"

"I'm not saying that."

"So what are you saying?"

"I don't know what I'm saying. You're twisting my words."

"I'm not trying to do that, Melanie. Do you think Max was involved with the theft?"

She turned bright red. "Not really." She sat up. "But if he's telling you that I was involved, he's crazy."

"Why would he think you're involved?"

"C'mon, I know what he told you."

"What did he tell me?" Decker prompted.

"Lemme see how I can phrase this so it comes out right." She stood up and began to pace. "Ken is a great guy, but tight with a buck, a quality that he passed on to my husband. I never ever buy things we can't afford, but if I can afford it, I don't see why I shouldn't buy it. I mean, why do you work a million hours a week and earn all this money if you're just going to have it molder in stocks and bonds. I realize that it's Rick's business, but he does have a family and why should our children do without when we can plainly do with."

71

She stopped pacing.

"Anyway, this is all very beside the point. I don't know anything about the theft. It's not like it's been preying on my mind. To tell you the truth, Tiffany isn't my style. I am all about sleek and modern. This one room is my compromise to Rick. I mean where would I even put the windows? Although I suppose if I did steal them, I wouldn't hang them out in the open. That would be pretty stupid."

Decker nodded.

"Anything else? I've got a nail appointment."

"Can you think of anyone in the family with money problems?"

"No . . . none of my business. I just wish they'd keep their noses out of my business."

"Anyone in the family who has an addiction—drugs, gambling, sex, bad business? Or bad business deals?"

"Ken's extended family is large: lots of cousins and second cousins. I'm sure there must be a couple with problems. Who doesn't have a family without problems?"

"But nothing jumps into your head?"

She thought about it earnestly. "No . . . not really. But Rick and I *try* to mind our own business. We're both way too busy to worry about other people. If other people don't have a life, that's not my problem. Are we almost done?"

"Just a few routine questions that I'm asking everyone on the list. When was the last time you were in Greenbury?"

"The funeral in the summer when Ken's cousin died. We came in and left the same day. We were with everyone else."

"So you haven't been to Greenbury or the crypt since then?"

"No. I've got better things to do than to schlep up to a musty old crypt in the middle of nowhere."

"Besides Max, who do you think might have wanted to steal the panels?"

She looked aghast. "I didn't say Max stole them."

"So who do you think did it?"

"How would I know?"

"I'm not saying you would know. I'm just asking your opinion."

She stood up, examining her nails that looked perfectly groomed in contour and color. Then she shrugged. "No idea. All I know is it wasn't me."

Two phone messages, three texts, and five missed calls: all from McAdams. The kid either missed his company or had info. Decker dialed his cell. Harvard was peeved.

"What's the purpose of giving me assignments and telling me to call back when you don't answer your phone?"

"I was in the middle of an interview. What do you have for me?"

"Since I outrank you, what do you have for *me*?"

Decker smiled. He recapped the interviews.

McAdams said, "She sounds like a nutcase."

"She's intense."

"We should look into her financials."

"Great idea except we have no legit reason to pull paper on her. Now it's your turn."

"Well, it seems that grave robbing and stealing from cemeteries are time-old traditions. I found quite a few cases of people stealing from cemeteries. The items usually taken are for personal use, things like urns, planters, gravestone decorations, and statues. The thieves usually live close to the graves and were caught with the items displayed in their houses or yards. Then there are the practical thieves who lift things like lawn mowers or weed whackers or shovels for their own gardening purposes."

"Okay. What about valuable items?"

"I don't know how relevant it is to our case because it's old, but I'll tell it to you anyway. A very well-known art dealer named Alastair Duncan was caught selling a stolen Tiffany window to a guy in Japan. It was looted from a local cemetery by a guy named Anthony Casamassima who used to work as a caretaker there."

"Where's there?"

"Salem Fields, New York. It's a massive cemetery on the Brooklyn/Queens border. And it has a lot of Jewish mausoleums because a lot of the families used to belong to Congregation Emanu-El in Manhattan, which used the cemetery to buy plots for its membership. That's the synagogue I told you about with a Tiffany window."

"Where is it?"

"On Fifth Avenue in the Sixties. It's open to the public and from what I saw online, pretty damn ornate. You might want to take a look at it. The Met has some gigantic Tiffany works if you want to get a feel for the art. It's right off the Temple of Dendur."

"The what?"

"A re-creation of an Egyptian temple built by some Roman official. It's a little touristy but a nice space."

"As long as I'm here, I'll try to take it in. What happened to this Duncan guy?"

"Twenty-seven months in prison and $220,000 in restitution. I don't know how much time he actually did and how much of the fine he paid, but he's still considered an active authority on art deco. My guess is it's highly unlikely that Duncan had anything to do with our itty-bitty theft."

"Don't say that to Ken Sobel. When did that theft take place?"

"In the 1990s. Duncan was sentenced in 2012, I believe."

"What about this Casamassima guy?"

"He appears to be a thief of convenience. Like I said, the cemetery was in the neighborhood. I don't think it's likely that he'd travel upstate to steal. And even less likely that he'd bother replacing the stolen windows with fakes. Plus since the original case was solved and they were exposed, all eyes are on both of them."

"Sometimes old habits are hard to break. How was the case solved?"

"I don't know the ins and outs of the investigation but I do know that an FBI informant posed as a hired thief. Graveyard thefts are relatively common. Now if you want to go into actual art thefts, there are lots to choose from: mostly items taken from museums and homes. They also dwarf in size and scope our cemetery break-in."

"Give me an example."

"Let me pull up my notes." Shuffling over the line. "Okay. Here goes. The most famous art theft in this area was paintings stolen from the Isabella Stewart Gardner Museum in Boston."

"Is that the one where they still have the empty picture frames hanging on the walls?"

"I'm impressed, Old Man. How'd you know that?"

"It's called reading the paper. I also remember getting the notice over the lines when I was in LAPD. When did the Gardner theft take place?"

"That was also in the nineties. Thieves posed as police and tied up the guards and walked away with hundreds of millions of dollars of artwork: a Manet, a Vermeer, several works by Degas, and Rembrandt's only known seascape. I don't see this having any connection with our case."

"I agree with you. Anything else that's vaguely similar . . . a theft from an odd place?"

"I did find one theft that was more our scale. And it's still unsolved. But it's also very old."

75

"Let's hear it."

"Hold on . . . okay . . . here we go. It took place twenty-five years ago in Marylebone, Rhode Island, about an hour away from Greenbury. Four mosaics were taken from the iconography of St. Stephen's, a Russian Orthodox church. The mosaics were fashioned after the ones at the Church of San Vitale in Ravenna, Italy. Would you like to know about Ravenna, Italy?"

"First I'd like to know what an iconography is."

"Oh, sure . . . you know that most churches are laid out like crosses."

"Yeah, the transept, nave, and apse . . . I do crossword puzzles."

"Okay. On the transept wall—that's the wall that forms the shorter end of the cross—leading up to the nave where the priest leads the service, there are often images of the saints or the Madonna or Jesus. It can be statues, gold work, bas-relief, oil paintings, and in this case, they were mosaics. Would you like to hear about Ravenna now?"

"Sure."

"Let me get my notes . . . here we go. Around 400 Common Era, there were essentially two parts to the Roman Empire—a western Rome that was under siege by the Ostrogoths and an eastern Rome that still had its territories in eastern Europe and the Levant. Justinian along with his general Belisarius recaptured and reunited a large part of the Roman Empire. But Justinian was also a religious autocrat and that resulted in a schism with the pope in Rome. So Justinian's solution was to move the capital of the western Roman Empire to Ravenna, Italy. The city was influenced more by Venice—then a city-state—than by Rome. Venice, in turn, was way more influenced by Byzantine Christianity than Roman Christianity because Venice did its primary trade down the Adriatic to Greece and Turkey.

"At Ravenna, inside the Church of St. Vitale, there are these incredible mosaics done in Byzantine style, influenced by the masterpieces in the Hagia Sophia in Istanbul, which he rebuilt as well. The tile work in Ravenna was commissioned by Justinian and his coruling wife, Theodora. Their faces are on the models in the mosaics and she is featured almost as much as Justinian was. And—point of information—neither one of the Roman rulers ever lived in Ravenna as its capital.

"There's a point to all this rambling. A lot of art nouveau was influenced by the incredible tile work of this period. So it's not uncommon that tile workers in the Greek Orthodox or Russian Orthodox churches at the turn of the twentieth century would model their works with Ravenna or Hagia Sophia in mind, only they'd throw in an art nouveau riff. These particular mosaic icons were the work of a Russian artisan named Nikolai Petroshkovich who had worked on all the Romanovs' palaces—Peterhof, the Catherine Palace, the Hermitage—doing restorations. He immigrated to New York in 1910 when he saw which way the winds of discontent were blowing. The iconography in the church was considered a prime example of art nouveau mosaic work done in the Byzantine style. And it was a major heartbreak to the church when it was stolen."

A long pause.

McAdams said, "I'm done unless you want to know more history about Justinian and Theodora."

"No, I'm fine for now. I'm just thinking . . ." A long pause. "We are interested in this case because . . . it took place around the same geographical area and a break-in involved a theft from an unusual place—a church and a graveyard—not a museum or the home of an art collector."

"And they both involve art nouveau items."

"Right . . . that's good, McAdams. And the church case was never solved?"

"I haven't found it on the Internet. I'll delve a little further. What are you thinking?"

"It could be someone local who's paying for stolen art. But if the cases are related, it's someone who has been collecting for personal use over many years. We're not talking museum thefts, we're talking thefts that would go under the radar. Someone who started stealing in his twenties through forties and would now be between his fifties and seventies."

"And still active."

"Someone with champagne taste on a beer budget. Like an art historian, a curator, or maybe a professor." Decker paused. "Maybe an art history prof at Littleton because it's an art college. But first I have to rule out the family. And that will take a while."

"Take all the time you want. Nothing is happening here."

"McAdams, could you find out who the detectives were on the case? If they had a few *local* suspects in mind, they can tell us what roads to travel."

"Well, whatever roads they traveled were bad ones because the case wasn't solved. Besides, I didn't find anything about the detectives on the Internet."

"That's why you need to call up Marylebone and get the names. Then I'll call up the old-timers and pump them for info. I can relate better than you."

"That's for sure. You know if these guys are still alive, they must be like eighty."

"Haven't you heard, McAdams? Eighty is the new sixty."

CHAPTER SEVEN

After walking through a sally port, Decker and Rina walked into a mirrored-wall gallery fronted by display cases filled with gems, jewelry, and objets d'art. A twig-thin blonde of forty was perusing the wares, her face and eyes registering indifference at the pieces being shown to her. Decker supposed it would take something massive to compete with the rock on her finger. As he regarded her face, he thought about the difference between the coasts. It wasn't that L.A. didn't have its fair share of "look at me" gals, but the women seemed to relish their bling. This Park Avenue princess seemed to delight in her disinterest.

On the black velvet tray was a mine's worth of ice that had been set into earrings, bracelets, and necklaces. Maxwell Stewart looked up and gave Decker a nod. He was dressed in a black suit, white shirt, and plaid bow tie. As the woman talked, he listened and brought out another piece of serious sparkle. He seemed professional but not fawning. A minute later, he pressed a button. Another forty-year-old woman, wearing an emerald dress and pearls, came through the back. She had curly red hair and a big, white smile.

Max said, "Could you excuse me for a moment, Dawn?

I have an appointment that I can change but I have a feeling that Detective Decker can't."

"Detective?" Dawn's face finally registered an emotion: a speck of curiosity. "What's going on?"

"Nothing important." He smiled at Decker. "No offense."

"None taken."

Dawn looked Decker up and down, her eyes completely ignoring Rina.

Max said, "Jill knows the inventory better than I do. She can help you find whatever you want." He lifted up the countertop and came over to Decker and Rina. "Welcome to the gallery." His eyes on Rina. "Maxwell Stewart."

"Rina Decker." She held out her hand. "We can wait until you're done with your client." Her lips formed a big smile. "We don't mind browsing."

"Speak for yourself, Lone Ranger," Decker grumped.

"You could get into a lot of trouble here," Max said.

"Thankfully I'm limited by my wallet."

"Nonsense. We have something for everybody."

"Let's hear it for jewelry ecumenicalism," Rina said. "Why don't I have a look around while you two gentlemen talk? There's a lot here to keep me occupied."

"Enjoy yourself. But I feel compelled to tell you that our best pieces are downstairs."

Decker said. "Is that where you're hiding all those Tiffany lamps that I saw online?"

"I'm not hiding anything," Max said. "This is not a museum. Everything is for sale. That's how I pay my mortgage. Would you like a tour?"

Decker looked at Rina who said, "Sure, if you wouldn't mind."

"Not that we can buy anything," Decker said.

"Not right now but there's always the lottery," Rina said.

"Exactly." Max was already headed down the stairs. "And

when you do strike it rich, remember me with fondness."
He flicked on the lights and the modern world of technology suddenly gave way to an elegant life of yesteryear.

Dozens upon dozens of Tiffany lamps in all shapes, patterns, and sizes, some of them geometric in design but more of them highlighting nature. The shades included, but were not limited to, dragonflies, lilies, daffodils, poppies, peonies, dogwood, cherry blossoms, woodbine, lemon leaf, and the graceful blues and purples of the draping wisteria vine—one of the most desirable shades, Max explained. The swirling glass was infused with rich colors, fashioned with such precision that the final work had depth as well as sparkle. Each one was spectacular: as a gestalt, it was eye popping.

The lamps were set on tabletops designed by masters of art nouveau furniture: the free-flowing signature pieces of Louis Majorelle along with the precise inlay work of Émile Gallé. Cabinets and display cases contained Tiffany desk items in all kinds of patterns. Original Alphonse Mucha posters, featuring images of girls with swirling hair and free-flowing gowns, hung on the walls. Along with the artwork was a poster of a painting by Gustav Klimt—odd because it was mass produced.

Max said. "It's one of my favorite works. If I can't own the original . . ."

While Decker was taking in Max's lecture on Tiffany, Rina stole away and took a closer look at the poster of *The Kiss* by the Austrian master. Amid the swirls, squares, and starbursts of color and gilt was a very erotic painting, the man smothering a beautiful woman's face with a passionate kiss on the cheek. She studied it until she heard her husband's voice.

"Are you with us, darlin'?"

Rina scooted over to his side. "Sorry."

Max said. "The original *Kiss* is in Vienna. But if you want a close-up look at one of Klimt's masterpieces, the Neue Museum on Fifth has the original portrait of Adele Bloch-Bauer I. If you haven't seen it, you should."

"I have seen it," Rina said. "I just forget how arresting he is. You have to wonder how a mind works to have created something so beautiful . . . dreamlike."

Max said, "He was influenced by a lot of ancient art, specifically the Byzantine mosaics at Ravenna."

Talk about perfect timing. Decker raised his eyebrows. "St. Vitale Church. The mosaics of Justinian and Theodora." When Rina and Max stared at him. "Imagine commissioning all that artwork in a capital where they never even lived."

Max said, "You've been to Ravenna?"

"No, but it's on my bucket list."

"Since when?" Rina asked. "Where is Ravenna? Greece?"

"Italy," Decker said. "It was once the capital of the western Roman Empire."

"Now you're just showing off," Rina said.

Decker smiled. "Impressed?"

"You had me at St. Vitale Church." Rina turned to Max. "Thanks for showing me your unbelievable pieces. I think I'll go upstairs and stare at the bling. I promise I won't interfere with your client."

"Dawn?" Max gave a dismissive wave. "She's one of those women who's status rich but cash short. We've been working together for years. She buys a piece from me retail and then sells it back to me wholesale in order to buy another piece . . . which she pays retail. It's a happy arrangement. I make money and she appears to have an extensive jewelry collection. As far as her friends are concerned, she is dripping in diamonds because she never wears the same piece twice."

*   *   *

After Rina had left, Max gave a sly smile. "So where'd you pull that rabbit out of your hat? Or is art history a secret love of yours?"

"We detectives are tricky folk." Decker walked over to a green Majorelle love seat. "Can I sit down or . . ."

"The furniture is not only beautiful, it's usable. Be my guest."

"Thanks." He gingerly put his rear on the cushion. Max sat opposite. Decker said, "I interviewed your sister-in-law."

"No love lost, correct?"

Decker's shrug was noncommittal. "After doing hundreds of these kinds of things, you get feelings when someone is lying. She's not lying. She didn't have anything to do with the theft."

"I believe you. Did she implicate me?"

"Not seriously." Decker took out a notebook. "So if it's not you and it's not her, give me some direction with the list." He handed it to Maxwell who studied it for a few minutes.

The dealer finally said, "I'm really sorry, Detective. Nothing is jumping out at me."

"No ne'er-do-well with an addiction problem?"

"Oh, I see where you're coming from." He pointed to a name. "Rubin and Anne Sobel. Rubin is a first or second cousin to Ken. Both of their kids have had some substance abuse problems as teens. Campbell is doing all right from what I last heard."

"Is that a boy or girl?"

"She's twenty. I think she's at Hampshire. Her older brother, Livingston, has been in and out of rehab. I don't know if he even lives in the New York area anymore. But just because he's had problems doesn't make him a thief."

"Of course not. Did he go to college?"

"Dropped out after a year."

"Where'd he go?"

"Uh . . . Brown, I believe."

"So inherently, he's a smart guy."

"Yeah, he is smart. I see him more of an Occupy Wall Street guy than a thief. Honestly, Detective, it would surprise me if it were someone in the family."

"Well, I don't think I'm working with amateurs," Decker said. "If it were amateurs, they'd steal all four panels at once. And they certainly wouldn't bother making replicas. But if it were a truly professional job, it wouldn't have been done piecemeal like it was. So I'm looking for something in between, which makes it hard for me to get a handle on what is truly going on."

"Any ideas?" Max asked.

"I was going to ask you the same thing. Put yourself in my shoes. Where should I be concentrating my efforts?"

Max was silent. Then he finally said, "Well . . . the thief was definitely trying to hide the crime with those poor replicas. He or she didn't want anyone to notice."

"Okay. That's a lot of work to go into hiding a theft. Why would someone do that? What outcome would be worth that much effort?"

"For one thing, it would buy time for the thief to sell the panels to the highest bidder," Max said. "Also if the theft wasn't reported, an auction house could conceivably buy them, which would give the thief more options."

Decker started to scribble in his notepad. "That makes sense. So who would you be looking for if you were me?"

"Usually dealers who dabble in stolen art don't sully their hands directly. I'd say the dealer definitely hired out."

"So you think it's a dealer?"

"Possibly."

"Is there anyone in the family who's an art dealer?"

"Besides me?" When Decker smiled, Max said, "Do I like where this is going?"

"I'm talking to you about it. I'm being very up-front."

"We're the only gallery in the family. And since I didn't steal them, I have no idea who is calling the shots."

"Okay. Let's put that aside for a moment. If the guy hired out, who would he hire?"

"Obviously someone who could do stained glass. Or maybe he'd hire someone who would hire someone who could do stained glass."

"Put a little distance between him and the theft."

"Exactly. From the looks of the pieces, I'd say maybe it's a hobbyist or an art student."

Decker nodded but didn't say anything. It very well could be a student who was hard up for money. "Do you know which institutions teach stained glass?"

"All the art schools I would imagine. What about Littleton in the Five Colleges? That's in your own backyard."

"It's on my list. But as you so aptly pointed out, I may also be looking for a dealer. If you could give me a list of dealers with . . . how can I put it . . . questionable morals . . . maybe you've heard some rumors for instance?"

"You always hear rumors. We're in a venal business."

Decker laughed. "Anything that you could do to help me would be appreciated. In the meantime, I still have to run down the list of family members."

"Even though you don't think any of them had anything to do with it."

"I have to keep an open mind. Maybe someone in the family teamed up with a dealer for quick cash."

"I don't see it. I can't even see Melanie doing that. She isn't capable of that much executive planning. Besides, her husband makes a fortune."

"What does he do?"

"Hedge fund. They did very well last year. I should know. I have money with him. And I know that Rick got a huge bonus."

"Okay . . . so let's leave the family aside for a moment. I want to go back to art thefts. Is that a problem for you—people breaking into your gallery?"

"Not yet, thank God. My security is excellent!"

"What about thefts from other galleries in the area?"

"You mean like Mark Lugo?"

"Who's he?"

"He lifted a Fernand Léger from a local gallery in the Carlyle. Wasn't the first time he stole. He lifted a Picasso in San Francisco."

"He was a dealer who sold the pieces for profit?"

"No, he was a sommelier who kept the paintings in his apartment in New Jersey."

"A sommelier?"

"Yes, and I bet he had an extensive wine collection as well. That one popped into my mind because it's recent, but there are probably dozens of them. You can probably look up gallery thefts on the Internet."

"Getting back to our case. What about other thefts from graveyards or mausoleums?"

"Sure, there are people who steal from graveyards all the time. The most famous theft that I know of was Alastair Duncan who was convicted of stealing a five-hundred-pound Tiffany window and selling it to a Japanese collector for over two hundred thousand dollars. He was teamed up with someone who lived in Queens."

"Anthony Casamassima. Salem Fields Cemetery. He claimed he was liberating broken-down treasures in very poor condition. That one was solved using an undercover FBI agent."

Max stared at him. "I see you've done your homework."

"It's all at the click of a button, Max. My partner also found a very old art theft from a Russian Orthodox church in Marylebone, Rhode Island. That one interests me a little more because it's still unsolved and the thief took items in the art nouveau period. Would you happen to know anything about that?"

"The Petroshkovich icons. That was before my time, but I do remember my dad talking about it. It was a big deal." A pause. "Now that was a professional job."

"What makes you say that?"

"Because the thieves only took the Petroshkoviches, nothing else in the church. There were things that were a lot flashier. They knew what they wanted."

"Just like the thieves knew that your father-in-law's pieces were real Tiffany."

"I do not deny the value of Tiffany . . . Lord knows that's how I put bread on the table. But the Petroshkovich icons are way more valuable because they're rarer. When did the theft take place? It must have been around thirty years ago."

"Yep. It's an old case and a cold case, but it's still wide open. And that makes it interesting." Decker folded his notebook and stood up. "I don't even need wide open, Max. I have confidence in my skills. All I need is just a toe in the door."

CHAPTER EIGHT

Once outside the gallery, Decker and Rina walked glove in glove down Fifth Avenue, dodging the crowds of shoppers, executive and middle management suits, and tourists who didn't mind braving the cold to get the winter discounts at the hotels. There were a couple of kosher restaurants nearby and it was around twelve-thirty, so lunch was in order. They nabbed one of the last tables at a meat restaurant in Midtown. Erelong, there wasn't a chair to be had. Service was slow, but that gave Decker a chance to make a few phone calls, confirming interviews with other Sobel family members.

Forty-minutes later, the waiter served two hamburgers that were slider sized at prime rib prices. Still, it felt good to get out of the small town. He could actually feel his pulse rise. "How's your food?"

"It's tasty . . . perfect if it were a first course."

"And therein lies the rub."

Rina smiled. "Once when I was visiting Sammy, I went out to lunch with an old friend while he was busy. I ordered a niçoise salad appetizer. I needed a magnifying glass to see it."

"Yeah and a pair of tweezers to pick it up." Decker was trying to figure out how to eat the burger in more than two bites. "Thanks for coming with me."

"You're welcome. Not that I learned anything juicy about Max or anyone else for that matter."

"So what did you learn?"

"Gallery has been around for years. I asked if Max owns it and Jill said he works there side by side his father, Keith, whom I met."

"Nice guy?"

"He was running out the door when I was introduced. He seemed fine. Also, there's a cousin who mostly does the jewelry buying. Her name is Katy Mendel. Jill says she's lovely."

"Any strife between any of the relatives? Or you probably didn't ask."

"No, I didn't ask." Rina picked up a pickle that was bigger than the burger. "Jill didn't give off any vibes of conflict. She's been working there fifteen years. Are you still considering Max a suspect?"

"I can't see him stealing four small Tiffany panels, ruining his name, and committing a crime, when he has such a vast inventory to steal from. And he could probably alter the books without anyone noticing for a while. So for the moment, he's near the bottom."

Rina said, "So what's your plan now?"

"I'll go down the list of family members and people who knew about the panels and see what I can dig up. What's the jewelry woman's name again? Katy what?"

"Mendel."

"Thanks." Decker wrote the name on his notepad. "I did find out from Tyler that stealing from graveyards isn't unusual. The most likely culprits are the caretakers and people who live around the cemeteries."

"What do they take when they're not stealing Tiffany?"

"Planters, urns, statues, architectural decorative elements, lawn mowers, shovels, even gravestones."

"So maybe your thief is closer to home."

"Whoever did this put time and money into replacing the panels so no one would notice. He probably had a buyer lined up before he stole the first panel." Decker regarded his empty plate. His hand made a beeline for the breadbasket.

Rina stopped him. "You want to split another hamburger."

"Not at these prices. And plus we're taking the family out tonight. I'd like to go home with some money in the bank."

"We can afford another hamburger." Without asking, Rina summoned a waiter and ordered another burger. She gave him a wide smile. "Tell them to be a little more generous on the beef. You're not feeding supermodels, okay?"

Decker laughed as the waiter huffed away. "Before we leave Manhattan, I'd like to check out the Met. They have Tiffany glass panels that I'd like to see. Also there's a place . . . Emanu-El? Do you know it?"

"Sure. It's been around since the mid-1800s. It's reform." She began playing with her phone. "Started by German Jews. Prime example of Moorish Revival . . . ah, there's a Tiffany window there. That's why you want to see it."

"Not that I need to see it, but as long as I'm here I figure I should educate myself." He looked up. "Want to come with me?"

"I'd love to." She stowed her phone back in her purse. "So are you going to tell me how you suddenly became an expert on Byzantine mosaics?"

Decker smiled. "McAdams gave me a history lesson about fifteen minutes before we met to go to the gallery."

"Why?"

"It had to do with an art theft that happened thirty years ago. Four mosaic icons from a Russian Orthodox church in Rhode Island made by an artist named Nikolai Petroshkovich. What was stolen was done in the style of the mosaics at Ravenna. The timing couldn't have been more advantageous."

"You sounded casual but very impressive. What does an old art theft have to do with your case?"

"Probably nothing. I asked McAdams to look up all major art thefts around our town and I'm not about to punish him for being thorough."

"For once."

"Yeah, for once. Mostly he just clocks in the hours. Why he signed up for Greenbury Police is still a mystery. He seems to hate everything about his life there."

"I'm sure there's a backstory."

"My opinion? I think he's secretly writing a screenplay and that's why he joined any police force that would take him. The guy is pure Hollywood to me."

"I'm sure it'll all come out one day."

A pause. Decker said, "I'd like to talk to the detectives who worked that Rhode Island case if they're alive. Find out the steps they took to attempt to trace stolen art. I'm hoping that they still live in the area."

"Maybe we should extend our visit to another day to give you a little more time."

"You mean more time with Lily."

"And more time for the twins, too. There's nothing wrong with that." The second burger came. Rina pushed it toward her husband. "You take the whole thing. I'm full."

"You're just being nice."

"Honestly, I'm okay." She took her husband's hand.

"Peter, we moved back east to be closer to the kids. Also, you retired from the big city so we wouldn't be so rushed about everything. We could stroll instead of jog. It's so lovely that we're going to see the Met and Emanu-El together. Please try not to slip into LAPD work mode just because you finally have a real case. Besides, you have Tyler to handle the slack."

Decker picked up his miniburger and managed not to eat the entire thing in one bite. "You're right. There is work I can do here and an extra day wouldn't hurt. I'll call Mike. I'm sure it won't be a problem."

"Thank you."

"You're welcome," Decker said. "But let me tell you something, woman. If there's a cat in a tree that doesn't make it because Tyler's too lazy, I'm going to put the blame squarely on your shoulders."

After seeing Rina off, Decker made several phone calls while sitting on a park bench. Temperatures had climbed to the high thirties with no wind: practically spring climate compared to the icy conditions and gray skies in Greenbury. The fresh air felt bracing on his face and woke him from his usual afternoon torpor.

His aim was to narrow the playing field by crossing off as many members of the Sobel family as he could. First to go were the distant relatives who had professed ignorance about the family mausoleum in Greenbury. Next, he spoke to those who did know of the mausoleum's existence but had never stepped foot in the town. All their claims were verified by quick calls to Ken Sobel. Then he called up Katy Mendel—the jewelry buyer for Max Stewart. She also seemed to be a straight arrow. His leads were disappearing as he checked off each name on his list.

He'd been sitting for over an hour and the chill was starting to get to him. He walked back to his car, cranked up the heat, and spoke from his office on wheels, ignoring the honks and the pleading eyes of motorists aching for his parking spot.

The most interesting group was close family members: those who had been at the funeral last summer and probably knew about the expensive glass panels inside the vault. On the surface, they seemed like poor candidates for hands-on criminal enterprise. Most of them appeared to have the trappings of wealth: good jobs, stable marriages, and tony addresses. When questioned, they seemed appalled by the thefts and even more outraged that he was looking at them with a detective's eye.

Between phone calls and interviews with the family, the Met and Emanu-El were perfect places to visit with Rina. The museum was open until six. The temple was open tomorrow between ten and four and visitors were welcome without an appointment. Then it was off to Philadelphia to see Cindy, Koby, and the kids.

It was close to six in the evening when Decker headed back to Brooklyn for the family dinner. He was also starved so he hoped that wherever Rachel and Sammy had chosen, the place believed in large portions. The minihamburgers had long been digested, leaving a raw ache inside his stomach. At this point it was all about quantity rather than quality. As he drove, he started thinking about the theft, wondering if McAdams had dug up anything since the last time they spoke.

Arriving in Brooklyn at the kids' apartment, he was tired and grumpy, but the baby's smile cheered him up. Soon the space began to shrink as the crowd grew. It was wonderful to see everyone. There were hugs, kisses, and lots of laughter and that was before dinner. Finally, everybody was assembled and Rachel had finished giving the babysitter last-minute instructions. The brood stepped out into the cold night air, Decker's children walking ahead, catching up with one another's lives. They talked about movies, songs, and television series that left Decker in the dark.

"Do you know what they're talking about?" he asked Rina.

"Kinda. You know, we do have Netflix. You can stream a lot of series. That means you watch them all at once."

"I know what streaming is, Ms. Flipphone."

"It serves me perfectly well. All I do is make calls and text. Why should I get a new one, especially in a small town where we don't need an app to know every single gas station or movie theater within a thirty-mile radius."

Decker felt his own smartphone vibrate. Without checking the caller, he let the call go to voice mail. He watched his kids joke around with each other. "We did something right. They all seem to get along." His phone vibrated again. He took it out of his coat pocket and checked the prefix. "It's the police station. Probably McAdams. I should probably take this."

"Why are they calling so late in the evening?"

"Yeah, that ain't good." He slowed his walk. "Go on with the kids. I'll meet up with you."

"Do you know where the restaurant is?"

"Actually, I have no idea." He dithered so long that the call went to voice mail again. He debated whether or not to call back. "Whatever it is, I suppose it can wait until I get fed."

"That certainly is a change in your previous attitude."

"Yeah, the difference between being the person in charge and being a peon. Besides, how can I help? I'm three hours away." They were almost at the entrance of the restaurant when the phone buzzed a third time.

95

Rina said, "It must be important."

"Yeah, I guess. Go in with the family. I'll be with you in a few minutes." He pressed the button. "Hey, Harvard, what do you have for me?"

"It's not McAdams, Pete, it's Mike Radar."

Decker had asked the captain for another day in Manhattan so he had expected to hear back. But not at eight in the evening. And not with the tone of voice he was using: all business.

Mike said, "How soon can you get back here?"

"How soon do you need?"

"Ten minutes ago."

"What is it?"

"Homicide. First real one we've had in twenty years and it's nasty. It should make you feel right at home."

Decker went back to Sammy's place and grabbed the car, insisting that Rina stay in Brooklyn and visit Cindy, Koby, and the boys tomorrow. They'd be disappointed if no one made the trip, and he'd most likely be very busy for the next twenty-four hours.

He made it back to Greenbury in two hours and fifteen minutes.

He was famished, although he barely noticed his pangs because as soon as he pulled up in front of the apartment building, his heart began to beat in full throttle. The "crime scene" was a mess and teeming with people who didn't belong. Nothing was taped off so everyone was tromping around the complex, destroying things like possible shoe prints and tire tracks and trace evidence.

The neighbors were out in droves. Greenbury PD was small. Often, the guys and gals took turns doing uniform duties and detective work. So in a very short time, Decker knew the entire force by name. Stacy Steven, bundled in outerwear to protect her from the frigid temperatures, was guarding the doorway to the building. She was very young and seemed relieved when she spotted Decker. "The captain's inside. Unit 14."

"Anyone else here besides you?"

"Yeah, everyone from the department is here. Mike put me in front and told me not to let anyone in or out."

"When was it reported? The homicide."

"I don't know. Mike called all of us down about two hours ago." She jumped up and down and rubbed her hands together.

"You've been out here for two hours?" When she nodded, Decker said, "Let's see if we can get a change of guard. Actually we should have a few people out here, shooing away the neighbors and putting up some crime scene tape." No response. "You do have crime scene tape."

"Honestly, I have no idea." She paused. "We have traffic cones somewhere."

"That'll work. Hang in, Stacy. I'll be back in fifteen minutes with some help." He quickly made his way up to the apartment unit, the living room stuffed with police personnel. The windows were wide open letting in the cold night air.

Kevin Butterfield, a ten-year veteran of Greenbury, came up to him. "The body's in the bedroom. Young and female. Probably a student at the colleges."

"Is this considered campus housing?"

"It's a little distant from the main campus, but the colleges have spread out so much over the past ten years, I really don't know."

"Anyone from campus police here?"

"Maybe Mike called someone down."

"I didn't see any wagon outside. Has anyone from the coroner's office been here?"

"Mike would know." He pointed in the direction of an open door. "There's where all the action is." Kevin shook his head. "This must be one hell of a welcome for you."

"Maybe it's me, Kevin. I just bring sunshine and good cheer wherever I go."

"Angeline Moreau, twenty-two, a student at Littleton." Mike ran his hands through his hair and looked up. "That's according to the school ID that we found in her desk. It's kind of hard to make a definite ID because the face is distorted. We may need dental or DNA."

Decker was looking at the surroundings as the captain spoke. It was a brutal scene. "Did you find a purse and a cell phone?"

"Nope . . . we looked. That immediately brings to mind a robbery, except that she had cash and jewelry in her desk. Maybe he was looking around when she surprised him by walking inside her apartment and all hell broke loose. He took her phone and her purse and made a beeline for the door."

Decker nodded. "Do you know if the body has been moved?"

"I was here when the manager opened the door and I haven't left except for a piss. Believe me, no one has touched her. Since it's a homicide, I'm waiting for a city coroner with homicide experience, not the local doctor who certifies death."

"Good idea." Decker's eyes were on the walls: blood spatter was everywhere. There was ripped bedding and upended furniture—a battle had taken place. "Has anyone started interviewing the neighbors to find out what they heard or saw?"

"I put Jack and Carol on it."

"And?"

"Nothing yet."

"Mike, look at this place. It's a war zone. There had to be plenty of bumps and thumps. We got nosy neighbors in this town. Someone must have parted their blinds."

"The problem is that the apartment is mostly student rented even though it's off-campus. It's a noisy environment—lots of parties with music blasting all the time."

Decker was still dubious, but he kept it to himself. He didn't know how the captain would react to being challenged. "This is a huge mess. Do we have tech people who know forensics?"

"We're working on that as well." Mike was troubled. "I want to do justice to this girl, Pete. No one wants this screwed up."

"We all want the same thing." Decker stared down at the heap that once was a human being. She was already deep in a state of decomposition. "How were you notified? Did someone complain about the smell?"

"Yep."

"Who opened the windows?"

"I did. It must have been a hundred degrees inside when I got here."

"Okay." Decker paused. "Someone cranked up the heat to help the body rot. Did you happen to notice the exact temperature before you opened the windows? If you take into consideration the stage of decomposition and the temperature, it might give us an idea of when she was murdered."

Mike looked pained. "No, I didn't. This is what I mean by screwing things up. Can I be frank with you?"

"Always."

"I can work a homicide. Ben can work a homicide. Kevin can work a homicide. But none of us has done it in years. I'm thinking about calling in reinforcements."

"Up to you."

"But then I start thinking, this is my town. I don't want hotshots walking all over us and telling me how to handle my people. You, on the other hand, are fresh from the trenches. So if you're up to leading, I think we should give it a go. What do you think?"

"If this were LAPD, I'd say no problem. I could do the whole thing solo. But I am new here . . . neighbors don't know me well . . . and we're not exactly high tech." Decker shrugged. "Give me twenty-four to forty-eight hours to feel everything out and I'll let you know."

"Fair enough."

"Right now, we need a police photographer."

"Jenny photographed every inch of the body that we can see. Like I said, we haven't moved her."

"Just make sure that we have doubles and triples of everything and from every angle. It might help us down the line. How long do you think it'll be before someone from the coroner's office gets here, Mike?"

"No idea. We're in New York so it should be them. But we're closer to Boston. I called both cities. Let's see who shows up. And I also called CSI and Forensics. If you can think of anything else, I'm listening. Want me to close the windows?"

"No. Keep them open. It'll slow down the decay." Decker thought a moment. "She was a student at Littleton—that's the fine arts college, right?"

"Yes, it is: arts, theater, and acting. You're thinking about a connection to the cemetery theft?"

"Someone was making phony stained glass. Even if it has nothing to do with the theft, we need to get a team out there to start questioning friends, teachers . . . her classmates. Find out more about who Angeline Moreau was."

Mike raised an eyebrow. "This is going to be an issue, Pete. It's not that I don't have faith in my staff. I think we've got a great bunch of guys and gals here. And if this was a homicide that had to do with a bar fight or a domestic or even burglary, I'd feel good about assigning any one of our people.

"Problem is, handling the colleges is a delicate situation. We need a seasoned guy. I know you can't be two places at once, but I can supervise the techs once they get here. I can talk to the coroner. Maybe you should do the interviewing."

"That's fine. Just give me a few minutes to think. Do you have a tablet?"

"You mean like an iPad? Not on me, but I suppose I can authorize the money."

"I was thinking low tech: a notebook and something I can write with."

Mike smiled and handed him his pad and a pencil. Decker took it and squatted next to the body.

Angeline Moreau was fully clothed and wasn't positioned sexually: Her pants hadn't been pulled off and although her top had flipped up, Decker could see that her bra was clasped. There was nothing to suggest sexual assault, but a rape kit would be ordered anyway. Sometimes the killer orders the victim to put her clothing back on. Or maybe she had recent, consensual sex and that could be a lead.

Since it was wintertime and the windows had been closed tight, there was no insect activity. No flies, no maggots, and no way to date the body using the critters. The flesh hadn't been eaten up by external factors, but the body gases were exploding from the inside out. She had a bloated, eggplant-colored face that was shedding skin. Eyeballs had sunk into her sockets. Because of the swelling, it was hard to decipher things like ligature marks and bruises. Even things like knife wounds close up with the swelling. But Decker could discern dried blood that had leaked from the nose and a split lip. As he examined the face further, he noticed dark spots that could have been bruises.

"Looks like she might have been punched hard in the face." Decker stood up. He ripped out a few blank papers of the tablet and started scribbling. "This is your department and your call. But this is what I'd suggest."

"Please."

"First of all, Stacy is freezing out there. Rotate a couple of people every two hours outside so no one gets frostbite. Second, let's cordon off the area. If you don't have crime tape, have someone get some traffic cones and we'll tie string around them. We need to keep whatever we have left intact. Third, get everyone out of the apartment except a few of your select chosen. Put all the rest on canvass duty. Assign them to talk to every single neighbor within a couple of blocks. If this is mostly a student apartment, the kids aren't going to feel loyal to Greenbury so we may hit a wall of silence. There's a dead girl here and we need to push. I'm not saying we run roughshod over the kids, but we need them to know that we're not going to go away. So if they know something, they'd better come forward now. No one wants to feel idiotic. Last . . ."

He sighed and shook his head.

"We've got to do a notification. It's the proper thing to do, and maybe talking to her relatives will give us a direction."

Mike nodded. "I'm sure the school has the name of her parents."

"I know you didn't find a cell phone. Did you find bills in her desk?"

Mike walked over to the desk drawer and pulled it open with a gloved hand. Inside was a massive pile of paperwork. "Be my guest."

Decker gloved up and took out the stack. He found what he was looking for and held it up. "Her phone bill from last month . . ." Scanning down the list. "You know, let me go to the station house and I'll start calling some of these numbers. I could use some help with that." He looked around. "Uh, where's McAdams?"

"He was looking green around the gills so I sent him home."

"He went *home*?" Decker felt his fury rise. "What the hell is wrong with him?"

"Pete, he didn't come to the department through usual channels. The mayor put him with us as a favor to his father. He didn't sign up for this shit, and frankly I don't want flak from the town biggies. I told him he could leave."

"You are way too nice."

"If you need him, I'll call him back."

"I don't need him, but he needs to be here. I'll make the call." Decker pulled out his cell phone. "Because if I don't see his sorry ass down at the station in fifteen minutes, he'll have a lot more to worry about than losing his lunch."

CHAPTER NINE

While waiting for McAdams to make an appearance, Decker downloaded the photographs from Jenny's camera to the station-house computer. She'd done a thorough job, taking dozens of pictures from all different perspectives. It gave Decker a chance to really study the body without distraction and noise since the place was basically deserted. Then he started going down the phone numbers. He picked out a few with out-of-town prefixes that were frequently called.

The first number kicked into a male voice: *Leave your name and number and I'll call you back if I feel like it.*

Obviously not her parents. After the beep, Decker said, "This is Detective Peter Decker from Greenbury Police. Call me back as soon as you can."

The next number also went to a voice mail, but this woman on the message was soft-spoken and sounded older. Decker tried to be as gentle as he could. "This is Peter Decker from Greenbury Police. If someone could please call me back as soon as possible, I'd appreciate it. Thank you very much."

He hung up the phone and thought about the case. He

had to give kudos to Mike. The captain wasn't territorial. He wanted a quick resolution: to do justice for the victim, to put the town at ease, and to do a good job.

Decker picked up the receiver to make a third call just as McAdams walked into the station house. The two of them exchanged looks. Tyler sat down at his desk and said nothing, fiddling with paperwork while wearing a hound dog face. The kid wasn't much older than Hannah and something about Tyler's expression brought out the parent in him. He hung up the phone and tried to keep his face neutral. "You okay?"

McAdams looked up and then he looked down. "Yeah, fine. What do you need?"

Decker crossed his arms and regarded him until the kid looked up again. "Tyler, first times are the hardest. Almost everyone gets a little sick when you see something like that. Nothing wrong or embarrassing about it. But should something like this happen in the future—which is very unlikely here—this is what you do. You grab a nearby bag and place it over your nose and mouth to try to slow down your breathing. Sometimes that works. If not, and you have to throw up, you throw up in the bag, not in the toilet because there might be forensic evidence in there and you don't want to contaminate anything. Then afterward, you wash your face with cold water and go back and do your job. No one will say anything because we've all been there, okay?"

"Yeah . . . yeah, you're right. Sorry."

"No problem. So take out a notebook and let me bring you up to speed. Let me get everything out before you ask your questions."

Decker recapped his conversation with Captain Mike Radar. The kid was silent but he did take notes. "I have the victim's phone bill. I'm going down the list, trying to find her parents so I can do a notification. That's a lousy job even for someone experienced, so I'll do that."

He slid the phone bill across his desk over to McAdams's desk.

"This is last month's phone bill so it's out of date, but right now it's all we have. What I'd like you to do is to go down the numbers and find out what matches to what. If you find her parents, give the call to me. As soon as I make the notification, we'll go to Littleton and start interviewing friends and acquaintances to see if we can get a feel for who she is—"

"Sorry for leaving, Decker. That was really unprofessional."

"It's past history, Tyler. Let's just move forward because we have a lot of work—" His cell rang. Decker looked at his phone window. "This may be the parents. Hold on." He depressed the button. "Greenbury Police."

"I'm looking for a Peter Decker."

A woman's voice. He said, "This is Peter Decker. Who am I talking to, please?"

"This is Karen Bronson. What's going on?"

"Are you related to Angeline Moreau, ma'am?"

"I'm her mother. Is Angeline in trouble?"

The expected panic. "There's no easy way to tell you this, ma'am. There was an incident in her apartment. I'm very sorry, but Angeline is deceased."

The wailing was immediate. Over the phone, Decker heard a male voice asking what was wrong. Then the female voice screaming, "Angeline is dead!" Then there was a lot of shouting and even more voices followed by sobbing. No matter how many times Decker did this, it never, ever got easier. It always made him sick in his gut.

The man came on the line. "Who is this?"

"Detective Peter Decker from Greenbury Police. I'm very sorry for your loss."

"Are you positive it's her?"

Decker paused. "Sir, I'll tell you everything I know, but it would be better to do this in person. Who am I talking to?"

"Jim Bronson. I'm Angeline's stepfather. You didn't answer my question."

"I know. We don't have a positive ID because of the condition of the body. We may have to do a DNA test. I can get a twenty-four-hour turnaround if you bring me her toothbrush or hairbrush."

"So it's possible that it *isn't* her?"

The expected hope. "Yes, it's possible. But we're proceeding as if it were her. Because we found her in her apartment with ID on her. I'm so sorry, but I do need to talk to you and it would be helpful to talk in person. Where are you located? This looks like a Florida prefix."

"It is. We're on our way as soon as I hang up. God, can't you tell me anything?" He lowered his voice. "Murder?"

The wailing in the background had intensified. "The coroner does the official ruling . . . but it looks like a homicide. We can get into the details face-to-face. I know this is very difficult, but did Angeline ever speak to you about having any problems up here?"

"Angeline is an A student."

"I'm thinking personal problems. Maybe she had a beef with another student or a teacher?"

"I don't think so, but I'm in a fog right now."

"I know this is hard, but could you ask your wife? Anything you could give us in this very early stage of the investigation might help."

"God . . . hold on." Decker heard muffled conversation

108

and the woman shouting no, no, no. Jim came back on the line. "She can't think of anyone."

"Did Angeline have a boyfriend?"

"Uh . . . uh . . . what the hell was his name? Karen, what's the name of the boy that Angeline was dating?" A female voice and then he came back on the line. "She *was* dating Lance Terry. He had been her boyfriend for several years, but they broke up a while ago."

"Do you know who broke it off?"

"Hold on." A moment passed. "Karen said that she did. No problems afterward supposedly."

"Is Lance Terry a student at Littleton?"

"Somewhere in the colleges."

Decker said, "Okay . . . what about friends?"

"Hold on." A pause. "My wife says that her two closest college friends are Julia Kramer and Emily Hall. I can't believe—" He choked up. "I really have to go. Do you have a number where I can reach you?"

"I'll give you my cell. Feel free to call it twenty-four/seven if you think of anything else or even if you just want to talk."

"It'll probably take us a while to get up there . . . God, I don't even know about flights at this time of night. I need to call the airlines. If we drive out, we won't get there until tomorrow at the earliest."

"No problem. Just call me when you arrive. And if you drive, please drive carefully. Don't worry how long it takes. I'm not going anywhere." Gently, Decker hung up the phone. "I've got some names for you, McAdams: Julia Kramer, Emily Hall, and Lance Terry. Two friends and the ex-boyfriend."

McAdams pushed the phone bill back across to Decker's desk. There were three circled numbers. "The 917 belongs to a male voice . . . no identification in the voice mail.

109

The 314 belongs to a girl named Emily and the 310 belongs to Julia. Not many calls but a ton of texts going back and forth. No one talks on the phone anymore. I'd probably be better off texting them if you want to talk to them."

"Do it. Then let's get out of here."

McAdams looked up. "Where are we going?"

"To Littleton College to talk to Angeline's friends." Decker regarded Tyler's stunned face. "I'll do all the talking. You just take notes and listen. I want you along because a younger person might inspire the kids to talk a little more."

"So I'm like your secretary?" When Decker glared at him, McAdams reddened. "I didn't mean it like that. Sorry. Can I use my iPad to take notes?"

"As long as you don't get distracted and start looking up mustached babies who dance the tango."

"Is that a real YouTube?"

Decker rolled his eyes. "Let's go, Harvard. See what was going on in Angeline's life. Because right now, we don't have a clue about her death."

Stepping out into the frigid night air, the two of them began the slow trek in ankle-deep drifts toward the colleges. Academia sat about a mile away: a pleasant walk in the daytime. But as the hour got late, the damp air seeped into the bones and stiffened the muscles.

McAdams's phone beeped. "It's a text from Julia Kramer. She wants to know what's going on."

"Tell her we're on our way. Ask her where we should meet."

"That doesn't answer her question."

"And in not answering her question, we say a lot, don't we."

"True that." McAdams texted her back. They walked for another minute in silence until his phone beeped again.

110

He read the text aloud. *"Come to my dorm. Maple Hall, 4D. What's going on?"*

"Tell her we'll be right there. Don't tip her off. I want to read her face when we get there and break the news." Decker tightened his scarf and rubbed his hands together. "Tyler, ask her if she has a roommate? We may want some privacy."

"Sure." The kid's hands flew over the pop-up keyboard of his smartphone. A minute later, he said, *"Angeline Moreau. Why?* . . . Okay, then. What should I text back?"

"Tell her we'll be there in ten minutes," Decker said.

"Done."

"It looks like Angeline has an official dorm room on campus. The apartment is officially registered in her name. Is she paying for the off-campus place or is someone else footing the bill?"

"Should I write that down as a question?"

Decker smiled. "I was thinking out loud, but sure write it down. And write this down as well. Did her parents know she was living off-campus? Probably not. Why would they continue to pay the college for her room and board? And if she was mostly living off-campus, it might explain why Julia, her roommate, wasn't worried when Angeline hadn't shown up after the weekend."

"It's only Monday night," McAdams said. "Maybe Angeline didn't have class on Monday and she is a senior. Maybe she goes away for the weekends. Maybe she has a boo who goes with her."

"By boo you mean boyfriend?"

"Yeah."

"That brings us to another question. If Lance Terry is out of the picture, does she have a current boyfriend?"

"I still don't know who the male voice is. Maybe he's the new guy in town."

111

"Could be. Mike, Kevin, and Ben are combing her apartment and the complex for any information they can dig up. But there still may be something in her dorm room that can help us out." Decker held up a package. "Hence the gloves and evidence bags. Don't touch anything without latex fingers."

"Don't you need a warrant or something to search the room?"

"First off, she's dead and that changes everything. Second, the dorm is the school's property. If I need it, someone can surely grant me permission in these circumstances."

"Does the school even know about the homicide?"

"Mike has contacted the school. And the school should know it's in its best interest to keep this *very* quiet."

"Are we going to keep it quiet?"

"Depends on how cooperative Littleton is."

"Are you going to threaten to expose this if they don't cooperate?" A pause. "And if you do that, isn't that the definition of blackmail?"

"Whoa, whoa, whoa," Decker said. "Blackmail, besides being against the law, is a very loaded word." He smiled to himself. "I prefer to think of it as . . . leverage."

The Five Colleges of Upstate were not all built in a day. Duxbury was the oldest and most elite, and was originally founded as a men's college but went co-ed fifty years ago. It most closely resembled the prototype of an eastern college: imposing limestone buildings, a magnificent brick and stone library with stained-glass windows, and of course the stadium where the five colleges played football among themselves. It took up the most real estate, leaving the other four colleges as stepsiblings. Clarion—the women's college—was built forty years after Duxbury. Morse

McKinley was erected in the postwar boom in the late 1940s when brick and concrete and straight lines were all a building needed to look modern. Now it just looked like a big dingbat apartment house. The smallest of the colleges was Kneed Loft and was nicknamed Nerd Loft because it specialized in math, science, and engineering. The architects more or less gave up on this one. It was way more bunker than building, but it didn't stop the college from turning out brilliant students, most who went on to graduate school or government labs.

The last college was Littleton, noted for its artsy teachers, its spacey students, and its clear-cut agenda of social activism. It was considered the only college composed of co-eds who *cared*. It prided itself on being different. The students had palpable disdain for Morse McKinley and its greedy Wall Street ways. They were way cooler than the robotic dweebs of Kneed Loft, and of course, they were much less pretentious than the snobs at Duxbury. Clarion didn't even factor into its equation.

Ten years ago, Littleton underwent a massive successful campaign to retrofit the college and turn it all green—from solar energy that ran the generators to the organic food in the cafeteria. Now it almost seemed like an aggie school with its numerous outdoor gardens—dead in the wintertime—and its four greenhouses happily providing tomatoes and zucchini squash to the cafeteria for its vegan entrées. The school's four main buildings had quilted roofs of thatch reed intermixed with solar panels that frequently had to be wiped down from the snowfall.

The dorms were recycled brick boxes, nondescript, interchangeable, and named after trees. The door to Maple Hall was locked. McAdams was about to text Julia that they were in front of the door, but then a student came running up to the door, swiped her card, and all three of them stepped inside. She bounded up the stairs and left them in the lurch.

The place was a sty with overflowing garbage cans and various jackets, hoodies, boots, and other articles of clothing strewn chockablock. It was also unbearably stuffy, stale, and smelly as well as loud and cacophonous. Anyone who could study or sleep in these environs was a freak of nature.

McAdams took off his parka, wiping his forehead with the back of his hand. "This brings back memories and none of them good. And Dad wonders why I'm not rushing to do it all again." He turned to Decker. "Did you go to college?"

"Of course not—because as you well know all cops are cretins by law."

"I didn't mean it that way. Jeez!"

Decker smiled, took off his coat, and started climbing stairs to the fourth floor. "FYI, I'm a lawyer. Passed the California bar and everything. And I hated every moment of it."

"That I can understand. The law's an ass and so are lawyers."

"So why are you going to law school?"

"Good question, Decker. What law school did you go to?"

"Some unaccredited job in L.A. I went at night and worked LAPD during the day."

"So where'd you go to college . . . undergraduate?"

"I didn't go to college. I had completed my training at the police academy and I guess that was good enough for my law school—that and full tuition."

"You went into LAPD academy directly out of high school?"

"No, I worked Gainesville police for a while. I was born

in Florida. And no, I didn't go directly into the academy out of high school. There was this little glitch called the Vietnam War. Uncle Sam had first dibs."

"Oh . . . right." A pause. "Did you go overseas?"

"Of course." Decker gave a mirthless laugh. "We weren't given choices, Tyler." He reached the third floor and paused. "I was drafted and went into the infantry. First time out on a mission, I saw the kid about twenty paces ahead of me step on a mine and blow himself up." He wiped his forehead. Man, it was hot. "Welcome to the jungle."

McAdams fell silent. "I don't like it when people pry into my life so I guess I shouldn't be prying into yours."

"I don't mind. Curiosity is a good feature for a cop."

"So can I ask what happened?"

"I survived. That's what happened." He shrugged. "It was a little more than that. I'll tell you how I survived and then we won't have to talk about this anymore."

"You don't have to tell me."

"Buddy, it's no secret. Within a short period of time, like you, I figured out how to work the system. I knew I'd wind up dead if I stayed in the front lines. A guy six foot four isn't built for guerrilla warfare. So I asked to be transferred into Medics because of my height disadvantage. It wasn't an unreasonable request. Plus I was an EMT in high school so I had some experience. I knew it was a long shot but nothing ventured, et cetera. Three weeks later, after days and nights of routinely seeing body parts flying through the air, I was transferred. Medics wasn't an easy division and it wasn't safe. We were the first called in when the fighting broke out. We were transported in choppers and we were always getting shot at. And, yes, we did get hit and have to land more than a couple of times. We even crashed, but there are crashes and then there are *crashes*. I was lucky."

115

"I suppose that's one word for it."

"It's the only word for it. Luck. And let me tell you, it was better than crouching in the dirt and shooting at Cong because I was actively doing something worthwhile. I saw a lot of horror, but I helped save a lot of lives.

"After I got back to civilian life, I drifted into the academy because it seemed like my best option. I do well with a chain of command. I'm not the gadfly, McAdams. I'm not the wise guy or the renegade and I don't like rogue cops on a crusade because they screw things up for the rest of us peons. I'm the drudge. I worked my cases with elbow grease. I worked them to death and mostly I got results. Do I have some cold cases that eat at me? You betcha I do. But maybe those cases will eventually be given a fresh pair of eyes. And if they call me for information, I will be happy to cooperate. All I want is justice for the victims. No ego, just solutions. Which brings us to the all-important question. Are you with me or not? Because I'm going to demand 110 percent."

McAdams nodded. "Whatever you need. And I'll try to keep my obnoxiousness in check."

"It'll come out from time to time, but that's okay. As long as you're dependable."

"I'm good at dependable."

"Great. So let's go find Julia in 4D and see if we can't get some justice for Angeline Moreau. I may not have been suited as a lawyer, but I'm a great advocate for the dead."

CHAPTER TEN

The door was partially open with no consideration of personal safety. Decker knocked and a female voice told them to come in. The girl was about five ten and a hundred and ten pounds judging from her sticklike arms. Long blond hair, bright blue eyes, a small upturned nose, thick red lips. She wore a wife beater and board shorts and had slippers on her feet. Skimpy dress to meet the police but it was hot inside. She stuck out a hand "Julia Kramer. You guys must be the police."

Yes, we guys are the police. Decker shook her hand. "I'm Detective Decker and this is Detective McAdams. Thank you for seeing us on such short notice." He turned to McAdams whose mouth was slightly agape. Julia smiled, obviously used to male attention. She plopped down on her bed and sat cross legged. "You guys can sit down if you want."

"I'm fine standing, but thank you." Decker looked around the room. It consisted of two beds that had been lofted on high legs for more space, two desks, two chairs, and two closets. "I'm actually here to talk about Angeline Moreau."

"Why?" Her blue eyes narrowed. "What's she done?"

"What makes you think she's done anything? Has she been in trouble before?"

"Not really. I mean not in serious trouble. I mean we had this anal RA. Not anymore, thank God. We forgot our room cards and, yes, it was late. But so what? I mean it's an art school, right. And she's getting all amped because we're a little tipsy. Yes, we were underage at the time. Not anymore thank you very much. But c'mon. Like the school cares?"

Decker pulled up a chair and sat down next to the bed, giving her some breathing room but not much. "Does the school care?"

"As long as it's in a red cup, everyone's down with that. But I'm guessing you're not here to talk about two girls getting wasted, right?"

"Right."

"So what's going on with Angeline?" She suddenly gasped. "Is she okay?"

"Let me answer your question with a question." Decker pulled out a notebook. "When was the last time you saw her?"

"Oh my God! She's *missing*?" She covered her mouth with her hands. "What *happened*?"

"That's what we're trying to figure out. Right now we're trying to get a timeline of her actions. When did you last see her, Julia?"

"Oh my God! I can't believe I'm actually talking about this!" Her voice was a whisper. "Not Friday . . . maybe Thursday of last week?"

"Morning, evening?"

"Morning, I think. It could have been Wednesday." She looked up at Decker. "She hardly lives here anymore."

"Why's that?"

"She rented another place . . . closer to town."

"So you know about her apartment."

"Of course. We're close . . . or we used to be close." Her eyes formed tears. "Did you guys check her apartment?"

"We're doing that right now."

Her eyes went from Decker's face to McAdams and then back to Decker. "Have you called her cell?"

"It goes straight to voice mail." That part was true. "Why aren't you close anymore?"

The girl looked down. "It's not like we had a fight or anything. We just drifted apart."

"I know about Lance Terry. What happened between the two of them?"

"That was over a year ago." Julia sighed. "She broke it off. Lance was very upset, but he's moved on. He has a new girlfriend."

"So . . . is she seeing someone else?"

"I'm not sure. We kinda stopped talking. It was gradual. It's okay. We all have our own lives." Tears streamed down her cheek.

"So you don't know if she has a new boyfriend. Because if you have a name, I need it. Time is important."

"She . . ." Julia stopped herself.

"What?" Decker motioned to McAdams to sit down and returned his attention to Julia. "Tell me, hon. We need all the help we can get."

"I honestly don't know about a new boyfriend, but I'll tell you what I do know." She bit her lip. "Angeline doesn't come from money . . . like a lot of people here. I mean it isn't as obvious at Littleton as it is at Morse McKinley because we're more socially conscious."

A pause.

"She suddenly started toting around very expensive

119

designer bags. The kind you can't even buy here. You've got to go to New York or Boston to get Celine or Nancy Rodriguez or Chanel."

"How expensive is expensive?"

"Over a thousand dollars retail. Not only that, her boots. I mean I didn't check the label or anything, but when she crossed her legs, I saw the red sole."

"Christian Louboutin," Decker said.

"Yeah . . . right. Exactly. It's not that she dressed expensively. Jeans and sweaters like the rest of the campus. But she did accessorize expensively. I finally asked her about them. She smiled and winked and that's as far as she got to telling me about it. I mean . . . *someone* had to be paying the rent on her apartment. I know she didn't have that kind of spending cash."

"Do you think she might have been doing something illegal to get extra money?"

"Like what? Hooking?"

"I was thinking more about pushing, but do you think she was hooking?"

"*No*. Who'd she ho with? The guys here get it for free and Greenbury isn't exactly crawling with sugar daddies."

"So what about pushing?"

"No way. You can't get that kind of money selling shit . . . uh, stuff. Most people get it for free at the parties. Besides, Angeline was more of a boozer than a pothead. Not that she binges that much. She's like all of us here." She wiped a tear away. "This is really upsetting."

"I know it is. But we need as much information as you can give us. Could she have found a rich boyfriend?"

"If she did, I don't know about it."

"Fair enough. Julia, do you know if Angeline has been having problems with anyone?"

She shook her head no.

"Think about it. A guy? A girl? An RA or even a professor?"

"No stalkers if that's what you mean."

"Was there *anyone* specifically that she complained to you about?"

"She complained about people, sure. Mostly that everyone here was stupid. Angeline was an intellectual snob. She would have rather gone to Brown, but Littleton offered her close to a free ride."

"So she felt a little out of place?"

"Not really. We had fun. I think at the beginning of the year, she came down with a major case of senioritis. She just kind of withdrew."

"What's her major?"

"Art history. Littleton specializes in the arts."

"Was she doing a thesis?" McAdams asked.

"Yeah, sure."

"Do you know the specific topic?"

"Yeah, actually I do. Asian export textile design in the eighteenth century and its influence on art nouveau. Why do you ask?"

Decker said nothing, but the two men exchanged glances. McAdams jammed his hands in his pockets and looked around. "I don't see a lot of textbooks here."

"Try her apartment. Like I said, she was almost never here anymore."

"I know dorm life pretty well. I just graduated a few years ago. It's hard to study in your room. Where did Angeline study before she got her own apartment?"

"You mean which library?"

"Yeah, I guess I do."

"Rayfield is our big research library but it isn't as big as Huntington."

"Huntington is at Duxbury?"

"Yes."

"Is that where she did her research?"

"Probably."

There was a pause. Decker waited for Tyler to finish with his questions. It was good to see the kid finally take initiative. When he remained quiet, Decker said, "Do you know if Angeline does stained glass?"

Julia paused then shook her head. "Not that I know of."

McAdams was playing with his smartphone. "Uh . . . it's taught as an elective at Littleton."

"I . . . don't know every course at the school so . . . there you go."

Decker let it ride. "Julia, I don't have Angeline's recent cell-phone records. But I do have an old phone bill. Can you help us identify the numbers on it?"

"I can give it a shot."

McAdams pulled out the bill and handed it to her. Julia looked up and smiled. The kid attempted to smile back but it came out as more of a grimace.

"Um . . . this is me, of course. This is Emily . . . Emily Hall. This is Lance . . . hmm; I didn't know they were even still in contact. This is take-out pizza. This is take-out Chinese. This is our nail salon . . . appears she was going without me, thank you very much." She sighed. "I must seem petty."

"You were hurt," Decker said.

"I was very hurt. She blew me off and I didn't know why. And the worst part was, she wouldn't talk about it." She looked down. "How long has she been missing?"

"We're trying to figure that out. Can you tell me when you last *spoke* to her?"

"I guess it was the last time I saw her." She looked up. "After she broke up with Lance, she changed . . . we didn't see that much of each other."

"Who else should we talk to about Angeline?"

"Maybe Emily Hall although I was closer to her than Emily was . . . I don't mean it to sound jealous, just the way it was. When she complained to me about Angeline's disappearance act, I was the one defending her. I suppose you could talk to Lance if they're still in contact." She thought a moment. "Maybe she'll just show up."

"Did she often take long weekends away?"

"Sometimes. Was she in class today?"

"No, she wasn't," Decker said. "Did she have class today?"

"I don't know her schedule anymore." She shook her head. "I mean, who reported her missing? Musta been her parents. Have you spoken to her parents?"

"We have."

"This is just terrible! Do you think she ran away or . . . ."

Decker said, "Do you have a water bottle?"

"Sure, in my minifridge. Help yourself."

Decker found a bottle, opened it up, and handed it to her. "There's no easy way to tell you this, Julia." He sat down next to her. "Angeline was found dead in her apartment."

"Oh! My! God!" The tears were instant. "Oh God! I feel sick . . . oh, God, oh, God!"

McAdams sprung up. "Drink, Julia."

"I can't . . . I feel funny . . . real dizzy."

"Put your head between your knees," Decker said. "Slow your breathing down."

But it was too late. Her eyes fluttered and rolled back into her head. She fell backward onto the mattress, dropping the bottle down McAdams's leg, water spilling inside his boot. The kid jumped up. "Shit!"

Drolly, Decker said, "Well, kid, it looks like you finally got your feet wet."

"Aren't you witty."

"You asked good questions by the way, Harvard. Keep it up." Decker moistened a tissue with the remaining water in the bottle and ran it over her forehead. Julia stirred and started breathing out loud. "You're okay, Julia. You're okay."

She tried to get up but fell back down.

"Slowly." He helped her sit back up. "Are you still dizzy?" She shrugged. He said, "Take a few minutes to catch your breath."

"Why didn't . . ." She was crying. "You shoulda *told* me right away."

"I apologize but I needed to talk to you first. Do you need some water?"

She nodded, downing the water bottle and then wiping her forehead, her face pale and pasty, her lips trying to talk but her throat not getting the words out.

"Her parents know," Decker said. "They're coming in from Florida."

"Oh my God!" The tears wouldn't stop. "Poor people!"

"Other than her parents and police, you're the first person we've told. We need to talk to Emily and Lance before they find out from someone else. Do they live in Maple Hall as well?"

"Emily is upstairs . . . 8C."

"What about Lance?"

"Elm Hall. I don't know his room number."

"I'll find it. Julia, I'll need you to keep this quiet until we've had a chance to complete our interviews."

"Does . . . the school know?"

"Yes. Before we go, we'd like to look around the room."

"Her stuff? Sure . . . I guess. Is it legal?"

"She's dead, Julia. These first few hours are crucial."

"Sure, look around."

124

The two detectives began to search: Angeline's desk, her closet, her bed, her personal life. Within the first few minutes, it was clear to Decker that the young woman had basically moved out of her dorm room. Nothing of interest, not even schoolwork. He smiled at Julia who had regained some of her color but was still in a state of suspended animation. McAdams was checking out the pockets of her clothing.

"Anything?" Decker asked.

"A comb, old lipstick, pens, pencils, squashed candy, loose change."

"Paper?"

"Store receipts, credit card receipts, and a few scraps of paper with notes written on them . . . mostly to-do lists. I'll bag them all up."

Decker turned his attention back to Julia. "Anything else that she might have wanted to hide from prying eyes? What about a diary?"

"I don't know."

Decker handed her his card and McAdams did likewise. "If you think of anything else, call anytime."

She nodded. "Are you going to talk to Emily now?"

"Yes, if she's in."

She said, "Once you tell her, can you have her text me or call me? I don't know if I want to be alone tonight."

"Lonely, sad, or are you worried about your personal safety?"

She looked down. "Is this something that I need to worry about?"

Decker said, "Honestly, I don't know. Is there a specific person who you're worried about, Julia? Someone out there who is giving you the creeps?"

"Not really." Stated without a lot of conviction.

"What's on your mind?" Decker asked. "Who are you worried about?"

"No one specific . . . really."

McAdams said, "But guys do get drunk and behave badly, right?"

"Exactly."

"Do you think that's what might have happened to Angeline?" She shrugged helplessly. Decker said, "In the next few hours, we'll be talking to a lot of people. Like I said, if anyone makes you feel uneasy, give me a call."

She let out a gush of air. "I'll call you, I promise."

"After I'm done with Emily, I'll come back to check on you," Decker said. "In the meantime, it's always a good idea to lock your doors."

CHAPTER ELEVEN

The interview with Angeline's friend Emily didn't provide any new insights, just a fresh batch of tears from another vulnerable young woman. Maybe a guy's perspective would be more enlightening. As they made their way over to Elm Hall, Lance Terry's dorm, McAdams said, "Looks like Angeline had lost interest in college. Typical for seniors."

Decker didn't answer, churning around his own thoughts. The men walked in silence for a few moments.

"Did I piss you off or something?"

"No, I'm not pissed at anyone. Why would you think that?"

"You're not answering me and I piss people off all the time."

"Just thinking." A pause. "Even brain-dead cops do that from time to time."

"Are we really having this conversation—*again*?" When Decker didn't answer, the kid exhaled. "Look. I know I'm an arrogant ass . . . with a weak stomach. But I'm not stupid. I told you I'm in this all the way. So if you deign to share your thoughts, I might deign to add an insight or two."

"You do have insight. So you tell me what you're thinking and I can shoot you down."

McAdams smiled. "Like everyone else."

"In the biz, we call it a discussion. You go first . . . please."

"Since you said please." McAdams collected his ideas. "I don't think the crime had anything to do with the college per se. Angeline was psychologically gone . . . all but graduated. And when you add the designer purses and shoes, I'm thinking that someone had to be giving her money, right?"

"Makes sense."

The kid grew animated. "I'm thinking she was making a lot of money on the side and probably doing it illegally. Since both Emily and Julia didn't like our hooker/pusher theory, and since Angeline was an art history major, and since stained glass is taught at Littleton, it is not inconceivable that Angeline might have had something to do with the forgeries and the thefts in the cemetery. And that may have something to do with the reason behind her excess money and her murder."

"Go on."

"So I suppose the next step is to find out if she took a stained-glass course."

"And if she didn't?"

"Well, it still doesn't rule out that she knew how to do stained glass."

"Now you're thinking, Harvard. If she was attempting to forge Tiffany, do you think she would be good enough to attempt it with just a single course?"

"No, that's a very good point. Did we find anything in her apartment to suggest she was doing stained glass?"

"Nothing obvious, but the guys are still looking."

"Do you think she had anything to do with the forgeries?"

"Actually, I'm thinking that if she attempted forgeries, she was probably doing stained glass for a while. And it is possible that Angeline knew that the police had discovered the forgeries with all the action that's been going on at the cemetery. She might have dumped all her equipment thinking that even if the police came around, she could deny everything."

"Okay, right. If she's been doing stained glass for a while, I bet her parents would know about her hobby. We should ask them."

"And we will do just that when the time is right. If I come in with accusations, they'll close up and that won't do anyone any good." They walked a few steps in silence. "Angeline was a scholarship student, right?"

"Right."

"And what do you do to get a scholarship besides get good grades and good test scores—the basic requirements to be accepted in these elite schools. What do you do to impress?"

"Besides the essay?" McAdams asked.

"Yeah," Decker answered. "You've gotten your grades, you've gotten good test scores, and you've written an amusing essay. You're applying to a liberal arts college with an emphasis on the arts. What would you do to impress the admission's committee that you're unique?"

"I dunno. Maybe make your own artisan cheese from a rare species of yak."

Decker laughed. "How about this? When my foster son applied to Harvard, he sent them several CDs of his playing. Angeline applied to a school specializing in the arts. I'm sure she sent in some kind of portfolio. We should look up her application. See if she mentioned stained glass."

"Right." McAdams nodded. "I'll check with the administration when it opens tomorrow morning. Unless you want to do it."

"You can do it, Tyler." A pause. "Just . . . use a little finesse, okay? Cops have different styles. But I've always caught most of my flies with honey rather than vinegar. And even when I use vinegar, it's sparingly."

McAdams rolled his eyes. "I know you can't be an asshole if you're pumping someone for information."

"See, that's it, Tyler. You're not pumping, you're *asking* . . . can you help me, *please*. Try to be disarming. The conversation shouldn't be adversarial even when you're trying to get a psycho to confess. When you point out how your suspect has just screwed himself, you may talk emphatically and with confidence, but seasoned detectives talk in a conversational tone."

"I *get* it, okay?"

"Fine." Decker threw up his hands. "You get it. End of discussion."

Tyler rubbed his eyes. "It's been a long night. And it looks like it's only going to get longer."

"If you want to turn in, I can handle it from here."

"It wasn't a hint. For the last time, I'm here for the long run, okay?"

"You're right. I'll stop needling you at least for the rest of the night."

The kid stopped walking and turned to him. "All I'm saying is try . . . just *try* to give me a little credit. I've been with upper-crust Manhattanites all my life. I know how to suck it up and how to suck up. I just choose not to do it anymore."

When the pair arrived at Elm Hall dormitory, Decker stopped in front of the secured door. "Go talk to the administration in the morning. If you have any questions, just give me a call. With Lance Terry, I'll do most of the talking but feel free to chime in. Like I said, your insights are pretty much on the money."

"Thank you." The kid started to talk but stopped himself. "Let's go."

Decker put a hand on his shoulder. "The image is going to bother you for a while—"

"It's not the image, it's the *smell* . . . God, I can't get it out of my nose. It comes in waves. Truthfully, I'm still a little . . . queasy."

"In the beginning—when I started working homicides—I carried Vicks VapoRub because it helps dilute the smell. Later on I stopped because it blocked out a very important sense, and smelling something putrid is better than not being able to smell at all. But I know what you're saying. It takes time for the stink to exit the olfactory nerves. To this day, every time I go to the morgue, I can't eat meat for a few days."

"It's okay. I'll deal." He bit his lip. "I know you think I'm a pussy—"

"No, that's not what I think. You're just trying to figure it out." Decker smiled. "Like all of your pussy generation."

McAdams laughed. "You got that right, Old Man." A pause. "Did your foster son get into Harvard by the way?"

"Yes, he did, but he wound up at Juilliard. He could have gotten in anywhere. He's exceptional but that's not what makes him a great kid." Decker pointed to his chest. "He's got heart."

"Yeah, I'm not known for my warm and fuzzy cardiac muscle, but that's to be expected. Genes are genes. And if you ever meet my father, you'll know what I mean."

There was a wall of sound in all directions, so when Decker knocked on the door, he didn't hear anything until a voice was shouting at him.

"Fuck off!"

"That's code for I'm fucking right now so fuck off," McAdams said.

"Even an old guy like me can figure that out." He knocked harder. "Police! Open up, Terry."

"Je-zuz!" Stomping. Then the door flew open. The guy who answered wore boxers but nothing else. "Who the fuck are you?"

The man was tall and built: football player but more a quarterback or a running back than defense. His hair was one step longer than a buzz cut. He had dark eyes, a big brow, and a jutting chin. Decker showed him his badge and brushed against him as he walked inside. McAdams followed. The girl in the bed had pulled the sheet covers to her chin.

The guy said, "You can't come in without a warrant!"

"You know that because you've seen it on TV?" No answer. Decker saw a pile of feminine clothes on the floor. He picked them up and laid them on the bed. "Get dressed under the covers." Decker turned to the young man. "I need to ask you some questions, Lance, like in right now. Something has happened."

"What's going on?" the guy asked. Quieter this time.

"I'm Detective Decker and this is Detective McAdams. We're from Greenbury Police—"

"Greenbury Police?"

"Yes, Greenbury PD. We're not from the school so you don't have to start flushing your joints down the crapper. But we'd like to ask you a few questions about your girlfriend, Angeline Mo—"

"That would be my ex-girlfriend."

"Right. Ex-girlfriend." Decker took out a notebook. "Julia Kramer told me that you've moved on. Would that be the young lady you're with?"

A voice peeped out of the sheets. "Yes." She emerged

132

from the covers like a butterfly shedding a cocoon. She was diminutive in size, dark in hair and eye color. She bounded out of the bed and offered a firm handshake. "Lucy Ramon. What did Angeline do?"

"Do you know her?" Decker asked.

"It's a small school with an even smaller senior class."

"What's going on?" Terry asked. "Did something happen to her?"

Decker nodded. "Unfortunately, yes. She was murdered."

Lucy gasped. Terry turned ashen. He took a few steps and stumbled. He managed to find the chair and hold on to the splat for support, but he didn't sit down. "That's . . ." He shook his head. "It's that guy she'd been seeing, right? Are you looking into that freak?"

"What do you know about the freak?"

"Not much . . . not much at all."

"Do you have a name for the freak?"

"John something."

"C'mon. You know his last name."

"I can't think right now."

"Well, if you think it's him, I need more of a name than just John."

"If you lay off, it'll come to me. Can I get dressed?"

"Fine with us," McAdams said. "I'm sure you can talk and get dressed at the same time."

Decker said, "So why do you think John's a freak and that he did it?"

"I mean . . . who else?"

"What did Angeline tell you about him?"

"Can I go?" Lucy asked.

"Not yet," Decker said. "This is a murder investigation. Would you two be willing to come down to the station and talk to us there? No sense making everyone in the dorm curious."

133

"Of course I'll go down," Terry said. "This is horrible!"

Lucy was biting her thumb. "I barely knew her."

"But I'm sure you want to help." Decker's eyes were on her face. "Right?"

"I've got a midterm."

"It's two weeks into the semester," McAdams said.

"Fine!" She rolled her eyes. "I'll go!"

"Don't do that," Decker scolded her. "Angeline was murdered. It was a brutal killing. This isn't a joke."

The girl had paled. Tears burst from her eyes. "Sorry."

"No problem. Thank you both for your cooperation." Decker said to McAdams, "Call up Captain Radar and tell him we have a couple of people who knew Angeline and are willing to help us out. I'll get us a car. In the meantime, can you please escort Ms. Ramon back to her room? She'll need a coat."

McAdams took out his phone and punched in Radar's cell number. "Where do you live, Lucy?"

"I go to Morse McKinley, about a ten-minute walk past Kneed Loft." She teared up. "Let's just get this over with." She stomped out of the room. McAdams had to do a two-step to keep up with her.

Decker turned to Terry who had sunk into the chair. It seemed to sag under all his muscle. "You went with Angeline for a while."

"Two years." He slipped on a long-sleeved shirt and a pair of jeans with Uggs on his feet. "The breakup was mutual."

Decker wasn't sure about that. "What happened?"

"Different interests." His eyes seemed far away. "We drifted apart."

"What was she like? Angeline."

His eyes focused on Decker's face. "How can you sum up a person in a few lines?"

134

"Tell me why you liked her."

"She was very sexy . . . she loved sex. She was adventurous . . . try just about anything once." A pause. "She was really smart . . . funny . . . sometimes over-the-top sarcastic. She could cut you with a few chosen words."

Decker's phone beeped. He read the text. "Our car will be here in a minute. We should wait downstairs."

Terry looked at his watch. "How long do you think this is going to take?"

"I don't know. Grab a coat. It's cold outside."

Decker split the kids up, choosing to interview the girl first, making the guy wait and more anxious. Nervous people talk even more freely. He told Tyler to take copious notes, then he opened the door to the first of two interview rooms that the station had. There were no other places for private conversation other than the jail.

"Thanks again for coming down." He handed Lucy a bottle of water.

"Do you have hot water?" she asked. "It's freezing in here."

"I'll get it," McAdams said.

The kid was learning. Decker said, "I know it's late. I'll try to make this quick. What did you know about Angeline Moreau?"

She shrugged. "Like I said, I barely knew her."

"I'm sure Lance told you things about her."

She tried to cross her arms. Awkward because she still had her bulky coat on. "If you want to know about what Lance thought of her, ask him."

"Right now I'm asking you." Decker pulled his chair closer to her. "This is just fact finding, Lucy. I'm not trying to box anyone into a corner. And whatever you thought about Angeline, no one deserves to be snuffed out like that. Help me out."

135

Her eyes watered again. "Honestly, she was full of herself. She was pretentious . . . an artsy, fartsy opinion on everything. I don't know how Lance put up with it for so long. He's kinda . . . basic."

"Why do you think he liked her?"

"Probably the sex was hot." She shrugged. "Isn't that usually the reason guys put up with crazy girls?"

McAdams came in with the hot water for her and two cups of coffee for them. "I don't know how you take it so I put in some sugar and milk."

"Thanks, it's fine." Decker took a sip. He wasn't used to the watered-down stuff. He liked his mud without any accoutrements. "We were just talking a little bit about Lance, Terry." He turned his eyes back to Lucy. "What do you mean when you say Lance is basic?"

"Well . . ." She sipped hot water, which must have warmed her up. She took off her jacket. "Lance plays football for Littleton . . . that's kinda like saying you're a caddy for Tiger Woods's caddy. Our sports teams aren't in competitive divisions other than tennis and maybe water polo. The football teams play small liberal arts colleges in the area as well as each other."

"Did Lance come here on a football scholarship?"

"No, his family has money."

"Where is his family from?" McAdams asked.

"Manhattan. The Upper East Side."

"Groton?"

"Horace Mann. I'm from Groton. Were you in Groton?"

"Phillips Exeter," McAdams said. "What's Lance's major?"

"Performing arts, acting. That's where we met."

"You're an actress?" Decker asked.

"*Actor.*"

"Right." Decker smiled. "Is that how you met Angeline?"

"No, she's an art history major. I'm an econ major

136

actually. Why else would I be at Morse McKinley? But I find that marketing and acting have a big area of intersection. Anyway, Lance used to bring Angeline to the theater parties. It's probably how we met, although I don't remember the specifics."

McAdams asked, "What was Angeline's substance of choice?"

"She liked whiskey and bourbon. Jack Daniel's. I don't do booze . . . too many calories."

Decker said, "What else did Lance tell you about Angeline?"

"Just that she was nuts. He didn't elaborate." She started chewing on her thumb again. "I know they still talked. Every time she'd call, he'd, like, turn around and talk quietly into the phone, protecting the call like I'd listen in. Finally I told him, 'Look, if you want a girlfriend, you've got to stop behaving stupid. Just cut her out of your life!'"

"Did he?"

She blew out air. "I don't think so."

McAdams said, "Booty calls?"

"If anyone did the booty calling, it would be her. According to Lance, they used to fuck all the time." She rolled her eyes. "God, as I'm talking about him, I don't know why I put up with it." She shrugged. "I guess I don't care all that much. I mean, it's a college fling. And he takes me out to nice dinners when we go into the city." She checked her watch. "It's two-thirty in the morning. I need to get some rest."

Decker said, "Just a couple more questions. Lance mentioned another guy. Someone he called a freak named John. What do you know about that?"

"Nothing."

"C'mon. Lance must have mentioned him when he was pissed at Angeline."

"All he said is that she's seeing some freak."

137

"How did he know?"

"Beats me. When he went on his tirades, I barely listened."

"Did he give the freak a name other than John?"

"No."

"Did he know where the freak lived?"

"I wouldn't know." A pause. "This could be totally wrong, but I got the feeling that the freak wasn't a student at any of the colleges."

"Tell me why?"

"Because Lance used to rant about how old he was."

"How old was he?"

"From the way Lance talked about it, he was around thirty."

"And he never said where the freak lived?" When she didn't answer, Decker said, "It's not a time to be holding back, Lucy. Angeline was murdered and I really need to talk to this guy."

"I don't know where he's from and that's the God's honest truth." A pause. "I don't know if this is relevant or not, but it sticks in my mind as odd, so I'll tell you. A few months ago, Lance asked if I wanted to meet him for a Saturday night dinner in the city. It was reading week so I didn't have classes anymore. I figured why not. I asked him what he was doing in the city. He said he had some family affair earlier in the day and if I could come down on my own, he'd drive me back up. I agreed. I made all these plans to hitch a ride into Manhattan. At the last minute, right before I was ready to go, he called me and said, change of plans. He was in Boston. Could I come up? I was pissed but he offered me a car service to come up and we'd drive down together."

"That was nice," Decker said. "Even a little extravagant."

"Yeah, it was. But we're closer to Boston than to New York anyway, so I didn't think much about it."

"Did you meet him?"

"I did. He took me out to a Spanish place. It was really, really good and we had a good time. But he was downing the pitchers of sangria like it was water."

"What did you think?"

"Well, I was kinda worried about him driving. But the meal lasted a long time and when we were done, he seemed sober enough."

Sober enough. Great. Decker said, "Do you know why he was in Boston instead of New York?"

"I asked him that. He told me he had an audition at Boston Rep and didn't want to tell me . . . that it was bad luck. And that made total sense. Lots of actors are very secretive about their auditions because the field is so competitive. And because he was drinking so much, I thought it probably didn't go well. So I dropped it."

"Does he have family in Boston?"

"No idea."

"Friends?"

"Probably. The city is full of colleges."

Decker said, "So what made you skeptical about his story?"

"Not exactly skeptical. More like . . ."

"Dubious?" McAdams tried. "Doubtful? Unsure? Uncertain? Hesitant? Cynical? Am I getting closer?"

She smiled. "I just think there was more to the story than an audition."

"Angeline often went away for the weekends," Decker said. "Do you think he could have been following her?"

"Possibly."

"Because it happened before?"

"Not like a stalker . . . I'm not saying that. More like

139

he was curious, I guess." She rubbed her arms. "Can I go home now?"

"Yes, you can." Decker looked at McAdams. "Take the spare squad car and drive her back, please." He handed Lucy his card. "If you think of anything more that could help us, please call."

"Sure." She stood up and smiled at McAdams. "Where'd you go to college?"

"Harvard."

"Thought so. You seem Crimson." She was still smiling as she slipped on her coat. "Why are you working as a cop? Gonna write the ultimate screenplay or something?"

"Yeah." McAdams held the door open for her. "Something."

CHAPTER TWELVE

Lance had fallen asleep in the interview room. In the big city, dozing was usually a sign of psychopathology. But in this case, it was three in the morning, Lance had been partying, and he was overwhelmed with exhaustion. Decker still had a good six working hours left in him, but McAdams was drooping. Maybe a little strategy planning would wake him up. They were looking at Terry through a one-way mirror.

"Did Lucy say anything on the way back to her dorm?" Decker asked.

"About Terry? No."

"Is she flirtatious?"

"Yep."

"She's cute."

"Not my type."

Decker shrugged. "Do you think she's Terry's type?"

"What do you mean?"

"Is she a rebound relationship from Angeline or do you think he really likes her?"

"He likes her enough to fuck her. College guys aren't noted for discrimination."

"Speaking of which, do you think Terry was still doing her?"

"Angeline?" Tyler nodded. "If she'd let him, sure."

"Think that's why he was in Boston? Meeting up with her for a tryst?"

"Makes more sense for him to just go to her apartment."

"What if Angeline was living with a guy?"

"The freak? If he exists, he probably wasn't there all the time. They could easily squeeze in a quickie." McAdams shrugged. "Besides, Boston seems like a long way to go for a nostalgic fuck with the ex."

"What do you think about Lucy's stalking theory?"

"I think stalking makes more sense than traveling three hours for a booty call."

"Why?"

"Because if all he wanted was sex, I'm sure he could have figured out how to do it closer to home." He faced Decker. "If Angeline dumped him, he'd think about her for a while. Who did she throw me over for? Who's the other dick? But eventually, he'd just let it go. That's how college guys are."

Decker said, "So let's see if we can rule him out as a suspect. Angeline was murdered recently, so we need him to retrace his steps over the weekend. If we can rule him out, then we can concentrate on the other guy a.k.a. the freak."

"Whatever you think, boss." When Decker was silent, McAdams took out his iPad and said, "That came out as sarcastic. I didn't mean it like that. I know this is serious stuff. And I know I haven't a clue. I cede to your superior knowledge."

"More like my experience. It's nothing you can't learn, Tyler. But you've got to want to learn it."

"I'm here, aren't I?"

"That's a good start."

"This weekend, this weekend . . ." Terry was having a hard time concentrating even with the double shot of caffeine. "Uh, starting on Friday?"

"Yes, tell me what you did on Friday."

"I was in school."

"How about Friday night?"

"I didn't murder her. I loved her."

"I believe you. This is just routine. Friday night, Lance."

"Uh, Friday night . . ." He hit his head. "I had a game on Friday night. We won."

"Congratulations. What did you do after the game?"

"Partied. Morse McKinley . . . that's where most of the parties take place." He cleared his throat. "The way it works is that Morse McKinley and Littleton are like one group versus Clarion, Duxbury, and Kneed Loft. I mean our swipe cards can get us into Morse McKinley's gym facilities, but not into Duxbury. Most of the time, Morse McKinley students use Littleton facilities because we're a smaller college."

"A consortium within a consortium," McAdams said.

"Yeah . . . I guess. We can still take classes at any of the colleges, but we're allowed to take more classes at Morse McKinley than at the other three colleges. We still have to take a certain amount of classes at Littleton unless our major is a 5-C major, meaning you can take classes in your major across the colleges. Angeline wasn't a 5-C, but she took a lot of classes at Duxbury because it's the most prestigious of the colleges. She thought she was all that."

Decker said, "Let's return to Friday night after the game."

"I told you I went to a party. There were like a zillion people who saw me."

"And what did you do after the party?"

"Went back to my dorm room and fell asleep."

"What time was that?"

"Around . . . four."

"Did you go back alone or did you go back with friends?"

"I went back alone. I was pretty wasted and needed to sleep."

"Did you swipe your card to get into your dorm?"

"Yeah, sure, of course."

"So there would be an electronic record of it."

"Yeah, you're right. Check it out."

"I'll do that. What time did you wake up the next morning?"

"Late . . . twelve, twelve-thirty. I made it down to lunch . . . that must have been around one. I went back to my dorm and showered. We had an acting seminar at three until six. Afterward, I worked out for a couple of hours . . . then I had dinner at the dining hall . . ."

Decker and McAdams waited.

Terry rubbed his eyes. "Can I check with my phone?"

"Sure."

Terry took out his phone and then said, "Ah . . . another party. This one was at Kneed Loft. I went with Lucy. We both got wasted, and then we went back to my room . . . she spent the night. We went to brunch in Greenbury on Sunday morning. Health and Hearth. I hate that place but she loves it." He continued to consult his schedule. "I worked out . . . I had an appointment at the writing center at four."

"Did you show up?"

"Yeah, of course. My tutor was Liz. We worked on my Native Americans of the Southwest paper. The Pueblo revolt of 1680 and the recapturing of the land by Spain under Diego de Vargas Zapata Lujan Ponce de Leon." He grinned. "The mind is still working."

"Good for you," Decker said. "What did you do after that?"

"I went to dinner at the dining hall. Then I guess I was in my dorm all night. My door was open. It's always open unless I'm doing my business with my woman. People coming and going. Lucy came over at around ten. She left at twelve and I went to bed."

"We are now at Monday."

"I had classes. Then I had practice. Then I showered and did a little work. And then Lucy came over and we went to a party at Palm Hall in Littleton. Lucy came back with me and . . ." He grinned a third time. "We are now up to date."

"I need phone numbers," Decker said. "We'll need to verify everything."

"Go ahead," Terry said. "I'm down with that. Angeline and I hadn't been together for a year. Like I told you, I moved on."

"But you've been in contact though."

"A few texts here and there."

"You've spoken to her on the phone as well."

"When she called me, I didn't hang up on her."

"Did you ever call her?"

"Not once I found out she had someone else."

"Yeah, the freak. John something . . . do you recall his last name? There are a lot of Johns out there."

"I've been thinking. Leather . . . Letter . . . it's something like that."

"Keep thinking. You'll nail it down. And in the meantime, tell me about him."

"Pretentious arty type."

"You've talked to him?"

"Well . . . no." Lance blew out air and took a swig of coffee. "No, he just looks pretentious. Really, really skinny.

Like he lives on air or something. He has a scrawny beard and a long braid down his back. He wears black—including a black hat."

"Hipster meets hippy," McAdams said.

"Yeah . . . like he can't quite decide. And he's old . . . old for her, I mean. Maybe thirty-two or thirty-three. He's just got the type of face that you want to put a fist through. Smug little bastard. I just don't understand what she sees . . . saw in him. I asked her about it . . . when she called me up. What the fuck do you see in him?"

"What'd she say?" Decker asked.

"She'd just laugh . . . like I couldn't understand. Bitch!"

"You sound angry."

"I'm angry at her for being conned."

"Maybe he was a secret prince?"

"Right . . . living in a one-bedroom shit house in Summer Village outside of Boston. The locals call it Slummer Village."

"So you know where he lives," Decker said.

Terry turned a deep red. "Uh . . . she told me. Angeline did. I said he looked old for a college student and she told me he wasn't a student. That he was some kind of lecturer or postdoc or something."

"Tufts University is in Medford, which is next to Summer Village," McAdams said.

"Yeah, I know," Terry said. "Angeline told me he was at Tufts."

"What was his field?"

"I didn't ask and she didn't tell me. We didn't speak that often after the breakup." Terry exhaled. "This isn't politically correct to say out loud but he looked gay. For the life of me, I can't understand what she saw in him."

"Could they have had something else going on?"

Terry was confused. "What do you mean?"

146

"Julia Kramer told me that about the same time Angeline broke up with you, she began toting around expensive handbags. Could they have been doing something illegal together?"

Lance was stoic, then stunned. "You don't think they were sleeping together?"

"I don't know. And it's possible that they were sleeping together and still doing something illegal. We're exploring everything. And if you say that he was a postdoc student, it appears she wasn't getting her money from him."

"I don't know where she got her money," Terry said. "I . . . was out of her life." He turned to McAdams. "Are you from Massachusetts?"

"I went to school there."

"Tufts?"

"Yeah," McAdams lied.

"Did you know him?"

McAdams said, "Lots of Johns in the school, Lance. It would help if I had a last name."

Terry went quiet. So did McAdams. Decker said, "Did you ever pay the mysterious John a visit, Lance?"

"No . . . why would I?"

"You knew he lived in Summer Village. And I know you were in the area when you went on your audition at the Boston Repertory Company," Decker said. "Maybe you took a little side visit."

Terry turned red again . . . this time out of anger. "Lucy told you about the audition?"

"She did. Now I'm not saying you were stalking Angeline—"

"I wasn't stalking anyone! I had an audition and it didn't go well. To blow off some steam, I drove by his apartment, taking great pleasure and schadenfreude in his shabby building. Je-ez! Can I go now?"

147

Decker took a chair and pulled it up close to Terry. "Lance, you're not a suspect—"

"Well, thank you."

"You're here to help us find a killer, okay? So if there was another guy in her life, I want to know about him . . . starting with his last name . . . which I know you know. So tell me."

Terry closed his eyes. "Latham. John Latham."

McAdams was already on his iPad. "There's a John Latham who's a stage actor in England who's fifty."

"The guy wasn't fifty," Lance said.

"There's a John Jeffrey Latham who won a Windsor Prize: Political Analysis of Prolekult and the Soviet Socialist Realism Art Movement."

"Well, ex-cuse me!" Lance said.

"Let me get an image." McAdams showed the picture to Lance. "Is this him?"

Lance stared at the picture. "Yeah, that's him. Do you know him?"

"Nope."

"What does the article say about him?"

"Not much . . . it mostly talks about the Windsor Prize. It's given to candidates every four years who have excelled in the fields of arts and politics . . ." McAdams looked up. "I know that Tufts is known for the Fletcher Graduate School of International Affairs. I bet he's either a postgrad there or maybe a lecturer—something like that."

"He's a prick, that's what he is," Terry said.

"Lance, do you know anything else about Latham?" Decker asked. "If you know something, tell me now."

"Only that he and Angeline like to go out for Thai." He bowed his head. "Okay. So I followed them a little in the beginning. Then Lucy and I starting hanging and I lost interest."

148

"Do you have any idea where Angeline got the money to buy expensive purses?"

"No." Said emphatically. "And it's really ironic. Because if she wanted nice things like that, I would have bought them for her."

"You went together for two years and you didn't buy her anything nice?" Decker asked.

"I took her out to nice places—restaurants, concerts, sports events. I took her to a couple of Jets games, a Knicks game. We went on a couple of nice weekends. But . . . I never bought her much of anything: T-shirts, books, flowers a few times . . . nothing expensive like designer handbags."

"If you loved her so much, why not?"

"Well . . . for starters . . . she never asked."

CHAPTER THIRTEEN

It was turning up dawn by the time Lance Terry left the station house. Decker offered to drive him back, but the kid elected to walk, saying that he needed to clear his head. Decker was putting on a fresh pot of coffee when his cell rang. He depressed the button. "Hey."

"Hey," Rina answered back. There was an awkward pause. "Just like old times."

"Sorry. I know this isn't what you bargained for."

"I'm fine, honey. You sound tired."

"A little."

"But you're also wired."

"A little." Decker smiled although she couldn't see it. "Did you go back to the city last night?"

"Not without you. I slept on the couch in the kids' nonexistent living room but that was fine with me. I got to wake up with Lily who seems to enjoy a predawn glass of milk. We're watching Elmo right now. Later, we'll go to the park, around eleven after she wakes up from her morning nap."

"You've got your work cut out for you."

"I do. I'm leaving for Philadelphia in the late afternoon

by train. The kids are taking me out to a vegetarian Indian restaurant called Spice and Chai. I'll save you samosas."

"I see my absence has made no dents in anyone's plans—as usual."

Rina ignored his self-pity. "I talked to Cindy last night. Of course, she's disappointed. But I represent the both of us. I should be back Wednesday afternoon. I'll send your love."

"Just like old times," Decker said. "And not in a good way."

"Peter, when was the last time Greenbury had a homicide?"

"A whodunit? Maybe like twenty years ago."

"So if you have to do this again in twenty years, I can live with that. They are very lucky to have you on the force right now. Does Mike know anything about procedure?"

"He's a smart guy, but he hasn't done it for a while."

"How's the investigation going?"

"Step by step." Decker chose his words carefully. "Rina, I love our decision to move east. I love living in a clean environment. I love being close to the kids, and I don't even mind the cold. I hope the homicide is a weird thing and I return to recovering stolen iPads and rescuing cats from trees. I don't need the thrill of the case to be happy."

"But what you're doing right now feels natural, right?"

"I guess it takes time to decompress."

"This case is basically feeding crack to an addict."

Decker laughed. "I'm slipping into all my old bad habits. No sleep and too much coffee."

"At least you don't smoke anymore. How's the kid working out? Or is he even in the picture?"

"Better than I thought . . . once we jumped a couple of hurdles."

152

"I heard that," McAdams said.

Decker covered his phone. "We're talking about the Summer Olympics. Hurdles are my favorite event." He returned to the phone. "Give Cindy, Koby, and the boys my love. Tell them I promise I'll visit real soon."

"Do you really want to tell them that you promise?"

"Yeah, you're right." Melancholy slipped into Decker's voice. "Maybe just give them my love and we'll leave it at that."

"I've made out a schedule for Lance Terry so we can check out his alibis." Decker pushed the list across the desk over to McAdams. "Make a few copies. It shouldn't take too long to verify everything."

"Do you want me to check out the alibi first or to talk to the administration when it opens?"

"Maybe, neither. Maybe one of the other guys can do it."

"Still don't trust me?"

"I might need you for something else."

"Like?"

Decker handed him a phone number on a scrap of paper. "This is the only number that I could find for John Jeffrey Latham in the Boston area. Give him a call."

"Sure." McAdams did. "Voice mail. Should I leave a message?"

"Give it here." Decker waited for the beep and then pressed the hash mark to go past the instructions. "This is Peter Decker of Greenbury Police Department. Can you please call me back as soon as possible? It's important." He left his cell number, the station number, and then he hung up. "It's seven in the morning. Where could he be without his cell?"

"Sleeping in bed."

"You of the information highway generation have your cell phones glued to your hands. The call should have woken him up. Try again in five minutes. Leave your cell number. Then he'll have two numbers to not call."

Five minutes later, on the dot, McAdams called and left his own voice mail. Decker was scribbling out his thoughts. "Can I have Angeline's phone bill from last month?"

"Sure." McAdams slid it across the desk.

Decker's eyes scanned the list. He gave it back to McAdams. "Do you see Latham's number anywhere?"

"Uh . . . no, I do not."

"Do you see any 617 area code numbers?"

"No, I do not."

"What are the other Massachusetts area codes?"

"If my memory is still intact, which I can't promise after being up for almost twenty-four hours, it has 857 and 781 . . . uh, why don't I just look it up?"

"Before you do, what's the point I am making?"

"That she made no calls to the Boston area."

"Which means?"

"Either Latham and Boston are dead ends or she had another cell phone."

"And why would it make sense for her to have another cell phone?"

"If she was doing something illegal, she wouldn't want a paper record of it."

"So what's our next step?"

"Search her place and see if we can find the other cell phone, which we won't find. Because if she was doing something illegal, she was using a disposable phone."

"Which means?"

"We won't be able to recover either a phone bill or a phone number."

"So what's our next step?"

154

McAdams sat back in his chair. "She had to buy the disposable phones somewhere. We need to hit the local phone stores."

"Tyler, you are truly worthy of your Harvard B.A."

"How about my two-hundred-thousand-dollar-plus tuition?"

Before Decker could answer, Mike Radar stepped into the station house. Clearly it had been a long time since the captain had worked through the night. Fatigue was etched into his face, sorrow in his eyes. "What's up?"

Decker said, "We're making a little headway. Did you get a coroner?"

"A CI came down from Boston. It's hard to find an exact time of death because of the decomp of the body. Remember, the room was very hot. Her best guess is that Angeline probably died sometime on Sunday night. There were ligature marks on her throat—also marks on her feet and wrists. Most likely it was strangulation, but we won't know for sure until the autopsy is done. The doc couldn't see any petechiae on her face because it was too bloated."

"Could she tell if the hyoid was broken?"

"No, but the CI thinks she saw cigarette burns on the body. She couldn't tell if that was done before or after she died. Her name is Bonnie McFee." Radar handed him a card. "In case you want to talk to her directly."

"What's a CI?" McAdams asked.

"Coroner's investigator," Decker said. "They are usually laypeople with some medical experience, like an EMT or a nurse. In big cities, they're the ones called out to take care of the bodies and get them to someone who's qualified to do an autopsy. Police can't touch the bodies until they've been seen by someone from the coroner's office." To Radar. "What about forensics?"

"Boston's Crime Laboratory Unit came in about an hour

ago. Ben and Kevin are holding the fort. Feel free to talk to whoever you want."

Decker's phone buzzed. He looked down at the text. "It's Angeline's parents. They're in southern Maryland, checked into a motel last night. They'll be here around eleven." He thought a moment. "Give me a minute to text them back." When Decker was done, he turned back to Radar. "Has the body already gone north?"

"Yes. They took it back to Boston. And with the city's murder rate, it might sit in the morgue for a couple of days. Now it's your turn. Tell me what's going on."

Decker gave him the story with as much detail as he could remember. The captain digested the information. Then he said, "So Lance Terry was stalking her?"

"I'm not sure if it was stalking or more like boredom. The next step is checking out Lance's timeline. If he was where he said he was, he was alibied pretty much all weekend."

"So he's out of the picture once we verify his alibi."

"More or less. Can Kevin do the verification? I can fill him in on everything."

"Any reason why you don't want to do it yourself?"

"I want to track down John Latham. I haven't reached him and that makes me feel uneasy."

"We called him twice," McAdams said. "Once Decker left a message and then I made a follow-up call. He's not answering his cell."

Decker looked at his watch. "Boston's about an hour and a half from here by car?"

"Probably two hours in this traffic."

"What about the train?" Decker asked.

"You have to go to Islewhite."

Decker's mind was whirling. "Let me see if I . . ." He dialed the cell number associated with his most recent

156

text. A woman answered the phone. "Hi, this is Peter Decker of Greenbury Police."

"It's Karen Bronson, Detective. I'm sorry we're so late . . . we just had to crash last night . . . it was too long a drive and we were both so exhausted."

"No, no, no, you did the right thing." Decker cleared his throat. "So you're planning on being here around eleven?"

"More like twelve . . . twelve-thirty. We're getting a late start."

"Okay."

"Is that a problem?"

"No, it's perfectly fine. We've been talking to a few of Angeline's friends and I do have a couple of questions for you. Could I ask them now?"

A sigh. "Go ahead." A pause. "Of course."

"Are you familiar with the name John Latham?" Silence. "Does it ring any bells?"

A pause. "I don't know the name . . . hold on, I'll ask Jim." Muffled voices and then she came back on the line. "Neither of us knows him. Who is he?"

"I don't know. He came up in conjunction with Angeline. I was just wondering if she mentioned him to you."

"No, she didn't. Is he important?"

"Anyone associated with Angeline is important. I think he may live in a suburb outside of Boston. Did your daughter make weekend trips to Boston?"

"I have no idea. She kept in touch with us, but she rarely spoke about her private life and I . . . didn't pry. I probably should have."

Decker heard the sorrow in her voice. "She was a legal adult. You couldn't have stopped her anyway." No response. "Okay, if he becomes important, I'll let you know. A few more questions. I found out from Julia

157

Kramer that Angeline was studying eighteenth-century textiles. She was writing her thesis on the subject."

"That's correct. Textiles are her first love. In high school, she did a lot of textile design on her own. She painted material by hand. She taught herself batik and laser print. She experimented with lots of different materials."

"Is that why she chose Littleton College?"

"Yes, of course. They have a wonderful art department. And she got a great scholarship. She deserved every penny they gave her. She's a one of a kind, very gifted . . ." There was a sob. "She was, very, very talented."

"I'd like to hear more about that. It helps me get a feel for who she was. Did she focus on textile design? Or was she talented at other things: drawing, painting—"

"Of course she could draw and paint. But she was excited by . . . how did she phrase it? She liked elevating crafts into works of art. Like her textile designs. She used to call it wearable art."

"What other crafts did she like?"

"I don't think Angeline ever met a craft she didn't like: weaving, macramé, papier-mâché, stained glass, pottery, glass blowing—"

"Stained glass?"

"Yes, she was very good at it. She started at around fourteen. I didn't relish the idea of her using knives and working with shards of glass, but she was careful. I think she only cut herself a couple of times."

"It's an unusual hobby."

"With Angeline, the more unusual the better."

"Any idea why she took up stained glass?"

"Like I said, she loved anything artistic and unusual. She was influenced by a woman named Clara Driscoll who worked at Louis Comfort Tiffany Studio—the lamp guy. She told me that the best designs were actually done

158

by her and not by Tiffany even though he put his name on them. That appealed to her as an artist and a woman. Why are you asking about her art?"

"Just trying to get a feel for your daughter. It may be significant down the road."

"Whatever I can do to help." Her voice cracked. "Ask your questions, Detective."

Decker said, "Mrs. Bronson—"

"Karen, please."

"Karen then. I wouldn't bring this up unless I thought it was important, so please forgive me in advance."

"What . . ." Anguish in her voice. "Was she pregnant?"

"Did she intimate that to you?"

"No . . . I mean just the way you're talking . . . was she pregnant?"

"I honestly don't know. I haven't gotten the report back."

Her voice grew very soft. "How did she die?"

"I won't know anything definite until I get the report."

"Do you have any ideas?"

"Nothing I want to talk about over the phone. I do have another question for you. Please don't take it personally. Before she was murdered, Angeline had acquired a collection of expensive handbags and designer shoes. Would you know anything about that?"

"No." A long pause. "How expensive?"

"Bags over a thousand dollars and exclusive designer boots."

"Oh my Lord . . . I . . . no, I don't know anything about it."

"That's all I wanted to know. We'll get to the bottom of it."

"She couldn't afford . . . maybe Lance Terry bought her gifts. He comes from money."

159

"We asked him. He didn't buy them. He did tell me that they broke up a year ago."

"They did, but I thought they remained friends."

That jibed with what Emily and Julia had said about Lance, that he had made booty calls to Angeline. "Any idea how she might have acquired those items?"

"No idea at all. She didn't have that kind of money. Did . . . did she have an older man paying for these items? Is that who this Latham character is?"

"The Latham I'm investigating is in his thirties and appears too poor to afford those kinds of accessories. I'm not even sure what his relationship is to your daughter. He isn't answering his phone, so I'd like to pay him a visit."

"Is there a problem with that?"

"Latham lives in the Boston area, which is about an hour and a half from Greenbury without traffic. If I go visit him, I might not make it back before you get here. Would you like me to wait for you? There are other things I could do in the meantime."

"How important is this Latham?"

"I feel he's very important. And there are things I need to do in Boston. We're too small to handle the lab work. The captain wanted it done correctly, so Boston sent out a team."

She cleared her throat, but her voice choked up. "Where is . . . the body?"

"In Boston."

There was a long pause. "Shouldn't we meet you in Boston? After all, you're not certain that it's her, right?"

"Karen, we can do the identification with a simple cheek swab."

"But I want to say good-bye!" Anger in her voice. "I need to say good-bye!"

"Karen, please give it a few days. Then you can give her a proper burial."

Her voice was a whisper. "You don't want me to see the body."

"It isn't necessary to put you through that anguish. I'll be back down by late afternoon. We'll get a DNA profile. And I'll tell you everything I know." There was a long silence. "Karen, are you still with me?"

"Go to Boston, Detective. Don't let us stop you from doing your job."

"I'll try to make it back as soon as I can."

"We'll wait. We'll wait as long as it takes. As long as it takes for you to get back and as long as it takes to get some answers."

CHAPTER FOURTEEN

McAdams sipped coffee from a paper cup while staring out the passenger window. Decker was behind the wheel. It was in the high twenties outside, but the skies were clear. It made for easy driving even with arid heat blasting in their faces.

"Any specific reason why you asked me to come with you?" the kid said.

"Why do you think?"

"You know you always answer my questions with another question."

"It's effective in getting people to talk. So why did I ask you to come?"

"I've been mulling several options in my head." He ticked them off. "I'm keeping you awake so you don't fall asleep at the wheel, I can drive home in case you do get too sleepy, you want me close so I don't fuck something up in your absence, or maybe, just *maybe*, I may actually be of some use to the investigation and you value my opinions."

"Bang on the money, Harvard."

"Admit it, Old Man. I'm growing on you."

"Mea culpa."

"Yeah, I'm kind of like lutefisk: strictly an acquired taste." McAdams put the coffee cup in the holder and rubbed his hands together. "I could tell by your conversation with the mom that Angeline did stained glass. So that makes her a strong candidate for the Tiffany forgeries. The thefts must have something to do with her murder."

"Maybe."

"Are you just being cagey or is that a sincere maybe?"

"This is what I think. The thefts weren't what caused her problems . . . it was you and me uncovering the thefts. Someone wanted to silence her. But do I really believe that someone would murder over a few Tiffany panels? Doubtful. We're dealing with something bigger . . . no offense to Tiffany . . . or Clara Driscoll."

"Who's that?"

"Karen Bronson, Angeline's mother, told me that Angeline liked stained glass because Clara Driscoll, a woman who worked for Tiffany, actually made a lot of the designs."

"Hold on, let me look her up." McAdams took out his iPhone. "It may take a minute. I think we're in a dead zone." He looked up. "For the phone, I mean. My brain, that's another story . . . what's it going on without sleep? Like thirty hours? How do you think, let alone stay awake?"

"That's why I brought you here, Harvard."

"I'm a fancified alarm clock. Okay, here we go. Wikipedia at its finest." McAdams paused while he read. "Clara Driscoll was indeed the head designer for Tiffany and worked there for twenty years. She chose the colors and the type of glass and designed some of his most famous lamps. Before her, the designs were more symmetrical and static. Her first design was the Daffodil, but she is also known for the Wisteria, the Dragonfly, and the Peony. She was given her just due when the New York Historical

Society gave her an exhibition in 2006 entitled 'A New Light on Tiffany.'"

"Angeline would have been about fourteen at that time," Decker said. "That's the age when she became interested in stained glass according to her mom. Maybe she saw the exhibition or read about it."

"How would Angeline have heard about it if she was in Florida?" McAdams said.

"There's a museum in Orlando that features lots of Tiffany. Damned if I can think of the name."

"Morse Museum of American Art."

"Yes! Exactly!" Decker turned to him. "Did you just look that up?"

"I've been there. My grandfather had a place in Bal Harbour."

"I also keep you around because you have a memory." Decker grinned. "Anyway, Karen Bronson told me that Angeline liked that Clara Driscoll because she appealed to Angeline's ideas of talented, strong women and the arts."

"Makes sense. Girls in college were always yakking about being strong and independent. God, it got so damn sophomoric. Just quit your bitching and actually *do* something."

"I can see that patience isn't your strong suit."

"You're right about that." McAdams gave out a mirthless chuckle. "Most of my classmates at Harvard were living away from home for the first time. But there were some like me: boarding school since first grade with absentee parents. Granted we were privileged as far as education, money, and connections go. And yes, we were spoiled beyond the point of ridiculousness. But we were independent. The first timers . . . man, they were still attached to the umbilical cord. They had absolutely no concept of how utterly dependent they were on mommy and daddy. God, how I envied them."

Decker was quiet.

McAdams said, "Don't mind me. Go on."

"Pour me more coffee. Just half full so I don't burn my fingers."

"Yes, sir."

"You're allowed to call me Peter."

"I prefer Old Man."

"Am I like your real old man?"

McAdams shrugged. "Yes and no. He's a prick in a bad way." He handed Decker his coffee. "You're a prick also, but in a good way."

"You have a way with words. Can we get back to the case now?"

"Gladly."

"Being that Clara Driscoll made the designs and Tiffany put his name on it, do you think that it might have mitigated Angeline's conscience when she was making the forgeries?"

"Huh!" McAdams was quiet. "She was doing to Tiffany what he did to Driscoll. I like it. Not that it helps us understand why she was murdered, but there is a sort of *lex talionis* to the whole thing. That means—"

"Eye for an eye, I know."

"Yeah, that's right. You were a lawyer. What kind of law again?"

"Estates and wills." When McAdams started to snore, Decker said, "Exactly. You know eye for an eye doesn't mean exacting retribution. It's actually tort law."

"How do you figure?"

"Because it's in the section of the Bible that deals with property law. You injure a guy's eye through negligence, you pay the victim for the value of what he would have earned with the eye versus what he makes because he's missing an eye. Courts do that all the time. It's called economic forensics."

"Yeah, I know. I interned for several white shoe law firms in my college days courtesy of Daddy." He took out his phone. "Where is the saying in the Bible?"

"Eye for an eye?"

"Yes."

"It's in Exodus . . . in the Hebrew section called Mishpatim if that helps."

"Hold on . . . Exodus 21 paragraph 22 through 25 . . ." He read. "It doesn't say anything about monetary compensation."

"It's in the commentary from Rashi. He was a great, eleventh-century—"

"I know who Rashi is. I took Moderation and Extremism at Harvard—Twersky's class—although he was dead by the time I took it. But people still refer to it as Twersky's course. The point is why should I believe some guy's commentary? Just go with the text."

"Law is always about interpretation. Nothing is ever face value. And the background of the biblical section deals more with torts than with capital cases."

"Aren't you the hotshot, biblical scholar?"

"This is pretty rudimentary, Tyler, but if you're impressed, I'm fine with that."

McAdams was still reading text. "The sections deal with tort law as well as capital cases. It's all mixed together."

"Traditionalists go by rabbinic law because the sages can interpret Jewish law better than the layman."

"You need a learned mind," McAdams said.

"Exactly."

The kid grinned. "Or a Learned Hand."

Decker groaned at the pun. "You were setting me up for that one, weren't you?"

"I was."

"Clever, but awful!"

"It wasn't awful!" McAdams sniffed. "It was just . . . Harvard."

The rural Northeast was white and stark, giving the region an aesthetic minimalism. Urban Northeast was gray and depressing. Grime mixed with snow equaled sludge, and the old factories and crumbling brick warehouses were bereft of any kind of beauty. The only saving grace today was the bright sunshine and the clear skies, which only served to highlight the sprawl. According to the GPS, Decker was only a mile from Latham's address. He said, "Are we near the university?"

"I take it you mean Tufts. We're not far in distance, but worlds away socioeconomically. If Latham was doing something illegal, it wasn't paying him big dividends."

"Or he chose the area because petty criminal activity might go unnoticed."

"That's certainly possible."

"Or Latham was a poor grad student who was strapped. Or he was just cheap." Decker pulled up to the apartment building and killed the motor. "Hopefully, we shall find out something about the lad." He clicked open the glove compartment and took out his gun.

McAdams said, "I don't think you'll need that in the daytime."

Decker strapped it into his harness. "I'm not leaving a loaded Beretta in the car."

"Why'd you bring a piece? I mean, do you routinely carry it in Greenbury?"

"No. Don't need it there. But here we don't know what we're dealing with so I like to err on the overcautious side." Decker opened the door. "Let's go."

"I'm with you, partner."

Together, they walked up to the apartment building—an

168

old square made of bricks and stucco. In a perfect world, the glass front door was locked for security. But the hasp appeared to be broken so they slipped inside, walking up a flight of stairs, down the hallway until they found Latham's unit. Decker knocked on the door. After a few minutes of futile banging, Decker gave up.

"What now?" McAdams asked.

"We leave a card, then we drive over to the morgue and see if they've started Angeline's autopsy. I'd like to get a blood sample for DNA. See if we can get a match from her toothbrush. If that doesn't work, we'll do a match with Mom. Anything's better than a visual identity. No parent should have to see a son or a daughter in that condition."

"Don't you need both parents for a profile match?"

"The lab can do a mitochondrial match. Unless there are other sisters missing, it's good enough for an ID." Decker took out his card and stuck it into the doorway. As he turned to leave, a neighbor came out. She lived two doors down and was wearing a housecoat. She was dark complexioned with gray hair: midsixties to early seventies.

"Finally!"

"Excuse me?" Decker said.

"You're the police, right?"

"Right."

"Well, it took you long enough to come down."

Decker smoothed his mustache. Then he took out a notebook. "When did you call?"

"Around ten last night. I couldn't take it anymore."

"Remind me of the complaint. I just got a notice to come down and talk to the man in this unit . . . I believe his name is John Latham."

"It's John. I don't know his last name. He wasn't very friendly."

169

"Okay," Decker said. "And you are . . ."

"Inez Camero."

"How long have you lived in the building?"

"Ten years."

"How long has John been here?"

"Under a year. And like I said, he's not very friendly. But at least he was quiet . . . until last night. Music was blasting so loud, my other ear nearly went deaf. You could have probably heard it in Cambridge."

"It was blasting all last night?"

"It started around nine-thirty. I know because my favorite show, *Real Estate Buddies*, was on the television. I had my tea, I had my biscotti, all set to enjoy a nice quiet evening, but nooooo. I called the police at ten during the commercial break. When nothing happened, I finally went over myself and banged on the door. That musta been around ten-thirty right after my show. Leslie Avila saw me. She was getting ready to do the same thing. Finally the jerk turned down the volume."

"Inconsiderate neighbors can be a real problem," Decker said.

"What's a real problem is an apathetic police department. What good are you if I have to do it myself because you don't show up until the next morning?"

Decker nodded. "I understand your frustration."

"Sure you do." Inez was actively glaring by this time. "Sorry to have disturbed you. I'm sure you have important stuff to deal with like where to get your doughnuts." With her parting shot, Inez marched back into her apartment and slammed the door.

McAdams said, "She wasn't very nice."

"She's frustrated." Decker swirled his tongue inside his cheek and thought a moment. He squatted down and sniffed underneath the door. While he was down there,

170

he saw the tip of a small white card. With deft hands, he pulled it out and read. "Officer James Marx."

"The police did come out."

"Apparently." Decker stood up and turned it around to the back side. "No time on the card. Maybe when Marx showed up, the music had stopped." He handed McAdams the card. "Give him a call. Find out when he came out."

"Now?"

"Yes, now." Decker bit his lower lip. "Someone was here last night inside Latham's apartment because someone turned down the music. But the card was still there under the door in the morning."

"Maybe he didn't see it when he left the apart— Uh, hello, can I talk to Officer James Marx, please?"

"Identify yourself first, Tyler."

"Right."

Decker dropped to a squat, once again sniffing under the door.

McAdams said, "Could you please have him call Detective Tyler McAdams of the Greenbury Police Department. We're in the area investigating a crime that occurred south of here. I'll give you my cell number."

Decker stood up. "I definitely smell something."

"Like what?" Tyler stowed his cell in his pocket. "Decay?"

"More metallic—like blood."

McAdams started to bend down. Decker pulled him up by his collar before his hands and knees touched the ground. "If there was a murder, everything on the floor is possible forensic evidence—"

"I know. Don't kneel, squat. My quads leave something to be desired."

Decker pointed to the floor. "Go on. Take a whiff."

The kid complied. "Yeah, it does smell a little funky in there. Can you help me up?"

"You've *got* to be kidding!"

McAdams took in a deep breath and managed to hoist himself back up on his feet. "If I get a leg cramp, can I apply for workman's comp?" When Decker didn't answer, he said, "I'm just trying to add a little levity in an otherwise grave situation . . . no pun intended."

But Decker was lost in thought. "There was a report of unusually loud music, which could have been used to mask criminal activity. The police card wasn't taken off the floor. And I think I smell blood." He looked at Tyler. "I'd say we have probable cause."

"Probable cause for what? You're going inside?"

"I'm going to try." Decker took out a credit card, worked it between the door frame and the lock.

"What if the guy's still there?"

The lock snapped open. Decker took out his gun. "This is basic police work, McAdams. Stay here and guard my ass." The kid had turned ashen. "You're not going to pass out on me, right?"

"No, no, I'm fine." A forced smile. "I don't have a weapon on me, Old Man."

"You've got the best weapon in the world, McAdams. Your vocal cords. You see anything hinky, just let out a scream."

Decker took out a single latex glove and sheathed his left hand, keeping his right hand bare and firmly on the grip of his gun. He pushed open the door with the barrel of his gun. Stepping inside chaos, his nose was assaulted with bad news as he took in the sight of a recent struggle, not unlike the one that had taken place in Angeline's apartment.

Upturned furniture, items pitched everywhere. He didn't

see any stereo receiver, but there was a TV and a dock for an iPad. The TV was off and cold and the dock was empty. It was hard to walk without disturbing something, including the blood on the floor and area rug. Distinct circles and ovals . . . drip blood from an injury, not splatter from an artery. He tiptoed very carefully across the room and into the kitchen.

There was more mess—overturned canisters, broken glasses, cutlery on the floor. More drips, but still no splatter, which meant no massive amount of blood loss. There were two wineglasses in the sink, and an open bottle of pinot on the counter that somehow remained intact. An empty knife block, its contents scattered on the floor. He couldn't tell if anything was missing, but strewn knives were never good signs of anything. He tiptoed out of the kitchen and down the small hallway. The bathroom door was open. More drips on the floor, bloody towels in the sink and bathtub. The smell was getting stronger and stronger, not just metallic but putrid—discarded feces, decay . . . fetid rot. When he opened the door to the bedroom, he found the source.

The nude body on the bed: multiple stab wounds, which often meant not only rage but up close and personal. This time the fury was overt because the man's penis and testicles had been severed and placed on his stomach. In addition to the stab wounds and the genital mutilation, his throat had been slashed.

"Decker?" McAdams called out. "You okay?"

"Don't move, McAdams. Stay where you are."

"Are you okay?"

"I'm fine. Just hold on." Decker tiptoed out of the bedroom and saw the kid standing in the hallway of the apartment. "I'm assuming you didn't touch anything and you were careful where you walked. There's blood evidence in the living room."

173

"I saw it. And yes, I was real careful where I put my feet." The kid swallowed hard. "You've been gone a while. I peeked in and saw the blood. I got nervous . . . like you were ambushed. I guess I would have heard something if you were ambushed. Sorry to disturb you."

"No apologies necessary. I said guard my ass and you guarded it. Sometimes I lose track of time."

"I'll go back and wait outside."

"I'll come with you." Once back in the common hallway, Decker gently pulled the door to the jamb, making sure it didn't close. He stowed his gun back inside his harness.

McAdams said, "James Marx called me back. He was out here at 10:42 P.M."

"After Inez Camero took action into her own hands. They probably both missed the killer by minutes." Decker took out his cell phone.

"*Killer?*" McAdams felt woozy, but kept his balance. "Latham's dead?"

"I found a desecrated male body." Decker punched in 911 and brought his cell to his ear. "If that was Latham, God rest his soul."

CHAPTER FIFTEEN

It was after three in the afternoon by the time Decker and McAdams had given their statements to the Summer Village detectives. Decker hadn't slept for over thirty-six hours and he could feel his brain starting to shut down. He needed to pull himself together for Angeline's parents, his scattered thoughts trying to focus on two horrific murders. The Summer Village Police Department was smaller and less bureaucratic than Boston PD, but big enough to have resources and actual detectives. That was a plus. Explaining why Decker and McAdams were there and why they broke into the apartment took up a lot of time. After the requisite questions, the detectives were generous enough to let them stick around while Summer Village brought in the coroner and their forensics team.

The apartment had not only been the scene of a struggle but it had been ransacked. No staging, at least to Decker's eye. The killer appeared to be looking for something. No one turned up Latham's phone, laptop, or tablet. There weren't any Tiffany panels hiding in a closet or under the bed. But a careful probe did turn up a hidden ring of unmarked keys. Decker was allowed to make a copy at a local locksmith: maybe it contained the key to Angeline's apartment thus providing a link between the two cases. He returned the originals to Summer Village detectives. Decker asked them if he could come back in a day or two and search for storage bins in the area. The lead detective equivocated, saying they'd be in touch. Good enough because he was way too tired and pressed for time to check today. He had to get back to Greenbury and Angeline's parents.

Summer Village would be stuck doing the notification for Latham. Although the body was mutilated, the face was still recognizable as the image that McAdams had pulled up on the Internet. That was in marked contrast to Angeline where time, heat, and gases had distorted everything, meaning that she was probably murdered first.

Decker's stomach was long past empty. His head was pounding and he knew if he didn't get more than caffeine into his system he'd pass out. "I need to eat something."

"You can eat after witnessing that . . . horror?"

"Survival, Tyler. Before we hit the road, I need to fill the tank and get some calories." He drove about a mile, neither of them speaking, until they reached a gas station with a Stop-N-Go. "You get the gas, I'll get food. Do you want anything?"

"I suppose I should eat. Whatever you get is fine. I don't even have the energy to be disagreeable."

Decker went inside the minimart and picked up a pack of six onion bagels, a tub of cream cheese, two cartons of orange juice, two bags of honey peanuts, two energy bars, and two giant coffees. They ate in the parking lot, making the most minimal of conversation. Ten minutes later, with a semifull belly, Decker put the key in the ignition and crawled through the streets until he hit the highway.

McAdams spoke first. "Are you sure you don't mind driving?"

"No, I'm awake. Thanks for asking. You can sleep, Harvard. You've earned it."

But McAdams continued to stare out the windshield. The sun grew stronger as it made its descent in the winter sky. "That was . . . intense."

"Gruesome even for someone experienced. Not part of your job description when you signed up in Greenbury?"

"Whoda thunk?" McAdams sipped coffee from a thermos. "Not that I was staring at the corpse. Au contraire, I was watching the pros . . . trying to hold down my stomach and learn a few pointers at the same time."

"Good for you."

"None of it sank in—shock and fatigue took care of that." His eyes remained forward as he spoke. His voice seemed to come from somewhere far away and deep inside. "I know that the Tiffany panels are valuable, but surely they are *not* worth the wholesale slaughtering of two human beings."

"Are you making an ethical judgment or are you talking about the motive for the crime?"

"Motive." He was still visibly upset. "The panels can't be the motive for something that abominable, right?"

"I've seen men gutted for a pack of cigarettes," Decker said. "But I know what you're saying and I agree. These cases are not just about the panels. All we can say so far is that we have two bad murders and the killings are probably connected. Next question: Are the two murders related to the Tiffany thefts?"

"What else is there?"

"There's probably way more. Right now, beyond the murders and the theft, do we know anything else?"

"Besides the fact that I'm exhausted and sick to my stomach?"

"Bagel didn't go down well?"

177

"I ate too fast. I always eat too fast. What do we know beyond the two murders and a theft?" He shrugged. "Beats me."

"The two murders were overkill."

"Yeah, I'll say."

"In both cases there was not only a struggle, but the apartments appeared genuinely ransacked. The murderer was looking for something."

"The Tiffany panels?"

"Possibly. But like you said, do you butcher your victims over stolen Tiffany panels?" Silence. Decker said, "Let's start throwing out some ideas."

"You go first."

"We have two victims we suspect were doing something illegal because Angeline suddenly came into money. She started toting around designer accoutrements and only did that after she met John Latham."

"Right."

"We also suspect that she might have been involved with the forgery of the two Tiffany panel replacements. Angeline did stained glass and she liked Tiffany."

"Right again."

"And the forgeries might have something to do with the murders."

"Correct."

"Tyler, if we think the forgeries are even one of the reasons for the murders, then it would behoove us to look at who was wronged by the forgeries."

"That would be the Sobel family. But I can't believe anyone in the family would do something that extreme. *That* doesn't make sense."

"I agree. The theft per se isn't the reason for the murder. As I said before, it was probably the *discovery* of the theft that put Angeline and Latham in danger."

178

"Because they were involved in other thefts and did them at the behest of someone. Meaning those other burglaries might now be discovered."

"Exactly. So any ideas?"

"Let me think." McAdams was tapping the dashboard.

"There's no right or wrong answer. Just say what's on your mind."

McAdams continued to drum the dash. "I looked at art thefts. I didn't find anything recent in the area. If someone has been selling stolen art, I'm thinking that he or she is a pro and has been doing it for a while. He—or she—just hasn't been caught."

Decker nodded. "And you know about the Art Loss Register, right?"

"Yes, I do know from my father. It's a stolen-art site. Before museums, auction houses, and galleries acquire any work, the purchaser looks up the piece in question to make sure the work wasn't stolen." McAdams started snacking on nuts. "Maybe I should start looking up cases on the register. I mean I'm not saying that our alleged buyer—" He paused. "Alleged? Is that even the right word? This person may be entirely fictitious."

"Alleged is fine, Harvard."

"Yeah, okay. I'm not saying our alleged buyer of stolen art is the same guy who arranged the hit on the Isabella Stewart Gardner Museum. But maybe he arranged some lesser thefts. Like the icons by Nikolai Petroshkovich."

"I agree. Did you ever find out the names of the original detectives on the case?"

"I . . . uh." He sighed. "I thought it was a dead end and I didn't bother. I know, I know. I should stop thinking for myself. My initial reaction is always to bristle at orders. I fucked up. My apologies."

"Just get it done."

"I'd call Marylebone right now, but I'm not getting a signal on my phone."

"Do it as soon as we get back. That way if they tell you something, you can write it down. Then go home and go to sleep."

"Why bother? All I'll have is nightmares."

"Believe me, you'll sleep. And yes, I think it's a good idea to start investigating more local art thefts. If Latham and Moreau were stealing things, they were probably small-timers who maybe hit on something big time."

"Makes sense."

"So we're now working on a possible assumption that the thefts are related to the murders and that the burglaries were done maybe at the behest of a third person who's calling the shots. That theory can change at any time. Don't get too wedded to it."

"Open mind."

"Right," Decker said. "With that theory in mind, we both think that the murders involve more than just the theft of Tiffany panels. We suspect that Angeline was doing the stained-glass forgeries. She was talented in more than one artistic field. Perhaps she was doing other forgeries as well."

"Like actual art painting forgeries?" McAdams said. "She's probably not that good."

"I agree. So maybe she was doing something that was easier to copy: like antique maps or old nature prints."

"She couldn't forge an Audubon, that's for certain," McAdams said. "He was a master at watercolors."

"But she could be stealing . . . taking old prints and maps out of books by razoring them at the binding."

"Again, not Audubon. Ever see a copy of his original book? I think his plates were like two feet by four feet."

"So not Audubon. Maybe someone not as valuable or big."

"Possibly."

"Or," Decker said, "maybe she was stealing outright: rare manuscripts or books. After you're rested, I want you to check out the local libraries at the Upstate colleges and see if some of their old atlases have been messed with or see if any rare books are missing."

"I should start writing this down." He took out his tablet. "Find the names of original detectives in the Nikolai Petroshkovich theft, talk to the Upstate colleges' librarians and see if any rare books are missing, check out antique reference material and see if maps or prints are missing . . . what else did you ask me to do? I'm a little fried right now."

"Expand your search for other smaller local art thefts."

"Right."

"Now for the crucial question. How do we link the murders to the Tiffany theft? Just blurt out the first thing that comes to mind, Tyler."

"I'm not a good blurter outer, Decker. I'm more the well-placed zinger type."

Decker sighed and didn't respond.

"Right, just shut up and answer the question. Okay. I'm gonna say that since you made copies of the keys that you found at Latham's apartment, you're going to valiantly attempt to open some storage locker with the faint hope that it holds the stolen Tiffany panels or other objets d'art."

"That is an avenue of exploration, yes. But unless Summer Village PD turns up a bill to a specific storage facility, that's a long shot. Let's go back to the beginning. If we assume a connection—murders and thefts—how did Angeline and Latham find out about the Tiffany panels in the first place?"

"Maybe they're professional grave robbers and they hit upon the panels by luck."

"Are those items or any items in a cemetery worth butchering two people?"

"Is anything in cemeteries worth butchering two people like that?" The kid thought a moment. "Perhaps. Just look at King Tut."

Decker couldn't help it. He laughed. "How about we stick to American cemeteries?"

McAdams smiled. "No, it is not likely that Angeline and Latham were murdered for items they pilfered from local cemeteries."

"Right now, we're working on the theory that someone hired them to rob the mausoleum. So how did Angeline and Latham discover the panels in the first place?"

"They were told by the person who hired them to steal them?"

"And how did the person find out?"

"That's actually a very good question," McAdams said. "Because according to my research, they haven't been featured in an art book or loaned out for any museum exhibit."

"Were they mentioned in the local papers?" Decker asked.

"I checked the *Greenbury Tattler* from the 1970s to present day and found nothing. I'll go back further if you want."

"Occam's razor," Decker said. "What's the most expedient way to find out about the panels?"

"Somebody who knew about them blabbed."

"And who knew about their existence?"

"This is very Socratic. Great preparation for law school."

"I'm this close to throwing you out of the car."

The kid smiled. "Who knew about the panels? Uh, the caretakers of the cemetery, maybe a few locals, and of course, the family."

"Bingo. The theft was either ordered by a family member or someone in the family yakked to the wrong person. We need to go back to New York."

"When?"

"Maybe tomorrow, maybe the day after tomorrow. I'm going to tell my wife to stay put. Let her enjoy the kids a little longer." A pause. "The murders have just given us ammunition to start asking the family very serious questions."

"You keep using first person plural. Is annoying little me tagging along?"

"You're not tagging along, McAdams. You're discharging your duties as a sworn officer of Greenbury Police."

"Between you and me, I never swore any kind of an oath."

"You can take notes on your iPad."

"That I can do."

"Do you have a place to stay?"

McAdams laughed. "I have several places to stay, all on the Upper East Side, FYI."

"Hence, my reason for taking you to the Big Apple. Your upper-crust upbringing and connections will come in handy. Unless you have loyalties to your East Side homies."

"No loyalties whatsoever." When Decker laughed, he said, "Blunt but true."

"Then I could use your insider perspective."

"I can certainly talk the talk."

"Tyler, all you need to do is walk the walk." Decker smiled. "Let me handle the talking."

CHAPTER SIXTEEN

Four fifty-three in the afternoon and a mile away from the station, Decker said, "Go home and get some rest, McAdams. If all goes as planned, I'd like to leave for Manhattan by seven tomorrow morning. That should put us into the city by ten."

"Are you going home?" McAdams asked.

"Not yet. I've got to talk to Angeline's parents and catch up on forensics."

"How long will that last?"

"I suppose it depends on what the parents have to say and if CSI came up with anything significant."

"Drop me off at the colleges and I'll start looking up antique books."

"You're not tired?"

"I'm beyond tired and into delirious. I probably won't get much out of anything, but I'll be damned if I quit before you do."

"This isn't a competition."

"With me, it's always a competition. How about if we meet up for dinner when you're done and we can swap notes?"

185

Decker studied the kid. "I don't know, McAdams. I just get a feeling that you're up to something."

"Because I'm trying to be conscientious?" The kid got huffy. "Can't win for losing."

"You're right. I should be applauding your work ethic. Okay, let's meet up for dinner. It might be late. What time do the libraries close?"

"College libraries close late, late."

"That's fine," Decker said. "I probably won't be done until late, late."

McAdams said, "Most of the restaurants in town aren't open late, late."

"What about the bars? They're open late, late and they serve food."

"They're a little loud for talking business. And sometimes stinky, too." McAdams paused. "I'm showing my age."

"And you call me Old Man?"

"Irony of ironies."

"You know, Tyler, when I was much younger, I felt much older. Now that I really am older and retired . . . well, semiretired . . . I feel young again. I think it's because I no longer have anything to prove."

"Good for you."

"I'm hearing sarcasm."

"Not sarcasm . . . jealousy. I've been jumping hoops since I was born: the right schools, the right university, the right friends, the right address, the right clothes, the connections, the right shit in the right gold-plated toilet. You can drop me off here."

Decker pulled the car to the curb in front of Duxbury's administration building. It was an imposing limestone edifice: Federalist in style and reminiscent of a courthouse. There were a fair number of students milling about, huddled and bundled as they trudged through the snow.

The skies were dark and clear, the campus grounds frosted in pure white. In the daytime sun, walkway sludge had melted to water. When the temperature dropped, the pathways froze over to a black sheet of ice. Despite the shoveling, the clearing and the salting, the local emergency room dealt with lots of slips and falls in the winter. Cleats would have been helpful.

"I think we both could use a good night's rest," Decker said.

"I think I could use some meaning in my pathetic life. And I don't think I'm gonna find it at Harvard Law." He got out and slammed the door.

Decker blew out air. He called up Rina and brought her up to date.

"So now you're dealing with two murders?"

"Yes."

"That's horrible. Poor victims." A pause. "Poor you."

"I'll be fine. I'm coming back to Manhattan. It makes more sense for you to stay put."

"You don't have to twist my arm. This actually works out perfectly. Cindy has the day off tomorrow and we were planning to go to King of Prussia. This way I won't have to rush."

Decker felt a twinge of envy. "Have fun."

"Do you need anything?"

"No . . . I'm just a little peeved that I always seem to be missing out."

"We're going to a shopping mall, Peter. A very, very big shopping mall. Last I heard, malls are your version of hell."

"Actually I'm dealing with real hell right now," Decker said. "King of Prussia has just been downgraded to purgatory."

* * *

The station hummed with activity. As soon as Decker stepped through the door, Ben Roiters got up from his desk and walked over to him. "Mike wants to see you."

"Where are Angeline Moreau's parents?"

"They're at Littleton, talking to someone in the administration. Since it happened off-campus, the college is punting to us."

"It might not have anything to do with college. We'll have to wait and see."

"I think the parents were planning on dinner after the meeting, but I'm sure they'll want to talk to you."

"Could you call them for me? Tell them I'm back and I'll meet with them whenever they're ready."

"No problem."

"Thanks." Decker walked into Mike Radar's office and shut the door. The captain's lair was tiny. There was a desk, a file cabinet, two chairs, and lots of pictures and plaques on the wall.

Mike pointed to the chair. "Did you ask for the coroner's office in Boston to send down any identifying marks on Angeline Moreau?"

"Yeah, I asked them to send it to your e-mail in case I got hung up."

"They sent me two tattoos so far. As the gases dissipate, the doc told me that more marks might become visible. I forwarded the tats to you: some kind of flower vine on her shoulder and a flower on the small of her back. I think they call those tramp stamps, although I'm not going to say that to the parents."

"Hardly. Can you bring up the tats on your computer?"

"Sure." Radar played with his keyboard. "Here." He turned the screen around for Decker to see. A wisteria vine cascaded down Angeline's shoulder, and a peony rested on the junction between her spine and buttock. It was of note that she had chosen flowers used by Clara Driscoll in the Tiffany glass lamps.

"Can you print them out for me?"

"You want to show them to the parents?"

"It's easier than showing them her body. I also told them to bring her toothbrush in case you wanted to confirm with DNA, but these might do it."

"Fine." Radar produced a latex glove and small paper bag. "Forensics found this with the vacuum. Be careful. We're talking sharp."

Decker put on the glove, opened the bag, and looked inside. He shone a light and then gingerly picked up a pinch of tiny colored fragments. "Stained glass."

"Angeline had been a busy girl. Where are the forgeries from the mausoleum? Did the family take them?"

"No, no, no. I've got them in bubble wrap and put them in the lost and found since it's the only cage that locks. We really should get an official evidence room."

"Become a real big-city police department."

Decker smiled. "Let's see if the fragments match to the forgeries. We'll need a big-city lab with equipment for something this sophisticated. Boston will probably do it since her murder is most likely connected to Latham's murder."

"That was Boston territory?"

"No, it's Summer Village territory, but they use Boston if they need something specific."

"Tell me about Latham." After Decker did a brief recap, Radar said, "That's one vicious murder."

"It was bad. I'd like to go back to his apartment when I have time and riffle through it myself. The Summer Village detectives seem like good guys and eager to share. But Latham isn't my case. I'd also like to return to New York and reinterview the extended Sobel family."

189

"Why?"

"Because I think that's how Angeline Moreau found out about the Tiffany windows."

"Someone in the family was behind the theft?"

"Or talked to her too freely. There were people I didn't interview because I came back to investigate Moreau's murder."

"Yeah, about that. How do you feel about handling the murder investigation? Are you comfortable with it?"

"I'm okay for right now."

"So then it's yours. If it becomes too much or too complicated—and it might be with Latham's murder—let me know."

"I'll keep you posted."

"How's the kid?"

"McAdams? Surprisingly motivated. I told him to go home and get some rest, but he insisted on doing additional research. I'd like to take him with me to New York."

"Why?"

"It's his home turf. He has connections there."

"Does he ever."

"You want to fill me in with that?"

"His father, Jack McAdams, is in international banking; his mother, Alberta, is currently married to someone else in international banking. But it's the grandfather with the real money. He did the backing for a lot of the high-tech companies when the field was in its infancy. He passed about six years ago and Tyler's father amassed most of the fortune. Jack went to Duxbury as an undergrad."

"Not Harvard?"

"Harvard Law School. Jack is not only a major benefactor of Duxbury, he sits on the board. He also built the new rec center for the town. Actually, it's about four years old but we still call it the new rec center. He is also instrumental in building the new stage theater and revamping the swimming center. It has endeared him to the mayor."

"Got it."

"So you're okay with the kid? That's good. He's a trust fund baby, you know. So I suppose it's laudable that he's trying to work, although I can't help but think that he has something up his sleeve."

"Me, too," Decker said. "What's your take on it?"

"I don't know. But why would a kid like that want to work with a small-town police department?"

"Probably this is the only place that would take him without a lick of experience."

"Yeah, you're right about that. I gave him a six-week crash course. He was a quick learner, very smart, but obnoxious. I don't get him. Why not go to law school, sit back on your ass, and spend Daddy's bucks? Something's on his mind."

"Maybe he wants to write a Pulitzer Prize exposé."

"Here? We're boring. Not a scandal in fifty years."

"Maybe he's after a screenplay with verisimilitude."

"Yeah, that would fit." Radar handed Decker the printouts of the tattoos. "All right. Go back to New York and see if you can't make something happen. If you happen to meet Tyler's old man, tread lightly."

"Tyler detests him, you know."

"Nobody likes him. Jack's a real schmuck. One day that man's going to wind up with a bullet in his back and no one will be surprised."

In another context, Karen Bronson might not be beautiful, but she might have appeared fit: a good figure, nice tan, brown, straight hair cut in a neat bob. She had a lithe body and long arms and legs. Her face was long with thin lips and light, red-rimmed eyes with deep circles under the orbs. Like Decker, she hadn't slept for many hours. Her husband also had an athlete's build—long and lean with broad shoulders. They appeared to be in their early fifties. They had dressed strictly for comfort: sweatpants and sweatshirts. Decker came into the small interview room holding the printouts and a cup of coffee.

"Can I refill your cups for you?" Both of them shook their heads. "Peter Decker." He shook their hands and sat down. The square footage of the place was very small. Intimacy was forced. "I'm so sorry for your terrible loss. This is my case and I'm going to do everything I possibly can to find out what happened and who did this."

Jim spoke up. "No offense, Detective, but this is a very small town. I mean . . ." He threw up his hands. "Have you done this before?"

"I was a Los Angeles Police Department lieutenant before I came out here. And I've worked hundreds of homicides. I promise I'll do everything I can. And I'll be sure to keep in touch. Like I said, call me anytime."

"So this was like a retirement job or . . ."

"Exactly."

"When did you leave Los Angeles?"

Karen broke in. Her voice was husky. "Jim, we can ask the questions another time."

"I want to make sure he's competent." Jim looked at Decker. "We're thinking about hiring private . . . if we don't get results."

"Sure, if you want. I'll coordinate with him if you do."

"And you're sure it's Angeline."

Decker clenched his jaw. "Does she have tattoos?"

"Oh God!" Karen's eyes watered. "Yes."

"We have some pictures." He slid them across the table. She gasped and then broke into open sobs. Jim held her shoulders and shoved the papers back to Decker.

"I'm sorry." When neither responded, Decker said, "I need to ask you some questions. They might be unpleasant. I'm sorry if they are."

"What did you find out about this John character?" Jim demanded. "Is he important?"

"John Latham. You're sure that you've never heard the name before?"

"No. Never. Who is he?"

"I know the bare minimum about him." Decker blew out air. "He was murdered by the time we got to his apartment. That's why he wasn't answering his phone."

"Oh my God!" Jim hugged Karen tighter as she continued to sob. "Just what the hell is going on?"

"Has . . . has Angeline ever been in trouble before?"

"What the hell does that mean?"

"I told you the questions might be unpleasant. I have to ask them. Has she ever shoplifted, for instance?"

"*Shoplifted*?"

"Yes," Karen broke in.

"She *did*?" Jim asked.

"Years ago. When she was eleven or twelve—during the divorce. She was having a hard time. Nothing since that one incident . . . actually it was two . . . two incidents. But I begged the owner to let me pay and not press charges and she was very kind about it. Two charges would have meant juvenile hall." Karen wiped her eyes. "What mess did she get herself into?"

"I'm not positive about anything." Decker took out his notepad. "Let me tell you what I do know. Last Friday night, one of the cemetery mausoleums was broken into. There were some items taken."

"What kind of items?"

"Valuable stained-glass window panels. Not all of them. Two original panels were still there. But the other two

193

panels had been forged. The forensic team found shards of glass in your daughter's apartment—"

"Yes, I was going to ask you about that," Karen said. "When you mentioned her apartment, I thought you meant her dorm room. But then her dean told us that it happened off-campus . . . that the university wasn't even technically responsible."

"Passing the buck," Jim said. "They're all fucking weasels!"

"Jim—"

"You know it's true. All they care about is their own asses. They are petrified we're going to sue. Well, I'll tell you one thing. We're going to sue someone. Somebody is to blame for my daughter's death!"

"Who gives a damn about money," Karen snapped.

"I'm just saying that somebody has to take responsibility!"

"That would be me," Decker said. "I'm responsible for this investigation right now. So if you want to yell at someone, yell at me."

"Why would I yell at you? You're trying to help."

"I am," Decker said. "So you knew nothing about an apartment off-campus?"

"Not a thing," Jim said. "We weren't paying for it, that's for certain."

"Okay. Going back to the apartment, we found glass shards in it. We also have the forged panels. Our next step is to see if the glass that we found in the apartment matches the glass in the forgeries."

"Even if it does match, it doesn't mean that Angeline did the forgeries," Jim said. "There could be dozens of people owning that glass—"

"Jim, just listen to what the man has to say, okay." Karen wiped her eyes. "You think she forged the panels."

"I have to consider it, yes."

"And she was *murdered* because of the forgeries?" Karen's eyes shed new tears.

"Maybe."

"How valuable are these panels?" Jim said. "Are they priceless or something?"

"Pricey but certainly not priceless."

"How much? Like thousands?"

"Probably."

"If she was carrying around expensive bags, you're thinking that she has done some other types of forgeries before and that's how she got the spending money," Karen said.

"Yes, that's what I'm thinking." He paused. "Could there be other illegal activities that she's done in the past?"

"Like what?"

"Drugs maybe?"

"No, not Angeline," Karen insisted. "Yes, I can see her . . . possibly . . . copying some art pieces, but not drugs."

"Why can you see her copying other art pieces, Mrs. Bronson?"

"Karen."

"Okay, sure. Karen. Tell me why you said that."

The woman sighed. "Angeline was every bit the typical college student, idealistic and a bit . . . radical. She often spoke about art, saying it should be available to the masses. In museums and public places, not holed up in big mansions. Her goal was always nonprofit . . . getting major pieces back to public places from private places. So . . . maybe she got carried away, imagined herself to be a modern-day Robin Hood."

Stealing from the rich and buying designer handbags. Decker said, "Anything else you'd like to tell me about her?"

"No." Karen wiped her eyes. "And I'm not saying she

did anything illegal. I'm just trying to give you background on my baby."

"I appreciate it."

"What's with this Latham guy? How does he fit in?"

"I'm working on that. It's not my case—it happened in Summer Village, which is a suburb of the Boston area—so I can't just charge in and demand answers. But when I find out, I'll certainly let you know."

"So he's not a student anywhere here?"

"I haven't checked every student on the roster, but I don't believe so. He's older. He lives an hour and a half away. I think he might be associated with Tufts University but I'm not even sure about that. Is there anything I can do for you two right now?"

Jim said, "When can we take her home?"

"I'll check with Boston. I'll let you know as soon as I know."

"When can we start packing up her . . ." Karen hung her head and stopped talking.

"I'll check with Forensics and let you know about that as well," Decker said. "Do you have a place to stay tonight? I can help you arrange something if you need it."

"No, we're . . . we're staying at the Greenbury College Inn for the next two nights."

"And you have my number?" Decker said.

"We do," Jim said.

"Call me if you need anything."

"We need a lot of things right now," Jim snarled out. "And it's nothing that you or anyone else can give us."

CHAPTER SEVENTEEN

Kennedy's Pub was one of the busier college hangouts because it had a reputation for cheap drinks and decent bar food. As the kid predicted, the place was arid hot, noisy, and stinky, especially at ten in the evening. They found a corner table away from the oversized and over-crowded bar. The dance floor was packed with students doing all kinds of moves and it took a while before a server was even visible. Finally, McAdams grew impatient, got up, and a moment later, a surly student took their orders: crudités and a Grolsch for Decker, a Manhattan and the lamb sliders for the kid.

"I like bourbon," he said. "One of the few things that my father and I have in common." He drummed his fingers. "That and we both live off my grandfather's money. Now that guy was a true visionary. Not the most grandfatherly type. I think I waved to him in passing when I was five. Real warm people the McAdamses are."

Decker nodded. "At least if he wasn't warm, he was generous."

"You take what you can get. The old man was married three times with a lot of lady friends in between. Lots of divorces and lots of alimony, but he had enough to go around." The server brought over their drinks and plopped them on the table. McAdams sipped the richly colored bourbon. "I like his third wife, Nina. Matter of fact, I'm staying with her in the city."

"How old is she?"

"Seventy-two. My grandfather would have been . . . eighty-six or -seven. He died six years ago. That's when I came into a small part of our inheritance. I know my other sibs got something but his third wife told me that, as the eldest and most precocious, I am due to get the lion's share, probably as much as my father."

"Oh boy."

"Yes, oh boy. It took our already explosive relationship and brought it that much closer to total obliteration."

Decker saw that McAdams had polished off his bourbon and ordered another one for him. "You're a smart kid. You'll figure it out."

"Maybe in a hundred years." McAdams pulled out his iPad. "I got the names of the detectives on the Petroshkovich theft. Douglas Arrenz and Allan Sugar. Both are still alive."

"Hold on." Decker took out his notepad. "Can you spell the names for me?"

Tyler complied. "Marylebone has a small police department, about the size of Greenbury's. The case was huge. It took up headlines for months. The department even brought in several experts on art thefts, but the case didn't go anywhere."

"Any theories about where the icons went?"

"I found a retrospective article on the theft that came out ten years ago. When the icons were taken, the iron curtain was still up. Now that there is easier access to Russia, the hypothesis is that they were sold to some oligarch to adorn the walls of his dacha. Petroshkovich is better known in Russia than here. No doubt they could command high prices from the newly minted bourgeoisie. I really don't see them as having any connection to the theft of two small Tiffany panels, but it's your call."

"I'm sure you're right, McAdams. However, if the detectives are on our way to the city and they're willing to talk to us about it, we should meet with them. Maybe they've come across some black market dealers."

"Sure." The server brought a refresh on the alcohol and the food. McAdams picked up the drink. "This is truly going to put me under. As if I'll need help. I have a very loud alarm clock. You still want to leave at seven?"

"Yep. Find out anything tonight?"

"I found out that the student libraries are open late, late, but not the reference desks. The biggest one—at Duxbury—closed at eight. There are hundreds of books of antique plates and maps in that one library alone. I've paged through seven of them and they all looked clean. Then I went to Rayfield at Littleton—which closes at nine. I went through another five—all clean. The assignment is going to take hours."

"God is in the details." Decker munched on a celery stick. "You should go to law school, Tyler. You'll be over-worked but at least you'll be compensated."

"And this coming from a man who walked away from the title esquire."

"I'm blue collar. You're not. You know the salaries of an average working detective. You're a rich kid. Why would you want to deal with all that jealousy from the department?"

"Are you jealous?"

"I might have been in my younger years."

"And now?"

"Now I don't need anything from anyone. You seem like a decent kid, Harvard. As a cop, you'll always be an

199

outsider. Why set yourself up?" When he didn't answer, Decker said, "Let me tell you what I found out this evening." He gave McAdams a recap while the kid typed away on his iPad.

Afterward, McAdams said, "Colored glass shards. So Angeline did the copies."

"Seems like it."

"Not surprising considering she shoplifted. Once a thief . . ."

"There were two incidents that her mom knew about. I'm betting there were more that she didn't know about. So yes, she seems like a good candidate for the forgeries. The questions are: Was she forging things other than stained glass and who was the mastermind behind it?"

"Latham?"

"Living like he was, I see him as a middleman, maybe a broker with connections to the rarefied world of art collecting."

"Why do you think he has those kinds of connections?"

"The Windsor Prize . . . art culture and politics. He's a better candidate for connections than Moreau. Find out about the Windsor Prize, okay?"

"Will do." McAdams typed it into his iPad. "We're still headed for New York?"

"Yes. I'm still interested in the Sobel family and Max Stewart. He's an art dealer, ergo he has connections. I'm not saying he's dirty, but he needs to be interviewed again. When I talked to him the first time, he played it close to the vest. When you were around at the cemetery, he seemed more relaxed, like the two of you were sharing an inside joke."

McAdams shrugged.

"I noticed that as well when we interviewed Angeline's friends. That they kept looking at you as an ally."

"Then they're delusional."

200

"I can read people, Harvard. You're young and you're relaxed around money in a way that I'm not. You're a good person to have around when I'm knocking on the co-op doors of Park Avenue."

"Glad to help even if I'm just a prop."

Decker smiled. "As of last night, you're pulling your weight. No complaints."

"Stick around and I'll give you plenty." When Decker was quiet, McAdams said, "I want you to know something. That rarefied world isn't me . . . even if I don't know what exactly me is."

"Frankly, I don't care about your existential issues. Two people were murdered. I've got a job to do. You can help in that regard."

"I'm down with that." He finished his drink. "And by the way, I don't mind being an outsider in Park Avenue or in Greenbury Police. In my opinion, popularity is highly overrated."

After making a dozen phone calls, Decker found out that Douglas Arrenz had retired to Florida. But Allan Sugar lived in East Hampton and agreed to see them any time after ten in the morning. That meant he was the first stop on their way to the city. The business districts of the beach areas were made up of quaint villages: cute little shops and cafés, one after another. The skies were gray and the sidewalks looked deserted with only a few hardy souls braving the snowdrifts.

Mansions abounded.

Since it was after the holidays, the residences that Decker could make out through the iron gates looked shut down for the winter. He wondered how a retired detective could afford this piece of paradise. That was made clear by the address. Sugar lived in what looked like the carriage house to the original dowager estate next door. It was a compact brick one-story with black trim around two multi-pane windows. Decker parked in a blanketed driveway, snow crunching underneath the tires. The chimney was emitting pine-scented smoke and there was a hint of ocean beyond the house.

McAdams said, "Looks like the Rhode Island PD pays well."

"How much do you think the house is worth?"

"Well . . ." He thought a moment. "It's small—about two thousand square feet. And it's in the wrong part of the Hamptons. But it is on the shore. Maybe around three, four million."

"Whoa." Decker was taken aback. "That's a lot of zeros."

"My grandfather's house isn't a whole lot bigger, but it has more property and it's in Southampton, which jacks up the price. It's also got a good beach front."

"Do you own that as well?"

"I have no idea. I do know it's in a thirty-year trust for the good and use of all the grandchildren. So I have access to it for the next twenty-four years. After that." He shrugged. "Who knows?"

"Somebody knows."

"That is true, but I'm not privy to that information. I rarely use it in the summer. The Hamptons are a scene. I actually like it at this time of year. There's something serene in the desolation."

"It's calming. I can understand that." Decker put on his jacket, gloves, and his hat and got out of the car. The kid followed, both of them stepping in fairly deep drifts. January was turning out to be a particularly cold month everywhere on the eastern seaboard.

"If you ever want to use my grandfather's house, let me know," McAdams said. "I'll slot it in for you."

202

"That's mighty generous of you, Harvard."

"Share the wealth."

They made their way up the walkway to a paneled front door painted in black and without a knocker. There also didn't appear to be a doorbell.

Someone wanted privacy.

Decker rapped as hard as he could on the wood with a gloved hand. Behind the wall, an elderly voice said, "I hear you, I hear you." A moment later the door opened and a gush of hot air blasted their faces. "Detective Sugar?"

"Yes, yes. Come in." He left the door open, turned his back, and shuffled across the mudroom floor and into the living room. The men followed. Sugar said, "Hope you found the place okay. The addresses can be confusing."

"No problem." Decker wiped his boots assiduously on the floor mat and dried them off with a provided towel. McAdams did the same. "Great house."

"Courtesy of a spinster aunt who willed it to me fifty years ago when the area wasn't hoity-toity and the roof leaked like a sieve. I almost sold it after my wife died. Thank God I didn't. The bluebloods next door are after me to sell it to them for some ridiculous price. You want some tea?"

"That would be great. Thank you for seeing us."

"Yes, yes." Sugar was around five five, with stooped shoulders, white hair, milky blue eyes, and a bony frame. He wore a thick cable-knit sweater and wool pants. Argyle socks covered feet that were tucked into slippers. "Sit anywhere you'd like."

Decker chose a green-and-red plaid sofa that matched two green-and-red plaid chairs. McAdams took a chair. There were coffee table and end tables made from particle-board and originally stained in a deep espresso brown.

203

Over the years—more like decades—they had suffered chips, scratches, and gouges where the lighter board was showing through. The floor was pine, covered in part by an area rug worn thin with use. Heat was pouring out of the radiator, and the flat-screen television—Sugar's nod to modernity—was on some kind of a game show.

When Sugar returned from the kitchen, he set the tray down on the living room table. He turned off the TV and turned down the heat. He poured himself a cup of tea. "Make it how you like it. I'm not a waiter."

Decker poured hot water into two mugs—for McAdams and for himself. After he made the introductions, he said, "How long were you with the Marylebone PD, Detective Sugar?"

"It's Allan and I was with them for thirty years. Wish I'd come up when you did, with AFIS and CODIS and all that razzamatazz. You don't even have to work anymore. Just plug in fingerprints or DNA and the machines pop out the answers."

"It's been a boon," Decker said.

"NCIC was just about all we had. That was back in '67 when J. Edgar created it. Probably to spy on the Reds but he dropped a few criminals in the files just to make it look legit. None of it was linked up to any computer. Everything was done by hand. It took forever to make a request and forever for it to get processed."

Sugar sat down.

"So you're interested in the missing Nikolai Petroshkovich icons. You and all Rhode Island. And the Russian Orthodox church—St. Stephen's. The thefts became an international cause célèbre. Did I pronounce that right?"

"I think you did."

"After I failed to get anywhere, they brought in all the experts." He made a quotation with his fingers. "Paid all

204

this money and not a damn clue closer to what the hell happened."

"What do you think happened?" Decker asked.

"Douglas and I entertained a number of possibilities. You know Douglas?"

"Detective Arrenz. He was your partner on the case."

"Yep. Retired in Florida. Not for me. I don't like to sweat." He sipped his tea. "The theft wasn't the cleanest job I'd ever seen. At first we considered vandalism. Back then, adolescent crime was confined to car stealing, petty theft, and graffiti done by the drunk, pot-smoking, or coked-up lads and lassies. It's worse now. All those designer drugs . . ."

"When are we talking about?" Decker asked. "The eighties?"

"Yeah, the late eighties. Douglas and I kicked around the possibility that it was a bunch of thugs and punks. We checked the regular troublemakers and didn't get anywhere. Even the worst of the town miscreants denied thieving from a church. After we found out how valuable the icons were, we fanned out in other directions. We talked to the professionals and found out, much to our chagrin, that churches are easy targets for theft. They're not occupied most of the time and they contain valuables. We also found out that there are thieves who specialize in hitting churches and synagogues. The common burglars concentrate on fencing things like silver candlesticks and silver chalices. The more sophisticated thieves concentrate on the artwork contained within the hallowed walls of God. That kind of material, as you might imagine, is much harder to fence. You need a specialized dealer."

"Black market dealers."

"Of course. The thing is that most of the black market

art dealers are or were respectable dealers who dabbled in the underworld."

"Did you get names?"

"We got a lot of names. None of them got us anywhere."

"Do you still have those names? Maybe they can point us in the right direction."

"They didn't do much good for us, but you're welcome to try. They're all in the case files. I've got a copy for you so there's no need to ask. The dealers are ancient by now: senile, in jail, or dead. But knock yourself out."

Decker took another sip of tea. Since Sugar had turned down the heat, the room was more comfortable. "Since the Petroshkovich thefts became a cause célèbre and the Russian Orthodox Church became involved, I take it you ruled out random vandalism."

"In the end, we all decided it was a professional job made to look like amateurs. Wasn't the first time iconography has been stolen and it won't be the last."

Decker seemed perplexed. "What other cases of stolen iconography have you come across? I wouldn't think it would be a very common occurrence."

"Not here in the US of A. But there once was a Soviet Union that devalued religious art—opium of the masses and all that razzamatazz—so it happened more often than you'd think. Even great artworks, if they had religious contents, were denigrated. Lucky the Reds never got hold of Italy, otherwise we might not have the Sistine Chapel."

Decker smiled. "They might have made an exception to Michelangelo."

"You'd be surprised. Look what they did to St. Isaac's."

"Which St. Isaac's?" McAdams asked. "I'm assuming there is more than one in a country as big as Russia."

"St. Isaac's in St. Petersburg."

206

McAdams immediately started typing on his iPad. "Do you have a password so I can connect to the Internet?"

Sugar rolled his eyes. "I think it's the word *Admin*. Never use the damn thing but when the grandchildren visit, I can't get them here unless they can use their gadgets."

"Uh, that worked." McAdams smiled. "Thank you."

"What happened at St. Isaac's?" Decker asked.

"Ancient history," Sugar said. "After years of trying to recover the Petroshkovich icons and all the research I did for the case, I became interested in Russian Orthodox religious art. The first thing I did after I retired was take the wife to Russia. It didn't help me make headway with the Petroshkoviches but it did make me feel better that even a big city like St. Petersburg hadn't fully recovered all its stolen art."

McAdams read out loud from what he had pulled up. "St. Isaac's was built in the mid-eighteen hundreds after a design by Montferrand . . . Frenchman who studied with Napoleon's architect and designer, Charles Percier. The cathedral is in honor of St. Isaac's of Dalmatia. Interior artwork originally done by Karl Bryullov. When the original oil paintings started to deteriorate because of cold and moisture, Montferrand had the artwork re-created as mosaics."

"And truly spectacular mosaics they are," Sugar said. "In quality as well as quantity. It's meant to dazzle and it does."

"You know, I think I might have been there . . . in this church." McAdams looked up. "I'm sure I was."

Decker said, "You were in St. Petersburg?"

"Yeah, when I was eleven or twelve. I was in boarding school so every summer my mother made it her mission to drag me to Europe from one church to another for a cultural experience. I must have seen one hundred

207

churches over the years. They all begin to look alike especially if you see one right after the other. At that age, all I wanted to do was go to a Yankees game. I was resentful . . . stupid me." McAdams chuckled. "Anyway, correct me if I'm wrong but St. Isaac's is the tallest building in St. Petersburg."

"It is. Which was why it was of use during the Second World War," Sugar announced. "St. Petersburg was bombed badly. All the famous palaces that the tourists see were rebuilt, including the Hermitage."

"The Hermitage?" Decker asked. "You mean the art museum?"

"Yes, indeed. It was built as a palace."

"It was bombed?"

"Left to rot in ruins. They have pictures there of what it looked like. It was a mere shell of its former glory until the Russian artisans rebuilt it."

"What happened to all the artwork inside? Don't tell me that was destroyed as well?"

"No, the Ruskies knew they were in trouble. They stored it all in the basement of St. Isaac's, which the Nazis did not bomb wholesale. Because St. Isaac's was the tallest building in the city, the Luftwaffe used it as a navigational guide for its Messerschmitts. It's one of the few buildings that, except for some random shelling, remained intact."

McAdams was still reading. "I can't find anything about St. Isaac's being used for art storage . . . or for the Nazis using it as a navigational guide," McAdams said. "Matter of fact, it says that the dome was painted over to avoid enemy aircraft detection."

"Young lad, you are missing critical parts of the tale because you're probably using some condensed encyclopedia site. If you really want to know history, you have to read something with more depth. Or take the lazy man's way out and just go to St. Petersburg again as an adult and listen to one of their many well-informed guides."

Decker said, "What does St. Isaac's have to do with the Petroshkovich icons?"

"Nothing as far as I know," Sugar said. "I just found it interesting because the cathedral had works missing from its iconography that have never been recovered."

"Are they also Petroshkoviches?"

"No, nothing to do with Petroshkovich. These works were done in an earlier period."

"Okay," Decker said. "And you don't think there's a connection."

"Can't see how. The thefts were years apart."

"Any ideas on who was responsible for the St. Isaac's thefts?" Decker asked.

"Not a clue. When the Reds took over, the church was converted into a museum for scientific atheism. It was looted and then it fell into disrepair. During the war, it was used to store sacks of potatoes. If you'd see the church today, you'd realize how appalling that was. The refurbishing started in the fifties under Khrushchev. The mosaics were black, but otherwise in good condition. Good thing the original paintings were turned into tile art. Otherwise they'd probably be sold out or stolen as well."

Decker turned to McAdams. "Anything on St. Isaac's stolen icons?"

"Images of what was there." McAdams read to himself. "And there was lots of looting of churches by the Germans during the war."

"Between the Reds and the war, it's a miracle that any religious institution survived," Sugar remarked.

Decker said, "No connection between those lootings and the Petroshkovich thefts."

"Nothing," Sugar said. "Not that I was trying to find a

link: different cities, different countries, different times. I just relate it to you as a cautionary tale. If a major city like St. Petersburg can't find its own treasured artwork, you can see what you're up against."

"This is more than an art theft case. It's a double murder."

"All the more reason why I think you're up against something bigger than yourself. But I realize you still have to try. Good luck."

Sugar placed his teacup on the scarred coffee table, then he shuffled over to a hutch and opened the bottom cabinet. He pulled out a box and lifted it to his chest, his legs sagging under its weight. Quickly Decker relieved him of the box. "Lot of forests died for this file. Are you going to read every page?"

"Maybe even twice," Decker said.

"Tell me if you find anything I might have overlooked. I'll help you in any way I can. My brain isn't what it used to be, but this case is burned into the gray matter. It's the one that got away."

Decker said, "We all have those."

"Yes, we do. For me and the Petroshkovich artwork, time is running out. I'm happy to pass the mantle onto someone younger and more clever."

"Younger is a fact," Decker said. "The clever part remains to be seen."

CHAPTER EIGHTEEN

When he opened the door to the West Side condo, Decker heard a tiny female voice.

"Hello?"

He and McAdams stepped inside. Decker was holding a bag and a thermos of coffee. Tyler dropped the Petroshkovich file box on the floor. Yasmine Nourmand was at a small, round table, papers spread out so that the surface looked more white than wood. She looked up with her big brown eyes and flipped her black hair off her shoulder. "Oh, Lieutenant." She stood up. "I'm sorry. Gabe said you went back upstate."

"No apologies necessary. I did go back. Unfortunately we have more business in the city. Are you staying here, honey? We can move somewhere else."

"Oh no, definitely not! I can go to the library."

An awkward pause.

Yasmine said, "Gabe told me you might be coming and going." She stood up straight—all five feet two inches, one hundred pounds of her. "I just study here sometimes. It's a little quieter." She managed a tight smile and stuck out her hand to McAdams. "Yasmine Nourmand. I'm Gabe's girlfriend." A pause. "Do you know who Gabe is?"

McAdams cocked a thumb in Decker's direction. "His foster son." He shook her hand. "Where do you go to school?"

"Barnard. And you?"

"Graduated."

"Lucky you."

"It depends on the day."

Another forced smile. Yasmine said, "I'll just gather up my things—"

"You can study in the bedroom if you want," Decker said. "You won't bother us. If anything, we'll bother you with our talking."

"If you don't need the bedroom, I'd really prefer to study here. I'm not real good with dorm life. I'm a little claustrophobic."

McAdams looked around the spotless, modern apartment: gleaming dark floors, a sleek white couch, a simple oak table with four Plexiglas chairs upholstered in white leather backs and a baby grand Steinway. Good light from two big windows. It had an over-the-rooftops view of the park. "This is definitely preferable to a dorm."

"Is Mrs. Decker coming in?"

"I'm meeting her tonight."

"Okay. Say hi."

"Would you like to go to dinner with us?"

A genuine smile. "That would be great." A pause. "I'm not much on dorm food, either. It might be late. Like eight. I have a lab class. Is eight okay?"

"Eight is perfect. I'll have Rina choose a place and make a reservation." He turned to McAdams. "You're welcome to come, Harvard, but I suspect you made plans."

"You suspect wrong."

"Then come."

"Thanks."

Yasmine said, "Can I bring my roommate? I'll pay for her and everything. Her parents were real nice to me. They live in Long Island."

"Absolutely and you don't have to pay, honey."

"In that case, can I bring my grandmother?" McAdams said. "I'll pay for her and everything."

Yasmine blushed. Decker said, "Tyler, behave yourself."

"I'm serious. She has expressed a genuine interest in what I'm doing and she wants to meet you. And I know she'll pick up the tab—"

"Harvard—"

"I'm just saying."

"My kids might be coming."

"Nina's always up for socializing. It will be a veritable party. Probably the first I've been to in two years."

"Amen to that," Yasmine said.

"A kindred spirit."

She began gathering up her books and papers. "Everyone I know hates parties yet everyone goes to them. I mean what's the point?"

"I see you don't drink."

Decker laughed. "Do you know when Gabe will be back?"

"Two weeks if his agent doesn't extend the tour."

"Must be hard with him away so much."

"Actually, Lieutenant, I'm okay with that. I'm not a natural student. I have to study real hard to get my grades and Gabe . . ." She made a face. "I love him to death, but he takes up a lot of my time when he's here." Another face. "Don't tell him I said that."

"It'll be our secret."

Yasmine stuffed her material into a backpack. "See you later." She disappeared behind a door.

213

McAdams said, "She reminds me of a cricket . . . all little and bony and chirpy and big eyes."

"She's Persian and comes from a very sheltered environment. I've got to hand it to her. She followed her dream by coming out here and being with Gabe."

"The delusion of love." Tyler picked up the box of files and laid them on the table. "What's the plan, sir?"

"Eventually I'll look through the files with a fine-tooth comb. Right now all we're looking for are names of art dealers that Sugar and Arrenz interviewed. I want to run them by Maxwell Stewart. See if he or his dad knows them."

"When are we meeting with Stewart?"

Decker checked his watch. It was twelve-thirty. "I'd like to pop by the gallery at three-thirty."

"You didn't make an appointment?"

"No, I did not."

"How do you know he'll be in?"

"Someone will be there. I assume whoever it will be has the capacity to call him up."

"No need for sarcasm."

"Pot . . . kettle . . . black."

"Ha ha and ha." McAdams opened the box. There were ten stuffed file folders inside. "What if Stewart's name is in the file?"

Decker gave him a closed-mouth smile. "Then that should make my interview with Maxwell all the more interesting."

At three-thirty in the afternoon, the sun was sinking behind the skyscrapers, casting long shadows over the avenues. The winds were strong and icy especially coming off the park. The skies had slowly dimmed as if someone had a rheostat to the ethers. Decker rang the bell to the

214

gallery. Redheaded Jill looked up, recognized him, and buzzed them inside the sally port. A moment later, he and Tyler were standing inside warmth, light, and a lot of sparkle from gems he couldn't afford.

"Is Max expecting you?" Jill asked.

"No, ma'am, but we'd like to talk to him."

"Of course. Good news, I hope." When Decker didn't answer, she said, "He's downstairs. I'll let him know you're here."

"Thank you."

She rushed downstairs and a minute later, she bound back up, "He'll be up in a minute."

"We can wait if he's with a customer."

"No, he's . . . can I get either of you coffee or tea or hot cocoa?"

McAdams took off his coat. "Tea is fine. Herbal if you have it. And could you hang this up for me?"

Jill took Tyler's coat and turned to Decker. "Can I take your coat as well?"

Decker took off his coat. "Thank you."

"Tea?"

"That would be great."

Jill took the heavy overcoats and came back a minute later with two teacups and saucers. "I hope it's okay. It's mint." The phone buzzed. "Excuse me a moment." She lifted the handset. "Okay. Sure." She hung up. "Max says you can come down."

"Thank you." Decker picked up his tea and McAdams followed.

The overhead lighting was reduced to emphasize the Tiffany lamps, which seemed to twinkle and dance when illuminated. Max was sitting with a man in his early twenties in front of a display case of art nouveau desk items. They both stood up as the two detectives came down the stairs. The young lad was very lanky with a full, dark beard and limp hair that grazed his shoulders. His shoulders sagged and his head drooped. He wore jeans and a sweatshirt. Max had on his usual suit and tie. He wore a tense expression that he was desperately trying to mask with a forced smile. Decker's eyes were on the men, McAdams's eyes were on the objects.

Max said, "You saved me a phone call, Detective. Please sit."

"Where should we put our cups?" Decker asked.

Max took them and put them on the floor. He said, "This is my first cousin-in-law, Livingston Sobel."

"The expat from Brown," Decker said to Max.

"Indeed. Liv, this is Detective Decker and Detective McAdams."

The men shook hands. Decker said, "Thanks for seeing us on short notice."

"Actually it was no notice, but that's fine. Any news?"

"Not yet, I'm afraid."

"In that case, Livingston has just been telling me a very interesting story. I was about to phone you, but since you're here, why not hear it from the primary source."

"Sure." Decker took a chair and sat as delicately as he could. The chairs were collectibles.

McAdams took out an iPad. "What's your password so I can get on the Net?"

"Why do you need to get on the Net?" Max snapped.

McAdams looked up at the sharp tone of voice. "I don't really need it. It's just that at every interview we've had, I seem to be looking material up. The pad is much faster than my phone." He took out his smartphone. "I'm getting bars. Don't worry about it."

"I haven't given it a single fret. Why are you here?"

216

"I'll fill you in. But first I'd like to hear Livingston's story."

Max glared at Livingston. "Tell them what you told me." When the kid started muttering, Max said, "There is no way they can understand you, Liv. You think you can talk a little clearer?"

The kid let out a sharp exhale. "There's this girl I know." He stroked his beard. "I met her like . . . four years ago . . . when she came to Brown as a prospective student. When I was still in Brown. We kind of clicked right away as friends. We're both artsy people."

McAdams threw Decker a glance. "Name?"

"Angelina Moreau," Max said. "By strange coincidence, she goes to school in Littleton. And she's an art history major."

"Angeline," Livingston said. When Max looked up, the kid said, "Not Angelina. Angeline."

Decker said, "Go on, Livingston. You met Angeline and . . ."

"We've been like friends for about four years."

"Define friends for them, Liv."

"It's nothing serious."

"FWB," McAdams said. "Nothing wrong with that."

Livingston looked at him with grateful eyes. "Exactly. We're not destiny but she's okay . . . kind of a free spirit."

"More like a dishonest spirit," Max said.

"For the millionth time, Max, we don't know that she did anything."

"Can you finish the story for me, Livingston?" Decker said.

"She had a boyfriend and that was always fine with me. As a matter of fact, I know him from the parties around here. Lance Terry. I don't care who she screws, but I really don't know what she sees in him—other than his money. That might be enough. Anyway when she comes down to the city, we get together for a few hours and talk—"

"Can you say booty call?" Max said.

Decker held up his hand. "Let him finish, please?"

Livingston stuttered out, "What is wrong with that? You sound jealous."

"Just green with envy."

"I don't love her but I like her. She helped me through some rough times. We could talk to each other."

"And you did," Max said.

Livingston glanced at him. "Yes, we talked and, yes, we talked about art and, yes, I mentioned the Tiffany windows to her. I told her about them like three years ago so if she wanted to do something illegal, she could have done it a long time ago."

"And she probably did," Max snarled. "The kicker of this whole thing is that since we've discovered the theft, the girl is suddenly not answering her phone. You need to find her and ask her about it. My father-in-law is going to freak when he finds out. Maybe if you call, Detective, she'll know you mean business and have the decency to answer the phone."

Decker said, "When did you tell Max about knowing Angeline, Livingston? Just now?"

The kid nodded. "It's probably nothing. If I would have known that Max would be so pissed, I would have kept it to myself."

"Brilliant."

"Ken talks way more than I ever did. You know that's true."

"He doesn't talk to random girls in a drunken stupor."

"Oh fuck this!" He started to get up, but Decker stood up as well.

"We're not done just yet. Please."

Livingston sat back down. "Honestly, I can't exactly see her breaking into a cemetery and stealing the Tiffany glass windows. I could actually see Lance doing it as a joke."

Max said, "So now we have two people you should talk to. Give them Angeline's number, Liv."

"We don't need it," Decker said. "We have it."

Stewart was taken aback. "You're already investigating her?"

"We're investigating her murder."

Livingston turned pale. "Angeline was *murdered*?"

"Yes," Decker said. "We think she was killed last Sunday afternoon or early evening. That would be right after you left to go back to New York. I suspect our presence at the mausoleum may be behind the murder." Both Livingston and Max had registered shock: wide eyes and mouths agape. Decker continued. "We're actually looking into two murders: hers and a man named John Jeffrey Latham who might have been Angeline's boyfriend or a friend or partner. Does that name ring a bell, Livingston?"

He didn't answer right away. "Wha . . . what *happened*?"

Decker said, "That's what we're investigating. Where were you over the weekend, son?"

"Me?" Liv pointed to himself. "I was here . . . in the city." He was breathing hard. "You don't think . . ."

"Where in the city? I need a timeline: Saturday and Sunday."

"I . . . have to think."

Max finally spoke. "You want to tell me what's going on?"

"If I knew what was going on, I wouldn't be asking all these questions," Decker said. "We have two murders that happened after your visit to the mausoleum. Do I think the murders are related to the thefts? Yes. Do I think Angeline and this Latham character were up to something?

Yes. Do I think Angeline had anything to do with the forgeries? Yes. Is any of this worth killing two people over? No. So I'm missing a lot of pieces. And that's why I'm asking questions." To Livingston, "Where were you? And take your time because you're only getting one shot to get it right."

The kid looked up, down, and then up. "Saturday?" A pause. "I was home the whole day. I went to a party in the evening . . . like around nine."

"You were home the entire day?"

He nodded.

"Who saw you?"

"My mom, my dad, the housekeeper."

"Did you have your cell on you?"

"Yeah, sure."

"Can I have it?"

Wordlessly, he handed it over to Decker.

Scrolling through to Saturday's calls, Decker spoke out loud. "Over twenty texts and ten phone calls . . . none of them Angeline's number . . . or Latham's number . . . what is his area code again? Seven oh six or Oh seven six?"

"Oh seven six."

Decker handed the cell to McAdams. "Write down the numbers and we'll check out them out later. Since it's a cell, if we need to check towers, we can." McAdams began typing on his iPad. To Livingston, Decker said, "Do you recognize the name John Latham?"

"Who is he?" Max asked.

"I don't know details on him, just the basics. He was murdered in the Boston area so it's not my homicide and not my jurisdiction. But we're trading information. Livingston, who is John Latham?"

The young man ran his hand down his face. He rubbed his eyes. "I . . . she . . ."

"What!" Max said.

Decker turned to him and said, "You're not helping." Back to Livingston. "Look, son, unless you murdered her or stole the artwork, you're not in trouble—at least as far as the police are concerned. So just tell me what you know about Angeline and Latham and then you're a free bird."

"Let me think." The barrage of information had thrown the kid into a tizzy. "Okay. I knew that Angeline broke up with Lance about a year and a half ago."

"Go on."

"I knew she was dating this older guy. I don't know his last name but his first name was John." Livingston rubbed his nose. "She told me that he was brilliant and from Oxford, that he came to the U.S. because he got a prestigious fellowship at one of the universities. Sounded like bullshit to me."

"Why did it sound like bullshit?"

"This is going to sound terrible, but I'm going to say it anyway. Angeline didn't grow up in the most sophisticated of families. She was easy to snow. She'd do any guy who she thought had connections. Why else would she put up with someone like me? I was terrible to her." His eyes watered. "It's probably what she liked about this asshole. She thought he was connected. If he was, he probably treated her terribly, too. That's probably why she stuck with Lance for so long. He was rich and connected but a little dull in the cranium. I mean anyone with money who has gone to the right prep schools can do better than Littleton, for God's sake." He looked at McAdams. "I know I sound like an asshole, but it's just the way it works."

"Don't look at me. I grew up around the block. Park and Sixty-Eighth."

"Why don't I know you?"

221

"Probably because I was shipped off to Phillips when I was a kid."

"Phillips Andover?"

"Phillips Exeter."

"Oh. Do you know Joey Seldano?"

"He was two classes below me. First string point guard. Did you play basketball?"

"Yeah. Joey and I used to go one-on-one all the time." Livingston looked at him. "You're a cop?"

"A Harvard-educated cop," Decker broke in. "What else did Angeline tell you about Latham?"

"Just what I said. He was some kind of university fellow."

"That part is true," McAdams said. "He did win a fellowship . . . the Windsor Prize."

Livingston shrugged ignorance. "She also told me that he was connected."

"Connected how?" Decker asked.

"She didn't elaborate and to tell you the truth, I wasn't that interested. I had other things on my mind."

"She must have told you something, Livingston," Decker said. "Did she say he was rich, that he was political, that he had friends in high places . . . think!"

"A novel concept," Max muttered.

"Please," Decker pleaded. "What did she tell you about him?"

"Just that he went to Oxford and was brilliant. That he knew a lot of really rich people. When I asked her to name names, she wouldn't do it. I thought she was pulling the story out of her butt."

Decker thought a moment. "Do you know if Angeline ever worked in any city art gallery?"

"I don't know."

. McAdams said, "I can make phone calls to some of the galleries."

"Yeah, we should do that."

Livingston said, "How was she killed?"

"I couldn't tell you. I haven't gotten the coroner's report back."

"So how do you know she was murdered? Maybe she ODed or probably drank herself to death. She binged, you know."

"So I've heard."

"So how do you know it was murder?"

"Because where we found her was definitely a crime scene."

"God, that's nauseating," Max said.

Livingston put his hand to his mouth and then looked at his watch. "Can I go now? I was just trying to be a Good Samaritan and as usual, it backfired."

Decker nodded. The kid got up unceremoniously, grabbed his coat, and was off. When he was gone, Max said, "I didn't comport myself very well. I apologize. He gets under my skin. He gets under everyone's skin."

"Do you think there's a chance that he was in on the theft? It would make a difference in how we handled the investigation."

"Well, he came here to tell me about it. If he was in on it, I don't think he would have done that." He sighed. "What did you want to see me about?"

"Can you spare me an hour?"

"I need coffee and a nosh first. There's a sandwich place around the corner."

"I don't want to talk in a public place," Decker said.

"I'll have Jill order out then." Max rubbed his neck. "God, what a mess! And here I was worrying about a few Tiffany panels. How old was she—the girl?"

"Twenty-two."

"God, that's terrible. Her parents know?"

"Yes."

"My kids are little, under someone's care all the time." He regarded Decker. "How do you ever let them go?"

"You pray a lot and hope for the best."

"And you think the girl's murder is related to the theft?"

"Yes, especially now that I found out that she knew about the Tiffany panels' existence."

"So what's the next step?"

Decker said, "That's why we're here to talk to you. But get your food first. I'd love some coffee and a bite to eat. I'm sure McAdams would as well."

"Blueberry muffin if they have it and coffee would be fine," McAdams said. "Cream no sugar."

"And you, Detective?"

"Black coffee. Maybe fruit—apple, orange, or banana." Decker fished out a twenty, then thought better of it. This was Manhattan. He fished out two twenties. "On the department."

"Sure. Let's go upstairs. We'll talk in my office." He shook his head sadly. "Look, we can talk now. I can wait to eat."

"Max, I make it a rule to never talk to anyone on an empty stomach—his, yours, or mine."

CHAPTER NINETEEN

The office was cramped with desktops filled with paperwork. Max had cleared a small spot for the food and coffee.
No coasters were needed. The furniture was weathered
and scarred. As he ate a muffin, Max's eyes scanned down
the list of names. His expression was strained. "If the
Rhode Island detectives didn't find anything to indict the
dealers on, I don't see the point in adding to the rumor
mill."

Decker kept his frustrations in check—almost. "You
know we're beyond locating the stolen Tiffany panels or
solving the Petroshkovich icon thefts. We're looking for
dangerous people who slaughtered two human beings.
We're going to check out everyone on the list. I'm just
asking you where to start."

Max played with the knot in his tie. "Check out Jason
Merritt on Sixty-Third. Not that I think he's done anything
wrong. The Merritt gallery has been in family hands for
almost a hundred years."

Decker waited.

Max said, "His grandfather dealt in Russian icons. Like
Armand Hammer, he was one of the few people who had

225

access to Russia when it was dominated by Soviet rule. I've never heard that he looted anything, but he probably paid bottom dollar for religious items because postwar Russia was in shambles. People needed money and no one was interested in anything religious. Since the gallery still deals in Russian icons, it's a good place to start." Max turned quiet. "The second murder happened in Boston?"

"Outside of Boston," McAdams said. "In Summer Village near Tufts."

"I'm curious why you think someone in New York is responsible when both murders took place north of here."

"The Marylebone detectives also started in New York. But if you have something you want to tell me about other cities, I'm here to listen." Decker regarded the man's downward eyes. "What's on your mind?"

"Nothing. I'm just making a simple statement—that there are lots of galleries other than the ones in New York."

Decker said, "Max, people who are not psychotic or psychopathic murder for mundane reasons: to keep a secret, unrequited love, pathological jealousy, to usurp power—and *money*. You want to find a killer, go down the money trail. The New York galleries deal in the big money. That's why I'm here."

"I can't help you with a killer. That's a fact." Silence. "Detective, my family has spent a lifetime building up this gallery. I really don't want to get involved in something pernicious."

McAdams said, "It was your father-in-law's pieces that started the whole thing." He shrugged. "You're already involved."

"This is just a nightmare!" Max looked down. "I'm not accusing anyone of anything, okay. This is just a thought. Chase Goddard bought a Boston gallery two years ago. It

226

is now the eponymous Goddard Gallery. Chase first opened a fine arts and antique store in New York in 2006 or 2007. Needless to say his timing was off because of the recession and he closed two years later. Then I heard he was up in the Boston area."

"What kind of art does the Goddard Gallery deal in?"

"Not Russian icons." Stewart shrugged. "If it's similar to his New York gallery, it's mostly small antique pieces, but some fine arts. I've never been there so I don't know what he specializes in."

"What did he sell in the New York gallery?"

"It featured eighteenth- and nineteenth-century genre paintings, English and continental antique furniture, and smaller objets d'art of the period. A few twentieth-century pieces . . . nothing to write home about. In the main, it was a little of this and a little of that."

McAdams showed Decker his smartphone. He had pulled up the Goddard Gallery website. "A little of this and a little of that."

"Can I see?" Max asked.

"Sure."

Max perused the website for a minute. "Yeah, like his New York place."

Decker said, "If Goddard folded shop in 2007, where did he get the money to buy the new gallery?"

Max bit his lower lip. "Some people were asking the same question. Chase not only bought out the lease, but a good portion of the old inventory, which, judging from the website, isn't superpricey. But there's a lot of it."

"Okay." Decker sipped coffee. "What else?"

"What makes you think there's a 'what else'?"

"I read people for a living. You've come this far. Don't stop now."

"Chase would buy from a lot of different sources," Max

said. "That's not unusual. We all do. Our inventory depends on many different sources. But Chase had a reputation of skirting around provenance."

"He bought hot items?" Decker asked.

"I didn't say that. Just that he wasn't as meticulous as maybe he should have been. We all slip up. We all get burned. Chase seemed to have more incidents of slipping up. I have nothing more to add. I've given you a starting point—several starting points. Good-bye and good luck."

"Thanks for your time."

But Max didn't move. He bit his thumbnail. "The panels are still missing and now there are two murdered people. Do I have any reason to be concerned for my safety?"

Decker held up the list. "I'm just checking out art dealers who were in the Petroshkovich file. No reason it should come back to you."

"The Goddard Gallery isn't on the list," Max pointed out.

"Latham's murder took place up north. So it's reasonable for me or Summer Village PD to check out galleries in the area."

"I'm nervous."

"I understand. You have security at the gallery. It might make sense to beef it up until we know more."

"Could I ask a favor of you? Could you not come here anymore? I'll talk on the phone but unless you have something urgent, could you stay clear of my family?"

"No problem. Thanks for your help." Decker got up. "Maybe the next time we talk, I'll give you good news."

"That can be done on the telephone as well."

They shook hands and left it at that.

Decker and McAdams walked out the door and into a blast of cold. It was five-thirty in the evening, dark, frigid, and depressing. The kid rubbed his gloved hands. "What now?"

"It's too late to go over to the Merritt Gallery. We'll do it tomorrow. Let's walk back to my stepson's apartment and go over the Petroshkovich files."

"I see you don't believe in cabs?"

"It's a ten-minute walk."

McAdams had to pick up his pace to keep up with Decker's long stride. "Do you think he's in danger?"

"Max?" Decker shook his head. "Not really. But if he wants extra security, why not? If anyone's in danger, it would be us. We're the ones stirring up the pot."

"Peachy!"

Decker smiled. "No one forced you to join up, McAdams."

"Greenbury is the new Mayberry. Nothing ever happens there."

"Until it does."

"Thank you for allaying my fears."

Decker laughed. "I'm just messing with you, Harvard. Just about every detective I've ever known has retired safe and sound with a good pension. If anyone gets whacked, it's usually the poor patrolman on a routine traffic stop."

But McAdams remained troubled. "For the record, how often do detectives get whacked because of what they're investigating?"

"Rare."

"Can you quantify your answer more precisely?"

"No."

"Have you ever gotten shot?"

"Yes."

"Tell me it happened in 'Nam."

"No, it happened when I was chasing down some stupid kid around twenty-five years ago. I was shot in the shoulder." Decker lifted and rotated his arm. "All healed."

229

"This is not reassuring."

"If you're nervous, you know I can go it alone. You've got nothing to prove with me, Harvard. Do I think anything will happen? No. Can I guarantee it? No. But if it's going to prey on your mind, you won't be able to concentrate. You have my blessing to remove yourself from the case, no judgment and I mean that sincerely."

"You're not worried?"

"I'm a drug addict, Tyler. I thrive on adrenaline. This is the happiest I've been in six months."

The kid was quiet. Then he said, "I'm here as long as you want me here."

"Okay. But if you change your mind, no harm, no foul."

"The truth is, Decker, for the first time in my life, I've actually felt useful. I feel energized and the danger only adds to it. Yeah, I'm a little scared. But what really disturbs me is I like being a little scared."

"A little scared is good. It keeps you on your toes. It's when you're cocky that bad things happen."

"What if you're cocky and scared?"

"Then you've just described the ideal homicide detective."

With a glide in her walk, Nina McAdams came in on the arm of her stepgrandson. She was thin, blond, and beautiful, wearing a black chiffon skirt and a silk top. What was truly humbling was that she was only ten years older than Decker. While he'd just gotten used to working with people young enough to be his son, he was now working with someone who was young enough to be his grandson.

The woman looked around the crowded table filled with Decker's children, stepchildren, spouses, and significant others as well as Yasmine and two of her roommates, Jenny Lee and Katy Bera.

"My Gawd, this isn't a dinner, it's a party." Nina regarded Decker. "Are all these yours?"

Tyler said, "Behave yourself."

"Why should she?" Jacob said. "No one else does."

"We are happy to claim ownership to all of them," Rina told her.

Nina sat between Tyler and Decker. After all the introductions were made, Nina patted Decker's hand and said, "You have a veritable UN here."

Tyler turned red. Decker smiled. The woman spoke the truth. Koby was from Ethiopia, Yasmine's family was from Iran while her two roommates, Jenny and Katy, were from Taiwan and India, respectively. Hannah's fiancé, Raphy, was a Colombian Jew.

Rina said, "If the state ever mandates diversity within families, we will have complied."

"Have a drink, Nina," McAdams told her. "Or . . . maybe not."

"How about we all have a drink?" She picked up the wine list and perused the selections. She sniffed. "I don't believe I know any of these labels."

"Probably because they're kosher wines," Rina said. "A lot of them are very good."

"How about this one?" She pointed to the most expensive bottle. "Herzog To Kalon? Did I pronounce that correctly?"

"You did." Rina winced. It was over two hundred dollars a bottle. "Sure, let's get a bottle."

"One bottle? Let's get four. And don't worry, young lady. I'm paying."

"Told you," Tyler said to Decker.

"We invited you, Mrs. McAdams," Decker said.

"It's Nina and pish on that. I know what poor Tyler makes. It's appalling! And even with your pension from

231

somewhere, this is a large crowd. It would be my pleasure and I won't hear of anything else. So let's spend a lovely Wednesday night eating, drinking, and being merry." To punctuate her sentence, she picked up a menu and everyone else did likewise. Within moments, the table buzzed with conversation.

Decker spoke across the table to Cindy and Koby, "Thanks for making the trip."

"If the mountain won't come to Mohammad . . ."

"I'll come. I promise. I'm dying to see my boys again."

"They miss Grandpa," Koby said. "I miss him as well."

Decker smiled. "Who's watching the boys?"

"My partner, Mary, and Koby's classmate, Alicia," Cindy said. "They met at a party at our house and are now an item."

Nina said. "So you have the gay thing covered as well."

Tyler put his hands to his forehead. Sammy said, "This is nothing." He cocked a finger at Decker. "You should meet his mother."

"Leave Ida alone," Rina said. "She's lovely."

Rachel said, "I think I'm getting the short ribs." She looked at Jacob's girlfriend, Ilana. "You want to split it?"

"Sure, I'll split it with you."

Jacob banged a spoon against some stemware and stood up. Everyone looked at him. Hannah said, "Make it quick, Yonkie."

"Just a few words."

"It better be, Yonkie, I'm hungry," Sammy turned to Tyler. "He likes to make announcements."

Hannah said, "He's sentimental."

Cindy said, "In all fairness, how often are we all together?" She looked at Yasmine. "You're here along with Gabe's spirit."

"I'll fill him in when he gets home."

"Where is he?" Hannah asked.

"Uh, Japan . . . Osaka."

"A lovely place," Nina said. "Especially compared to Tokyo." She turned to Rina. "Have you been?"

"It's on my list."

"The cherry blossom time is simply exquisite."

"Nina, he's trying to talk," Tyler said.

"Oh, pish!" She turned quiet.

Jacob said, "It's impossible to keep this family's attention for more than thirty seconds."

Ilana patted his hand. "Make it quick, sweetie."

Jacob cleared his throat. "First of all, I'd like to say congratulations to our baby sister on her recent engagement to Raphy." Everyone let go with a mazel tov or a hear, hear. "This is a day that I am sincerely looking forward to because I have been making notes about her since she was two and I have a lot of dirt on her."

"Blackmail worthy?" Hannah said.

"I'm keeping it PG."

"I'm hun-gry," Sammy said.

"Second of all." Jacob grinned. "Everyone here knows I move a little slow and I couldn't take another wedding with a 'soon be you' so . . ." He took a deep breath, and then he took Ilana's hand. He got down on one knee. The women gasped. Instantly, Ilana teared up. Rina squeezed Decker's hand. Jacob took out a small box and said, "I know this was a long time coming, but will you do me the honor of being my wife? And if it's no, please say yes anyway so you don't embarrass me in front of my family."

Ilana couldn't answer, but she nodded and the table broke out into applause. Ilana opened the box and gasped. She still couldn't talk as Jacob put the ring on her finger.

"Fin-a-lly!" Sammy put the menu down. "I'm having a steak."

Rachel hit him. "It's your brother. Can you show a little emotion?"

"It's been seven years."

Rachel hit him again.

Nina said, "How grand is this? Now it's truly a party. Let's get champagne." She summoned the waiter and asked for four bottles of champagne along with four bottles of To Kalon, which put the bar bill well over two thousand dollars.

There were kisses and hugs all around. Everyone admired the ring. The girls were in their element while the boys talked food. Rina said, "You have to call up your parents, Lani."

"They already know," Jacob said. "They helped me pick out the ring. They're coming for dinner. I'm assuming you wouldn't mind."

"When did you do all this?" Ilana finally said.

"I'm a sneaky guy."

"Gawd, with all these people, you should have rented a hall!" Nina turned to Ilana. "Would you like a bridal shower, dear?"

"Nina, I'm sure her friends will do that for her," Tyler said.

"I'm sure they will. But with my friends, she'll have a completely different present pool: deeper pockets. Don't deny me this, dear. We're always looking for an occasion to dress up and show off."

Tyler rolled his eyes. He leaned over to Decker and handed him a piece of paper. "New York art galleries. A lot of them closed at five, but some were open until eight. I called up a few to find out if any of them employed Angeline Moreau."

"Any luck?"

"No. And I didn't say I was a cop. I told them I was

from the bursar's office at Littleton College and was trying to reconcile some numbers for her W2 form."

"Good work." Decker's eyes scanned the list of galleries. "I got a call back from Jason Merritt. I set up an appointment at ten. Let's meet at Gabe's apartment at nine and figure out a strategy."

"Sounds like a plan."

"For once can you *not* talk about work?" Rina scolded. "Especially in light of what just happened?"

"I brought it up," McAdams said. "I apologize."

"Don't you dare let him off the hook," Rina said.

Decker said, "I won't talk about work. But then you can't talk about wedding stuff. I have nothing to add on the seemingly endless topic. And even if I did, no one would listen to me."

Hannah said, "You haven't said anything to me."

"Whatever I said never got past your mother's veto."

"That's not fair," Rina said. "Well, maybe it is a little fair."

Decker laughed, leaned over, and kissed her forehead.

"I'd like to have your input, Peter," Ilana said.

"Ilana, that would be a first. But honestly, weddings are outside my bailiwick."

"How can I not talk about weddings?" Rina protested. "Especially now."

"Two weddings in . . ." Sammy looked at his brother. "Are you planning in months or years for the actual date?"

Ilana's eyes were on the ring. "There's no hurry."

"Oh, don't say that to him," Rina said.

"I'd at least like to finish my internship."

"How long is that going to take?" Rina said.

"Like maybe two years."

"Two years sounds about right." Jacob stood up and motioned over a couple who were walking toward the table, both of them with grins on their faces. "Dad, could you just be nice?" he asked. "And if you can't be nice, can you at least not be grumpy?"

"Don't ask for the moon, son, and you'll never be disappointed," Decker said.

"He's just grumpy because he's hungry," Sammy said.

Rachel said, "Like father, like son . . ."

"I fully admit it."

"This event should have been catered," Nina said.

"Stop it," Tyler said.

Ilana's parents sat down and again kisses and hugs and oohs and aahs were exchanged. The server finally came over with several bottles of champagne and a bucket of ice.

Nina said, "Keep it flowing, darling. It looks like everyone could use a little mellowing."

When all the glasses were poured, Jacob held the glass up and said, "L'chayim."

"L'chayim," the chorus responded.

"That means to life," McAdams told Nina.

"I know what it means, Tyler, I wasn't born in an eggshell." Nina pulled out a handkerchief and dabbed her eyes. "Besides, who in America hasn't seen *Fiddler on the Roof*?"

CHAPTER TWENTY

The Merritt Gallery's address was in the Fifties between Park and Lexington, one of the many smaller studios that occupied a glass and chrome skyscraper. Inside, it was small and spare with religious articles in cases as well as Byzantine art painted on canvas, board, or wood planks. There were several Madonna and child, the Christ babies looking very elongated and with adult features, as if the artist was astigmatic. The babies were very different from the plump Renaissance Jesus that Decker was used to seeing in museums.

A man dressed head to toe in black looked up from the desk. He was in his thirties, balding and lean, but with big arms that strained his long-sleeved T-shirt. "Can I help you?"

"I'm looking for Jason Merritt." Decker gave the man his card. "He's expecting us."

"Police?" The assistant frowned. "Is something the matter?"

"Just gathering information about icons," Decker said. "It has to do with a thirty-year-old case that we're reopening."

The assistant pushed the intercom on his phone. "The Greenbury Police are here . . . Certainly, Mr. Merritt." He looked at Decker and then at McAdams. "His office is in the back." The assistant got up and started walking. "Are you working on the Petroshkovich icons? We're all wondering if the case would ever be reopened."

"It was never closed."

"Well, I for one am glad to hear that someone's breathing new life into it."

"And you are?"

"Victor Gerrard." He knocked on the door.

"It's open."

Gerrard opened the door.

The trio was welcomed into a small but tidy office. The art dealer was in his fifties with thinning dark hair and dark eyes. He was slight and had manicured nails. He was immaculately dressed in a pinstriped gray suit, white shirt, and a red tie. Black, polished lizard skin shoes on his feet. He listened intently while Decker explained why they had come.

Afterward Merritt said, "I'm still a little confused, Detective. I don't have anything to do with art nouveau or art deco. You should try Max Stewart."

"I've already been there. Now I'm interested in learning about the Petroshkovich icons that were stolen from Marylebone, Rhode Island."

"And what's the connection between a thirty-year-old case of stolen Russian icons and stolen Tiffany?"

"Not much except that both of the thefts appeared opportunistic. Meaning that the thief would need someone to market the stolen items. And he'd need high-end clients. I'm wondering if you could point us in the direction of dealers who . . . may be less meticulous with the object's ownership."

Merritt looked at Gerrard. "You should be getting back to the gallery."

"Of course." Gerrard smiled and nodded. "Good luck."

Merritt turned his attention back to the detectives. "Why exactly have you come to me?"

"Your name came up as a dealer who specializes in Russian icons."

Merritt made a tent with his fingers and brought them to his chin. "I still don't understand why you're so interested in the Petroshkovich icons when you're investigating stolen Tiffany." The man's expression grew cold. "Is this interview really subterfuge?"

"I beg your pardon?"

"If this is about my grandfather, I have nothing to say to you."

Decker was expressionless. "Your grandfather?"

Merritt considered the baffled look on his face. He blushed. "Never mind."

"No, no, no. You can't throw something out like that and say never mind."

The art dealer sighed. "It's not relevant."

"Sir, I don't have a lot to go on. Everything is important."

Merritt said, "If you speak to enough people, you might hear things about my grandfather stealing Russian art. That kind of drivel is not only completely false, it's pernicious."

"Okay." A pause. "Could you fill us in a little?"

"Why bother? It's all a pack of lies."

"I could either hear the truth from you or the lies from your enemies."

Merritt considered his words. "Some reprehensible people have had the nerve to say that my grandfather looted from Russian churches."

Decker took out a notepad. "Who's your grandfather?"

"August Merritt. His father—my great-grandfather—was Wilson Merritt. He was one of the few businessmen who dealt with Russia postrevolution. It wasn't an easy thing to do. It involved many layers of bureaucracy from both countries."

McAdams said, "What business was he in?"

"He owned textile mills down south. He imported cloth to third world countries. That included the Soviet Union when it was heavily ostracized. After the revolution and WWI, the Russian people ended up in a bad state—as was most of eastern Europe. Food was scarce, fuel was scarce, supplies were scarce. Bolts of woolen cloth may not seem like a lot, but it saved many people from freezing to death. My great-grandfather and my grandfather were rewarded for their humanitarian acts with visiting privileges at a time when the Soviet Union was off limits to most Western countries."

"So how did these rumors get started?" Decker asked.

"Jealousy." The art dealer made a point of sighing. "Wilson Merritt had always been interested in Byzantine art. As a matter of fact, he started the Merritt Gallery just to display his massive collection and later on, my grandfather went into the retail aspect. Wilson's detractors claim that he had acquired the pieces by using his favored status in the Soviet Union. And that part is true. It's the theft part that's a lie. The art world can be very vicious."

"Finance is pretty vicious as well," McAdams said. "When you mix the two, there is a high probability of corruption."

"Well said."

"How do you think the rumors got started?" Decker asked.

"As I told you, Russia was in terrible straits. The country

240

needed fuel. Thousands of religious items were burned for heat. What wasn't incinerated was thrown away as obsolete relics of an undesirable past. Wilson and my grandfather August made it their mission to save as many of those works as they could from total destruction. Of course that included items from churches left to rot. August wasn't a thief, he was a hero."

Decker looked up from his notepad. "Anyone specific who's spreading the gossip? Some names would go a long way."

"I have no proof. So I take the high road. Having been a victim of the rumor mill, I loathe hurting anyone even if that person or persons deserve it."

"How about if I name a name?"

"I can't stop you, can I?"

"Chase Goddard. What do you know about him?"

"No comment."

"Do you know if he's ever purchased stolen items?"

"I know of one case where he bought a very expensive pair of French silver candlesticks from the seventeenth century. They had been stolen from a Catholic church in the Chicago area. But as soon as it came to light, he refunded the money to his seller and gave the items back to the church."

"Was it an honest mistake?"

"It could have been. It could have also been prevented had he done proper homework."

"How was he caught?"

"The whole thing came to light when someone saw the items on an old website." Merritt looked at him. "And you didn't hear that from me."

McAdams said, "Was this when he was in New York?"

"Yes," Merritt said. "It happened about six or seven years ago before he went under."

"His New York gallery went under, but the website of his current gallery in Boston has a lot of inventory."

"So you've noticed."

"Care to speculate?" Decker asked.

"I'll leave the hearsay to others."

"Have you ever done business with him?"

"Good heavens, no."

"Has he ever approached you for business?"

"Several times . . . minor icons. I wasn't interested for a variety of reasons."

"What constitutes a minor icon?" Decker asked.

"Too recent of an age, poorly done images, and the piece as a whole is in bad shape."

He stopped talking. Decker waited for him to continue. Merritt finally said, "There was a onetime exception to the trash he usually showed me. It was when he was still in New York and his reputation hadn't yet been so sullied. But he was still someone we all watched."

"What happened?" McAdams asked.

"Goddard claimed that he had just gotten back from a European buying spree. He presented me with a truly magnificent icon. I won't go into the specifics but it was spectacular. The detail, the color, and the artist." A deep sigh. "I still bristle when I think of the lost opportunity."

"Why didn't you buy it?"

"I came that close to purchasing it." He pinched off a distance between his forefinger and his thumb. "But then he told me it came from Germany. He claimed to have checked out the provenance and that it went back a hundred years. I went on the Art Loss Register. I went through as many books on religious items as I could find. I couldn't place the object anywhere. Perhaps the provenance was legitimate. But it was an expensive item and I couldn't take the chance."

"Okay." Decker thought a moment. "Why did you have a problem with an object that came from Germany? Did you think that the icon was looted by the Nazis?"

"That's exactly what I thought."

Decker digested the information. "I'm not a history buff but I seem to recall that Hitler's invasion into Russia was a big disaster, that it was the turning point of the war. They bombed the cities, but the Germans never got into Moscow with boots on the ground. My dad used to tell me that the Russian winters did more to decimate Hitler's armies than all the bombs of Europe."

McAdams was already on his iPhone looking up a condensed piece of history. "Operation Barbarossa was the code name of the Soviet invasion by Hitler. Huge invasion . . . successful at first. And . . . eventually it was an utter failure."

"As far as a war tactic, yes, it was a failure," Merritt said. "And it was the turning point of the war. But the big picture doesn't tell the whole story. St. Petersburg—Leningrad back then—was under siege for two and a half years. The Germans didn't occupy the city because they didn't want to feed the residents in times of shortage. So with the Finns, the Germans closed all the access roads in and out of the city, hoping to starve the population before they'd take over the land. But the city wasn't impenetrable. German soldiers went in and looted. And some lucky individuals got out mostly through Lake Ladoga, which was how the Red Cross got its meager supplies into a starving population."

"Okay," Decker said. "So you're telling me that Nazis crossed enemy lines to loot Russian art while the city was under siege?"

"To that statement I say to you that someone dismantled the original Amber Room before Catherine's Palace was bombed to smithereens."

243

Decker turned to McAdams. "Want to look up the Amber Room for me?"

"Already on it."

Merritt said, "You don't know about the Amber Room?"

"It rings a very faint bell," Decker said. "If I had to guess, I'd say it was a room with a lot of amber in it."

"The original room was covered in amber with twenty-four-carat gold mirrors and precious and semiprecious stone inserts," McAdams said. "The repro is still in the Catherine Palace. I saw it. I remember it in detail because I've never seen anything like it before. There was an intimacy about it even though it was over the top. The history of how it came to exist eludes me at the moment . . . Hold on, let's see what I have. Okay, originally constructed in Prussia, but Friedrich Wilhelm I of Prussia gave it to Peter the Great in order to secure the Prussian-Russian alliance against Sweden."

Merritt sniffed. "Even the repro is magnificent in its craftsmanship. One can only imagine what the original was like. It must have been unworldly remarkable."

McAdams said, "What's unworldly remarkable is that two major countries had to form a pact against Sweden."

The art dealer managed to crack a smile. He said, "Everyone knows the room was dismantled by the Nazis. Twenty-seven crates were moved to East Berlin and then the crates went underground in Konigsberg, supposedly destroyed in a fire."

"You have doubts?" Decker asked.

"I do. If for no other reason, it's a romantic notion."

McAdams was still pulling up information. "This article says that the original cartons may now be located in the bunker in Auerswalde near Chemnitz, Germany."

"Perhaps the boxes will magically surface. You should go to St. Petersburg, Detective. See it for yourself."

"You're the second person who's told me that within twenty-four hours."

"It's a fascinating city, specifically in its scope of grandeur."

McAdams said, "The whole city is like Park Avenue on steroids."

Decker said, "I was told that most of the great artworks of the Hermitage were stored in the basement of St. Isaac's and remained there until the end of the war."

"That's true," Merritt said. "Most of the great pieces survived, specifically the two Da Vinci masterpieces, but there was looting. The Hermitage did get its ounce of revenge, however." He smiled. "Inside the museum, there are several out-of-the-way rooms entitled the Hidden Treasures. You have to look for the rooms to find them. They display marvelous works of impressionism and post-impressionism. So why aren't the works with the Hermitage's spectacular permanent collection?"

Decker thought a moment. "Stolen art?"

"The Russians would call it disputed art."

"Depends whose ox is being gored."

"You're correct about that. It is clear that the paintings were looted from Germany. For fifty years, they sat in the basement of the Hermitage until the museum decided to do the audacious and display the pieces. Whenever the German government starts making waves about the ownership, the Russians come back with the Amber Room.

"There are quite a few people out there whose full-time occupation is recovering looted art. Most of the time, the art is hiding in plain sight. Look at the Gurlitt collection in Munich. Everyone around knew about Hildebrand Gurlitt for years, including the German government. But no one said a word. What is really needed is for violating countries to start fessing up."

"That's not going to happen," McAdams said.

"I agree with you," Merritt said. "The Vichy government looted thousands of pieces. Most of the paintings never made it back to their rightful owners. It's rumored that billions of dollars of art is languishing in the basement of the Louvre. The museum can't display it for obvious reasons. They won't even admit they have it. And France was an Allied country. You'd think it would rush to do the proper thing. But where money is concerned, ethics fly out the window."

"Politics and art," McAdams said. "In the case of Soviet art, they're one and the same."

Decker nodded. "Does the name John Jeffrey Latham mean anything to you, Mr. Merritt?"

The dealer appeared to give the question some thought. "No, I don't think it does. Who is he?"

"How about Angeline Moreau?"

"Neither name is familiar. Who are they?"

"Could either one be a client?"

"Spell them for me, please?" When Decker complied, Merritt sat down at his computer and typed on the keyboard. "Not on my current list. What do they have to do with your case?"

"Supposedly, Latham was an expert on Soviet art," McAdams said.

A long silence. "You used the past tense," Merritt said.

"Our case has branched out from stolen Tiffany." Decker gave him a brief and startling recap. "We know the theft isn't big enough to warrant two bestial murders."

"That's . . ." His face was white. "Just horrible."

"That's why we need any help we can get."

"I can't help you at all. Nor do I think that I want to get involved."

"A few more questions then we're out of your hair,"

Decker said. "Just give us some direction. What would be worth murdering over?"

"Murder is not my area of expertise, Detective."

"But art is. What, in your opinion, what art is worth murdering over?"

"That question is obscene."

"So is homicide. Help me out."

Merritt sighed. "There are tens of thousands of priceless masterpieces out there."

"I'll narrow it down for you. What kind of *Russian* art work could lead to murder?"

"Oh dear . . ." He sighed. "Since we've been talking about Nazi looting . . . I suppose if you had the crates that contained the original Amber Room . . . well, it's something that would be very near and dear to many a Russian heart."

CHAPTER TWENTY-ONE

After numerous calls, neither Decker nor McAdams could find a connection between Angeline Moreau and any of the New York galleries. The same was true with John Jeffrey Latham. No disappointment because Decker didn't expect anything, but it was a procedural step that had to be done. He and Rina spent Shabbat with the kids in Brooklyn, sleeping on a pull-out sofa, while McAdams luxuriated at his grandmother's apartment on Park. The trio left the Big Apple on Sunday evening at nine, arriving in Greenbury a little before midnight. He and Harvard had switched off driving while Rina slept in the backseat.

The colleges were beacons of light in a little dark town. As Decker drove past the campuses, he heard the punctuation of drunken shouts as party-hard students wended their ways back to the dorms. A light flurry of snow was falling, enough to use the windshield wipers. As soon as Decker pulled up in front of Tyler's house, Rina woke up and took a quick intake of air. "How long was I out?"

"About two hours," Decker said.

McAdams opened the passenger door and in came a

gush of cold air. "I'll see you tomorrow, Old Man. Have a good night, Mrs. Decker."

"You too, Tyler." Rina got out of the car and moved to the front seat. "You shouldn't have let me sleep. Now my schedule will be all messed up."

"Maybe you needed sleep after caring nonstop for your grandchildren."

"Isn't that the truth? There's a reason for having children when you're young."

"You are young, especially compared to me."

She leaned over and kissed him. "Your mother is ninety-three. You have many more years on this planet . . . if you don't wear out your engine with homicide cases."

"I hear you." Decker parked in front of his house and killed the engine. Outside was deadly silent. "We're going up to Summer Village tomorrow. I'm hoping the detectives had better luck with Latham because I'm not getting anywhere."

"You can't just call them?"

"I've already called them. They don't tell me anything over the phone. I need a face-to-face. I've got an appointment with Chris Mulrooney. After him, I want to start looking into some of the Boston galleries since New York was a bust."

"Are they open on Monday?"

"Some of them are. The one I'm interested in, isn't open usually, but I have an appointment."

"So you really think the murders have to do with the art theft?"

"Right now, it's the only thing I have to go on."

They both got out of the car and went into the house, Decker flicking on the hallway light. He hung up his jacket and Rina's jacket as well. He took off his boots, his scarf, and his mittens and turned on a living room lamp. Inside it was warm and cozy. Greenbury was beginning to feel like home. Rina had put on a kettle. "Tea?"

"Love some." He sat down on the couch and threw his head back.

Rina sat down and put her hand on his knee. "Tell me where you are in the case."

Decker explained what he knew so far. "Now that we have the connection between Angeline and the panels, I can at least go forward. If she and Latham were fencing stolen material, they'd need a middleman. Since Latham lived up north, I'll try hunting around the Boston area."

"You can do that without stepping on Summer Village's toes?"

"That's why I want to see them personally. We can compare notes and since they're busier than I am, maybe they wouldn't mind a little help."

Rina nodded, and then she went into the kitchen to fetch the tea. They sipped a while in silence, watching the snow fall from the living room picture window. There was a light outside the house emphasizing the delicate white flakes: a live screen saver. She said, "Are you taking Tyler with you?"

"It always helps to have another point of view." A pause. "Before we left for New York, Tyler was in the middle of searching for valuables that could be stolen from a library: things like old reference material with original prints or vintage maps or collectors' books that could be sold on the black market. If they were stealing from graveyards, I wouldn't put it past them to steal from libraries."

"Makes total sense."

"The problem is none of that material is worth killing over. Even if their fence was caught, the most he'd get is a slap on the wrist. So far I have nothing that says that Angeline was anything more than a two-bit hustler. I have nothing on Latham. I'm going to exhaust all my leads very soon. I'm missing something." The room fell silent. "It's times like this when I really miss Marge."

"You do own a phone."

"I don't want to bother her."

"While Ventura is a bigger city than Greenbury, it isn't LAPD. I'm sure she's going through 'homicide withdrawal' as well. And I know she loves hearing from you. It's not late on the West Coast and you know she's not working on Sunday. Call her up."

Decker checked his watch as if to verify the time. "Why not? At the very least, it'll be nice to talk to someone who doesn't call me Old Man."

Halfway through the ride to Boston, Decker said, "I spoke to my old partner last night." A beat. "Not my *old* partner, my *former* partner. She's younger than me."

"Isn't everyone?" McAdams snapped.

Decker raised his eyebrows but said nothing. It appeared that he had hit a jealous nerve in the kid. It was always surprising what set people off.

The kid fidgeted. "Why'd you call her? Never mind. It's none of my business. Unless you were talking about the case. Then it is my business. Aren't you the one who told me to keep my mouth shut?"

Decker ignored his 'tude. "Her department isn't nearly as big as LAPD, but it's in a major city and she has access to a lot more databases than we do. I've asked her to look into any art crime that might have involved homicide within the last five years. It'd be interesting to see if she comes up with anything new."

McAdams was silent. He sipped coffee from a thermos.

"Anything left in that thing?" Decker asked.

"Dregs."

They drove for five minutes without speaking. Then Decker spotted a Dunkin' Donuts. "Let's get a refill."

"Doughnuts and coffee. Very cop of you."

"You want something to eat? I'm going to get a bagel." When McAdams remained silent, Decker said, "I'll take that as a no." It took him five minutes to make the round-trip. When he came back, he unwrapped his bagel and took a bite. "Sure you don't want anything?"

"I'm *fine*, okay?"

"Sure." Decker continued eating.

McAdams blew out air. Then he got out of the car and came back a minute later with his own bagel and a cup of coffee. "Did she have anything illuminating to add to the case?"

"She's smart enough not to offer opinions without having the facts in front of her. Mostly she just listened to my frustration. She agrees with us, that it has to be something more than just a couple of Tiffany panels."

"Insightful, that woman is. What's her name again? Maude?"

"Marge Dunn. She and her fiancé may come out in the summer to visit."

"How old is she?"

"Marge is a little older than Rina's age . . . early fifties. We both left LAPD at the same time. I don't miss the department, but I do miss her. You're with someone that long, it's like a marriage."

"Was she your little piece of action on the side?"

Slowly, Decker smiled. "No, she was not my little piece of action on the side. I don't have action on the side. I'm a true blue guy. But I thank you for the compliment: that I could get action on the side . . . had I wanted it."

McAdams just shook his head. "You are absolutely unflappable."

253

"I've asked Marge to look up Jason Merritt, Maxwell Stewart, and Chase Goddard. See if any of them has ever been in trouble before. It would help to know Goddard's background before we see him."

"What'd she tell you?"

"I called her last night." Decker checked his watch. "It's seven in the morning on the West Coast. I'm hoping to hear from her in a couple of hours. In the meantime, we can talk to the Summer Village PD, a guy named Chris Mulrooney. They're done with the search of Latham's apartment. Mulrooney was generous enough to share what they found . . . which doesn't look like much so far. We're meeting with him at eleven."

"What about Latham's computer?" McAdams asked.

"The dees didn't find his computer. They're trying to find his e-mail server via his phone service but that takes a warrant. They're hoping to have it today or tomorrow along with his phone and text logs. If he was using a throwaway phone like Angeline, we probably won't find much, but no stone unturned, right?"

The kid rubbed his eyes. "Do we know that Angeline was definitely using a throwaway phone?"

"We do. Ben Roiters texted me last night during dinner. He found the mobile phone store where she bought her throwaways. Sorry, I forgot to tell you."

McAdams's face darkened. "No prob, boss. What I think doesn't matter anyway."

Decker shrugged and finished his bagel. He wiped his hands, put the key in the ignition, and started up the engine. "There's a CPR class at the hospital this Sunday. It's given by the local Red Cross. I could use a refresher. Want to come with me?"

"No, I don't . . ." McAdams stopped himself. "Yeah, sure, why not. I'll come. Never can tell when a date might choke on a potato chip." He stared out the window. "Next thing I know, you'll be asking me to come down to the shooting range."

Decker pulled the car onto the highway. "I'd be happy to give you a few pointers."

"I don't own a gun."

"That can be remedied. I'm most comfortable with a Beretta 92FS or 92F 9 mm: they're standard LAPD issue. Do you know anything about guns and ammo?"

"Mike taught me a few things about slugs and casings and bullets from different types of guns. Since it hasn't been remotely relevant to anything I've done here, I don't remember much."

"It won't take you long to learn if you're interested."

"I'm interested."

"What about going to the range with me?"

The kid sighed. "Sure."

"Good. I'll get a gun for you and we can start whenever you want."

McAdams clenched his jaw. "I'm having a hard time figuring you out . . . whether you're friend or foe."

"I'm, neither, Harvard. I'm a professional. I want a partner who knows CPR in case I choke on a potato chip. As far as the guns go, I don't expect it to happen, but should we ever be in a situation with our backs to the wall, I'd prefer a partner who could shoot. And I do apologize for not telling you about Ben's text. It was during the family dinner and Rina said no business. And then because I'm senile, I forgot to tell you."

"I know I'm being touchy and obnoxious." A pause. "So you consider me your partner."

"I've been assigned to ride with you, so yes, you are at present my partner. And for a rookie who hasn't had much formal police training, you're not half bad. And if you'd lose the chip on your shoulder, you could be very good because you're not only smart, you're organized and that's even more important than smart. And since you are my current partner, I'd appreciate if you stopped calling me Old Man. I don't need to be reminded of my age."

McAdams tried stifling a smile. It didn't work. "I don't mean anything by it, but if it's important to you, I'll stop."

Decker waited a beat. "Maybe I'm being touchy. I'll stop calling you Harvard if it bothers you."

"It did bother me at first . . . like you were mocking me." A pause. "Were you mocking me?"

"Of course."

"You can call me Harvard although it's not such a badge of honor. Lots of mediocre minds there." A smile. "I'm just not one of them."

Decker smiled and pointed to the kid's iPhone. "As long as I'm driving, start phoning the Boston galleries on the list. They should be open by now. Let's get a schedule going so we won't be wasting time. We can start meeting with them at around 12:30. Our appointment with Chase Goddard isn't until 3:00."

"I can do that." McAdams picked up the phone and regarded the list the two of them had prepared. "A lot of them are on Newbury Street. I'll start there and pick up as many as we can do on foot. Parking is terrible. Once we find a spot, we'll want to camp out as long as we can. I know you don't mind walking. You certainly do a lot of it."

"When you're old like me, you take any exercise you can get."

"I hope I'm as sharp as you are, Decker, when I'm your age. I don't mean that as a compliment, just a fact." The kid started making phone calls. His voice sounded pleasant but professional. He was focused and all business. And

256

that was the way it should be. He was doing the job. If the job was done well, the trust and finally friendship would come later on. Tyler had a long way to go before he'd prove himself. But he was getting there, working without complaint. In this so-called *entitled* generation, that was pretty good.

CHAPTER TWENTY-TWO

Opening a locked cabinet, Detective Chris Mulrooney took out a spiral blue notebook with gloved hands. "We found it this morning, hidden behind a paneled door in the bathtub enclosure where a Jacuzzi motor should have been. The pipes were capped off." He opened up to a random page. "English letters, Greek letters, Cyrillic letters, Hebrew, Arabic, Chinese, Japanese, crap that looks like cuneiform. It's some kind of code."

Decker slipped on a latex glove. "Can I take a look?"

"Knock yourself out." Mulrooney was short, squat, and bald with a constant smile on his face, like he loved what he was doing and loved life in general. He wore a sweater over an oxford weave shirt, slacks, and rubber-soled shoes. "You find anything in code in the girl's apartment?"

"No, we didn't." Decker felt McAdams peering over his shoulder, mouthing words in a whisper. "You make any sense of this, Harvard?"

"Can I take a closer look?"

"Yeah, but glove up," Mulrooney said. "We've dusted it for prints and came up dry, but we'll give it a second go. Our victim might have been some kind of language guy. I know he was smart. He won some kind of prestigious award."

"The Windsor Prize," Decker said.

"Yeah, that's it. I put a call into the committee office and got an answering machine. I don't know if I'll get a call back soon because the prize is given every four years. When I talked to the people in his department, they told me that he got a two-year lectureship because of the award."

"What did his colleagues have to say?"

"The usual. They're all shocked by his murder, he was a quiet guy. And he was young: a lot younger than the professors around him."

"What was he lecturing in?"

"His research was . . . hold on, let me get this right." Mulrooney took out his notebook. "Political art and propaganda in the Soviet Union during the period between the two world wars. If I didn't know about your vic and the stolen Tiffany windows, I would have assumed that he was one of these nerdy academic types who was killed for his research or something stupid like that . . . except, well, you saw the body. Someone was royally pissed off. That was one horrific crime. Not the cozy professor kind of killing."

"Are we sure that this codebook belongs to Latham?" Decker said.

Mulrooney paused. "You think otherwise?"

"It could have been stolen. Both Latham's and Angeline's apartments were tossed."

"Whoever did it had a lot of languages at his disposal." McAdams was turning the pages. "We need a cryptologist to break this down. There are dozens of them at Harvard and MIT. They'd do it for you for fun."

"Yeah, this city is filled with people who can do

260

everything," Mulrooney said. "Before I show this to anyone outside the department, I'd like to know what we're dealing with. Latham was one nasty murder."

"Latham came to Tufts for a lectureship?" Decker asked.

"A joint appointment for two years with the art department and IR. What Soviet art has to do with Tiffany panels, I don't know. But he's obviously an art guy. One art guy talks to another art guy and pretty soon, you're an expert in something."

"Where did he study before he came to Tufts?" Decker said. "I heard he went to Oxford."

"Don't recall seeing that. Hold on, lemme see what I got on him." Mulrooney peered through some file folders. "Uh, he had a master's of arts from the Center for Russian, East European, and Eurasian Studies. Sounds like something political or an online scam."

"CREES," McAdams said. "It's a legitimate university program. Hold on." He started playing with his iPhone. "It's for people who have an interest in foreign languages of those regions and who want to work for government and diplomacy. There's a CREES at Harvard, there's one at U Mich, there's one at Kansas University, there's one at Stanford, there's one at U Texas—"

"What about the Five Colleges of Upstate?" Decker asked.

"Let me check." His fingers went flying across his phone. "Good call. There's one at Morse McKinley that offers a B.A. as well as an M.A."

Mulrooney said, "Then why didn't he list the college on his résumé?"

"Yeah, that is a little weird," Tyler said. "Maybe he didn't finish the degree."

"And yet he got the Windsor award and a lectureship,"

Decker said. "Any kind of college job is pretty hard to snag these days, let alone one at a major university in a major city."

"Something isn't making sense," Mulrooney said. "And I don't see any Oxford here."

"Could be he was padding his C.V. and no one bothered to check." McAdams thought a moment. "Betcha he had connections. That's really the way it's done."

Decker said, "What about his family? Any connections there?"

"Nope. They're fairly local—grape farmers in the Finger Lakes District."

"You mean wine?" Tyler asked.

"No, I mean grapes . . . Concord table grapes. They were devastated when we told them the news, but they didn't have a hell of a lot to add. He hadn't kept in touch with any kind of regularity. Packed out when he was eighteen and except for the occasional Christmas phone call, he had pretty much vanished from their lives. They had no idea who'd want to murder him. They didn't even know that he went to college."

"They were that out of touch?" Decker was skeptical.

"I think they were telling the truth, but I didn't press them too hard. They'd just lost their son." Mulrooney held up his hands in a hopeless gesture.

"If he was from the Finger Lakes District, he probably knew about the Five Colleges of Upstate. It would make sense that he'd choose Morse McKinley. But at his age, he wouldn't have overlapped with Angeline Moreau . . . well, maybe with a master's."

Tyler had gone back to looking at the codebook. He was mouthing some of the words out loud.

"You read Russian?" Mulrooney asked.

"I can read it although I don't know what I'm saying.

262

The same with Greek." He looked up. "We were required to learn the classic languages in prep."

Decker pointed to two words. כאאבאאת אממפתתוּר "This is Hebrew."

Mulrooney asked, "Does it say anything?"

"I don't know Hebrew so I couldn't tell you. I can read it, but they don't seem like real words. You'd never have two alefs in a row. Maybe it's Yiddish, which uses Hebrew letters."

Tyler said, "Is it possible to get a copy of the notebook?"

Mulrooney frowned. "How many pages is it?"

"About twenty."

"Give it to Frosty. She's down the hallway, first door to the left. Tell her I'm saying please." He looked back at Decker. "Sometimes you get a case where there's nowhere to go. This case, we've got too many places. Is it an art theft, something personal, something with the university, something with the estranged family that they're not telling me? We still have to look into all those keys he had, we've got codes and someone who was involved with something international. And we've got a real, real vicious crime. The bad people are real bad. It'll take a while to sort this one out."

"Anything I can do to help?" Decker said.

"Yeah, your girl looks simpler than our guy. If you find something, pass it on. What's your next step?"

"We're going to visit some art galleries in Boston." Decker gave a brief recap of his discussion with Maxwell Stewart and Jason Merritt. He purposely left out his appointment with Chase Goddard.

If something came up, he'd share it after the fact. No purpose in telling him about another blind alley that would no doubt turn into another dead end.

*　　*　　*

McAdams was poring over the file as Decker, stuck in traffic, tried to make his way to Newbury Street. "Now I know why I moved to a small town."

The kid didn't answer, engrossed in his business. A moment later, Tyler sat up. "It's Latin."

"Pardon?"

"The words . . . at least the words in Greek . . . Greek script but Latin meaning. Words that don't mean anything specific . . . like ipso facto or e pluribus unum. It's a code within a code. I bet if we got someone who knew Chinese or Arabic, those words wouldn't mean anything in the native language but would transliterate into Latin words also."

"Wow, kiddo, that's impressive." Decker nodded. "Good for you, Tyler. Well done."

The kid tried to stifle a smile. "If I show you the Hebrew, could you read it out loud?"

"Yeah, I could do that. Wait until I'm stopped at a light."

Tyler waited and then showed the page.

Decker stared at the letters. He repeated them several times to himself. "Wait a sec . . ." A beat. "Kav-i-at em-f-tur . . . or maybe the fey is a pey . . ." He turned to the kid. "It's caveat emptor."

This time, Tyler grinned. "Really?"

"Really. Good work."

McAdams couldn't keep the smile off his face. "Now all we have to do is find the code within the code. Once we translate the words into Latin, we can work translating it into English. Not me, personally. Someone who can do codes."

"You don't do codes?"

"Not these kinds of codes. I haven't a clue. But I know someone who can. What would a trip to Boston be without a stop at the big H. Shall we?"

"We need to tell Mulrooney about it first."

McAdams's face soured. "Do we really have to do that?"

"Yeah, we do. This codebook is his baby and he was nice enough to let us in. Besides, Latham's murder was gruesome. I'm sure the killer would do it again in a heartbeat. The more people who know about what we're doing, the better off we are. The bogeyman can kill off Latham and Moreau, he can even try to whack us, but he can't kill off an entire police department."

Two hours, six galleries, and no significant information later, they stood in front of the Chase Goddard Antique and Curio Gallery. The sun was out in full force, the temperatures in the high thirties, which meant melting snow and ice off the eaves and rooftops. Dripping water created puddles on the sidewalks. The gallery was on a side street off the main drag of Newbury, in a turn-of-the-twentieth-century house that featured plaster molding, a big picture window, and a green-and-white-striped awning over the doorway. On the left side was a bakery with a few inside tables for coffee and a snack, and on the right was a linens store specializing in lace and embroidery.

Since it was only two-thirty, they had time before the interview. They elected to sit in the bakery rather than the car, which was beginning to smell a little dank and rank. The bakery was cute and warm and the aroma was heavenly. After ordering, they sat down and waited for their cappuccinos and snacks, neither of them speaking until the coffee came.

Decker sipped. "Man, that's good."

"Yeah, it is." McAdams was still paging through the book, trying to figure out as many words as he could. "This is going to take a while."

"Maybe you shouldn't do this right now."

The kid looked up. "No one's here. Besides, you told me to bring it with me."

"Well, maybe it's best that you put it away just in case someone has been tailing us."

McAdams closed the notebook. "Very funny."

"Maybe not."

"What?" The kid dropped his voice. "What are you talking about?"

"Hyundai Accent silver van, maybe two years old. I noticed it when we left the police station in Summer Village. No front plates. About five minutes ago, I saw something very similar across Newbury Street right before we made the turn toward Goddard Gallery. I think the person spotted me looking at the car because he or she took off and unfortunately I was too far away to read the back plates."

McAdams was quiet. "Is it the same vehicle? I mean there must be hundreds of silver Hyundai Accents."

"I wouldn't say hundreds."

"Are you doing that on purpose or do you like to see me sweat?"

"I'm sure it was a coincidence. But two people are dead so I thought I'd mention it, in case we see the van again."

"Right." McAdams sipped coffee. "Your eyes. They're never in one place for long unless you're trying to spook someone. Do they teach you that at detective school?"

"My suspicious nature is all my own doing. It has served me well."

"I know I've asked you this before but *should* I be worried?"

"Honestly, I don't know, Tyler. You said you're in it for the long run, but if you wanted to walk, I wouldn't blame you."

"No, I don't want to walk. It's just getting interesting."

McAdams bit his lower lip. "What should I be looking for, Decker? What makes you suspicious?"

"Things that repeat themselves . . . like seeing the same car or the same guy. Also, things that don't belong. In a small town, that's a little easier, but harder in the big city. And then there are the basics. I lock my doors and pull down my shades and always give a twice-over before I leave my house or my car. Like I said, detectives are seldom whacked. But seldom isn't never."

"We live in Bumblefuck, USA. How can this happen?"

Decker smiled. "You know what they say about good things coming in small packages. Sometimes big-city bad things come to very small towns."

Chase Goddard couldn't figure out what to do with his hands. First he clasped them together. Then they dropped by his side. Finally he elected to shove them into his tweed jacket patch pockets. He was in his fifties with a long face, short blond hair, blue eyes, thin lips, and a Roman nose. Under his jacket he wore a pastel blue V-neck sweater over an open-collar white shirt, and he had on dark trousers and black boots. His nails were clipped short and his left hand sported a gold wedding band. Goddard continued to fidget. Maybe it was the lack of space. The three of them were standing, crammed into his office, a small room with a chair, a desk, and piles of paperwork.

"John Latham?" Goddard thought about the name for a decent amount of time. "No, I don't know him." A beat. "I certainly don't know the name."

"What about Angeline Moreau?" Decker asked.

Again, he didn't speak right away. "No, I don't know her. Who is she?"

"She is our murder victim," Decker said. "Latham's case belongs to Summer Village. We think the two of them were working together on something illegal and were murdered because of it."

Goddard winced. "And you're from . . . where again?"

"Greenbury, New York."

"Ah, near the Five Colleges."

"Yes. Do you have any association with the colleges, Mr. Goddard?"

"No, no, but of course I've heard of them. They're quite respectable."

"But they're not Harvard," McAdams said.

Goddard said, "There are other universities, Detective."

"Not to me."

The art dealer paused. "You're a Crimson man, I take it."

"Graduated almost four years ago."

"And you're working as a policeman?"

McAdams simply shrugged. "There's a real world out there that Harvard chooses to ignore."

Goddard raised his eyebrows. "I was in Harvard ages ago, when there was still a Radcliffe. As a matter of fact, I was there when it went co-ed."

"Seventy-seven," McAdams said. "My father had just started law school. James McAdams."

"James McAdams . . . James Mc— Do you mean Jack McAdams?"

"That's my dad."

"Well, that does take me back. I'm sure he wouldn't know me. Your father was a big man not only in the law school but in general." A pause. "What's he doing now?"

"He was in law. Now he fills his time by managing his inherited fortune from my grandfather. It seems to be a full-time job."

"Oh . . . right." Goddard colored slightly. "I know this sounds terribly crass, but if he's interested in buying or selling . . ."

268

"I'll pass the word on."

He gave Decker a forced smile. "Anything else?"

"I do have a few more questions."

Goddard sighed. "Can I interject something?"

"Of course."

"You know Summer Village has a high homicide rate. It's not unusual for murder to take place in that area."

"The homicide of a visiting lecturer is not routine for them. And the murder of a college student in Greenbury is not routine for us. Neither are art thefts."

"Tell me again what happened?"

Decker bit his lip. The guy didn't need a recap, but he gave it to him anyway.

Goddard tented his hands. "So from a small break in at a local mausoleum, you've constructed this . . . art theft ring that you think is responsible for two murders?"

"We haven't constructed anything, Mr. Goddard. We're just trying to make sense of what happened."

"I don't know what I could possibly tell you. I don't deal in stolen art."

"You deal in antiques. You must get people trying to sell you things."

"I do and most of what is brought to me is worthless."

"But not all."

"I get the occasional gem. And I do my best to make sure the piece is genuine and the ownership is flawless. And that is why most of what I buy is from private clients and estates. Over the years, I've worked very hard to establish a list of people who stay with me because I'm as fair and competitive with anyone out there."

"*Fortes fortuna adiuvat*," McAdams said.

Goddard smiled. "Well, fortune certainly doesn't appear *ex nihilo*." An awkward moment of silence. He took his hands in and out of his pockets several times. "My business is strictly on the up-and-up. I wouldn't deal with scum because it is not only dishonest, but it's also bad business practice. In this field, all you have going for you is your knowledge and your reputation."

"You've never accidentally bought something with a less than a perfect provenance?"

Goddard made a sour face. "If you'd look around the gallery, you would see that there are a variety of objects from inexpensive to very expensive. I work hard to check out provenance but if some youngster comes in with a piece of Meissen and tells me it's from his grandmother's attic, I might not go through the provenance as rigorously as if he had brought me a . . . Thomas Moran or Frederic Church for instance. Now if that same youngster came in a day later and brought in a piece of Daum and a day later, brought in a piece of Hester Bateman silver, I would be suspicious. The pieces have no relevance to one another and the piecemeal sale would make me think, he's stealing. I've been in this business a long time. You know what's legitimate and what isn't."

"You had a gallery in New York, didn't you?"

The dealer huffed. "I'm sure you know I did. And I'm sure you know that I didn't have a lot of success. And that was because I was attacked by a hateful campaign started by some unscrupulous dealers. Their venal little clique isn't open to anyone else unless you pay homage to them. I refused to play the game and they spread vicious rumors. I've never ever done a deal mala fide. Anything else?"

"What can you tell me about the Petroshkovich icons?"

"Good Lord, that happened years ago."

"It did. Have you ever dealt in icons?"

"I'm not sure I like what you're implying."

"I'm not implying anything. Just asking a question."

"Then I'll ask you one. What do *you* have to do with the Petroshkovich case?"

Decker said. "It's an unsolved art theft case. And like our theft, it happened in a small town. The items were stolen from a church, not from a museum: easy pickings and the thieves knew exactly what they were looking for."

Goddard was quiet. Then he said, "Icons are a specialized item. You should talk to Jason Merritt in New York."

"We have. He says he doesn't know anything about the theft."

"I'm sure he would say that." A pause. "Did . . . Jason sic you on me?"

"Your name came up."

Goddard's cheeks colored. "Like grandfather like grandson."

"What can you tell me about his grandfather?"

"Nothing. It's all just rumors and having been the victim of flapping tongues, I should know better than to pay credence to idle talk."

"Jason told me that his great-grandfather and his grandfather had special privileges in Russia during the Soviet regime. In the early years, they picked up a lot of religious art and icons at discounted prices because no one wanted it."

Goddard looked upward, debating what to say. "Discounted prices may be an understatement."

"Meaning?"

"Let's just say the regime was unstable and a lot of looting was going on. And that's all you'll get out of me."

Decker knew when to push and when to move on. "I know you don't recognize the names of the victims. Could I show you pictures? Maybe they used different names."

A sigh. "Why not?"

271

"This is Angeline Moreau," Decker told him. "She was an art major at Littleton College. She made frequent trips to the Boston area as well as trips to New York City."

Goddard barely gave the photo a glance. "I've never seen her before in my life."

"Okay." Decker wondered why people made statements like that. How do you know everyone you have or haven't seen? "What about John Latham?"

It took Goddard even less time to blow Decker off. "I've never seen him, either."

The man was reaching the end of his tether. Decker said, "And you're sure you've never had any contacts—"

"I don't know them, sir, and I've certainly never dealt with them. Is there anything else?"

McAdams said, "Would you mind if we took a look around the gallery?"

"Whatever for?"

"How can I tell my dad about you if I don't know what you have?"

"Oh . . . yes, of course. I'm sorry if I seem so rude. All this nonsense and rumors with New York has stirred up old memories. It was a bad time for me."

McAdams said, *"Fortis in arduis."*

"Isn't that the truth!" Goddard sat down at his desk. "Of course, take a look around. And I won't hover. I'll be doing paperwork if you have questions. If not, please enjoy."

The two men left his tiny office and began perusing the inventory. Goddard had everything in no particular order. Some of it was displayed, some of it seemed incidental. There was furniture, paintings, silver, porcelain, old lamps and lighting fixtures hanging from the ceilings, carpets on the pine floors. There were sets of china, antique linens, vintage cookware, and fireplace accoutrements. Shelves

272

and racks and rows of curios were stuffed into every nook and cranny. Decker said, "Do you know anything about antiques?"

"Only to say that this is pretty standard stuff: eighteenth- and nineteenth-century European. Not the right place to fence Tiffany." McAdams picked up a Rosenthal cobalt platter.

Decker pointed to the wall. He whispered, "Framed antique map."

"I noticed." The kid put the platter down. "Also antique plant prints."

The men continued to hunt around. McAdams whispered, "I was using phrases from the notebook by the way."

"I gathered that."

"Tried to work them in as seamlessly as possible."

They regarded a shelf of silver. Decker said, "Go tell him good-bye and I'll meet you outside. He likes you better than he likes me."

McAdams smiled. "Must be my charm."

A moment later, they were walking back on Newbury, headed toward the rental. It was dark, cold, and misty, but the street was well lit, which mitigated the gloominess.

"Do you want to pick up some coffee before we head back?" Decker asked.

"Sure. Let's go to Dunkin' Donuts. I've developed a taste for cronuts."

Decker got into the driver's seat, turned on the motor, and warmed up the engine. "Want to tell me what the Latin meant?"

"Sure. *Fortes fortuna adiuvat* means 'fortune favors the bold.' *Fortis in arduis* literally means 'strong in difficulties': sort of what doesn't kill us makes us stronger. He used the phrase *Mala fide*, which means—"

"In bad faith." When McAdams looked at him, Decker said, "Not hard to figure out. Also law school."

"Right." McAdams rubbed his hands together.

Decker said, "Who do you know at Harvard who does codes?"

"A professor I had. Brilliant guy. Codes are his hobby."

"Hold on." On speakerphone, Decker called Mulrooney and asked the Summer Village detective if it was all right to show the notebook to a third party at Harvard.

"I could probably find someone at Tufts," Mulrooney said.

"Latham worked at Tufts," Decker said. "I'd rather use another university."

"That makes sense," Mulrooney said. "What's that guy's name?"

"Dr. Mordechai Gold," Tyler told him. "He's a tenured professor in the math department. I took his class on game theory. I doubt that he'll remember me, but he's brilliant and I know he's an expert at code cracking. He's probably not going to be able to help us right away, but at least we can drop off the notebook."

Mulrooney said, "Yeah, you can call him up. Let me know what he says. Keep me in the loop, guys."

"As soon as we have a clue, we'll pass it on." Decker hung up his cell.

McAdams was on his phone. "Okay, I've got a department number." He punched in the numbers. "Do you want to talk to him or should I?"

"You do it."

"Right." McAdams pressed the green button. After being put on hold, he was finally connected to Professor Gold's office. "It's a machine." He waited. "Hello, Professor Gold, this is Detective Tyler McAdams from Greenbury Police Department in upstate New York. I took your game theory class four years ago and I remember your expertise in code cracking. My partner, Detective Peter Decker, and I are working a puzzling case and could use some advice. If you could call me, I'd appreciate it." Tyler left his cell number, Decker's cell number, and then he hung up.

"Perfect," Decker said. "You didn't tell him anything specific but you piqued his interest. You're turning pro, McAdams. I now have a partner instead of dead weight."

"You have a way with words, Decker."

"Don't I though? Clearly your brains are paying off." Decker put the car into drive and grinned. "Now all we have to do is work on the brawn."

CHAPTER TWENTY-THREE

Fueled up on coffee and carbs, Decker drove back to Greenbury on the highway, keeping an eye out for silver vans and black ice. He thought McAdams was dozing off, but then the kid suddenly sat up and dry washed his face.

Tyler checked his watch. "Six-thirty. It feels like eleven. I hate winter: the long, dark, cold nights. No wonder there's so much drinking and screwing in college."

"Don't blame that on winter," Decker said. "California universities have just as much drinking and screwing." A pause. "What's your take on Goddard? Anything in the shop worth beaucoup bucks?"

"Nothing worth killing for. His shop has a little of this and a little of that: a perfect front to fence stolen items."

"Like the framed antique maps and prints," Decker said. "And he had some antique books behind the glass case. I noticed *The Long Goodbye* by Raymond Chandler. That has to be worth something."

"If it's a first edition, yes. There was also a *Swann's Way* by Marcel Proust."

"Given his reputation in New York, Goddard as a fence

doesn't seem like a stretch. But do you see him as a murderer?"

"No. He'd never get his hands dirty. Maybe he hired someone."

"Do you see him arranging contract killings? Knowing those kinds of people?"

"I know this sounds pedestrian, but I watch those true crime shows. It seems pretty easy to get some lowlife to shoot someone. It doesn't even take that much money."

"But Latham's murder did not have any hallmarks of being an amateur hit. Someone was proving a point. You fuck with me, this is what happens. Do you see Goddard setting up a professional hit?"

"Maybe not." McAdams took off his jacket. It was warm in the car. "So what do you think about Goddard?"

"Instinctively, I don't like the man, but that doesn't mean he's a killer."

"I saw some Tiffany pieces from the grapevine collection, but those aren't major Tiffany. So are we back to thinking that Maxwell Stewart is the bad guy?"

"I don't see that, either." A pause. "I keep coming back to the Petroshkovich icons."

"Why? That happened ages ago."

"Because Latham was butchered and his field was Soviet art. Plus, he had this weird codebook in educated languages, which sounds international—and I like Russian mobsters as bad guys."

"Russian *mobsters*?" McAdams made a face. "How'd you get from stolen Tiffany to Russian mobsters?"

"Well . . ." Decker bit his lip. "With the codebook, I think Latham had been doing something illegal for a while. I think he was the intended target."

"Agreed."

"I think Latham had underground illegal contacts for

stolen art mostly in his field of expertise, which was Soviet art. And since he did have dirty contacts, maybe he fenced lesser stuff on his own to make a quick buck. Things like stolen books and antique prints. Things like Tiffany panels that he found out about from Angeline Moreau."

"Okay. So why was she murdered? And so brutally!"

"She put up a struggle, she was hit, but she was probably strangled and maybe stabbed. But wasn't *dissected*. Latham was. He was the main target. He bore the brunt of someone's uncontrolled anger. I think she was killed because of her association with Latham. Someone was nervous that she knew too much, that Latham had told her too much."

"She was murdered first, Decker."

"Yeah, you're right. You'd think Latham would be first on the list." He thought a moment. "Angeline was murdered Sunday night . . . right after we met with Sobel and Stewart at the crypt, right?"

"Well, not right after . . . but soon after, yes."

"Suppose the killer saw us investigating the break-in . . . or at least got word that we were investigating the break-in. He comes up to Greenbury, murders Angeline, then works his way up the coast."

"If you're saying he's working his way *up* the coast, are you assuming he's from somewhere south of here?"

"Good point. Maybe we should go back to New York."

"Sure. Whatever you think, boss."

Decker was quiet. "We do know that both of their places were ransacked. The killer was looking for something."

McAdams held up the codebook.

"Exactly," Decker said. "We need to get it translated. If Gold doesn't call back soon, we'll try someone else."

McAdams nodded. "This is the thing I'm confused about.

279

The Petroshkovich icons happened decades ago. Why would that theft suddenly result in murder?"

"Okay. Let me throw this out. Suppose through his studies in Soviet art, Latham found out who is in possession of the Petroshkovich icons. Suppose it was someone in Russia who was very rich—like an oligarch."

"Okay."

"Suppose Latham made contact with the guy who has the Petroshkovich icons and presented him with another opportunity to buy something of value that might not have been obtained through regular channels. Suppose an agreement was reached. But then suppose his 'client' found out that Latham had hired someone else to do his illegal work. Plus, the client found out that Latham was involved romantically with his hired help. You know . . . pillow talk. Maybe the client got nervous that too many people were involved on this buying opportunity."

"So why didn't the 'client' just back out?"

"Because Latham knew the client had the stolen Petroshkovich icons in his possession. So he had both of them killed."

McAdams shrugged. "Over some thirty-year-old stolen icons?"

"Okay." Decker nodded. "Maybe you have a point. So let's go back to motive, Tyler. What's worth killing over? And think Russian."

"The twenty-seven cartons that supposedly contain the original Amber Room."

"Could be."

"Uh, I wasn't serious." When Decker didn't answer, Tyler made a face. "I think the Amber Room might be a little bit hard to fence."

"Maybe not for Jason Merritt with his extensive client

list who, by the way, mentioned that the Amber Room was worth killing over."

"After we pushed him to say something. It didn't flow trippingly off his tongue."

After a pause, Decker said, "No, I don't think it's the Amber Room, maybe not the entire Amber Room. Maybe it's a couple of cartons that suddenly showed up. I was looking it up last night. Every so often some German claims to have original pieces."

"How would they know if the pieces were original or not? Amber is a fossil. It's impossible to date."

"I did not know that," Decker said. "Yeah, it does sound a little cloak and dagger. But we do know that Merritt has contacts in that region. He and his family have been involved there for decades. I keep thinking that we're looking for something priceless and unique to Russia that was looted by Merritt's grandfather."

"So you like Jason Merritt as a bad guy?"

"Maybe."

"I don't like him as the bad guy. He was too transparent with his family history."

"Maybe he wanted us to hear the rumors from him rather than someone else like Chase Goddard, who wasn't as gossipy about Jason Merritt as I would have expected."

"And Jason Merritt didn't tell us much about Chase Goddard, either."

Decker said, "But both implied that the other was crooked."

"Maybe they're in it together."

"I am completely open-minded at this point."

"We should probably just wait for the codebook before we draw any conclusions."

"I'm not one to wait around. If we assume that Latham was an opportunist and was peddling stuff on the side, he needed a quick source of valuable things. Tomorrow I want you back at the libraries in the colleges and continue looking through antiquarian atlases, print books, and missing rare books."

"And while I'm sitting at a carrel ruining my eyes, what will you be doing?"

"Rereading the files on the Petroshkovich thefts from Allan Sugar and going down the list of art galleries," Decker said. "I know I'm missing something." He thought a moment. "We should drop the codebook off at the station. But the security there isn't very good. I have a gun safe at home."

"I have a safe also. It's a combination lock. My father's birthday."

"Probably be better if you kept it," Decker said. "If anyone comes poking around, he'll come to me before you."

His eyes shot open and his heart started thumping in his chest.

The one thing that Decker appreciated about Greenbury was the quiet at night. It was possible to hear anything out of the ordinary. Next to him, Rina was sleeping soundly. Gently, he shook her shoulder and when she aroused, he put his finger to her lips. Her eyes widened and she brought her hand to her mouth.

Decker whispered, "Get under the bed."

Rina knew better than to question. Silently, she slipped out of bed and slid under the bed frame. Once she was taken care of, Decker crept to the walk-in closet and the gun safe. Within moments, he had his loaded Beretta ready for action. He dropped down and showed Rina the gun. She nodded.

Then the two of them waited. By now, they could both

hear the rustling sounds of someone going through their stuff in the living room.

Decker had a decision to make. Should he confront the burglar or should he wait until it was over? With Rina in the house, the decision was made for him. If there was more than one bad guy, he'd be putting her at risk by leaving her alone. No sense doing that unless it was absolutely necessary.

If it were punks, they probably wouldn't come into the bedroom. They'd swipe the electronics and Rina's purse and call it a day.

Decker's mind kept racing, tumbling thoughts and scenarios.

How did kids get into the house? He didn't have an alarm, but Greenbury was safe: often neighbors didn't even bother locking their doors. But even with that, he was a stickler. All the doors had deadbolts. All the windows were double paned and locked solid.

It had to be professionals.

The sounds grew louder—and closer.

Professionals.

Silently, Decker got up from the floor. With a few deft strokes, he made the bed, stuffing pillows under the duvet to make it look like people were still asleep. Then he crouched down next to Rina, his eyes just above the mattress and locked onto the doorway.

And then he waited.

And waited.

And waited.

The doorknob slowly turned.

Crunch time.

He'd been there before. His heart rate suddenly slowed as his brain cleared with the single thought of survival. Within a second, all his life experiences were cataloged as he pulled out the needed index card to continue on in the world.

The door opened and a dark shadow came inside. It raised an arm straight out, the gun pointing toward the bed. Decker shouted, "Police! Freeze!"

In slow motion, Decker saw the flash of his own gun at the same time the shadow pivoted toward his direction. As soon as the bullet hit, the figure stumbled. But he managed to remain upright, gun in hand, and took off, grabbing his shoulder and dripping blood while he fled.

If Decker had been alone, he would have given him chase. But he dared not leave Rina in case there was more than one bad guy. She suddenly emerged from her prone position under the bed. Decker barked at her. "Get down!"

"Oh my God! Are you *okay*?"

"I'm fine. Stay down, Rina." Decker heard a car screech down the street. His heart was now beating at allegro tempo. He flicked on the lights, grabbed his landline phone on his nightstand, and then realized the connection had been cut. Stupidly, he kept his cell plugged into an outlet in the kitchen. "Where's your cell?"

"In the closet. What's going on?"

Decker didn't answer. He grabbed her cell and called 911. He started to relate the information to the emergency operator when he heard Rina's voice say, "Peter, what about *Tyler*?"

"Oh *shit*!" He spoke into the phone. "I need patrol cars sent immediately to . . . what the *fuck* is his address?" Decker was pacing now as he spoke. "Send out cars to Detective Tyler McAdams's house immediately. It's on Hamilton Drive . . . no, I don't know the address! If I knew it, I'd give it to you!" He grabbed Rina while talking in the phone. "Just send someone out there *now*!"

Decker clutched the phone in his right hand while

pulling Rina with his left. Running through his living room, he found Rina's car keys, grabbed them, and sprinted out the front door.

"I know his house," he said to her. "It's quicker this way." They jumped into Rina's Volvo, which mercifully started right away. He put on his seat belt, gunned the engine, and then jammed the gear into reverse. He peeled out of the driveway and skidded down the street.

"Be careful, for God's sake!" Rina snapped on her seat belt. "No sense getting us both killed."

Decker wasn't listening. He tore down the street. "Keep your head down." He pushed her head. "Down, dammit!"

"It's down, it's down!"

No moon out. Just a black sky except for the sporadic streetlamp.

There was also no traffic.

Decker sped through the traffic stops as well as the traffic lights.

Rina was crouched down in the front seat. "Give me my phone. I'll call him. What's the number?"

He gave her the phone. "God, I can't think straight."

Then it came to him. Not only were Rina's hands shaking, her entire body was convulsing. It was adrenaline, it was the cold, and it was pure fear. Still, she managed to punch in the right digits.

"He's not answering."

It didn't matter much. They were already outside the house. No car outside. Decker gave Rina a crowbar and then cocked his gun. "C'mon."

They ran to his front door. He pulled her behind him and then started pounding on the wood. "Tyler?!" A pause. "Fuck it. Take my gun and cover me."

"Got it."

He took a three-step running start and shoved his

shoulder into the wood. The door splintered but didn't cave in or fall down. But the hole was enough for him to stick his hand in and undo the lock.

Rina gave him the gun as he opened the door and turned on the room light. "Tyler?" The living room was empty, but it had been tossed. He continued to scream the kid's name. "Are you there?"

No response.

"Stay behind me." As if to prove the point, he shoved her until she was hidden by his back. "I need to clear the rooms."

Again, he yelled out Tyler's name. In the ensuing silence, he heard a distant motor come to life. "Rina, call in a silver Hyundai Accent van. And no, I don't have the license number, but if it's in the area, I want it stopped."

"I'm on it."

Quickly, Decker went through the living room, the kitchen, and the bathroom: all empty. He went to the spare bedroom and by the time he hit the main bedroom, he could hear the distant sirens. He flipped on the lights. "Tyler! Are you here?" A pause. "Answer me, buddy."

They both heard the groan at the same time, but it was Rina who saw blood seeping out from the bullet-ridden closet door.

It was locked.

Again, Decker shoved it with his shoulder. It didn't budge. He took the crowbar and after three lumber jack swings, he managed to splinter the plywood. He unlocked the bolt, swung the door open, and pulled down the string to turn on the closet light.

The kid was crouched in the corner, his eyes wide open, his face covered in blood. Decker bent down, his eyes focused on the splatter on his temple. When he touched it, Tyler flinched.

A graze wound, thank God. Decker said, "Can you hear me?"

The kid didn't respond, either frozen with fear or something worse. He was clutching his arm. "Let me see what's going on, buddy."

Decker had to peel his hand away to see the damage. He was hit with a through and through: a small hole in the front with a bigger exit hole. It seemed to be a flesh wound but he couldn't tell for certain.

"Can you hear me?" He touched the kid's face and locked eyes with him. "Can you hear me, Tyler? Answer me, please!"

"I'm woozy . . ." he panted out.

"You can talk." To Rina, Decker shouted, "I hear the ambulance. Go direct them."

"Right away."

To Tyler, he said, "Can you move your fingers?"

He winced. "Yeah . . ."

"What about your toes? Can you wiggle your toes?"

Another grimace. "Yeah . . ." As if on autopilot, he tried to stand but immediately collapsed before he could get a knee off the ground. Blood was oozing out of his leg. His skin color was ashen. His forehead felt clammy.

"Tyler, you have to stay still. Real still. It'll slow down the bleeding." Decker ripped off Tyler's pajama bottoms and to survey the damage to the legs.

He'd been hit in the thigh. On the surface, the bone didn't look broken, but he had no way to assess the damage that the bullet made. A half foot higher and the kid would have had a lot more to worry about than a shattered femur.

Decker pulled a blanket off the closet shelf and covered Tyler to minimize the shock. He kept his voice low and soothing. "Can you feel pain?"

287

"Fuck yeah . . ."

"That's good. You'll be fine. Ambulance is already here."

The kid lifted the blanket to look at his groin.

Decker said, "Your dick is fine."

"Don't lie."

"I wouldn't, Harvard. You're totally intact."

Tears were streaming down the kid's cheek. "Not that it's getting much use."

Decker broke into nervous laughter. "You still have your wits."

"I'm really dizzy."

"Just hold on." Decker attempted a smile. "You must be the only person in the world who has a locked closet."

"I keep cash . . . the safe." He was breathing hard. "The notebook is there." Tears were blurring his vision. "I think I'm gonna pass out."

"You'll be fine, Tyler, I promise."

The paramedics came into the bedroom, followed by several uniformed officers. Decker stood up and pointed inside the closet. The EMTs carefully lifted Tyler onto the gurney and then went to work: an oxygen mask over his nose and mouth, an IV in his veins . . . dressing the wounds, trying to stanch the bleeding.

Tyler's eyes beseeched Decker's. Although the kid couldn't talk with the mask over his mouth, Decker knew what he was thinking.

"I'm not letting you out of my sight. I'm riding with you." He turned to Rina. "Have one of the officers drive you to the hospital."

"I have the car."

"Rina, you can't be alone!"

"Right. Of course. I'll meet you there."

Several minutes later, the kid was loaded in the ambulance. Decker sat on the bench as the paramedics continued to work on him. Decker took the kid's clammy hand and when he did, Tyler closed his wet eyes.

Thoughts jumbled inside Decker's brain.

Detectives are seldom whacked. But seldom isn't never.

For the first time ever, Decker wondered if he was truly over his head.

He had told the kid that he could walk away from the case. Maybe he should take his own warning. Going out with a whimper and long life were much better than going out with a bang.

His head was throbbing, his heart was pounding, and he was sweating profusely even though it was cold and, in his rush, he hadn't bothered with a jacket or coat. He continued holding Tyler's clammy hand, hoping that his own body heat would warm the kid up. With his free hand, Decker wiped tears from his eyes.

Bumblefuck, USA.

He had been bored with the job, had longed for the excitement he had left behind.

Now his overzealous wishes were coming back to bite him in the ass.

CHAPTER TWENTY-FOUR

The story became rote after repeated recitations. Decker was trashed in body and in mind. He sat on a hard plastic chair in the hospital, waiting to hear any news from the surgeon. Rina was next to him, curled up in a ball, dozing on and off. A half-dozen officers had been at the hospital when the ambulance had arrived. Mike had reassigned them to hunt down the Hyundai silver van after a reported sighting about four miles from Decker's house. The quiet streets of Greenbury now crawled with black-and-whites. Unfortunately the silver van remained illusive.

Mike Radar had stayed on at the hospital. "So you have the codebook on you?"

"It's in the kid's safe. The code is his father's birthday, which I don't know." Decker had already explained this all to the captain but Radar was talking from nerves. Every time there was a protracted silence, the captain asked another question. Decker checked his watch against the wall clock. Both timepieces said 4:45. It was Tuesday morning. "Even if it had been stolen from his safe, it wouldn't have mattered. Summer Village has the original."

"Maybe the thief wanted to see what was inside?"

"Yeah, of course. Did you get hold of Mulrooney?"

"About twenty minutes ago. I told him what happened and he thanked me. Don't think he'll be falling back asleep. He has the original codebook under lock and key." Radar was still pacing, bleeding off adrenaline. "No news on the silver van, dammit. How could such a conspicuous car just vanish?"

"We'll find it," Decker said.

"That's just wishful thinking." When Decker didn't answer, Mike said, "How did this *happen*? This is Greenbury, for God's sake."

"Bumblefuck, USA," Decker said.

"Excuse me?"

"It's what kids say when they're talking about a place that no one has ever heard of. They call it Bumblefuck. McAdams asked the same question: How was this happening? I told him he should walk away from the case." A sigh. "Actually told him he could walk away if he wanted to. And he didn't want to. But it doesn't matter now. We're both in too deep."

Rina inhaled and woke up with a start. She stretched. "Anything?"

"He's still in surgery."

"What time is it?"

"Almost five."

"So he's been in for two hours."

"Yes."

"That's not so long when you consider he was hit twice. Actually three times including the graze wound on his temple."

"I still think you should call his parents," Radar said.

"He specifically told me not to call them as they were wheeling him in," Decker said.

292

"What if something happens?"

"Mike, he's twenty-six, he's an adult, and he's not going to die."

"You never know."

Decker gave him an angry glance. "He's not going to die. He ordered me not to call his parents. The least I could do is honor his wishes."

"The mayor won't like it when he finds out."

"So let the mayor call them."

Rina patted his knee in an effort to calm him down. It didn't work. Decker got up, paced a few steps, and then he gently hit the wall several times. "If I'm going to get whacked in the line of duty, I'd at least like to know why!"

Rina said, "I'm sure you'll know a lot more once the codebook is squared away."

"Who's this guy that McAdams called?" Radar asked.

"Mordechai Gold. He's a professor in the math department at Harvard."

"How do we know he's trustworthy?"

"If you or Mulrooney have a better person, make the call."

"I still think you should call his parents."

"Mike, we're going around in circles."

The captain scratched his head. Then he sat down. "The silver van, Decker. You first noticed it when you left Summer Village PD?"

The same questions over and over and *over*. Decker said, "I noticed it tailing me after I left Summer Village PD. After I got on the highway, it pulled back then I lost sight of it. Second time I noticed it was when Tyler and I grabbed a cup of coffee while we poked around the galleries on Newbury. When I heard a motor being gunned, I figured that maybe it's the van. But I don't know. I'm probably full of shit."

"I doubt that." Radar was still pacing. "If you first noticed the van in Summer Village, the main focus has to be Latham's murder, not Angeline Moreau's death."

"I agree."

"So . . ." Radar smacked his lips. "I think the time has come to let the pros handle it."

"Excuse me?" Decker said.

"Not that you're not a pro, Peter. But I think it's in all our best interests to let Summer Village and Boston handle the investigation. They're bigger, they're more equipped, and they have more manpower."

"Mike, some son of a bitch broke into my house and would have shot me dead if I hadn't gotten to him first. Someone thinks that I know way more than I do. They're not going to stop until either they're stopped or I'm dead."

Radar made a face. "Then maybe you and your wife should take a vacation."

"Mike, I'm a cop, for God's sake. I'm not going to run away. They'd just track me down." He turned to Rina. "You, on the other hand—"

"Oh, no you don't!"

"I can't babysit the kid, babysit you, and do my job."

"Peter, since we've moved here, I've gone to the shooting range every time you've gone. I'm an excellent shot. And, FYI, I don't need your babysitting."

"Darlin', maybe you should visit your parents. Your father is ninety-five."

"Don't you play the parent card on me."

"Do you know the temperature in L.A. yesterday? A sunny, seventy-two degrees."

"Well, bully for L.A. And someone has to keep an eye out for Tyler, because—like you said—if you're watching him, you can't do your job."

"There's no job for him to do," Radar said. "I'm giving

294

the case to Boston. Let them coordinate with Summer Village—"

"No, no, no," Decker said. "That's not going to happen—"

"You said you'd tell me if it was too much for you to handle."

"I didn't say it was too much to handle. I've been a detective for almost thirty years. I've been in combat. I can handle this. Let me just see this out."

"Not on my watch."

"That's bullshit!"

"Don't swear at me."

Rina cleared her throat. The men turned in her direction. "Uh, as much as I hate to agree with my husband, I think he's right, Mike. Pulling him off isn't going to take the heat away from him. If anything, it'll make it look like Peter really knows something and that you're trying to protect him." Silence. "And from a personal point of view, I might also add that you will never find a detective as good as Peter is."

"Thank you," Decker said. "Thank you very much."

"You're welcome."

Decker looked at Radar. "Well?"

"What about Tyler?" Radar said.

"We can send him back to New York."

Rina said, "These guys are pro. Tyler's way more vulnerable in an anonymous city than he is in Greenbury. It's easier to take care of him here because anything unusual will stick out."

Mike said, "I'll put an officer on him."

"Agreed," Decker said. "But I still want Rina out of here." He looked at his wife. "You need to go to L.A."

"Peter, I'm not involving my parents in this mess."

"I'll put an officer on her, too," Radar said.

Rina said, "Have Tyler move in with us. That way you

only need one officer and I can shoot a gun should the occasion call for it."

"You can't be serious," Decker said.

"It's actually not a bad idea, Pete. It'll be a lot easier to guard one house than two. And it'll be easier to rotate people because we'll have more manpower."

"So it's settled," Rina said. "Tyler will move in, Mike will put a guard on the house, and Peter is still on the case."

Radar said, "I don't want you going at this alone."

Decker said, "If I could team up with an old colleague from L.A., I'd agree with you. But it takes a long time to get a trust and a rhythm between two people. I'm better going solo."

"No, no, no, no," Rina said. "You are not doing this alone."

"Last night, if I hadn't been so worried about Rina or Tyler, I could have chased down the perp. I'm not training someone new."

"Speaking of which, Marge called."

"When?"

"Last night. I forgot to tell you."

"Great."

"I can't think of everything!"

Decker said, "Sorry."

"Who's Marge?" Radar asked.

"An old colleague from L.A."

Radar made a face. "So now you're outsourcing?"

Decker felt sheepish. "We worked together for years. We keep in touch."

"Decker, if she called you *back*, you must have asked her to do something."

"He's got you there," Rina said.

"Whose side are you on?"

"Flexible."

Radar said, "What did you ask her to do?"

"Look up Chase Goddard and see if he's done anything arrest worthy in his past. Her police department has bigger databases than ours."

"Well, as long as the cat's out of the bag, she told me to tell you that she didn't find anything on him. She's going to try to see if the LAPD database might have something."

"Chase Goddard," Radar said. "The gallery man you visited yesterday afternoon when you saw the silver van."

"Yep."

"I'll see what I can find out about him from Boston," Radar said.

"Thank you." No one talked for a moment. Then Decker said, "So it's settled?"

"You are not working solo, Peter," Rina said. "I'm in your corner but you have to be reasonable."

"I agree," Radar said. "You're a target. You can't handle this alone."

"I'm not going to involve anyone on the force, Mike. Not with this bull's-eye on my head."

"For God's sake, Decker, we're all cops! We know what we signed up for. I am the captain of Greenbury PD and I'm calling up Ben Roiters. You cannot work alone."

"Then I'd rather you pull me off the case than involve Ben," Decker said.

"Peter, why don't you call Scott?" Rina said.

"Am I senile or wasn't he just shot a year ago."

"Who's Scott?" Radar asked.

"Peter, every time you talk to him, he complains how bored he is with retirement."

"That doesn't mean he wants to start working again."

"Who's Scott?"

"Why don't you ask him? What harm would it do?"

"Who the fuck is Scott?" Radar asked.

"Scott Oliver," Rina said. "He and Marge Dunn were partners."

"The woman you're using to outsource," Radar said.

"Old relationships die hard, Captain," Rina said. "Marge is currently working as a detective but Scott had retired. He's not married, he doesn't have any hobbies, and he's going out of his mind with boredom. When he isn't yakking to Marge about how tedious life is, he's calling Peter. The main thing is he's a great detective."

"He's old," Decker said.

"He's the same age as you are."

Radar said, "He's good?"

"Great," Decker admitted. "Very experienced."

"And he's cool under pressure. You've always told me that he's the one guy you'd want in a hot situation." Rina turned to Radar. "What do you think?"

"It's a possibility. I'll need to interview him."

Rina said. "At least *call* him, Peter. If he doesn't want to do it, he'll say no."

"He won't say no. He'd do it for me. I know that because I'd do it for him."

"He'd do it for the joy of feeling alive again . . . like someone else I know."

At that moment, a doctor in green scrubs came out to the group. Decker, Rina, and Radar stopped talking and looked anxiously at the man who introduced himself as Doctor Alex Harrow.

"He's out. And he's a very, very lucky man. A few millimeters more and the bullet would have hit the femoral artery."

"Thank God," Rina said. "He's going to be all right, then."

"After a fashion. He's still got some recovering to do. The bullet in his leg did knock some bone. It's cracked—a little bigger than a hairline fracture, but the bone didn't break apart. The orthopedic surgeon thinks there's enough bone to regenerate what the bullet nicked away. If not, he may need a bone graft. It's too early to tell."

"I take it he won't be able to walk," Radar said.

"He'll be in a leg cast for six weeks. He'll need a wheelchair. When he gets his strength back in his arm, he can probably manage with crutches."

"Can we talk to him?" Radar asked.

"In a couple of hours. He's still in recovery." The surgeon looked around. "Any wife or parents?"

"No wife," Decker said. "He didn't want me to call his parents."

"Yeah, he probably didn't want to worry them. But it might be a good idea to call them now that he's out."

"Thank you and of course, you're right." Radar waited until the surgeon left and then he eyed Decker. "Call them."

"Mike, he doesn't want them here."

"This isn't a request, it's an order."

"He told me—and I quote—'I fucking hate my parents. Don't call them.'"

"He was delirious. They have to be notified, Decker."

"He's a grown man."

"I'm not going to argue about this. I said it's an order."

"Fine. I'll call them."

"Good." He exhaled forcefully. "I'm going back to the station house. I'm going to bring everyone up to speed with what I know—and they're going to bring me up to speed with what I don't know. We'll get a murder board going because it's clear this isn't going to be a simple solve. Then, after that, I'm going to work out a watch rotation for your house. I don't want your lovely wife to feel endangered."

"I appreciate that, Captain," Rina said.

"And I'll be damned before I'll be the first captain in this quaint city to lose a man in the line of duty. I have my pride. And I do care about all of you."

"I feel the love, Mike."

"Don't get mouthy on me, Decker."

"Just trying to add a little levity."

"I suppose I should find out about this codebook. I'll call Summer Village."

"If I'm still on the case, let me do that."

"Fine, make the call while you're waiting for Tyler's parents to arrive. You're not going anywhere until you talk to them, understood?"

"Done."

"And while you're on the phone, I suppose you can call your buddy when it's a decent hour in L.A. Let me know what he says. If he wants to come out, I'll talk to him but no promises. I not only have to approve him, I'm going to have to figure out how to pull money out of my butt to get him hired on as a consultant."

"I understand."

"Let me know when Tyler wakes up. I want to be there when he tells his story." Radar licked his lips. "He didn't tell you anything about what went down?"

"He heard someone. He locked himself in the closet. That's all I know."

"I want the full story from him. You call me right away. And also call me when the parents arrive. I don't care what time it is. I want to talk to them personally."

"That's good because I'm sure they'll want to talk to you," Decker said. "Judging from the way Tyler talks about them, I don't think they usually deal with underlings."

300

CHAPTER TWENTY-FIVE

After Decker spent a half hour, meticulously explaining everything, the kid's sole comment was, "So I'm being replaced."

"No . . . no, not at all." Decker rubbed his eyes. "You're still actively involved. But because of the obvious circumstances, you can't do the legwork. If you want to heal properly, you can't be running around."

"I wouldn't be running around. I'd be in a car. I can put on a seat belt."

"As my kids would say, I'm not having this conversation." Decker had to be blunt. "McAdams, if someone starts shooting at the car, you're a sitting duck because you're immobile. We have to keep you protected—"

"I don't *want* protection." A pause. "Well, I do. But I don't want to be sitting on my ass while you get all the glory."

"The glory is all yours, McAdams."

"*I* figured out the codebook."

"Absolutely—"

"I still have a working brain—"

"And I intend to use it. Summer Village is giving the

301

codebook to Mordechai Gold. When he has something, I'll go up there—"

"With your new partner."

Decker treaded gingerly. "He's not my new partner, Tyler. You are my partner. But Radar will pull me off the case unless I have someone to ride with me."

"So use someone else from Greenbury."

"The dees in the town are already stretched. They're hunting down the van, they're canvassing the area, they're calling hospitals left and right because I nicked the guy at my house. They're also knee deep in forensics combing through *two* houses. That's one of the reasons why I wanted to bring in a third party."

"Your cop buddy."

"Tyler, he's a great cop and we work well together." Decker knew his words were a mistake. He tried to back-track. "He's bored. I'm doing him a favor."

"Fuck it, Old Man. I don't give a shit." The kid sunk back in his hospital bed. "I'm tired. Leave me alone."

"I called your parents."

"So you not only dumped me, you're now a traitor. Get the fuck out of here."

"Just shut up and listen. I had to call your parents. If I didn't do it, Radar would have called them. So I did it. You should be giving me sympathy, not sass."

"You and my father deserve each other."

"You're moving into my house by the way. That way the cops here only have to guard one location."

"I don't need a guard."

"Don't be stupid. Of course you need protection and so does Rina. She was there when Mr. Shadow tried to take us both out. Mike's putting a twenty-four-hour guard on the house and on the two of you. So whether you like it or not, you're involved up to your neck."

McAdams clenched his jaw. "You're actually moving me into your house?"

"Rina's idea not mine."

"Figures." A pause. "Where's the new guy staying?"

"Oliver? If Radar approves, he'll stay with us as well. It's a three-bedroom house. He's no threat to you, Tyler. He's an old guy just like me."

The kid was still sulking. "When you talk to Gold, I want to be there. It was my idea to call him."

"You cannot be there in person, McAdams, but we'll Skype you in. You'll have the codebook in front of you and you can ask as many questions as you want."

"How long is this interloper going to be here?"

"Until we get a solve. It won't be permanent."

"I can't believe you called my parents against my wishes."

"We're crossing the same road, Harvard."

He blew out air. "Are they coming in?"

"Of course, they're coming in. They were very concerned."

"Right. Let me guess. My father started screaming—his default way of communicating. First, he started swearing at me, calling me an incompetent moron, and then he probably turned his wrath on you, saying that you were also an incompetent moron and everything that happened was your fault." When Decker didn't answer, the kid said, "How am I doing?"

"He called me an idiot not a moron."

The kid managed a smile. "My mother probably listened for a moment, and then she put you through to her secretary for the details."

"You know the first thing out of their mouths?" Decker said. "They asked me if you were okay."

"Yeah, yeah."

"They care, Tyler." Decker stood up. "I have to call Radar. He wants to come down here when you make your statement."

"I already told you everything."

"I was supposed to call him when you woke up and started talking. But I didn't. If you could, pretend that you just woke up and you're telling your story to both of us for the first time."

"You wanted to hear everything from me first."

"Yes."

"So you're asking me to lie to protect your ass."

"It would be nice."

"What's Mike doing now?"

"He's directing forensics. You were shot with a .32-caliber bullet, probably a revolver because so far CID didn't find any casings. Too bad the asshole didn't drop the murder weapon when I shot him."

"Maybe he picked the casings up."

"I think I surprised him when Rina and I crashed through your door. He wouldn't have had time to pick it up. But we did find two stray bullets in the closet."

"Any prints?"

"I don't know." Decker waited a few seconds. "How do you feel, Harvard?"

"Like a truck ran over me."

"Do you want me to call in a nurse for more pain medication?"

"No." He shook his head. "No."

"You're sure?"

"I'm sure. I fucking hurt. But it's good to feel something real for a change."

The shooting had brought the mayor down to the hospital. Logan Brettly was in his fifties, average height with a barrel chest and curly white hair. He came into Tyler's room just in time to intercept Jack McAdams's wrath, which had been previously bestowed on Decker, Mike Radar, and of course, his son. Tyler had listened wordlessly as his father heaped insults without pause. The senior McAdams was a tall, good-looking man in his fifties: dark curly hair, big chin, flashing blue eyes, and a foul mouth. He ranted endlessly about being surrounded by idiots, morons, and cretins. Then came the inevitable mention of lawsuits.

"Dad, I'm not suing anyone." Somehow, Tyler had managed to interrupt his diatribe. "And even if I wanted to—and I don't—I have no case."

"Oh, shut up. If you would have gone to law school, you wouldn't be in this mess right now." The senior McAdams turned his fury on the mayor. "Logan, you assured me that this job was a cakewalk, a mere formality so the kid can pass a couple of years doing something other than jerking off. What the hell was that all about?"

"Jack, nothing like this has happened in this town in years. I know you're upset—"

"Of course, I'm fucking upset. I'm pissed off!" He pointed to the bed. "Look at him!"

The nurse walked in. "Sir, this is causing quite a ruckus."

"Get out of here!" Jack snapped.

The nurse turned wide-eyed. The mayor nodded and she turned tail and ran. The room fell silent, but not for long. Big McAdams launched another tirade. Decker had enough. He didn't mind having his ass reamed, but the man's berating wasn't doing Tyler any good. "Your kid is lying in a hospital bed, having been shot by God only knows who. Can you dial it back, please?"

Jack turned on him. "I damn well know what happened. And let me tell you something. You'd better have good representation right now, Old Man. I hold you responsible for sending my son out in the line of fire."

Decker said, "I will take full responsibility—"

"You'd better pray that your pension is untouchable because after I'm done with you, you'll be lucky to get a job as a guard at an old age home, which is where you belong."

"Dad, enough!" Tyler got out.

"Shut up!"

"I'm serious, Dad. That's enough!"

"Fucking moron!"

"We're all idiots and morons: I get it!" Tyler blew out air. "Can you cap it for a second so I can catch my breath?"

No one spoke.

Tyler said, "Dad, I'll be in Boston by August, ready to join the ranks of all the fine minds of law who came before me. So it's all good, okay?"

For the first time, the senior McAdams had managed to lower his voice. "I've heard that before."

"I'm serious."

McAdams weighed the kid's words. "You're finally going to do it?"

"I never said I wasn't. I just wasn't ready to do it right after graduation."

"You've been stalling to spite me. And now look at you!"

"If I had a crystal ball to see into the future, I might have reconsidered. But I didn't, so it is what it is. Can we move on?"

"We would have been all set up by now—"

"That's not moving on, Dad."

Jack McAdams looked at his watch. "I have to be back in New York. I have an eight A.M. breakfast meeting tomorrow."

"I'm sure I speak for everyone when I say you can leave."

"I don't want you left alone, Tyler. I know you think I'm an asshole but I really do care about your safety."

"At least until I enter law school."

"Stop it."

"Go, Dad. Just . . . go."

"I'll be with him," Decker said.

"How reassuring!"

Tyler said, "Dad, he saved my life. You might try a thank you."

"He put you in jeopardy in the first place."

"He didn't put me in danger, *I* put me in danger. I took the job, which means I should have learned to use a firearm a long time ago. I fucked up. So if you're going to sue anyone, sue me. And you know my assets better than anyone. You could walk away with a bundle."

"Stop it, Tyler. Just . . . shut up!" Then Jack said, "When's your mother arriving?"

"Tomorrow. I told her I was okay and after very little convincing, she took my word at face value." A pause. "I didn't want you two here at the same time."

"That was smart."

"Can you please leave? We've got it all figured out."

"Who's we?"

"Detective Decker and me. I'm moving into his house—"

"Are you out of your mind?" The senior McAdams was pacing again. "You're coming back to New York just as soon as you're discharged."

"No, I'm not. I'm staying here until I know what's going on. I don't want anyone else getting hurt, including you believe it or not."

"Don't be an idiot!"

"Do you want me in law school, yes or no?"

"Tyler—"

"Let me handle this, Dad. Let me do it my way—"

"I've seen what happens when you do it your way."

"Move . . . on!" Tyler snapped. "You are incredibly impossible. Is it any wonder that I defy you all the time? If you shut up right now, I promise I'll make the plunge."

"You know how *important* that is."

"I know but ultimately, I hold the cards. So don't piss me off and we'll both be happy. Now could you kindly go so I can get a little rest?"

The senior McAdams looked at his watch. "I'll be back in an hour."

"Just go home."

"I don't want to go home. I want to come back in an hour. Any objections?"

"Would it do any good if I did object?"

"None whatsoever."

"Fine. I'll see you in an hour."

Jack turned to the mayor. "I'm hungry."

"I'll take you out, Jack."

"You damn well better take me out, Logan, if you know what's good for you."

Decker could hear Jack's voice even after the two of them were down the corridor. He tried out a smile. Mike Radar didn't even bother to fake it. "I think I'm going to go make myself useful. I'd rather deal with just about anything than take abuse like that."

"I apologize," Tyler said.

"No, I owe you an apology," Radar said. "You didn't want me to call them and I did it anyway. My mistake."

"Exactly how much money does he give to the town?"

"Enough to make the mayor keep his mouth shut while he berates public servants."

"Again, I apologize."

"How are you feeling, Tyler?"

A forced smile. "Once he leaves, I'll be a lot better."

To Decker, Radar said, "So you'll stick around?"

"Yes. I have a little thinking to do and I could use Tyler's brain. Let's meet up at the station house at around six in the evening. I'm going to bring Rina with me. I don't want to leave her alone at night right now even with a cop outside our door."

"That sounds fine."

"Who's outside my house?"

"Wickel until six. Then I have O'Brien from six to twelve. I'll keep him there even if no one's home. Kramer's taking the graveyard shift."

"Thanks. At some point, I'm going to need to sleep."

"It's not a problem. We've got a post outside the hospital room so you can leave whenever you need to." To Tyler, Radar said, "Heal up, son. That's your sole job."

After he left, Decker blew out air. "You should probably get some sleep."

"I'm too pissed to be tired. I was just starting to feel like I'm doing something positive and then . . ." He threw up his hands. "It's like . . . why bother?"

Decker was about to give a pep talk, but changed his mind. He switched gears. "Why is he so keen on your going to law school?"

"Following in the old man's way."

"There's more to it than that."

"Yes, there is." Silence. "I suppose I owe it to you to tell you what's going on."

"You don't owe me anything."

"That's not true. Let me ask you this, Decker. That night . . . how long did it take you to realize that I might be in trouble?"

"I didn't." Decker felt sheepish. "Rina realized it moments after I made the 911 call."

McAdams laughed. "Well, you're honest."

"I almost broke my shoulder for you if that counts."

"Maybe a teensy bit. Remind me to send your wife a dozen roses." The kid tried to shift his position, but his leg was in traction.

"You need help?" Decker asked.

"No, I'm okay." Tyler said, "My father's right about one thing. I have been putzing around just to spite him." He grimaced. "We both can't fully inherit until I finish Harvard Law. Neither can Harvard Law. My grandfather left a shitload of money to them with the proviso that they take me and I graduate. Needless to say I could sit on my ass drooling for three years and I'd still matriculate. To prevent that, Grandpa stipulated that I have to pass three bars—New York, California, and Massachusetts. So I do actually have to learn something. We get a chunk when I enroll, another chunk when I graduate, and the final chunk when I pass all the bars. And until I do, both Dad and I are on a generous but fixed income. I don't care. But he does."

Decker raised his eyebrows. "Wow."

"Yeah, wow."

"Are you under a time pressure to accomplish all this?"

"I have until thirty to enter school. Then I have another ten years to pass all the bars. It's not a problem. I've always been an excellent test taker. I'm not worried about passing or anything. I'm just procrastinating."

"Why?"

"I don't know. Of course, I'm going to go. I'm not self-destructive. I can't figure out what I'm waiting for other than spite and even that's worn off."

"I suppose you'll do it when you're ready."

"You know if I die, Dad gets his share, the school's share, and my share, so I guess it's to his credit that he hasn't bumped me off."

"Tyler—"

"We should find out if he's rented out any silver Hyundai vans." The kid shook his head. "I'll go this August." He looked lost in thought. "The department will be happy to get rid of me. I know I've been a pain in the ass."

Decker didn't deny it. But he didn't confirm it either. "Tyler, if your father's inheritance depends on you, why do you let him talk to you that way?"

The kid shrugged. "It's unseemly to bring it up every time I have it out with my father—which is all the time. It's dirty fighting."

"Good for you. You're a better man than I."

"I suppose deep down I'm hoping for some kind of relationship after I've come through with the goods." He looked upward. "Of course, he may blow me off anyway. I'm prepared for that. But I don't want to give him ammunition. Can you change the subject?"

"How are you feeling?" Decker asked.

"I have a several tubes in my arm, a tube up my dick, I'm nauseated, and I can't move. I hurt almost everywhere and the few places I don't hurt, I'm plain sore. But other than that, I'm perfect." He forced a smile. "I believe it was you who said no whining? Something about no one wants to hear me bitch?"

Decker changed the subject. "I have an assignment for you if you want it."

"Thanks for the sympathy." The kid looked up. "What?"

"Are you able to use your iPad?"

"Yeah, of course. First of all, I'm right-handed and I got hit on the left side. Second, both my hands are fine. What do you need?"

"Once you're out of here, I still want you looking through the libraries for pilfered items."

"Why? The case is obviously beyond a stolen book or a few stolen antique maps."

"If Moreau and Latham were improvising with their own petty thefts, they had to fence their wares somewhere. We both saw the books and the maps in Goddard's gallery. Not unusual for him to have things like that, but if we could find him holding stolen goods, we'd at least have a connection."

"I would think he'd want to chuck anything that would tie him to them."

"When it comes to chucking valuable things, people are funny. That's why we find things like bloody clothes, bloody shoes, and murder weapons. Not to mention photographs and texts and phone numbers in cells. People don't cover their tracks that well. And even when they do, they slip up. We need to check as many angles as we can think of. Are you in or out?"

"I'm in." A beat. "Only because you're still using the pronoun 'we.'"

"Of course it's a 'we.'"

The kid gave a genuine smile. "I'm up to it."

"I'd also like Rina to come sit with you. I'll have an armed cop watch both of you. And she can help. She also knows how to shoot." A pause. "You'll all have to go together to the restroom."

"She's already seen me with a catheter. I'm beyond embarrassment. I'll gladly do whatever you need. You might as well exploit me while you can."

Decker patted the kid's arm, and then he slumped in his chair. "We both could use some rest."

"Go home."

"Not a chance."

"I could probably get a cot in the room if you want."

"Don't bother." Decker took off his shoes and put his

312

feet up on the end of the hospital bed. "I'll just doze in the chair."

"As soon as I'm up and about, I want to learn how to shoot a gun."

"You don't have to wait. I can take you to the range while you're still in a wheelchair. We all could use a little brushing up."

"Does the 'we' include your buddy?"

"I'm sure he hasn't been to the range since he retired. So, yes, it probably does include Oliver."

"Oliver is the last name, right?"

"Yes. His name is Scott Oliver." Decker closed his eyes. Within a minute, he started drifting off until Tyler's voice woke him up.

"What's he like? Oliver."

"He's got a wicked sense of humor and dresses like a dandy." Decker yawned. "He loves good clothes. It's his weakness. He's always looking for sales and outlets."

"The *GQ* cop."

"The *GQ* cop with a cop's IQ. You two have a lot in common."

"Like what? I don't care about clothes."

"No, not the threads." Decker stretched out. "You've both got the fire." He closed his tired eyes. "You both want to feel useful again."

CHAPTER TWENTY-SIX

Retirement hadn't treated Scott Oliver kindly. He had gone soft around the middle and walked stoop-shouldered with a drawn face. His once dark hair was almost white. It dawned on Rina that he'd probably been rinsing it for a while. Even his clothes reflected a defeatist attitude—all function with little flair that once was his trademark. The only glimmer of the former detective was the twinkle in his brown eyes when he presented Rina with a gift pack of three expensive kosher wines.

"Might be hard getting these out in the boonies."

"How thoughtful of you, Scott." Rina gave him a peck on the cheek. "No trouble finding the place?"

"I may be fading but I still know how to read a GPS." He set down his suitcase and took off his hat, his scarf, his gloves, and his jacket. "Where's Deck? Working on a Sunday? Like I need to ask."

"He's making up for the days he lost tending to Tyler in the hospital."

"Makes total sense. Deck did it right, you know. Getting a change of scenery but refusing to pack it in."

"The move has its pluses but a few minuses . . . starting

315

with the temperature outside." She pointed to his jacket and accoutrements. "Can I hang those up?"

"I'm not a guest, I'm hired help."

"Of course you're a guest."

"Rina, I don't want to be a guest. Think of me as old Oliver. Well, not *old* Oliver."

"The Oliver formerly known as Detective Oliver," Rina said.

He laughed. "Just show me where I'm staying and I'll make myself comfortable."

"Down the hallway, first door to the right. How about some tea or coffee?"

"Normally, I'd say coffee but I'm so cold, tea sounds great."

"Do you want me to turn up the heat?"

"No, I'll be fine. Which door? I really need to do something, Rina. I'm going nuts."

"First on your right. Tyler's staying across from you."

"Yeah, how's the kid doing?"

"Grumpy, but that's to be expected. How's your arm doing?"

"Stiff . . . especially in the cold." He rubbed his arms, and then lifted the handle on his suitcase. "I'll just settle in." A pause. "The Loo said it was your idea to call me."

"The case has jumped from puzzling to dangerous. He needs someone with experience."

"Thanks for thinking of me, Rina. I'm happy you did."

"You're welcome. There are clean towels on the bed. You have your own private half bath, but you're going to have to share the shower with Tyler."

"No problem for me, can't talk for the blueblood." He went to his room and closed the door.

Rina started the kettle for the tea. A minute later, she heard Tyler's wheelchair rolling down the hallway. He came into the kitchen with a scowl on his face. "The enemy has landed."

316

"Tea?"

"Sure." He wheeled himself to the kitchen table. "How's he doing?"

"He looks tired."

"So now I have to deal with two codgers."

"Two experienced homicide detectives, you mean?"

McAdams smiled. "At least it's not Dad." He sighed. "I assume Decker told you?"

"It's all over the precinct. Your dad's mouth has taken on legendary proportions."

"Man oh man oh man." He rolled his eyes. "So between getting shot and his charming personality have I garnered enough support for the sympathy vote?"

"Apparently not because Peter is putting you back to work." When Tyler perked up, she said, "He wants us to start going through the reference library books tomorrow."

"Yeah, right. Busy work."

"Which is 90 percent of detective work." She mussed his hair. "You know, I got a call from the provost of the college. He's not happy about our having an armed guard with us. I reminded him that one of his students was murdered and the case is still unsolved."

"So what did he say?"

"Not much . . . a little bluster followed by a lot of BS. But he didn't say no, so you and I have a date with some musty old books."

"Best offer I've had in a year."

The front door opened and Rina pulled out a drawer and extracted a revolver. Tyler's eyes went wide. She put her finger to her lips.

"Hello?"

Peter's voice. Rina stowed the gun back in the drawer and shouted, "In the kitchen."

Decker stepped in a moment later and kissed his wife. "Hello, gorgeous." To Tyler. "How are you feeling, Harvard?"

"No one wants to hear my bitchin' so I guess all right."

Decker smiled. "Is Scott here?"

"He arrived around five minutes ago," Rina said. "He's settling into his room."

Decker took off his coat and scarf. "I'll just hang these up and go say hello." To Tyler, he said, "Seriously. Are you feeling better?"

"Ready to take on the library, Old Man." A pause. "Actually, it'll feel good to do something even if it's menial."

"It's not menial, but it is tedious. Get to know your adjectives."

"Did you hear back from Professor Gold about the codebook?"

"Mulrooney gave him a copy, but I don't know if he's looked at it yet. I'm planning to see him tomorrow. Maybe being there in person will spur him on. I need a warm body in the car with me before Mike and my wife will let me go do my job. Scott will serve that purpose."

"I'm sure." McAdams looked pissed. "For one thing, he knows how to shoot."

Rina patted the kid's shoulder. "Anything new with the case. Peter?"

"Well . . . we've called just about every hospital within a hundred-mile radius and have come up empty. Maybe I just grazed him."

"I heard the unmistakable thud, Peter. You definitely hit bone."

"You can't go around for long with a gunshot wound. He has to have been treated somewhere. Maybe he has a private doctor who knows how to extract bullets and doesn't ask too many questions."

318

Rina said, "Someone he knew he could go to in case he got shot?"

"Yep." Decker turned to McAdams. "That's why I'm thinking a group of people are involved."

"And you're wondering why I don't want you traveling by yourself," Rina said.

"I'll be fine." Decker knew he shouldn't be talking in front of her. After what happened four days ago, she was still scared. But often she had interesting things to add. More important, it wasn't fair to keep her in the dark when she could be in danger. She should know everything he knew, which, at the moment, was paltry.

"Are you interested in dinner?" Rina asked.

Mercifully, she had switched the conversation. Decker said, "Always."

"Then go change. I just have to warm everything up."

"Need help?"

"You can set the table."

"I can do that," McAdams said.

"You baked the cake, he can set the table."

Decker grinned. "You baked a *cake*?"

"Apple with a cinnamon streusel," McAdams said. "Damn good especially considering I did it from a sitting position."

"That is a feat. Did you meet Scott?"

"Not yet. I figure we'll be forced to talk to each other over dinner."

"It won't be a strain. He's a friendly guy, Tyler."

"He may be . . . but I'm not."

After a good meal and flowing wine, Oliver had shed ten years in his face.

In vino veritas.

Decker cleared the dishes while Rina brought out coffee

319

and Tyler's cake. "I'm full right now. I'll leave you gentlemen to your business."

"Not this time." Decker patted her seat. "You need to know what's going on."

"He's right," McAdams said. "Someone tried to kill you. And I'll be insulted if you don't try my cake."

"And here I was thinking I could eat it by myself with a big cup of coffee." She turned to Oliver. "The one thing about living in a cold climate is the sheer joy of curling up in front of a fire with dessert and a good book."

"You know how I hate to get you involved, Rina, but this is an exception." Decker smoothed his mustache. "And I can always use a different point of view."

"I can grow six inches and pretend I'm Marge." Rina poured coffee for all and then she sat down. "Marge was the designated barista and I'm sure not by choice."

"I made coffee." Decker was offended.

"Not cappuccino."

"No, not that. But I made many a pot of rotgut coffee in my time at LAPD. And speaking of Marge, I got a report on Chase Goddard. Hold on, I'll go get it."

"Who's on watch tonight?" McAdams asked.

"Sam Brook."

"Sam?" He shook his head. "All righty dighty."

"What's wrong with Sam Brook?" Rina asked.

"Nothing if you like your guards around twelve years old and weighing ninety pounds."

Decker said, "He's a good shot."

"Well . . . then he has one up on me."

After Decker left, Oliver turned to McAdams. "How do you feel?"

"It sucks."

"Yeah, it does. Deck likes working with you."

"Now that's a lie."

320

"No, it isn't. He didn't at first, but now he does. Tell me what's going on."

"Decker didn't tell you about the case?"

"Of course he did. But I'd like to hear what you have to say." Oliver took out a notepad. "Whenever you're ready."

"Let me go get my iPad . . . which I should have had with me." He wheeled himself from the dining room and down the hallway.

Decker came back. "Where'd the kid go?"

"To fetch his iPad. Then he's going to give me a rundown on the case."

"Why?"

"Because it's good for him to do it, good for Rina to hear the basics, and good for us to hear his point of view."

"Still got the gray matter, Scott." Decker grinned. "It matches your hair."

"Excuse me, Mr. AARP, I think going au naturel shows the sign of a confident man." No one spoke. "Do they sell Grecian formula here?"

"Yes." Rina sliced the cake. "The population here is either college age or retirement age with very little in between."

McAdams returned and proceeded to give a complete recap up to the point of his getting shot.

Oliver tapped his pencil against his pad. "You didn't see anything?"

"As soon as I heard the noise, I locked myself in the closet."

"Why?"

"Because Decker had spooked me with the silver van that was tailing us, and it was a good thing he did." He looked down. "He tried to shoot the lock, but the closet is double reinforced wood and has a Medico."

321

"What was in there that's so valuable?" Oliver asked McAdams.

"I have a safe with a lot of cash." No one spoke. "Fifty grand."

"Whoa!" Oliver said. "That's a lot of greenery to keep around. Maybe someone was out to rob you, son."

"My first thought . . . until Decker showed up. Besides no one knew about the money."

"What's wrong with the bank?" Decker said.

"People talk around here . . . even bank tellers. I was hoping to fly under the radar."

"It's true," Rina said. "People do talk."

Oliver turned back to McAdams. "What else do you remember?"

"Not much after I got shot. Sorry."

Rina distributed slices of the cake, licking her fingers when she was done. "So any theories as to what's going on?"

"The whole thing sounds nutty," Oliver said. "If you're a professional, the last thing you want is attention from the heat. And the quickest way to bring heat on is to take swipes at police officers."

"In America, that's true," Decker said. "Only stupid people try to bring down cops. Not so in foreign countries. Look at Mexico or Latin America. Gangs and cartels are always taking down cops."

"You think this is the work of a Mexican gang?"

"He thinks we're dealing with Russian mafia," McAdams said. "Bratva is the local name for it."

"Because of some stolen Russian icons?"

"The Petroshkovich icons . . . which is a thirty-year-old case, FYI," McAdams said.

Decker said, "I think it has to do with Russian mafia because John Latham was the primary target and Latham's specialty was Soviet art. I've worked what . . . three hundred homicides? This one feels foreign. These guys don't care about cops because they're not beholden to American law. And then when you throw in this codebook."

"Yeah, it is kinda spy versus spy," Oliver said.

McAdams said, "It could be a red herring—the codebook."

"Someone went to all that trouble to produce a very complex and educated red herring?" Decker said. "I don't think so." He opened the manila envelope and pulled out the fax. "Marge's report on Chase Goddard." His eyes scanned the page. "Nothing much. A couple of DUIs in Miami."

"He had a gallery in Florida?" McAdams asked.

"Uh . . . ten years ago . . . about two years before he moved to New York. He's certainly hopped around."

"So maybe we are dealing with a drug cartel," McAdams said.

"Why do you say that?" Decker handed Oliver the fax.

"Isn't Florida an entry point for drugs?" McAdams said. "Maybe the codebook has nothing to do with art. Maybe it has to do with shipments of drugs from Florida."

"So now we're tagging John Latham as a drug dealer?"

"It was one of your theories early on," McAdams reminded him.

Oliver held up his hand. "Let me get this straight. Chase Goddard has had art galleries in Miami, New York, and Boston."

"Not to bolster my theory, but maybe he's distributing," McAdams said.

"Or maybe he's just following the money," Rina said. "Most galleries are in big cities or resorts because who else can afford art and antiques."

323

"Where there's money, there's drugs," McAdams said. "And like Oliver said . . ." He turned to him. "Do I call you Oliver or Scott?"

"Oliver's fine."

"Like he said, who shoots up the police unless they're in a chase or a shoot-out or they have utter disregard for the law. Drug dealers have utter disregard of the law."

"Do you see Chase Goddard as a drug dealer, Deck?" Oliver said.

"Not really. He's a little old and most dealers aren't Harvard educated. Plus he was obsequious when Tyler mentioned his father. He seems to want business. I can see him buying stolen art and drinking too many martinis. I can't see him in the back room castrating bodies and cutting heroin with quinine."

"Heroin's cut with quinine?" McAdams asked.

Oliver said, "Quinine, powdered sugar, caffeine, powdered milk, gypsum, baby formula. That's the powdered stuff. With black tar heroin, dealers will cut it with brown sugar, coffee . . . heat it all up into one big goop and then smoke it."

"I don't see Chase Goddard as a drug dealer," Decker said.

"What about John Latham dealing drugs?" Oliver asked.

"No indication."

"No indication he was an art thief, either," McAdams said.

"He had an association with Angeline Moreau who most likely forged the Tiffanies," Decker said. "And you know she didn't steal or fence them on her own."

Rina said, "It sounds like you could go in a thousand directions. What you do know is that someone wants you two dead."

Oliver said, "If it had to do with Latham's death, why haven't the triggermen shot at the Boston cops?"

"Summer Village," Decker corrected.

"Whatever," Rina said. "They were the ones who found the codebook. So if that's the key, they should be targets just like you two."

Decker said, "First off, they're a bigger force so there'd be too many to kill. Second, maybe Harvard and I are much closer than we know. The problem is the triggerman probably thinks we know more than we do."

"Who's on the radar right now?" Oliver asked. "Just Chase Goddard?"

Decker shrugged. "It'd be nice to tie him to the case but I don't have anything on him."

"What about . . ." Oliver flipped through his notes. "Justin Merritt?"

"Jason Merritt," McAdams corrected. "He's the specialist in Russian art. His gallery is in New York and we don't have a damn thing on him, either."

"Just like John Latham," Oliver said.

"No, John Latham's field of expertise was Soviet-era art," McAdams told him. "It's an entirely different field than Russian art. And Soviet art is not very collectible."

"Why not?"

"Because most of it was propaganda. I'm not saying it's worthless. Some of the posters are pricey. But because it's so stylized, it's more important as a recording of history and culture than as fine art. That's what John Latham won the Windsor Prize for: Soviet art as a tool for dissemination of propaganda during Stalin's administration."

"How'd you find all this out?" Decker asked.

"I've had time on my hands, Old Man."

"What about Russian art?" Oliver asked. "You don't hear of great Russian artists like you do French impressionists."

"That's because the czars were way more interested in

western European culture than promoting their own heritage," McAdams said. "The Hermitage is loaded with great Western art. Most of Russia's own homegrown painters have been relegated to storage. And once the Bolsheviks took over, they denigrated anything that smelled of Western society."

Oliver said, "But you just said that the Hermitage is filled with great western European art."

"That installation came later when Khrushchev made it a point to rebuild all the incredible buildings that the Nazis had destroyed. Probably that was propaganda, too. He wanted to show the West that Russia wasn't a back-water country." McAdams thought a moment. "I was talking to my dad in one of the rare moments when he wasn't screaming at me. We got on the subject of the Hermitage . . . which actually I brought up because I knew my grandfather had been to the Soviet Union when it was mostly closed off to Westerners. Dad told me my grand-father had seen the Hermitage way back when . . . in the forties or fifties maybe. It was an absolute mess . . . just piles and piles of all this invaluable art. The Soviets originally put it on display to show the extreme wealth of the aristocracy at the expense of the proletariat."

"So you're saying that there is no valuable Russian art?" Oliver asked.

"No, no," Decker said. "The older stuff is quite valuable because a lot of it was destroyed in the revolution. Mostly religious stuff like icons."

"So is there any kind of Russian art worth killing for?" Oliver asked.

Decker and McAdams spoke at the same time. "The Amber Room." They gave Oliver a rundown on World War II Russia. Decker said, "Supposedly twenty-seven cartons of the dismantled room were shipped to a castle where the cartons along with the building were destroyed by fire. Since then the trail has gone cold . . . or cool, I should say. Because pieces of amber from the original room keep showing up. The amber and the jewels are not only worth a small fortune, the room has national significance."

"So maybe we shouldn't be looking at Russian icons at all," Oliver said. "Maybe we should be looking at Nazi-looted art. Maybe that's what the kids were onto—a cache of looted art. If a wealthy and prominent collector had a disputed painting, it might be worth killing over."

"You're thinking that John Latham was blackmailing a wealthy collector and the guy hired a hit man or hit men to whack him?" When Oliver shrugged, Decker said, "It would make way more sense for the collector to pay him off. Certainly he wouldn't be stupid enough to try and take down the police *unless* you are foreign and you don't like Americans and you get a thrill out of mutilating bodies as part of the retaliation."

McAdams said, "He still likes the Russian mob."

"I'm just saying it feels foreign."

"Maybe it's a collection of looted art," Oliver said.

Decker said, "The Gurlitt stuff is worth a small fortune. And he's still alive and kicking. It doesn't feel like a German crime."

"Well, I still like drugs," McAdams said.

"If you like drugs, then go back to the college and talk to Angeline Moreau's friends again. Find out if she has any hint of dealing dope."

"Uh, I'm not too mobile right now. Besides we've already blanked out on that one."

"Which is why I'm still pursuing an art angle," Decker said. "Once that's exhausted, we'll try drugs again."

"Maybe it's both . . . like drugs hidden in art shipments from Florida," McAdams suggested.

327

"One thing at a time, Harvard. You and Rina go back to the reference libraries at the Five Colleges and make it a point to ensure that all the valuable books are intact. Start with Rayfield at Littleton. Since Moreau specialized in textiles, see if there are any antique print books on textiles that she might have pilfered from."

"I agree with Deck and the art angle for what it's worth," Oliver said.

"I knew you were going to be trouble," McAdams said.

"I'm not saying you're wrong, kid. I'm just saying that you have to approach it going from most reasonable to most unreasonable."

Decker said, "Tomorrow Oliver, Chris Mulrooney, and I have an appointment to see Professor Gold. We'll find out what he has to say if anything."

"I thought you were going to Skype me in with that."

"We'll Skype you in when we know something. In the meantime, I'll send him your regards."

"He won't remember me."

"I'm not sure about that, McAdams." Decker patted his good shoulder. "From what I've observed, you seem to make your mark wherever you go."

CHAPTER TWENTY-SEVEN

Rina showed the library guard her deputized license as well as her concealed weapon permit. The provost, who was accompanying them to the third floor—where Rayfield stored its reference material—gave a sniff of contempt. "Do you have to make it so obvious?"

"Would you rather I set off the metal detector with my gun?"

The man's cheeks pinkened. He was in his forties with glasses perched on his ski slope nose. He whispered, "You have an armed officer. How much do you need?"

"I don't know, sir," Rina spoke softly but definitely not in a hush. "How much protection do you need after someone tried to kill you?"

McAdams bowed his head and stifled a smile.

Greg Schultz, the armed guard, cleared his throat. He was a retired mechanic in his sixties who often helped out Greenbury PD and FD when they needed extra brawn. He was built like a tractor. "We're causing a backup line." He unlocked the brake on Tyler's wheelchair. "Can I take him through now?"

Quickly, the provost escorted them through the metal

detector, the guard bypassing Rina's purse. The four of them squeezed into an elevator. On the third floor, there was a long table in the corner with books of old textile photographs along with several pairs of white gloves. Natural light was provided by a window with a view to the outside quad, students milling in the snow like ants in spilled salt. The glass also let in a draft. Rina had dressed in layers. She took off her overcoat but kept on her sweater over a sweater.

The reference librarian was a young woman in her thirties with a short bob of straight blond hair and deep green eyes. Her name was Lisa Pomeranz and she recognized Tyler McAdams from his previous research foray. Her eyes tried to hide the shock at seeing him so disabled. "I read about the incident in the papers. I'm so sorry."

McAdams tried to put her at ease. "Neither rain, nor sleet, nor snow . . . especially snow."

"I thought that was mailmen," Schultz said.

"If the shoe fits . . ."

Rina said, "Any more adages, Tyler, or can we get to work?"

McAdams smiled. "I'll be fine, Ms. Pomeranz. The bullets missed all the crucial areas so I count myself as very lucky."

"I'm not supposed to do this, but I can get you some hot water. It's chilly up here."

"I wouldn't want to spill anything," Rina said. "Not even water. We're fine."

"Speak for yourself," McAdams said.

"I'm speaking for both of us." Rina donned the white gloves and sat down. "Thank you."

"Anything I can do to help, don't hesitate to ask," Lisa said.

After she walked away, McAdams said, "Man, she did a one-eighty from the first time I was here."

Schultz took up a seat that afforded him a view of the elevator as well as the staircase. "I'll just sit here and try not to fall asleep."

"I'm sure we'll be fine." Rina pulled two magnifying glasses from her briefcase and laid them on the table. Then she carefully pulled out the first reference book entitled *Textiles of the Far East*. It was published at the beginning of the twentieth century. Placed on the inside cover was a sign-in sheet of those who had used the book as a reference. She whispered, "Tyler, look at this." She put the book in front of him and pointed to Angeline Moreau's name. She had used the book six times.

"It was her thesis," he said.

"To quote my daughter: I'm just saying."

McAdams picked up *Mid-Eastern Textiles from the Silk Route in the Fifteenth Century*. He regarded the sign-up sheet. "Looks like Moreau was a busy bee." He turned to Rina. "Shall we?"

"Let's."

Simultaneously, they opened their respective books to the title page. The room fell silent except for the gentle swish of paper turning, each of them carefully studying the binding of the prints with the magnifying glass to make sure that a razor blade hadn't done any mischief.

It was going to be a long and tedious day.

By ten in the morning, Decker was on the way to the Summer Village Police Department to pick up Chris Mulrooney. While riding on the highway, he and Oliver kept a constant lookout for tails. With another set of experienced eyes, Decker could relax a tad. Being with Scott felt like home, the two in conversation that ran the gamut from the good old days to the puzzling case of present days. Drinking coffee and chomping on bagels, they exchanged ideas both logical and far-fetched. Neither had much to add from last night.

"Kid seems okay, manning up under his trial by fire," Oliver said.

"I think he'd be a great detective. But he's doing the smart thing and going to Harvard Law."

"Too bad. He certainly won't get this kind of adrenaline rush there."

"Ordinarily this job is very banal."

"Right now, I'd definitely take banal over retirement."

"Send out applications. You could have your pick of any small town."

"A good idea, better than feeling sorry for myself." He was quiet. "I'm thinking about Florida. I don't like the cold."

"Want me to talk to my brother?"

"Where is Randy?"

"Miami PD. But I'm sure he could make inquiries in smaller towns. Unless you want to go big again."

"No, not big . . . but bigger than Greenbury. Marge was real smart. Can't get more perfect than Ventura PD. Man, it's beautiful up there."

"So why don't you apply to Ventura?"

He shook his head. "No, it wouldn't be the same. We're both in different places now. I wouldn't mind a change of scenery. I'm willing to uproot myself."

"What about your kids?"

"They're scattered and busy. If they want to see me, I'll get a spare bedroom in my seaside condo that must have a pool. Certainly enough of those around in Florida."

"You might have a problem, though," Decker said.

"What?"

"A single man around all those widows."

Oliver laughed. "Stand in line, ladies, there's enough to go around."

332

"Here we are." Decker pulled into the Summer Village PD parking lot. He called up Chris Mulrooney who came bounding out five minutes later holding a briefcase. He wore a parka bomber jacket, thick denim jeans over bulky boots, shearling gloves, a knit hat, and a black scarf. Decker made the introductions after Mulrooney had slid into the backseat. He peeled off his winter wear in the hot car's climate.

Mulrooney patted his leather valise. "Got a copy of the codebook right here. We can follow along with the professor."

Decker pulled out several sheets of paper. "The kid has been looking at it for the past three days. He's been counting phrases and is using them to plot a frequency chart. Not that he knows for certain if the phrases correspond with letters but he figured it was a good start."

Mulrooney's eyes scanned over the deciphered words. "How's he feeling?"

"He's laid up in a wheelchair but I've got him working in the library."

"It'll do him good to work." Murooney stowed the papers in his briefcase. "We've been going through Latham's papers, trying to locate things that might be opened from that janitor ring of keys we found. No local storage units yet. And the keys that open safe-deposit boxes aren't local either. His local bank had two hundred and fifty-six dollars, forty-eight cents in a check deposit. Two credit cards with small balances. He had a bundled account for cable and Wi-Fi. No landline. Utilities and rent were paid up every month. Didn't seem to splurge on himself except for the occasional restaurant and bar bills. We checked them out. The ones who do remember him said he was just a regular guy. We did pass around the picture of Angeline Moreau. Couple of bartenders thought that she looked familiar but they couldn't be sure. They certainly couldn't put her with him at a specific time."

"That's too bad."

"They do remember Latham often chatting up the ladies, but not being obnoxious about it. He was okay just being a guy, watching the Celts and the Patriots on the screen with the locals. He owned his car. To me, he's suspicious because he was so unsuspicious. For a guy who was murdered so brutally, he was trying to keep his outward appearance squeaky clean."

"Did his colleagues have anything to add?"

"Nope. Just a typical visiting lecturer. He shared an office with four other lecturers but they rarely see one another because their schedules are different. One of the gals I spoke to said she doesn't even work there because the space is so small. She works at home and only uses the shared space for posted office hours with her students. People don't remember him hanging around the campus too much. But everyone I spoke to about Latham did say he was very knowledgeable about his field, which was . . ."

Mulrooney flipped through his notes.

"Here we go. The official title is History of Art and Propaganda in the Soviet Union. It was an upper-division class for majors in art, history, and art history; and he had forty students, which is a very big number. We've interviewed almost all the students and have come up empty. If the codebook doesn't tell us something, we're shooting in the dark. And that's really making all of us nervous after what happened to you guys down there."

Oliver said, "Deck thinks we're dealing with foreign criminals."

"Yeah, even stupid people usually don't take out detectives. And when they do try, it's usually to prevent

testimony. Somebody clearly doesn't know the rules."
Mulrooney hesitated. "Which foreign country? Are you thinking Russia because of Latham's specialty?"

"Yes, exactly," Decker said. "Latham's takeout was very surgical. Maybe it's not even the Russian mob. Maybe it's Russian spooks."

"That would be very bad," Oliver said.

"It certainly would mean we're over our heads. But I don't have anything to go on other than a queasy feeling."

"This is making me very, very nervous," Mulrooney said.

"Yeah, you and me both," Decker said. "But I'm not about to back off before I find out why someone wanted me dead. Maybe the answers will be in the codebook."

No one spoke for a minute. Then Mulrooney said, "Maybe we should take the book to Quantico. I know we don't have anything to tell them, but we can't figure out the code on our own and I'm nervous about involving a Harvard math professor in something so potentially dangerous."

"I hear you, Chris, and I was thinking the same thing last night. And that's why I called Gold up and gave him a brief rundown over the phone. I told him about what happened to me and McAdams. I told him he may be setting himself up for trouble by getting involved. You know what he said? He insisted we come up and that he's absolutely fine with it."

"But are we absolutely fine with it?"

"I wasn't at all until Gold told me where he learned all about codes."

"He's CIA?"

"Retired CIA. I don't think he saw much fieldwork but he did spend ten years doing codes in Virginia. He developed some of the programs way back when, that the

CIA still uses for electronic hacking. And he says he can shoot, goes to the range whenever he can. But it's your book and your call, Chris."

Mulrooney shrugged. "I guess he's in no more danger than we are . . . if that's any comfort." A pause. "If he knows what he's getting into, we might as well talk to him."

"That was my thought," Decker said. "You know, Gold, Oliver, and I have one thing in common besides being over sixty. We're all looking for action. Problem is we seem to be looking in all the wrong places."

CHAPTER TWENTY-EIGHT

After combing through piles of the antique textile and art books with zero results, Rina suggested a break. She had been working for two hours straight and her eyes needed to rest. She—along with McAdams and Schultz—left the library and found a school café called The Hop. The place made an attempt to resemble a 1950s malt shop: red fake Naugahyde stools at a fake linoleum countertop that was even cheesier than the original cheesy decor. Rina bought coffee for the three of them and they sat in an outside patio under a heat lamp. She took out a sack lunch that she had prepared for Tyler and herself, but there was certainly enough to go around in case Greg Schultz hadn't brought his own food.

During the first five minutes, the gang ate in silence. Tyler took out his iPad and was lost in concentration. Rina made small talk with Greg, asking him about various cars: always a good topic with guys but especially good with someone who had worked with vehicles for the past thirty years.

McAdams finally spoke. "I was looking up vintage prints and not all print books are the same in value—as if that should be a startling revelation."

"Go on," Rina said.

"Not surprising, it appears that the older the book, the more valuable the prints are. Prints in Basil Besler's book published in 1613 are selling from eighteen hundred to five thousand whereas prints in Dr. John Robert Thornton's book, published between 1799 and 1805, sell in the thousands." He continued searching on Safari. "But Dr. John Robert Thornton's book *The Temple of Flora,* published just ten years later . . . those images sell for a lot less."

"Probably depends on the rarity of the book."

"Yeah, of course. All I'm saying is the prices really swing and without knowing what is valuable, we're kind of shooting in the dark with choosing which books to look at. To make it worthwhile for a thief, he'd have to steal from the expensive books, which are rare and damn near impossible to find." He looked up at Rina. "Thanks for the sandwich, by the way."

"Yeah, thanks a lot, Mrs. Decker," Schultz said. "Way better than what I packed for myself."

"You're both welcome."

Schultz stood up. "I'm going to make a quick pit stop. Keep your eyes open."

"No problem." Rina patted her purse. "We're fine." After Schultz left, she said, "The prints you saw in Chase Goddard's gallery. How much is he asking for them?"

"I can tell you in a minute." McAdams clicked away on his pad. "They're priced between a hundred and three hundred each. I should really put his inventory as a favorite place."

"What about his vintage books?"

"He doesn't have that much inventory. He has a *Swann's Way* and a Chandler, *The Long Goodbye,* but without the dust jacket. That's the most valuable. The rest are in double digits."

"Not worth stealing," Rina said.

"No one thinks that Goddard was actually stealing. We were just wondering if Goddard was buying hot merchandise. And if he was purchasing stolen items, it probably makes sense for him to buy things that don't attract that much attention . . . like cheap prints."

"I agree." Rina stared out at the barren landscape. Nothing seemed suspicious. But would she even recognize "suspicious"? "Even if Goddard is buying small items of hot property, it's certainly not worth murdering over."

"Unless he's trying to keep his reputation unsullied, except that heretofore it had already been sullied."

"Even if he did pay Moreau and Latham a few bucks for stolen art prints, you certainly can't amass designer bags with a couple hundred extra bucks."

"Right." McAdams sat back and sipped coffee. This morning he had removed the sling from his arm and felt better with the freedom of motion. It still hurt, but he could move it and his balance was much better. Within a few days, he'd probably be on crutches. "No offense, but I think your husband is on the wrong track. I think this is a total waste of time."

"Not that I'm defending Peter, but he's more right than wrong. If he thinks the library needs to be checked out, I'm not going to argue."

"I know he's trying to tie Moreau to something more than Tiffany windows, but I still can't see her being a mover and a shaker in the nefarious world of looted art. Maybe her murder had nothing at all to do with the stolen panels. Her ex-boyfriend was pretty shaken when she dumped him. He followed her to Boston and even went by John Latham's apartment. I know he had an alibi for both murders, but friends lie for one another all the time."

"Was it just one person who alibied him?"

"No, it was several people who saw him. And he was in class like he said. But no one can perfectly account for every minute of his day. And people get the time wrong."

Rina said, "Peter feels that some foreign entity is involved."

"The Russian mafia." McAdams rolled his eyes. "Even if I agreed with him on that end, what would that have to do with Chase Goddard and a few stolen prints?"

Rina went silent. Then she said, "Tyler, can you look up on your iPad to see if there are any rare *Russian* books that have an auction history?"

"That's a thought." He nodded. "Give me a minute."

Schultz had returned and that made Rina feel a lot better. She said, "All's quiet."

"That's exactly what I want to hear."

McAdams said, "There is a book by D. A. Rovinski—five books actually published in St. Petersburg, 1881. *Russkie Narodnye Kartinki* better known as *Russian Folk Pictures*. They sold for auction in 2013 for 11 million rubles. And that would convert to . . . wow, that's surprising . . . 315,500 dollars." He continued typing. "God, the prints are gorgeous. Want to take a look?"

"Love to." She looked as he swished through the images. "They're beautiful."

"Yes, they are," McAdams said. "I'm assuming that is a very, very rare book and not the kind of thing that would be sitting around Rayfield Library collecting dust."

"Unless the library doesn't know what they have."

"That's why you have a reference librarian. She should know her inventory."

"It's worth a shot to ask her," Rina said. "What else goes for big money?"

"Books by Pushkin . . . *Eugene Onegin* . . . okay, this sounds interesting. A book commemorating three hundred years of Romanov rule, published during the diamond jubilee in 1913. This one went for . . . roughly 115,000 dollars. At least these books are in the vicinity of worth killing over." A pause. "I don't really see Chase Goddard dealing in them. Maybe Jason Merritt."

"Does it say anything about who owned the books and who bought them?"

"Nope." His eyes were still on his pad. "I don't believe this! Son of a bitch!" He looked up. "Sorry."

"What?"

"Nikolai Petroshkovich . . . a signed copy of his *History of Iconography* with original prints of his designs and works. One of twenty original editions. Two hundred pages, forty plates published in 1926 . . . 4 million rubles three years ago, which was, hold on . . . 115,000 dollars."

"Petroshkovich?"

He winced. "Yes."

"So maybe Peter's not so far off."

He exhaled. "Maybe not."

"How far is Marylebone from here?"

"About an hour."

"Where's the nearest big reference library in Marylebone?"

"In Rhode Island, I'd say Brown, but we're almost as close to Marylebone as Providence. And there are a slew of other colleges in between."

"Okay," Rina said. "When did Petroshkovich live?"

"I will tell you in a moment . . . 1889 to 1949."

"He was sixty when he died?"

"Fifty-nine . . . hold on . . . he did the Marylebone iconography in 1938, but he also did a lot of other work in and around New England. His icons at St. Stephen's, Marylebone was considered his pinnacle."

"So he was somewhat famous when he died?"

341

"He was pretty well known. If his book is going for 115 grand four years ago, you could only imagine what the icons would be worth today."

"Worth dying over?"

"More than a Tiffany."

"You said he worked in and around New England. *Where* did he live?"

"Hold on . . . Wowzers!" McAdams exhaled. "Good call, Rina. His workshop was in Bellingham, which is ten miles away from the Five Colleges."

"So if you're well known, older, and sick—and you want to leave copies of legacies in the form of your book somewhere . . ."

"Certainly worth asking about." McAdams put down his cup. He turned to Schultz. "Would you mind wheeling me into the bathroom? Once inside, I can take it from there."

"I'll meet you guys in the library," Rina said.

Schultz said, "How about if we all go together?"

"I can't come in with you." Rina laughed. "Even if I could, I wouldn't. I hate urinals."

"Deck says you're good with a pistol." Schultz smiled. "How about if you can stand guard for us?"

Again, Rina patted her purse. "Have gun will travel."

Boston was a college in search of a city. What wasn't past history was current academia. Large in scope as well as top dog in its field, the Harvard campus sprawled over an endless white landscape. Brick buildings from yore battled with modern architecture interspersed with long expanses of white fields. Mordechai Gold's office was located in the Science Center—a modern-day ziggurat of glass and steel off Cambridge Street across from Harvard Yard.

342

Classes were in session, but there were some empty rooms with open doors, enough to see that functionality ruled over form. Institutional furniture crammed into the space, whiteboards filled with abstract formulas that meant nothing to anyone outside of the field. Gold's office was a corner on the fifth floor. The door was ajar, but Decker knocked anyway. They were invited inside.

The space was a step back to a previous time: walnut paneling, parquet floors, Persian floor rugs, wooden book-shelves, and a view of the plaza. It was warmed by an electric fireplace as well as modern heating. An enormous ebony L-shaped desk hosted the math professor who was sitting in a tufted leather chair. He stood up: a large man in height and girth, bald except for a ring of unruly gray curls around the base of his head. Bushy gray eyebrows arched over large brown eyes. He had a full face, a full nose, full lips, and a big chin. Decker could see that Gold in his younger years would have fit the mold physically for the spooks in Virginia.

Introductions were made and hands were shaken. Then everyone settled into cushy chairs. Gold smiled. "I know you gave me a brief recitation over the phone, Detective Decker, but I'd appreciate a recap of what happened now that we're face-to-face with everyone here."

"How long do you have?" Mulrooney said.

Gold checked an Oyster Rolex. "A little over an hour. Will it take longer? If so, I can make arrangements."

"It's complicated."

"That's grand," Gold said. "The more complicated the better."

Decker said, "I'll start with my involvement and then Detective Mulrooney can tell you what he's doing."

"Splendid." Gold paused. "How is Tyler McAdams doing? I was horrified when you told me about the shooting."

"He's fine and should make a total recovery," Decker said. "Do you remember him?"

"Five ten, slender build but not wimpy, long face, brown hair, hazel eyes. He dressed in sweaters and jeans and was always prepared. Now, I would very much appreciate a full story."

"Absolutely." Decker pulled out his notebook and the two other detectives did the same.

"My handwriting is atrocious." Gold pointed to his head. "I may ask you to repeat something just to encode it into long-term memory."

"Not a problem," Decker said.

The recitation took twenty minutes. Gold interrupted three times asking for clarification. After the recap was finished, Mulrooney took out his copy of the codebook and said, "Did you have a chance to look at the pages?"

"I always like to hear the complete picture before I embark on any new project." Gold took out the copy given to him by Mulrooney and put on his glasses. "So the answer is no."

"Tyler cracked part of it," Decker said. "The Cyrillic letters are actually Latin phrases. The Hebrew letters are Latin phrases as well."

"Ah yes. Very good. Please tell him I'm impressed." Gold's eyes continued to study the pages. "That poor boy. He must have been ill-prepared for police work of this sort."

"He didn't expect to get shot but who does? As far as the work, he's been a quick study."

"Yes, I remember that for a nonmath major, he caught on quite well. Quiet boy, but he always knew the answers."

Decker watched Gold's eyes bore into the text. "Do you have a photographic memory?"

"Yes, I do. But also I'm one of those weird people with high superior autobiographical memory."

344

"I read about that." Decker smiled. "Uh, I don't remember where I read it but it was an article about people who remember daily details about their entire lives."

"Correct."

Oliver said, "Is that a blessing or a curse?"

"I do remember the bad as well as the good. Lucky for me that most of the emotional valance is long gone. I can tell you the day and the date of what was happening for the last sixty years. But only in relationship to myself. If something historical had occurred and I wasn't aware of it, I'll have no direct memory of it. I remember Tyler McAdams well not only because I remember the boy, but also because I knew his father, Jack McAdams. I went to law school with him."

"You're a lawyer."

"I've done everything except medicine. Poor kid. Growing up with a father like that could not have been easy."

"He's aware of his father's peccadilloes," Decker said. "He handles him very well."

"Good. I admire people with spine." Gold went quiet. "The Eastern letters and symbols—the Chinese, the Japanese, the Korean . . . this is Amharic . . . whoever wrote this is really all over the place . . . anyway, the symbols and sounds point to Latin phrases as well."

"What about the Roman alphabet?" Decker asked. "They appear to be nonsense words but they must mean something."

"They are actually transliteration for Russian words . . . Greek words as well. If I translate from Russian into English, the words mean nothing. But . . . if I translate from Russian into German, they appear to translate back into Latin phrases."

The three men nodded solemnly. Mulrooney turned to Decker and Oliver. "You men ever work a case like this?"

"Never," Oliver said. "Hardly ever worked with the FBI."
He looked at Decker. "What about you?"

"I worked with the spooks once in a multinational child porno ring back in Foothill. I remember it well because believe it or not, they did wear sunglasses. My involvement was minimal."

"This is a first by me."

"Anything else you notice, Professor?"

"A few things here and there." Gold looked up and folded the codebook. "The parsimonious thing for me to do would be to translate all of what I can into Latin and then I can try to break the Latin code and see if it makes sense in English or German or Russian or whatever language the code was originally written in. I'll tell you one thing. This was either done by a polyglot or more than one person. There are a lot of idiomatic phrases. And while I recognize most of the idioms, it would take me a while to write them up in code."

He smiled and stood up. "I'll do my best, gentlemen."

"Thank you for helping, Professor Gold," Mulrooney said.

"You realize that this may be something you might not want to deal with. That it may be beyond police work."

"Tyler and I were targets," Decker said. "Before I relinquish control, I want to have a better idea of what's going on."

"It's a safety issue," Mulrooney said.

"Exactly," Decker agreed. "We have to know who the bad guys are. And once the spooks get it, they'll cut us out of the loop."

"I understand. But do be careful." Business cards were exchanged as well as handshakes. "This would be amusing for me except I know that real people were murdered." Gold shook his head. "I'll do whatever I can. Do send my best to Tyler. I hope his recovery is swift."

"I'll do that." Decker strolled over to the window and took one last look outside. The campus must have been ten times bigger than all the Upstate colleges put together. "Must be a great place to work."

"It is," Gold said. "Although in all honesty, despite all the trappings of this office and the prestige of Harvard, I could work in a closet and be happy. People like me . . . we live in our heads."

CHAPTER TWENTY-NINE

While Schultz kept watch, Rina pushed McAdams's wheelchair up to the historical reference desk, located on the third floor of Rayfield Library. It was in a separate, caged area where books of value and historical significance were kept, a step back into another time with musty red carpeting and walnut tables and chairs. The librarian in charge was a woman named Susan Devry. She was in her sixties with a curly nest of short, gray hair that framed a round, mocha face. Her frame was thin, her oversized sweater draping over a free-flowing midi skirt and black boots. She regarded Rina's request for the Petroshkovich book and frowned. "I have to see if it's back for loan."

"Back from where?" McAdams had to look up to talk.

"Pretoria College in Marylebone." She regarded the pair. "I suppose I don't have to tell you two about the art theft of the Petroshkovich icons."

Rina nodded. "We're aware of the heist, yes."

"How tragic," Susan said. "There used to be a lot of interest in Petroshkovich—a lot of papers and theses—especially right after the icons were pilfered. But Nikolai seemed to have had his day in the sun. And since the artwork was never recovered, students lost interest."

"Not everyone lost interest in him if his book went out on loan," Rina said.

"Yes, but it's usually more from an amateur detective point of view than from something scholarly." Susan smiled sheepishly. "I'm not saying that's bad . . . to be interested in the theft. I suppose anything that generates enthusiasm."

"I'm surprised that the library loans out something so valuable," McAdams said. "The book is worth six figures."

"It's not really on loan to Pretoria." Susan gave another sheepish smile. "It's actually coowned by the two libraries."

"How does that work?" Rina asked.

"We just courier it over when it's requested."

"How'd it come to pass that the libraries coowned it?"

Susan seemed apprehensive. Rina waited her out. Finally, the librarian said, "Long ago each library had a copy. There are only around ten original copies left. It's a very long story."

McAdams smiled. "We've got time."

Rina said, "I'd love to hear it."

Susan checked her watch. "Very briefly, Pretoria had some financial difficulties. And Littleton, being the newest college here, didn't have the largest of endowments. The book was given to Rayfield from Huntington Library because it was an art book and as sort of a welcome present. But Rayfield was still wanting for funds. This was years ago before the icons were stolen." She rolled her eyes. "It was agreed that one of the books would be sold and the proceeds would be split between Pretoria and here. They couldn't get away with that today!"

"Who bought the book that was sold?"

"The buyer was anonymous. But it was rumored that the book went overseas."

"To Russia?" McAdams asked.

"Who knows, but that would be logical." Susan's eyes were outraged. "Let me check on the one copy we have left."

"Curiouser and curiouser." McAdams's phone vibrated and he checked the text. "It's from the Loo."

Rina grinned. "Since when did you start calling Peter the Loo?"

"It's what Oliver calls him. I kinda like it. Anyway, they just finished up with Professor Gold and he and Oliver are on their way back. And Gold says hello." McAdams stowed his phone. "I'm sure he doesn't even know who I am."

Rina looked him in the eye. "Where did all the arrogance go, Tyler? I miss it."

He smiled. "Getting shot is a humbling experience. But fear not. I'm sure when I'm up and about I'll be my old obnoxious self."

"I'm sure Professor Gold does remember you."

"I dunno, Rina, I was pretty forgettable . . . quiet, believe it or not. I was only in the PC because of my legacy of my grandfather. Not because of my charm."

"PC? As in personal computer?"

McAdams laughed. "Porcellian Club . . . it's a final club."

"I . . . don't know what that is, Tyler."

"It's like an exclusive fraternity. We don't have a lot of Greek at Harvard, we have clubs instead. They're also called eating clubs because meals are served. The Porcellian Club, better known to those who hate us, which is almost everyone, is sometimes called the Pig's Club not because of its all-male members—although the appellation certainly fits—but because the club's tradition is to roast a whole pig."

"Not many Orthodox Jews in the mix?"

"Nary a one who'd admit it." McAdams slowly stood up in front of his wheelchair, supporting himself on one leg and a cane.

Rina knew better than to try to help. "Getting a little numb?"

"My butt is frozen. It feels good to be upright even if I am a little off-balance." McAdams took out his iPad and began to punch in topics using Safari. A minute later, he spoke in a whisper. "Ach, this isn't getting anywhere."

"What?"

"Trying to locate a book that was sold years ago."

"We could try the archives of Pretoria."

"It might be worth a trip." McAdams checked his watch. "It's taking a while, isn't it?"

"Yes, it is and this section of the library is small."

"Something's amiss." McAdams continued to play with his iPad. Five minutes later, Susan came back with a wooden box and white gloves. "I don't know how this happened, but it was misplaced." She handed them each a pair of white gloves and a cloth to set the book on while turning the pages. "I can only loan this out to you for two hours. And you can only look at the book at the tables here. You cannot take it anywhere else in the library."

"We understand." Rina donned the gloves.

"I'm not done." Susan stopped herself. "You have to sign up for it."

"Already done," McAdams said.

"That was the general sign-up sheet. On a book this rare, we have a specific sign-up sheet. Your name, your official ID number . . . I suppose you can use your driver's license or badge number . . . and your time in, and the book you are looking at—title and author, please."

McAdams smiled. "Whatever you say, ma'am."

Both McAdams and Rina inked the sheet. Then Susan

pulled out a large lockbox of index files. "Let's see . . . Petroshkovich . . . ah, here we are. You both also have to sign the index cards for the book. One for each of you. That way we can keep track of who's checking out rare books with art plates . . . precisely why I told you that I'd be shocked if you two found something missing. We're very careful."

Rina and McAdams exchanged glances. The thought came to both of them at the same time. Rina said, "You're the one who has the badge. Go for it."

McAdams said, "So . . . that means you have the names of everyone who has ever looked at the Petroshkovich book?"

"Not *everyone*." Susan shuffled through the cards. "These currently date back . . . three years ago. The rest have been archived."

"Can I see them—the index cards?"

Susan paused. "I don't know if I can show them to you."

"Ma'am, it's a murder investigation." No one spoke. "Please don't make me go get a warrant. It's very time consuming."

Susan didn't answer. Instead, she put the cards down and slid the pile across the desktop. "You have thirty seconds."

"Thank you." McAdams shuffled through them as fast as he could. One name gave him pause—he showed it to Rina—and then he continued on until he'd seen them all. He slid the cards back to the librarian and regarded the book box. It was custom made: around a foot by two feet. "Could you open the Petroshkovich box, please?"

"Me?"

"Yes, I'd really appreciate it."

"What's going on?"

"Please. It's important."

"All right." Slowly, she lifted the wooden lid. The actual book was in a cloth sleeve.

"Could you take it out for me?"

"Not unless you tell me what this is all about."

"It's about two people who were murdered and about someone who feels it's okay to shoot the police. Please just do it."

Susan flinched. "Yes, of course." She took the book out of the sleeve. The cover was old and water stained. "What next?"

"Can you flip through the plates?"

"Detective, one doesn't flip through plates. You turn the pages slowly."

McAdams held his tongue. "Can you do that for me?"

"I'm sorry if I'm sounding brusque. If you'd just tell me . . ." When he didn't answer, Susan began turning pages. When she got to the fourth plate, she paused for a moment. "This is a forgery."

"You're sure?" Rina asked.

"Of course, I'm sure! If you compare it side by side . . . the paper is original, but the quality is lacking." She looked at the duo. "Of course, you suspected this."

"We did," Rina said.

"It must have happened at Pretoria." She turned to the next plate, which was original. But the following two were not. "Oh my heavens! I must report this. I'm terribly sorry but I can't have you checking this out right now."

"We understand. And in light of what happened, we have other things we need to do right now." McAdams tried out a smile. "Do we have to sign out?"

Susan was still in shock. "Uh . . . yes, of course. I'm sorry. I'm floored. How did this happen? How did you know?"

354

Neither answered. They both signed out and slowly, Rina helped McAdams back into the chair while Susan watched. She said, "You must think I'm terrible . . . upset by a book when you've suffered so much. I am very sorry."

"Don't be sorry," McAdams said. "There are two dead bodies out there. I'm the lucky one. Thank you for your time."

"You're welcome."

Rina pushed him to Schultz. The guard said, "That didn't take too long."

"Something's come up," McAdams said. "We need to set our priorities elsewhere."

"You handled Mrs. Devry very graciously, Detective," Rina said.

"Wow. I never thought I'd hear gracious and me in the same sentence."

Rina laughed. Schultz said, "So where to?"

"The hallowed dormitories. Specifically Elm Hall."

Decker hadn't spent this much time in a car since his patrol days. On the road again, this time to New York City with the kid sitting shotgun while Oliver, Rina, and Schultz were squished into the backseat. It was five in the evening, traffic was terrible and everyone, except Rina, was tired and grumpy. She had the most reason to be in a bad mood. She was in the middle seat, but as usual she seemed oblivious, soldiering on with pleasant conversation that was answered with grunts.

After a half hour of stalling in traffic, Rina knew that if the men didn't get something to eat, the car would decombust. She reached down to the bag under Oliver's feet, took out sandwiches, and passed them around. Amid begrudging thanks, everyone ate. It wasn't a tricky thing to pull off. With cars backed up on the highway, they were moving about five miles an hour. Ten minutes later, Rina passed around coffee with lids and cookies and napkins.

"Thank you very much, Mrs. Decker," Schultz said. "Your cookies make it almost worth the traffic."

"Call me Rina."

"Thank you, Rina."

"What can truly compete against a fine chocolate chip cookie?" McAdams said. "My nanny used to bake them. At first I just watched. Then I participated. Hence my baking skills."

"Your *nanny*?" Oliver said.

"Yeah, of course I had a nanny. The wealthy don't raise their kids." McAdams took a sip of coffee. "Not that my mother ever worked a real job. Her days were filled with society obligations." A pause. "She does a lot of charity work. Her largesse never extended to me. As far as jobs go, I've worked a few internships but it's always been with connections. I just waltzed in ahead of everyone else. Man, I've worked more in the past couple of weeks than I ever have in my life."

Oliver said, "Why'd you pick police work?"

"To spite my father."

"And?"

"What makes you think there's an 'and'?"

Decker smiled. "You have a terrible game face, Harvard. If you ever decide to make policing your profession, you should work on that."

"Let *me* guess," Oliver said. "You wanted the experience to write a screenplay."

McAdams laughed. "Am I that transparent or did you get that idea from Decker? And BTW, it started off as a novel. Later, it morphed to a screenplay. Like the Loo said, I'm kind of Hollywood."

"And I stand by that statement," Decker said.

"I always thought that I was kind of Hollywood," Oliver said. "Then I met real Hollywood sharks. I'll take criminals over them any day of the week."

"What's it about, McAdams?" Decker asked. "Your screenplay."

"What do you think?"

"An art theft," Decker said. "Under the circumstances, you might think about debuting with something that won't get you killed."

"I deleted everything after I was shot. It was garbage anyway. My main character was obnoxious and derivative of everything I've ever seen on TV or in the movies."

"It takes time to develop," Rina said.

McAdams smiled. "Thanks, but the truth is, I have no imagination."

Decker braked hard. "I detest traffic. Also this kind of stop and go makes us sitting ducks."

"I've got my eyes peeled out my window, sir," Schultz said.

"Ditto," Oliver said. "I've seen a lot of noses being picked, a lot of women putting on makeup, and everyone's texting. Nothing suspicious, but my guard is still up. How much longer?"

"Maybe an hour for what should be a fifteen-minute ride."

"Just as long as we get there in one piece," Rina said.

"Amen to that, sister," McAdams said.

"How are you feeling, Tyler?"

"With no horrible pain, I could probably move up to crutches very soon."

"Don't push it," Oliver said. "You'll heal faster."

"I'm just happy to be out of the hospital and working again." He paused. "And you honestly don't think he took off?"

357

"Why would he take off?" Oliver said. "We didn't call him. He has no idea we're coming down."

"But he must know he's in trouble, right?"

"Maybe," Decker said. "And even if he suspects he's in the weeds, most people don't disappear underground. People with money hire lawyers."

"Which is why you don't call him," Oliver said. "No warning works to our advantage."

Decker said, "Anyway, it's moot right now. At this rate, we won't make it until midnight."

Rina yawned. "We'll be there by seven at the latest."

"Take a nap, Rina," Decker said. "You've certainly earned it."

"Maybe I will close my eyes for a moment. It's been a long day."

No one spoke for the next five minutes. Then McAdams said, "Maybe I should make my protagonist a woman."

"Good idea," Decker said. "Model her after my wife."

Rina smiled. "That's a lovely thing to say. Thank you."

McAdams laughed. "Call me crazy but I don't see an Orthodox Jewish woman who bakes chocolate chip cookies and makes sandwiches as a gritty crime fighter."

"Excuse me?" Rina said from the backseat. "Cookies notwithstanding, I've had as much input in this case today as you have, Tyler."

"You're right about that," McAdams said. "Don't take offense, Rina. You know how I am."

"I do. No offense taken."

"Like I said before I have absolutely no imagination."

CHAPTER THIRTY

The prewar building, fashioned in brick and stone, was located on the Upper East Side between Fifth and Madison: two ten-story towers with a six-story edifice connecting them. The street, framed by small, bare trees, was filled with slush, and the sidewalk and steps had been salted. Awnings and eaves dripped ice as well as ice cold water. The double glass doors were unlocked, so the three of them went inside where the temperature was warmer but still leaked cold from the doors. A uniformed man sat behind a desk off to the left side. A sign said that all visitors needed to be announced.

The doorman was about to call, but then McAdams reached over the desk from his wheelchair and put his hand over the phone. "We're all cops. Let's keep it low key."

"But—"

"If anyone gets pissed, I'll take responsibility. Seventh floor, 3A, correct?"

"Yes, but—"

"Shouldn't there be two of you down here?" McAdams asked. "Where's the other man on duty?"

"Karl's taking out the trash."

"I take it in a building this big, there's no specific elevator man."

"No—"

"So it's on automatic. Great."

"I think I should take you up."

"Don't bother." McAdams wheeled up to the doors and pressed the up button.

"I'm going to call up right now."

The elevator doors opened. "I wouldn't if I were you. It might get you in trouble." McAdams wheeled inside the cage with Oliver and Decker in tow and pressed the seventh-floor button. The doors closed. "Poor guy. Taking all this shit for around 40K a year."

"That's all they make?" Oliver said. "I thought it was unionized?"

"It is. But the cap is small. They depend on Christmas tips. Dad and Mom were always generous. I'll say that much for them."

"How do they live on 40K a year?"

"Well, for one thing, they don't live in the city."

Decker said to McAdams, "This is your baby. You do the talking about the Petroshkovich book. Keep your questions short. Don't give away anything prematurely."

"Got it."

"We might talk if we think of something," Oliver said. "Also we like to throw out questions just to keep them off balance."

"Sure."

Decker said, "I'll start then nod when you should go."

"Got it."

"You have your pad?"

"Yep."

Decker took out his own notebook. "Then we're all set."

The elevator dinged and the trio got out. The door to the apartment was already open and Lance Terry was waiting in the hallway. The kid had on a sweatshirt, jeans, and slippers. His eyes immediately went to McAdams's wheelchair, then up to Decker and Oliver. They held the terror of uncertainty. "What's going on?"

"Can we talk inside?" Decker said. "No sense making the neighbors curious."

"Yeah, sure."

The door swung all the way open. Terry took them down the hallway and into a traditionally furnished living room: hardwood parquet floors, crown molding, expensive-looking rugs, a crystal chandelier, and a roaring fire. On the coffee table in front of a jacquard silk white couch were two almost empty brandy snifters and an ashtray of butts. The throw pillows had been crushed. Terry plumped them up. "Sit wherever you want."

"This is Detective Oliver," Decker said. "You know Detective McAdams and me." He looked around. "Are you alone?"

"My parents are out."

"That's not what he asked," Oliver said. "He asked if you were alone."

The group heard a door open and turned to the source of the sound. "It's all right, Tee." The voice was male, and he slowly ambled his way down the hall until the long hair came into view. He was sloppily dressed but the material was expensive. When he stepped into the living room, Decker said, "Hello, Livingston. What brings you here?"

Sobel didn't answer. Instead, he sat down on the couch and poured brandy into one of the used snifters. His eyes went to McAdams. "What happened to you?"

"I was shot: the leg, the arm, and a graze to the head.

361

I wouldn't recommend it even for verisimilitude in a screenplay. The dude was serious."

Sobel went mute. Terry sank down next to him. His voice was a whisper. "What the fuck is going on?"

"Why'd you take a leave of absence, Lance?" Decker asked.

It took him a while to find his voice. "I needed a break."

"In your senior year of college?" Oliver asked.

"It wasn't just Angeline's death, it was the way she died. Everything went weird, the way people looked at each other, the way they looked at *me*! I had to get out."

"What can you tell me about her murder?" Oliver asked.

"Nothing!" The room went silent. Finally, Terry said, "You guys know I couldn't have done anything. You checked out my schedule. I was totally telling the truth. I don't know *anything*!"

"Detective Decker filled me in, but I'm new here," Oliver said. "You said people went weird after the murder. Maybe your friends have theories about Angeline?"

"You name it, they said it. She was everything from a prostitute and a drug dealer to a spy working for the CIA. And everyone was coming up to me for answers, like I was holding back. I'm sure some idiots think my absence means I'm guilty of something. But I swear I don't know any more than anyone else. The break is temporary. I'm coming back for spring semester."

Decker looked at Terry, then at Sobel. "So when did you two get so tight?"

"I called him up when I came back home," Terry said. "We both knew Angeline. I . . . just wanted to talk to him."

"You were suspicious of me," Sobel said. "You were feeling me out."

"And you were feeling me out," Terry said.

"Fair enough." Sobel regarded Decker. "It appears we're both in the dark." He swallowed hard. "We heard that the Latham guy got chopped up."

Decker said, "Who told you that?"

"Word gets around," Terry said.

"I know people in Summer Village," Sobel said.

"He wasn't chopped up," Decker said. "But he wasn't pretty to look at, either."

"Oh God!" Terry hit his forehead. "Why are you here? I hadn't been with Angeline for over a year . . . longer."

Decker nodded to McAdams who said, "I was in Rayfield Library this morning—the reference desk."

Terry shrugged. "Good for you."

"I was looking for a specific book called the *History of Iconography*." When Terry didn't respond, McAdams said, "Want to tell us about it, Lance?"

"Tell you what?" A pause. "I have no idea what you're talking about."

"You don't remember a book you checked out only two months ago?"

A pause. "Is this some kind of trap?"

"Let's try it again. The *History of Iconography* by Nikolai Petroshkovich." The boy looked blank. "Doesn't ring any bells?"

"Not a one."

"You need to sign your name on an index card to check out this particular book because it's very valuable. It's worth six figures."

"Interesting but it has nothing to do with me."

McAdams licked his lips. "Your name was on one of the index cards."

"You must have misread the card."

"No, I did not misread the card. Furthermore, the school ID number belongs to you. Try again."

"What was the book again?"

"The *History of Iconography* by Nikolai Petroshkovich. Published in 1926. An old art book with original plates?"

"I have no idea what you're talking about. I never checked out a book on iconography. I have no interest in iconography. I'm not even sure what an icon is. If you suspect it has something to do with Angeline's murder, then maybe she put my name . . ." He fell silent.

"What?" Decker asked.

"That little bitch!" Terry's face turned dark. "That scheming little bitch!" He sat down so that he was eye level with McAdams. "Angeline asked me if I could check out a reference book for her—for her thesis. She told me she'd do it herself, but she already had too many reference books out and they wouldn't let her check out any more. She caught me at a weak moment . . . on purpose . . . fucking whore!"

"Go on," McAdams said. "She asked you to check out a book for her and . . ."

"I don't remember the title and I don't remember the author. All I remember is that the book came in a big, wooden box and we had to wear gloves to look at it. We weren't even allowed to take it out of the reference library. She looked at it for about an hour, put it back in the box, and gave it back to me and that was that."

"So you were with her when she went through the pages?" McAdams asked.

"I was there but I wasn't sitting next to her. I sat at a different table across the room."

"Why was that?" Oliver asked.

"She didn't want me around! I sat next to her at first. But then she told me it made her nervous to have me peering over her shoulder. I wasn't peering over her shoulder. I wasn't even paying attention to her. I took out my computer and was playing a video game. So then the bitch told me I was making too much noise, which was ridiculous because I had the sound on mute. When I pointed that out, she had the nerve to tell me that the typing was too loud. So I moved to another table. I woulda left altogether but I had to return the damn book. The area is in a cage and you can't get out unless someone unlocks it."

"That's true," McAdams said. "You didn't think that her behavior was strange?"

"She was always acting strange . . . hot one minute, aloof the next. I have no idea why I didn't tell her to fuck off. I suppose I was hoping for another go-around. But obviously she only fucked me to get to the book. I swear I don't know who murdered her, but I'm sure that it musta been someone she pissed off!"

McAdams said, "And after my experience, I'd say he's still pissed off."

Terry blanched. "Sorry."

McAdams said, "Not your fault."

To Tyler, Sobel said, "Are you gonna be okay?"

"I'll be fine."

Decker said, "Lance, can you walk us through the day she asked you to check the book out for her?"

"Uh, I'm assuming you're not interested in the sex part."

"I want a timeline for you. If you two had sex, I want to know when and where."

"This was a while back."

"Take your time," Decker said.

"I guess we hooked up around eleven. I remember because I skipped my class. It took about an hour. Afterward, she said something about working on her senior thesis and that she needed to go to the library."

"And you said?"

365

"I said okay. See you later or something like that. Then she must have asked me if I was busy because I remember asking her what she wanted."

Decker was taking notes. "Okay. Go on."

"She said 'I need a favor'—in those words, 'I need a favor.' I asked what and she said that she needed a specific reference book for her thesis. But she had checked too many books out already. Could I check a book out for her? And since she had just done me a favor—mutual favors I'd like to think—anyway, I was in a good mood so I said sure. Because it wasn't outrageous that she'd be working on her thesis. She worked a lot and she often worked in Rayfield."

"Okay," Decker said. "So then what did you do?"

"We went to the library and I checked out the book in the big wooden box."

"Back it up for a minute," Decker said. "Where were you when she asked you to do her a favor?"

"We were in my dorm room."

"So she came to your dorm."

"Yeah. I was surprised when she showed up. No phone call or text or e-mail. She just showed up." He shook his head. "Shoulda known better."

"So she went to your dorm room, you two had sex, and then you two went to Rayfield."

"That about sums it up."

"And you took your computer with you."

"Always. I always have my phone, my pad, and my laptop. People steal things."

"How about Angeline? What was she carrying with her?"

"I dunno." He shrugged. "I didn't pay attention."

"If she was looking at the book for her thesis, she must have had her laptop, right?"

"Yeah, probably."

"Anything else?"

"I couldn't tell you. I don't even remember if she had her laptop."

Decker paused. "She was an artist, right?"

"Yeah. A pretty good one, too."

"Did she carry any materials with her?"

"Like an art box?"

"Or a portfolio case."

"Yeah, she carried her portfolio case everywhere, never let it out of her sight. Like I said, she was a good artist, but it's not like her stuff was worth anything."

McAdams said, "Can I get back to the library for a moment? You said that while Angeline was looking at the book, you were playing with your laptop and she was sitting away from you."

"Yeah."

"Where was the reference librarian?"

"Beats me. I know I had to ring to get her when I wanted to turn in the book, so I guess she wasn't at her desk the entire time."

The men exchanged glances. McAdams said, "Do you have a piece of paper and a pencil?"

"Here." Oliver tore off a sheet of paper and gave him a pen.

McAdams drew a map. "I was at the library this morning. As I recall, the reference area has six tables." He quickly drew up a schematic and gave it to Terry. "Where were you sitting?"

Terry looked at the map. "Do you want to know where *I* was sitting or where *she* was sitting? Because I remember *she* was sitting next to the window here. And I probably was sitting here; clear across to the other side."

"So you were sitting closer to the reference desk and Angeline's table was the farthest from the reference desk."

"Whatever you say."

"I'm not saying, I'm asking. Look at the map and tell me if I'm right?"

Terry glanced at the rudimentary drawing. "Yeah, sure. That looks about right."

"Could you see what she was doing?" Decker asked.

"I assumed she was looking at the book."

"Let me ask it this way," Decker said. "Was she in your direct line of vision?"

"Because it doesn't look that way from my map," McAdams said.

"I guess if I had been paying attention to her, I could have seen what she was doing. But I wasn't. Why are you asking all these questions?"

Decker said, "Her thesis was on textiles, not icons. Why would she want a book on iconography? Did you ask her about it?"

"No. I didn't ask her about it. Why would I care?" Terry looked at McAdams. "You said the book was valuable. Did she take it? Is that why she was killed?"

McAdams looked at Decker who said, "The book is still in the library. But some of the original plates have been stolen and replaced with forgeries."

"Just like the Tiffany windows," Sobel said.

Decker nodded.

"She's the connection, right?"

"Jury is still out." Decker quickly scanned his notes and then he looked at Terry. The thefts of the art plates didn't seem to come as a shock to him from the expression on his face. "Thanks for seeing us, Lance. I may have a few more questions later on."

"If you do, call instead."

"Some conversations are better in person."

"You didn't have to sneak up like you did. I would have

told you about the book in the first place, but I didn't remember. There was no reason to terrorize the doorman."

"We didn't terrorize anyone," McAdams said. "Besides, this is the Upper East Side. He's dealt with far worse than us."

"I have a question." Sobel pointed to McAdams. "I see what happened to you. Am I in danger?"

Terry looked up and down and didn't say anything. Decker raised his eyebrows. "Is there something you'd like to say to me?"

"Me? No . . . I mean, yeah. Are we safe?" Terry's voice grew loud. "This is just terrific. Another legacy that the bitch left behind."

"Are you sure you don't have anything to tell me?"

"No," Terry said.

"You never answered my question," Sobel said.

"I wish I had an answer," Decker said. "I'm carrying a gun. So is Detective Oliver. My wife is carrying a gun and has a full-time armed bodyguard."

Terry began to pace. "You know my fucking name is on that index card. Anyone can look at it and hunt me down."

"It's not available to the public," McAdams said. "I had to arm twist to get the librarian to give it to me."

"Why isn't that comforting right now?"

"I'll get it pulled, Lance," Decker said.

"I want it destroyed!"

"I'll get it pulled by one of the men and locked up in an evidence room," Decker said. "I can't destroy it just yet because it might be evidence."

"The whole thing is fucking whack!" Sobel said. "I repeat. What should I do?"

"What should *we* do?" Terry asked. "Like get out of town or something?"

Decker said, "Small towns make it very easy to find people."

"I can vouch for that one," McAdams said.

"So we sit around waiting to be shot?" Sobel said.

"It wouldn't hurt to take precautions," Decker said.

"You mean hire a guard?" Terry said. "You just waltzed right in. And if this asshole tried to take out a cop, what chance do I have?"

"I'm way more involved in this case than you are, Lance; I really don't think either of you is on the bad guy's radar."

"But you don't know."

"True. I don't know. If it were my kid, I'd look into armed protection. It's probably not necessary, but there's no harm in being cautious. Maybe even overcautious." Decker paused. "Overcautious is okay. It's usually the daredevils who get tripped up."

CHAPTER THIRTY-ONE

The stopover for the night was Nina McAdams's ninth-floor apartment on Park Avenue. It was an august Beaux-Art building of stone and marble, staffed with uniformed doormen who were aghast to see Tyler in a wheelchair.

"What in the world happened to you, Mr. M?" asked the shorter of the two front doormen.

"Nina didn't tell you?" No response. McAdams said, "Just a little accident, Jonah, but I'm fine. Is my grandmother upstairs?"

"She left for dinner."

"At nine at night?"

"Yes, sir."

"With whom?"

"A new one, Mr. M. I haven't seen him before," Jonah said. "But someone is still up there. Are you sure there isn't anything I can do for you?"

"No, I'm fine, but thanks for asking." McAdams wheeled over to the elevator. The taller of the two uniforms rushed over to push the button and everyone waited. Decker was perfectly able to ride the elevator up without help but the upper crust of New York City lived an infantilized life. There was a ding and everyone crowded inside the wood-paneled car.

"How are you this evening, Dicky?" McAdams asked.

"Just fine, Mr. McAdams. Are you sure you're okay?"

"I'm not perfect, but I'll be fine. If anything, I'm lucky."

"If you say so, Mr. McAdams."

The elevator opened up onto a spacious marble landing with only one door: Nina McAdams owned a full floor apartment. Decker knocked before Tyler could get out his keys, and when Rina asked who it was, he said, "It's your tired husband and friends."

She opened the door and the three men came into a wide marble foyer. McAdams forged ahead, wheeling himself into a majestic living room filled with ornate furniture, a large fireplace, a grand piano, a carved staircase leading to a second story, and big French doors that opened to a terrace with an over-the-rooftops view to Central Park. The space was adorned with molding and patterned hardwood floors covered in part by expensive-looking oriental rugs.

"I've been drinking tea and reading a book and luxuriating in a cashmere blanket." Rina smiled. "How aristocratic is that? Your grandmother is lovely, Tyler. It's so nice of her to put us all up."

"We're doing her the favor." McAdams looked around. "Where are Bonnie and Kate?"

"Bonnie went home about an hour ago. Kate is in the back doing the laundry. She didn't want to leave me alone at first. I don't know if she fully trusts me."

"That's just Kate."

Decker looked around. "Where's Greg Schultz?"

"He and Nina went out for a bite to eat."

"He left you *alone*?"

372

"No, I have Kate."

"She's over sixty and has a limp," McAdams said.

"You're not helping me," Rina said.

"I'll kill him," Decker muttered.

"Peter, I'm fine and I'm armed. Besides, this place has better security than Fort Knox. I insisted they go out."

"He shouldn't have listened to you. What's the matter with him?"

"He's a volunteer, remember? His brain needs to turn off. It'll make him more alert in the long run."

"She's right," Oliver said.

"Who asked you?" Decker was still standing.

McAdams looked at Rina. "Are you comfortable here?"

"Are you kidding me?" She tousled his hair. "Come on, guys. I'll show you where Nina has stationed us." She turned to McAdams. "Do you need help getting up to your room, Tyler?"

"Nope. The place has an elevator."

Rina laughed. "Nina didn't show me that."

"And I bet she didn't show you the secret passage that leads to a secret room. It's where my grandfather entertained his mistresses when his wives were out, leaving no evidence of the deed. All that ended when Nina came along. She boarded up the space. Then she opened it back up after he died. Lord only knows what she uses it for."

"Maybe if I behave, will she rent it out to me?" Oliver said.

"Maybe if you don't behave, she'll rent it out to you."

Oliver laughed. Decker said, "Where should we meet to talk?"

"The breakfast room. We can spread out."

Decker looked around. "Where is that?"

Rina said, "I'll show you. I think I've got the lay of the land."

McAdams opened a door and wheeled himself into an elevator cart. "See you in twenty."

It was more like thirty before everyone came down. By that time, Greg and Nina had come back and the oversized apartment hummed with activity. Kate had fixed finger sandwiches and there were also preopened bottles of sparkling water and port with small, crystal glasses. Nina had gone upstairs to get comfortable—whatever that meant—and Greg Schultz, revitalized from his hour on the town, showed the group a map of the area complete with alleys and hiding places. He had done such a good job that Decker didn't reprimand him.

Schultz said, "I also have the doormen looking out for anything strange. They know more about the area than I could ever hope to learn. Anyway, I hope you aren't mad about me leaving Rina alone. She and the lady of the house ganged up on me."

"I'm sure they did," Decker said. "You're off duty now, Greg. I've got it from here."

"Thanks. See you all in the morning."

The boys replenished their fuel intake with the sandwiches while Rina sipped sparkling water and nibbled on fresh fruit.

Nina came down in sweats and flats. Her face was perfectly made up and her blond hair was still coiffed. "Anyone for coffee or tea?"

Tyler grinned. "You're pouring?"

"No, I'm offering. Kate will do the actual pouring."

"You were scaring me for a moment, Nina."

She gave him a grandmotherly pat. "Silly boy."

"I'll take coffee, if you wouldn't mind, ma'am," Oliver said.

"It's Nina," she said. "And you are way too old to ma'am me."

"I am old, Nina, but in dealing with such a beautiful and charming woman, it's better for me to err on the side of respect."

Nina stared at him. "You're very good. Are you married?"

"Nina . . ." McAdams said.

"Hush up." She smiled at Oliver. "Not that marriage has ever stopped anyone."

"I'm not married." Oliver grinned. "And I have a lot of war stories from my days at LAPD if you're interested."

Decker rolled his eyes. Nina caught it. "So the stories aren't true?"

"No, they're true," Decker admitted. "He left the force because he was shot."

"Well, you'll have to tell me all about it," Nina said. The coffeepot beeped. "Kate, the coffee's ready."

"Coming."

McAdams said, "I think we can take it from here, Nina."

"You're kicking me out?"

Tyler stood up with a cane. He leaned over and kissed her forehead. "Yes, I am. But thank you for everything. You're a first-class woman."

Nina was speechless. A tear trickled from her eye. "That was gracious—so unlike you."

"It's just because I'm weak, Nina. Very weak."

She wiped her cheek "Good night to all." A brief smile and then she left. After Kate poured coffee, she disappeared as well. The ensuing silence was awkward. Rina asked how it went with Lance Terry. Decker gave her a synopsis of the conversation with the two young men.

Rina said, "Interesting that Livingston just happened to be there."

"It looked suspicious at first," Decker said. "But I

believed Terry when he said he called Livingston down."
A pause. "I still think he's holding back."

"Totally," Oliver said. "I'm wondering why he *really* left the school. He doesn't seem like the kind of guy who'd have a breakdown even if his ex-girlfriend was murdered. Furthermore, it was his final year of college."

McAdams said, "Maybe someone threatened him?"

"Yeah," Oliver concurred, "I think someone spooked him good."

Decker said, "We know that Terry didn't kill her. His alibi checked out. So did Sobel's. But were they involved in the murder?"

"Don't see it," Oliver said.

"Why not?" McAdams said.

"Just a gut feeling based on experience. Do you disagree?"

"Not necessarily. I'm just trying to figure out your conclusions logically."

"That's a mistake," Oliver said.

Decker said, "I believe Sobel when he says he hadn't seen Angeline for a long time. For now he's out of the picture. Terry's another story. I think something scared him enough to drop out of school and come running to the safety of home."

"At least they didn't shoot him," McAdams said.

"True. If someone had, he would have phoned the police." Decker sipped coffee. "We have a recent link of Lance to Angeline. The Petroshkovich book. But did he know that she was razoring out the prints?"

"He seemed genuinely surprised," Oliver said. "But the point is, even if Terry didn't know what she was up to, maybe someone saw them go into the library together. Maybe that someone thought they were up to mischief."

"So you think the murders had to do with the Petroshkovich book?" Rina said.

"No," Decker said. "The murders had to do with something very big and I don't see the Petroshkovich book as being that big. But it does point the finger at another forgery that Angeline was involved in."

Oliver said, "How did she reproduce the pictures if she never checked out the book? She would have had to have seen the originals, right?"

"Of course," Decker said. "The book was coowned by Pretoria College in Marylebone. If we checked out the reference library there, do you think we'd find John Latham's name on a sign-up sheet?"

Oliver said, "He took the plates, gave them to her, and she put the phony ones back when Terry checked the book out for her."

"I'll call Pretoria in the morning," McAdams said.

"Let's roll with that for a moment," Decker said. "Angeline and Latham now have some original Nikolai Petroshkovich plates. What's their next step?"

"To find a dealer," Oliver said. "What about that Goddard guy you were talking to in Boston? The shootings happened right after you two came up to visit Summer Village."

"What do you think?" Decker asked McAdams.

"Don't like Goddard for the fence," McAdams said. "The plates are too valuable to be sold as pretty works on paper. You need someone who specializes in Russian art."

"Jason Merritt?" Decker asked.

"Kind of small stuff for him," McAdams said. "I called him to ask about some items on his website as a prospective buyer for a fictitious museum. Like everything else in art, not all icons are alike. Some very old icons sell in

377

the thousands. His icons are in the hundred-thousand-dollar range because they are very old and in very good shape."

Oliver said, "Do you know if he deals in rare books?"

"No, I don't know," McAdams said. "Nothing like that is on his website."

"But if something came his way?"

"The Petroshkovich book is worth about a hundred thousand intact. A single plate would be worth much less. I don't see him selling anything like that. He'd have to know the plate was stolen."

"Not even once?" Rina asked.

McAdams thought a moment. "He prides himself on being a reputable art dealer. Why would he buy a single plate or even two or three? He'd be risking everything to make a few bucks."

"I still want to talk to him," Decker said.

Rina said, "Even if Merritt doesn't sell individual art plates, maybe someone in his gallery has a side business."

McAdams raised his eyebrows. "That's a thought."

"I get them every once in a while," Rina said. "What about the guy who works there? Victor Geronimo or something like that?"

"Victor Gerrard." Decker turned to Rina. "Want to come with us tomorrow, darling? You can assess Gerrard while we talk to Merritt."

"Sure. I've got nothing to do." Rina shook her head. "Other than luxuriate in this fabulous place."

Decker said, "Let's keep Schultz at the apartment, guarding Mrs. McAdams. Unless Oliver would like the job?"

"It's tempting but since you asked me out here to help, I might as well deliver."

Rina said, "What specifically would you like me to do?"

"Just be a good distraction."

McAdams smiled, "No offense to Rina's beauty, but in this case, I think I may be a better distraction."

"Already thought of that and that's why you're coming, too." Decker shrugged. "You can't tell with these art dealers so I might as well cover all bases."

CHAPTER THIRTY-TWO

Mulrooney said, "We found Latham's storage bin."

Decker switched his cell to the other ear. "That's amazing!" It was eight in the morning and he only knew it was Tuesday because of his watch. The days seemed endless and he needed something external to keep him grounded. He was finishing his continental breakfast of orange juice, tea, and a croissant and jam when he got the call. The table was set with fine china. He was balancing a scalloped coffee cup with one hand and the phone with the other. He tried not to drop anything. "What's inside?"

"That's the bad part. The place had been cleaned out except for one lone key."

"A key?"

"Yes, a key."

Decker sighed. "I already know the answer but any idea what it's for?"

"I wish. No identification other than the lock is a Schlage. But it wasn't randomly left behind. It was jammed into a corner and taped to the wall. If Latham was dealing in stolen art, I'm thinking he took his hot merchandise elsewhere."

"He probably knew that the police had found out about the forgeries. Maybe Angeline saw us poking around the crypt. Or maybe the tip came from another person. I'm betting the key is another storage bin and that puts us back to square one."

Mulrooney said, "Except that we do have a key. But why hide it in an empty storage bin? Why not in a safe-deposit box?"

Decker said, "If he got caught, we'd look for a safe-deposit box. But if we found out about his storage bin, we'd look and find it empty and we'd have nothing. Your guys did good to find it."

"Be even better if we found a bin with the art," Mulrooney said.

Decker said, "If he rented another a storage bin, we'll find it."

"We're doing the paper trail. Nothing yet but we'll keep at it."

"You know? Maybe this is where Angeline Moreau entered the picture. Maybe *she* took care of renting the bins."

"Did you find any bills for storage rentals?"

"No. But maybe she paid cash and used an assumed name. We know that they used throwaway phones. No doubt they were careful."

"Then she'd have a copy of the keys," Mulrooney said. "Do you have her keys?"

"I have some of her keys. They've been filed as evidence. Can you send me a copy of the key you found in the empty bin? I'll see if it matches up to anything we've got."

"I'll courier it over to Greenbury."

"I'm not in Greenbury. I'm in New York." Decker brought him up to date.

Mulrooney said, "Do you think Lance Terry was involved in the murders?"

"No, but something scared him away from Greenbury."

"A shooter?"

"If it was a shooter, he'd have gone to the police. Maybe a harassing phone call or someone tailing him. All of us think he's still hiding something. We all think that it could be that he was involved in the thefts."

"Could be if he took a header. I'll make a dozen copies of the keys and we can begin to search for the missing bin—if there even is one. When are you back in Greenbury so I can send you a copy to compare it with Angeline's keys?"

"I'll call up my captain and let him know. He'll take care of it."

"Good. What's your next step?"

"Since it appears that Angeline was stealing art plates from the Petroshkovich book, I'm going to visit Jason Merritt—the dealer who specializes in Russian art. It seems a little lightweight for him, but I have to check it out. Any word from Professor Gold?"

"Nope. I'll give him a call. Keep me informed."

"I will. Bye." Decker hung up, called up Mike Radar, and explained the situation.

Radar said, "So you want me to see if Angeline has an identical key on her ring. And if she does, to start looking for storage bins in our area."

"Exactly."

"I'll assign the hunt to Ben and Kevin. If there is a match, they'll let you know."

"So can you call Chris Mulrooney in Summer Village and set it up?"

"Yeah, sure. When do you think you'll be back?"

"Tonight, hopefully."

"Good. I'm going to Rayfield Library to pull Lance Terry's

383

card. While I'm there, I'll nose around, talk to some of Terry's pals, find out if the kid was actually threatened. We'll trade notes later in the day. Just watch your back. No heroics."

"I hear you." Decker disconnected the line. Oliver came into the breakfast room: he was back to his old dapper self—pressed white shirt, red tie, black suit, and polished shoes. He sat down and picked up a slice of toast. "I could get used to this."

"Don't bother. It'll only make it harder in the long run."

"I say live in the moment. Oh, before I forget . . ." Oliver pulled a sheet of paper from his pocket. "Courtesy of Detective Dunn. Mr. Merritt isn't Mr. Squeaky Clean."

Decker looked over the rap sheet. Merritt had been cited twice for drunk driving. The two incidents had been six years apart and the last one was eight years ago. Those priors weren't nearly as interesting as the fraud charge ten years ago.

"Two years' probation," Oliver said. "I'm thinking that he represented something as genuine when it wasn't."

"But to get the charge to stick, he had to have known it wasn't genuine."

"He pled a nolo. But that begs the question. If the item was fake, why didn't he just return the money?"

"Maybe he didn't have the money to return."

McAdams limped into the room, using a cane for balance. Oliver said, "Are you sure you should be walking?"

"I'm tired of people giving me pitiful looks when I'm perfectly healthy." He sat down. "The reference library at Pretoria doesn't open until nine. I left a message."

Decker thought a moment. "Give Allan Sugar a call. Ask him if he'd like to go to Pretoria and check out the sign-up sheets personally."

McAdams poured a cup of coffee. "He's kinda old to be running around."

"It was his case. Let's give him the courtesy."

McAdams took out his phone and made the call. A minute later, he hung up. "He sounded eager. Go figure."

"I know how old cops think because I am one," Decker said.

"It's the jones of police work," Oliver said. "It never goes away."

McAdams sipped coffee. "Anything new?" Decker brought him up to date. Then Tyler said, "Interesting but not shocking. Merritt's an art dealer."

"Are they particularly more dishonest than anyone else?" Oliver said.

"Probably not, but they deal with rich clients. More temptation to fudge because the stakes are higher." McAdams buttered toast. "I'd like to think I'm honest, but I've never been tested. Money isn't my thing. Of course, I have a lot of it."

"So what's your Achilles heel?" Oliver asked. "Power? Women? Drugs?"

"I dunno. Maybe power. How about you?"

"Women."

"What about you, Old Man? Are you corruptible?"

"I'd have to think about it, Harvard."

"What about your family? Would you protect them if they did something illegal?"

"I suppose it depends on what they did."

"Would you turn them in if they murdered someone?"

"If it was premeditated, yes. Even if it wasn't, I still think I'd do it. Going to the police is usually the best option, as long as you go in with a great defense lawyer."

"Hedging your bets."

"Just using the law to my advantage. What about you, Oliver? Would you turn your sons in for murder?"

"Probably, but I couldn't swear to it. The one thing I've

385

learned being a cop for all my life: justice isn't black and white."

"Ain't that the truth?" Decker said. "I remember once when Cindy was around sixteen. She wound up at a twenty-four-hour drugstore at three in the morning with her friends. She wasn't supposed to be out that late. Neither my ex-wife nor I would have known about it except unfortunately for her, the store was robbed. The cops took statements of everyone there."

"Poor kid," McAdams said.

"Yeah, her cover was blown. We were both pretty damn pissed. Anyway, the case was handed over to a robbery detective who called up my ex-wife and asked her if Cindy could make a statement. My daughter lived with her mom. When Janet didn't answer him right away, the detective— who didn't know he was talking to a cop's ex-wife—said if it was his daughter, he wouldn't let her do it. So Janet said no and that was that. She called me later in the day, which was very unusual. She never called me for any reason other than money. She must have been sorely conflicted. She actually asked me if she did the right thing."

"What'd you say?" McAdams asked.

"I said I agreed with her decision. First of all, it was a done deal so why make her feel bad even if she is an ex-wife. Second, I probably would have done the same thing. I know what these trials can be, the tolls that they can take on the psyche."

"But then you'd never make a case if everyone refused to testify," McAdams said.

"You're absolutely right. If Cindy had been an adult, she could have decided for herself. But she was still a minor, and therefore it wasn't her decision. All I can say in my defense is that with matters of personal safety, it's family first."

* * *

It was hard to tell the predominant emotion: outrage, anger, embarrassment, condescension, absurdity: Jason Merritt exhibited them all. Today he wore a black suit, blue shirt, and no tie with black ostrich boots on his feet. Russian art apparently did very well.

"Your accusations are monstrous," Merritt snorted.

Decker tapped his toe and let the words hang in the air. Rina was wheeling McAdams through the gallery rooms, looking at the art. Oliver stood in the background. No sense ganging up on the guy. Decker said, "You've never dealt in books or plates at any point in your career?"

"I've already answered that question."

"Even something as valuable as the Petroshkovich book?"

"Oh my God, how many times are you going to plow the same ground?"

Oliver broke in. "If someone offered you a good deal on the Petroshkovich, you wouldn't buy it?"

"I don't deal in rare books!"

"I couldn't help but notice," Oliver said. "There's a stack of books on the front table."

"Those aren't *rare* books," Merritt sniffed. "Those are current art books on the subjects I represent. I give them out to my clients as *reference* material."

Decker was scribbling in his notepad, more to look busy than anything else. "And no one has ever offered you the Petroshkovich book or any plates from it."

"That is correct."

"But you do know that Petroshkovich had left one of his copies to Rayfield Library and it was coowned with Pretoria College in Rhode Island."

"More repetition, Detective?"

"It's a habit, Mr. Merritt." Decker pointed to McAdams. "We're dealing with very serious stuff."

387

Merritt lowered his voice. "I'm sorry for what happened to him. But to come in here and accuse me—"

"We're not accusing anyone," Oliver said. "Just gathering information."

"Those charges you mentioned are decades old!"

"They are," Decker said. "But because of what happened, we're investigating everything. So please bear with us. So the last time you looked at the Petroshkovich book in the library was over two years ago."

"At least two years ago." Merritt had lowered his voice.

"At Littleton or at Pretoria?"

"I've been to both colleges, but I've not been to either recently. Look, I don't know how many times I have to say this. Despite that charge, I don't deal in stolen art. I pleaded a nolo contendere on the advice of my lawyer because I was in a no-win situation with a horribly aggressive man. I should have fought harder. But at the time, I just wanted this terrible chapter in my life to go away."

"So why didn't you just return the money?"

"I did return the money. He sued me anyway! And once he claimed fraud, it became a criminal charge and took on a life of its own!"

"And you won't tell me who it was?"

"I'd love to give you his name. But I won't as a matter of principle."

"We can check court records."

"You can't. Everything was sealed at the settlement. He was a horrible man. He did it to spite me. And, may I add, it took him forever to return the piece back to me."

"Did you give him the money right away?"

"There were some expenses that were incurred like shipping and insurance. I should have just absorbed everything but he made me mad." Merritt shook his head. "Suffice it to say, it was an expensive lesson. Now, I don't deal with anyone without references."

"He was a walk-in?"

"A Russian national with a big wallet." He waved Decker off. "I don't want to talk about it other than to say that I've had the piece authenticated by three separate dealers. But it's not for sale. It's hanging in my living room as a reminder of carelessness."

Rina wheeled McAdams over to Decker. "Lovely pieces," she said. "I noticed you wrote a book on icons. Can I buy it?"

Merritt said, "I'll give it to you." He looked at Tyler. "I'm sorry about what happened. That's terrible."

McAdams shrugged. "I consider myself lucky."

"Is there anything else?" Merritt asked.

"Actually, yes." When Merritt groaned, Decker said, "I believe you when you say that no one offered you any plates."

"Does that merit a thank you?"

"Merit from a Merritt," Oliver said. When the dealer looked at him, he said, "If I'm joking, it means you're probably off the hook."

Merritt looked at Decker. "Go on."

"Is it possible that one of your employees might be doing some shady business on the side?" When Merritt appeared stunned, Decker said, "Who in your employ would have access to your client list?"

"I don't give the list out to anyone just for the asking."

"But it's on your computer. How hard would it be to access?"

The man pursed his lips and considered the words. "It is just a file and I'm not at my desk all the time."

"Thank you for being honest," Decker said. "Has the gallery had any suspicious thefts in the last three months?"

"No."

Oliver said, "Did anyone in your employ recently take a sudden vacation?"

Decker looked around. "Speaking of which, where's Victor?" A long silence ensued. "Victor Gerrard. He was here when we first visited. Where is he?"

Another long silence. "It wasn't a vacation. Victor's father is ill. He asked for time off."

"Okay." Decker smoothed his mustache. "Uh . . . how long has he worked for you?"

"About a year. And I've had absolutely no problems with him at all."

"Where does Gerrard live?" Oliver asked.

"He rents a room when he's in the city during the week. He's in Philadelphia on the weekends. His cell has a Philadelphia area code."

"What about his father? Where does he live?"

"I believe he told me that his dad lives in Chicago or maybe it was Cleveland."

"How long has Gerrard been gone?" Decker asked.

"About two weeks."

"Right after the time of our visit, "McAdams said. "Has he called in?"

"No . . . he hasn't. And I haven't called him. I figured he must have his hands full. And business is traditionally a little slow in the wintertime."

"Can I have his number?" Decker asked.

"I'll call," Merritt said. "I'm not giving out any numbers without his permission."

"Then please go ahead and do it, sir."

"Very well." Merritt punched in the digits. A moment later he got voice mail and left a message. "I'll let you know when he calls back."

"No, no, no," Decker said, "We need to find his

whereabouts as in *now*. When he applied for the job, he filled out an application, correct?"

"Of course."

"Go pull up his application. Maybe he gave you his father's number for contact information."

"It might take a few minutes."

"Mr. Merritt, this is a murder investigation. We need the information. Please get me his application."

Merritt said, "Very well. I'll be right back."

After he left, Oliver said, "Think he's telling the truth?"

"I do."

"Me, too."

McAdams said, "Shouldn't someone be there when he makes the call?"

Oliver said, "He's being cooperative. Let's not push it."

"What we really need is the client list," Decker said. "Maybe we'll find a fence among the names. But he's not going to give it to us without a warrant."

"We can use eminent danger to get the list."

"Yeah, that might be worth a try."

Five minutes passed. Rina said, "Maybe I'll go grab a book."

"What do you think of him, Rina?" Decker asked. "Do you think he's lying?"

"I'm not an expert, but I don't think he's lying. He's just prickly."

"I agree with you," Oliver said.

"The iceman cometh," McAdams whispered.

"More like the snowman," Oliver said. "He's white."

Merritt said, "The application form in my computer has been erased. But I keep the paper applications in a separate file. On it, he claims his father died five years ago." He wiped his forehead with a handkerchief. "Dear God! What is going on?"

Oliver said, "We need your client list."

"I can't give it to you, Detective. It's confidential."

"We'll get a warrant."

"Then do so."

"And while we're doing that, whoever else is brutally murdered is on your conscience."

"That's a *horrid* thing to say."

"Don't get mad at him," McAdams said. "He just doesn't want you to wind up like me. At least I'm breathing. The next one may not be so lucky."

Merritt buried his head in his hands. Decker looked at him. "We need the list."

"What makes you think that Gerrard was dealing illegally with one of my clients?"

"Do I really have to answer that?"

Merritt nodded. "Wait here. I'll print it out for you."

"Thank you. You're doing the right thing."

After he left, Oliver said, "Who do we contact about Gerrard? NYPD? Philadelphia PD?"

"I'll do Philadelphia first. Cindy works there."

"Yeah, right. How's she doing?"

"She's fine. She should be moving up to detective soon."

"Good for her. And the boys?"

"They're ready to play pro basketball."

A moment later, Merritt returned with several sheets of paper in hand. "It goes back five years, but I haven't updated in years. Some of the people may even be deceased." He handed it to Decker. "And should someone ask, you didn't get the names from me."

"Got it." Decker scanned the names with Oliver looking over his shoulder. "It's your complete client list, though."

"It's the only list I have, yes."

"Could you look it over for me? Make sure no one important has been erased."

"It's over three hundred names." When Decker didn't answer, Merritt grabbed the list back and with an index finger went over the names. It took him more than a minute, which meant he was paying attention. "I'm not positive but it looks complete."

Rina stood on her tiptoes and whispered into Decker's ear. He turned to her. "Can you do that?"

"I can't. Maybe Tyler can."

"Do what?"

"See if the client list was recently updated," Decker said.

"I told you I haven't updated it in a while," Merritt said.

"And you also told me that it isn't hard to get access to your computer. We're wondering if this list was updated right before Gerrard left."

"How would I know that?"

"Check previous versions of the file," McAdams said. When the dealer didn't answer, he said, "I could check. If you have an automatic backup, it's not hard to do."

"You're not touching my computer."

"You can watch me."

"It's a murder investigation," Decker reminded him.

Merritt gritted his teeth. "I suppose it would be okay if I was there."

"We'll all come." Decker smiled. "If it's okay with you."

"Oh, for God's sake." The dealer marched off and the crew followed him to his office. It was a decent-size office but not meant to accommodate five people let alone a wheelchair. McAdams elected to leave the appliance outside. He hobbled over to the desk chair, sat down, and it didn't take long to find what he was looking for. "The list was updated three weeks ago."

"That's not possible!" the dealer exclaimed.

Decker said, "Tyler, can you pull up an older version of the list?"

"Yep." A few moments later. "Here we go. Can I press the print button?"

"Yes, yes." Merritt removed it from the printer and gave it to Decker who put the two lists side by side and started going down the names. Within a few moments, he found his first discrepancy. Two more followed, making it three clients missing from the updated version of the file. He showed the names to Merritt.

"Alex *Beckwith*?" Merritt said. "Why on earth would anyone delete him?"

"Who is he?"

"He heads the Cultural American-European Liaison Association."

"Which is?"

"Just what it sound like. Beckwith acts as a go-between when museums want to borrow from each other. For instance, if the Met was having a Renoir exhibit and wanted a painting from the Louvre, he'd liaison from one museum to another. He's a very prominent individual."

"Does he buy stolen art?" Oliver said.

"I won't dignify that with an answer," Merritt said. "His position is critical. Since Chabad's challenge to the pieces in the Russian Library, European countries are disinclined to loan anything out to the United States without an indisputable provenance."

"I should hope so," Rina said.

Merritt looked incredulous. "Art is above politics, my dear."

"Not when it comes to theft, sir."

Merritt bristled. "I'm afraid we are of two minds."

"Guess my mind comes from being the daughter of Holocaust survivors."

McAdams had already pulled out his iPad. "Twelve thousand religious items and fifty thousand books assembled over two centuries by the Chasidic movement are in the Russian Library in Moscow. In 1991, a *Moscow* court ordered the library to turn over the items to Chabad, but then the Soviet Union collapsed and the judgment was set aside by the Russians. Then an American court sided with Chabad, but the Russians are refusing to honor the judgment claiming America has no jurisdiction in Russia."

"That means loaned art—especially Russian art—might be seized in America," Merritt said. "It really has had grave consequences for museum loans."

"Such a pity," Rina said.

Decker couldn't quite hold back the smile. "Mr. Merritt, what can you tell me about the other two men left off the list? The names look Russian."

"They are Russian and, honestly, I don't remember them. Obviously they bought from me a while ago but I can't place their names with faces."

"Let me get this straight," Oliver said. "They bought Russian art from you here in the United States and took it back to Russia?"

"I have better art than most of the Russian dealers. Like I told you, the crème de la crème was bought by my grandfather when no one wanted it."

"If these men are clients, you must have invoice files on them," Decker said.

"I should." He sat down at his desk. After a minute, he sighed. "Their files are gone." He looked at Tyler. "Perhaps you can find previous files?"

"You read my mind," McAdams said. He poked away on the keyboard. "I can't find any copies. Maybe he trashed them." He kept typing. "Nothing in the recycle bin." He looked up. "You could get an expert to go into the hard drive and see what was erased, but I can't do it."

"Are we done?" Merritt asked.

"For the moment." Decker nodded. "Thank you."

"Do I still get my free book or have you changed your mind?" Rina asked.

"Of course." Merritt smiled. "I admire your grit."

"Tell that to my husband."

The crew left the gallery in search of a place open for an early lunch. McAdams said, "At least, we've narrowed down the list to three names."

"Good work, Harvard."

"I did the work, but I wasn't the creative part of the equation."

"A-hem," Rina said.

Decker laughed. "Thank you very much, my brilliant wife."

"You're welcome."

"So where does that leave us now?" McAdams asked.

"We've got names," Decker said. "We do it the old-fashioned way: legwork. Or in your case, McAdams, we can call it wheel work."

CHAPTER THIRTY-THREE

"No missing persons report has been filed," Cindy told him. "How long has this Victor Gerrard been out of contact?"

"Around ten days to two weeks." There was a pause on the line and Decker knew what Cindy was thinking, what any cop would be thinking.

"And you're just reporting it now?"

"I just found out about it now." He switched his cell to his other ear. "Look, honey, all I need is for someone to go over to his apartment just to make sure he's not moldering."

"I think someone would have reported a moldering body. It kinda stinks."

"Please?"

"And you're sure this is the right address?"

"No, I'm not sure."

"And you don't want to place an MP report? Make it a little more professional?"

"No need for the bureaucracy yet. It's possible that we could locate him in New York."

"So why don't you let me know what happens in New York before I do anything."

"It may take us a while. I just want to know if you have a dead body."

Cindy said, "This is what I'm going to do because I love you. I'll go to the apartment and see if I have a body. If I can't find a body, I'll see if something looks off. If something's off, I'll start the paperwork. But I'll do it all in about an hour because it's already been a while and I'd like to finish up my shift because it's bad form to piss off your partner."

"Thank you, Cynthia. You are the bomb. How are the kids?"

"Doing great. They love their new school. Come visit them for grandparents' day. It's in a few weeks."

"I'll be there."

"Call me a cockeyed optimist. I choose once again to believe you."

"Low blow. I'll be there, I promise. I love you, dear."

"Same." She hung up. Decker walked back to the table where the gang had been seated for lunch. It was an overcrowded kosher vegetarian storefront with long wooden tables and hardback chairs, making the wheelchair the most comfortable seating in the café. There were a half-dozen mixed appetizers on the tabletop that probably looked better than they tasted and a pitcher of diluted, organic tea.

"She's going over to his apartment in an hour, God bless her." Decker sat down.

"Do we think Gerrard is still alive?" McAdams asked.

"I have no idea." Decker picked up a mock chicken egg roll. Not too bad but then again anything fried, sugary, or salty always tasted okay. His cell rang. The window showed Radar's cell. He depressed the button. "Hold on, Mike. Let me get to a spot where I can hear you."

He stood up again and walked outside into the cold.

The skies were gray and there were snow flurries, but it wasn't as cold as it had been up north. He had gloves on his hands and a scarf around his neck, but he'd taken off his hat and left it in the restaurant. Icy flakes landed on his head like a bad case of airborne dandruff. "What's going on?"

"I just got a call from a retired detective named Allan Sugar. I have no idea who he is, but since he asked for you, I'm assuming you know something about that."

Oops. Decker said, "Sugar is the original detective on the Petroshkovich icon thefts. We think that Angeline Moreau was stealing plates from one of the original Petroshkovich books and subbing them with forgeries. To do that, she'd have needed copies of the originals and it would have looked suspicious if she checked the book out in her library. So I asked Sugar if he could go to Pretoria College and see who else might have checked it out since it was shared between the two libraries."

"You think John Latham pulled out the plates and gave them to Angeline to copy."

"Exactly. I knew you were short of manpower and I figured Sugar wouldn't mind. I should have filled you in but it slipped my mind. Sorry."

"Yeah, it's not cool to look like a doofus. Find out what he found out and call me back."

"Right away."

"In the meantime I went over to Littleton and spoke to a few of Lance Terry's friends, asked them what spooked the kid to leave midsemester."

"And?"

"Hang-up calls: several of them. And then Terry began to think he was being followed. His buddies tell me he became a little paranoid. In view of everything that has happened, I'd label the paranoia as being perceptive."

"I'll talk to Terry again. Maybe he noticed a silver van. Any luck with that?"

"We've checked about fifty of them in the area. All registered and accounted for. On a positive note, Moreau does have a copy of the key found in Latham's empty bin."

"Yes!" Decker pumped his arm, eliciting a few stares from startled passersby. "Our first tangible link between Latham and Moreau."

"We're getting warmer. And that means you need to watch your back. I'd like you here in Greenbury where bad things stick out. When are you coming home?"

"I've still got business down here." He gave Radar an update on his conversation with Merritt. "After lunch, we're on a hunt to find Victor Gerrard."

"Are you looking in New York or in Philly?"

"We're looking in New York. I've got feelers out in Philadelphia. And it looks like I should talk to Terry again. So I'm saying we'll probably be back by tomorrow."

"Tonight would be better. I'll keep Ben and Kevin on the storage bin hunt. You call up Allan Sugar and find out if Latham checked out the book. Then you let me know."

"I'll call you back right away."

Ten minutes later, Decker sat back down at the table with a smile on his face after speaking to Allan Sugar. The appetizers were gone and there were no entrées as of yet. He was starved, but in too good a mood to be his usual famished, grumpy self.

"Entrées should be here soon," Rina said. "Service is a might slow."

"I can tolerate the slow service. But I'm a little miffed that you didn't save me an egg roll."

"I thought you were off fried foods."

"I'm never consistent. You should know that by now. Good news." Decker brought everyone up to date. "So now we have two definitive links between Latham and Moreau—the same key on both their key rings and they both checked out the Petroshkovich book—or at least Terry did it for Angeline."

"Or maybe he didn't do it *just* for her," Oliver said.

"What do you mean?" McAdams asked.

"Ask the boss," Oliver said.

Decker hit his forehead. "He means there is a possibility that Lance Terry was in on the thefts and now he's scared."

McAdams raised an eyebrow. "Interesting."

"Didn't you mention that he was a theater arts major?" Rina said. "As in acting?"

"Yes, I did," Decker said. "Let's pay him a visit right after lunch."

"What about Gerrard?"

"It's been about two weeks, he can wait another couple of hours."

"Should I call Lance up?" McAdams asked.

"No. We'll pop in. I don't want him rabbitting. Eventually, we should check out Terry's key ring. Maybe he has a copy of Latham's key."

"Like he's going to incriminate himself in the theft?"

"If he doesn't show us his keys, it says something," Oliver said. "There's a reason he's running scared and it probably has to do with more than a few hang-up calls."

"His alibis checked out for both murders," McAdams said.

"He could have always hired out. He was rich enough."

"What are you thinking, Scott?" Rina asked.

"Maybe originally Terry and Angeline had this little art theft thing going on. And then Latham comes in and not only takes over the operation, he steals the girl. So Terry

401

cuts off his dick. 'You cut me, I cut you.' The Latham murder was personal."

"I don't know," Decker said. "This feels like something bigger than a love triangle and a few pieces of stolen art. I keep thinking about that codebook."

Rina said, "Maybe it started as something simple and Latham made it more complicated. And that's when the real bad guy decided to show up."

McAdams said, "It's crazy: a codebook, a missing storage bin, three names erased from Jason Merritt's client book, and we're still missing Victor Gerrard." The kid looked around. "I'm starving."

"Yeah, this is ridiculous." Decker got up.

"Be kind," Rina said.

But Peter had already stalked off. Five minutes later the entrées arrived. Different types of tofu meant to simulate meat, all of it drowned in tomato sauce and covered with cheese.

McAdams picked up his fork. "It looks awful. But at this point, they could serve me dog food in a chow bowl and I wouldn't say anything." He speared something oozy and gave it a taste. "Not bad." He finished chewing and turned to Decker. "While you were out talking to Radar, I looked up Alex Beckwith, Ph.D. For the last ten years, he had been trying to persuade European museums to curate a traveling Da Vinci exhibit that would eventually come somewhere in the U.S., probably the Met."

"That sounds ambitious," Rina said. "And unrealistic."

"Especially now," McAdams said. "Between Nazi-looted art and the Chabad thing that Merritt was talking about, no one is loaning anything to the United States. Everyone is afraid that the pieces will get confiscated. Beckwith's plans have clearly hit a roadblock." McAdams smiled. "Looks like the *Mona Lisa* isn't going anywhere."

402

"He was trying to bring over the *Mona Lisa*?"

"I was being facetious. But any painting by Da Vinci is priceless because there are so few of them."

"So that would be worth killing over," Oliver said.

"Yes, I suppose that's true. But even if you were bold enough and smart enough and connected enough to steal a Da Vinci, you couldn't sell it anywhere." McAdams was checking his notes. "I would think that Beckwith was working on something smaller in scope for an exhibition—like works on paper: also rare but not as priceless. Anyway, it's all moot."

"What about the other two Russians?" Decker asked. "Find anything on them?"

"Lars Dotter Hemellvich is actually Finnish. He lives in Norway and Croatia and is an art dealer who specializes in Byzantine Italian and Russian arts and mosaics. Martin Kosovsky is a Russian industrialist from Odessa."

"What kind of industrialist?" Oliver asked.

"Oil and natural gas. I didn't pull up much beyond that. For an oligarch, he keeps a low profile."

"He's an oligarch?"

"He's very rich and he's Russian and he isn't Putin. Isn't that the definition of an oligarch?" McAdams ate some mock chicken: it tasted like chicken. "I'll delve a little deeper when I have more time. So next is Lance Terry?"

"Yes," Decker said. "I'm hoping against odds he can lead us to Victor Gerrard."

Rina put down her napkin. "Not my best choice of restaurants, I'm afraid."

"It was fine," Oliver said.

"If you like bad food and slow service, it was great." Decker waited for Rina to punch him. Instead she just laughed. Decker kissed her cheek. "You're a good sport. I'm always needling you."

403

"That is true, but I love you anyway. Mainly because I get my way and needling is your attempt to balance the powers." She kissed him back and regarded McAdams. "Poor Tyler. You hardly ate."

"Not the most satisfying of meals, but maybe you did me a favor." The kid shrugged. "Victor Gerrard may be dead and moldering. So given my track record with corpses, it's best I don't go hunting on a full stomach."

CHAPTER THIRTY-FOUR

Arms folded across his barrel chest, Lance Terry was flushed and sweating. "You have no right to come down here and harass me. If my father was here—"

"If your father were here, I'd tell him that you were in danger and your best option is to talk to the police." Decker looked around the hallway. "You already think people are following you. Who knows? Maybe someone is spying on us right now."

The boy's face drained of color, red to white. "Is someone following you?"

"If he is, he can see us talking. So how about if we come in? It's a good first step."

"Yeah . . . right." Terry swung the door open and let the crew inside, his eyes on Rina, wondering about the new person in the mix. The place was quiet except for the distant clatter of laundry being spun in a dryer. There was a half-packed suitcase on the couch, another closed one on the floor.

Decker's eyes went to the valise and then to Terry. "Are you alone?"

"Yeah."

"Where's your housekeeper?" McAdams asked.

"I gave her the afternoon off."

Oliver said, "You didn't want her to see you packing and asking questions."

Terry said nothing. He wore a body-hugging long-sleeved gray shirt and jeans. There were hiking boots on his feet. His sandy hair swept across his damp brow.

"Where did your friend go? Livingston Sobel?"

"How should I know?" A pause. "He left last night. I suppose he went home." His eyes refused to focus on any one spot. "Do you really think I'm in danger or is that just a pretense?"

"Doesn't matter what I think," Decker said. "Obviously you think you're in trouble. You're packing way too much to be going back to school."

"I'm not going back to school," Terry said. "At least not this semester. Too much has happened."

"What are you worried about, Lance?" When Terry didn't answer, Decker said, "Why don't we all sit down and you can tell us the truth."

"I have been telling you the truth!" Terry insisted. "I didn't have anything to do with Angeline's death . . . or the dude."

"His name was John Latham."

"I didn't kill her and I didn't kill him!"

"I believe you," Decker said. "But you certainly know more than you've been telling us. There have been hang-up calls. You think you're being followed. We're here because we're concerned about your welfare."

Terry seemed to wilt. He sat down next to his open suitcase. "You showing up here isn't good for my health."

"On the contrary," Oliver said. "Our presence tells the bad guys that we got to you before they did. So hurting you wouldn't serve any purpose for them other than to spur us to redouble our efforts. Right now the more people you tell, the better off you are."

McAdams said, "What's your password for your Wi-Fi?"

"My password?"

"The password for the apartment. I'd like to get on the Internet."

"Terrypark. Capital T."

"Thanks."

Decker opened up his notepad. "Tell me about the hang-up calls."

He whispered behind his hands. "A blocked call would come through my cell. When I answered it, I'd get heavy breathing—to let me know someone was there. And then whoever it was would hang up. I put in a *82 feature on my phone . . . so no one could get through without revealing the number. The calls would still come through as blocked. It freaked me out."

"How long has this been happening?" Oliver asked.

"They began a few days after Angeline was murdered. And then after you guys were shot at, I—"

"Detective Decker was shot at," McAdams interrupted. "I was shot."

"I know, I know. I got nervous. I had to get out of there."

"And you thought you were being followed," Decker said.

"Could have been my imagination."

"Probably not," Oliver said. "Tell us about it."

"I'd see things. Fleeting shadows but then I'd turn around to really look and it wouldn't be anything."

"So you felt like a person was following you?"

"As opposed to a dog, yes."

"As opposed to a car, Lance."

"Oh. I get what you're saying. It's hard to tail someone

on campus with a car because you're walking across quads and fields and things that don't intersect streets. So no. I never noticed a car following me." He furrowed his brow. "Like what kind of car?"

Decker said, "Silver Hyundai Accent van. Maybe two years old."

Terry shuddered while he shook his head no.

"Detective Oliver is right," Decker told him. "The more people who know your secrets, the better off you are. So start at the beginning."

"I've told you everything."

"No, you haven't, Lance. So either tell us or you'll wind up telling someone who's holding a gun to your head."

He slapped his hands over his face. "It . . . God . . . it was so long ago." No one spoke. "Just a stupid dare." He looked up. "Hazing. To get into the frat."

Everyone waited.

"I had to steal something from the cemetery. Not the one near the school, the big one in Bainbridge about ten miles away."

"When did this happen?" Oliver asked.

"When I first started Littleton about three and a half years ago. That's why I'm having a hard time believing that this whole mess has anything to do with me!"

"What did you steal?"

"A stone statue. It was maybe about three feet high. Some stupid goddess dressed in a Roman toga. It was in terrible condition. One arm was broken off. I found it buried in some ivy bushes and covered with dirt. So I took it because it didn't look like anyone would miss it. Heavy motherfucker." He exhaled. "Not my finest moment, but I was drunk and eager to please. Anyway, it sat in my dorm room for about a month or two months. And then I met Angeline. A few months later—after we were an item—she asked about it. I told her what I did. She was cool about it."

Silence.

"More than cool. She was intrigued. She told me she had seen something like that at an antique store in Boston. She asked me if she could try to sell it and we'd split the profits. It was just sitting in my dorm so I said okay."

Decker said, "Do you know who she sold it to?"

"No idea but she told me she got two hundred bucks— one hundred for each of us, which I blew by taking her out to dinner. I'm a moron."

"Go on."

"Nothing more to tell. She sold the statue, we split the money, and I never saw it again."

"Lance, the statue was just the start. We know you did other thefts because *we* know the gallery owner who purchased the hot items." A little white lie? Decker preferred to think of it as an educated guess. "So just get it all out."

The kid deflated, drawing in his shoulders into his torso and then doubling over as if in stomach pain. "I can't believe how this blew up in my face. It was just a stupid college prank, something you do when you're drunk and when you're getting pus—" He looked at Rina. "Girls can do weird things to your mind."

"I'm aware of that," Rina said.

"Tell us the rest of it," Decker said.

"It was a couple of months later. She asked if I could get more things like it."

"Like the statue."

Terry nodded. "I told her I could look around." A sigh. "So I lifted another statue from Bainbridge again: a smaller marble one. And then I lifted a couple of marble urns. She sold them and we split the profits. Because they were made from marble, she got more money for them."

Decker turned to McAdams. "Check to see if the items are on the inventory list."

"Already on it."

"If you stole anything else, Lance, we'll find out about it," Decker told him. "So now is the time to tell us everything."

He lowered his head. "I told her I wasn't going to pinch any more statues. Too heavy and too risky a venture. So Angeline asked if there was anything else valuable in the cemetery that was smaller and less heavy . . . so I wouldn't have to take a big risk lugging it around."

"And you said?"

"God . . ." He shook his head. "I told her there was a meditation room that held cremated ashes in metal urns. Some of the urns looked like genuine silver."

"You stole people's remains?" Rina asked.

"No! No, I didn't. Just the urns!"

"So what did you do with the remains? Dump them on the floor?"

"No! Of course not." Everyone waited for Terry to continue. "She asked if I could get inside the room. I said the door wasn't locked, but I wasn't about to steal remains. That's bad karma. Instead she told me to take pictures on my phone of the silver urns. Detailed pictures: close-ups. She said it was for a project, but I knew she was lying."

"But you did it anyway," Oliver said.

"I sent her the pictures. I figured what she did with them was her own business."

"And what did she do with them?"

"She copied the urns but used a cheap metal that she painted silver. She even engraved them with the same markings using a dremel tool." A big sigh. "This took her about six months. When she was done, she cajoled me to go back just one more time."

410

A long pause. "So I swapped out the real ones for the cheap ones."

"This substitution is sounding very familiar." McAdams showed him a picture on his iPad. "Uh . . . take a look at this marble urn, Lance. Does it look familiar?"

"Maybe it was one of mine, but I couldn't swear to it." A pause. "Wow, he's asking a thousand dollars."

Oliver said, "What did you two do with the silver urns?"

"On some of them, Angeline was able to polish out the inscription. On the others where the inscription was too deep, she said they were no good on the retail market. So she melted them down for the metal price. But I want you to know that I did transfer the ashes into the cheap urns. So I didn't steal Uncle Gomer or Aunt Dottie. They're right where they're supposed to be . . . just not in a fancy package . . . not that it matters to them."

His self-serving declaration was met with accusing silence.

Lance blushed. "I'll reimburse out of my own pocket if you promise no jail time."

"Kid, right now, that's the least of your worries," Oliver said.

"What other items did you steal?" Decker asked.

"Nothing after that." Terry winced. "I swear it! I refused to go back to the cemetery. The last job gave me the creeps. Not that she didn't try to change my mind. But when she saw that cemeteries were out, she pushed me into other things."

"Like?"

"Razoring out antique maps from old atlases."

"When was this?"

"About a year and a half ago, must have been in the start of our junior year. And FYI, I refused to do it. For one thing, you saw how careful they are at the reference desks. I knew I'd get caught. Then Angeline suggested that we could go to local libraries along the Hudson. Small towns are often filled with antique books. And no one cares about them. But I told her no. If she wanted to do it, she was on her own. She dropped it, but I knew her schemes weren't over, especially when she showed up with a Movado watch on her wrist. She dumped me because I wasn't of any use to her anymore. Finally, when she started sporting expensive stuff, it dawned on me that she got herself a new partner."

"How'd John Latham come into the picture?"

"I don't know how she met him. Maybe her contact in Boston fixed them up."

"And you don't know who this Boston contact was?"

"No." A pause. "I thought you said you knew the contact."

"I want to hear what you have to say."

"I don't have anything to say! I never knew her contact but I damn well knew she was doing something: her bling got bigger, her ski equipment was top of the line, and her sunglasses and purses were plastered with designer logos. How else did she afford any of that shit if she wasn't doing something illegal?"

"And you have no idea how she met John Latham?"

"No, I don't know. Why don't you believe me?"

"Are you asking me that seriously?" When Terry reddened, Decker said, "When did you find out about Latham?"

"I already told you guys that."

"So tell us guys again." McAdams held up his iPad. "Just for my notes."

"About a year ago, I tailed her into Boston. I saw Latham. I turned around, I went home. I was pissed. I admit it. And I thought very hard about punching his lights out.

412

But I was tired after the long drive. And I guess the drive also cooled me off. I didn't kill him and I didn't kill her." He slumped into his chair, regarding Decker with beseeching eyes. "I'm scared. No offense, but I don't want to end up like him." He pointed to Tyler.

"None taken," McAdams said. "I'm not happy about it, either."

"What do I do now, man?"

Oliver said, "Stop stealing stuff would be a great start."

"I was a fucking moron. I'll reimburse whatever I took in cash. I'll write apology letters. I'll do community service. But badgering me won't help because I have no idea who killed either of them." His eyes moistened. "I repeat, 'What do I do now?'"

"A few more questions, Lance," Decker said. "Do you know a man named Alex Beckwith?"

Terry shook his head. "Who is he?"

Oliver said, "How about Martin Kosovsky?" When he didn't get a response, he said. "Lars Dotter Hemellvich?"

"Never heard of them. They sound Russian."

"What about Victor Gerrard?" Decker said.

Terry thought long and hard. "Is he kinda like in his early thirties?"

"He kinda is and he's kinda missing."

"Oh God—"

"What do you know about him?"

"The name sounds vaguely familiar."

McAdams did an image search and showed the pad to Terry. "Any of these faces ring a bell?"

Lance studied the pictures. "I think I might have met this one at a college party. He might have been a friend of Angeline's. Beyond that . . ." He shrugged.

Decker said to McAdams. "Show him a picture of Jason Merritt."

"Sure." McAdams punched in search letters. "Here you go."

Terry shook his head with conviction. "Don't know him."

"Take another look," Decker said.

"I don't have to. I don't know him."

Decker pointed to his suitcases. "Where were you planning to go?"

"I have an aunt who lives near Los Angeles. Actually, she lives in a small little town about seventy miles north of L.A. She has this converted garage that she rents out to surfers because she lives close to the shore. It's currently empty and she said I could use it. I thought I'd spend some time up there until this all blows over."

"I'll need the name of your aunt, the address, and her phone number," Decker said.

"No problem." A pause. "So I can go visit her?"

"You can go, but don't leave Ventura without telling me where you're going."

The kid's mouth dropped open. "How'd you . . .?"

"The end part of Malibu is around forty miles from L.A. Sixty miles is Oxnard, seventy miles plus is Ventura. Ninety miles plus is Santa Barbara. I know that because I spent thirty years of my life with the Los Angeles Police Department."

"Oh . . . so you were, like, in L.A.?"

"Yes, Lance, LAPD is indeed in L.A.," Decker said. "You know what that means? It means don't piss me off because over there, I have all sorts of friends in very high places."

CHAPTER THIRTY-FIVE

Oliver went to fetch the car while McAdams, Rina, and Decker shivered in the cold. McAdams was upright, resting on his cane as Rina and Decker tried to figure out how to fold up the wheelchair.

The kid said, "The Boston contact is Goddard."

"Could be," Decker said.

"But we have no proof."

"If Lance never met Angeline's Boston contact, we don't have a link."

"Back to Boston?"

"Maybe. First things first. How do you fold up this chair?"

"There should be a latch near the footrest."

"Ah. Right." Decker and Rina managed to squash the chair down to a flat rectangle of metal and wheels. "Even if there was a link between Goddard and Angeline, a marble statue isn't worth killing over."

Rina said, "Maybe the statue turned out to be priceless, like that Degas that was just sitting outside the French embassy for years."

Decker smiled. "I don't think so."

Rina smiled back. "Well, neither do I."

"Where are we off to in the immediate?" McAdams asked. "Victor Gerrard's apartment?"

"Yes, and that reminds me . . ." Decker pulled out his phone and punched in Cindy's number, got her machine, and left a message. He turned to his wife. "How are you doing?"

Rina checked her watch. "Rachel's home by now. I'd love to go see our granddaughter."

"Not without Schultz."

"He can come along."

"How about we drop you off at Nina's? And then you and Greg can take a cab to Brooklyn. We'll meet you there later."

"That sounds like a good plan."

"Be careful."

"Of course."

Finally Oliver inched over to the sidewalk with the car. Traffic, as usual, was terrible. It took a few minutes to load everyone up, to buckle everyone up, and to pull out into the cacophony of horns.

"We'll drop Rina off at Nina's and then we'll head out to Gerrard's New York address."

"I pulled up several images of Gerrard," McAdams said. "We can pass those around to the neighbors."

Oliver slammed on the brakes and the car skidded. "I hate this city."

"It's meant for carriages, not cars," McAdams said. "If you walk, there's nothing like it . . . in good weather . . . without a cane."

"You're doing pretty well with the walking stick, Tyler," Rina said.

"Yes, I am. Take the wheelchair back. I'd really prefer to walk."

416

"It's slippery out there," Oliver said.

"I'll manage. I hate feeling like a cripple." He sighed. "This whole thing has been truly humbling."

"You've handled it all very well," Decker said.

"I'll miss it . . . the job. I was finally feeling like I was contributing something."

Rina said, "You're leaving Greenbury?"

"He's going back to law school."

"Good decision," Rina said.

"That's what Jack McAdams says."

"You know law is one of those fields that you can do anything with," Rina said. "With what you've been doing, you can specialize in stolen art."

"When do you start?" Oliver asked.

"August." McAdams stared out the window.

Rina said, "It's a ways off. Who knows what could happen?"

"That's the good part about a future," Decker said. "It's always open."

Over the phone, Cindy said, "I got the manager to open up the apartment. Aside from the furniture that comes with the place, it's empty, Dad. Nothing in any of the closets or drawers. No personal effects anywhere. Even the trash was cleared and that's unusual. There's always scattered paper left behind. Wherever he went, it appears he didn't want to be followed."

Oliver ran over a pothole. The car jumped and shook. "Hope no one was holding coffee."

Decker talked into the phone. "Was Gerrard's rent paid up?"

"Through the end of the month."

"So he left in a hurry. He's running."

"Who's running?" Oliver asked.

"Hold on, Cindy. I'll put you on speaker so McAdams and Oliver can hear." Decker depressed a button and Cindy's voice, made tinny by the phone speaker, rang through the space.

"Hey, Scott."

"Hey, Cindy. How's it shaking?"

"Pretty well. And you?"

"Not bad for an old guy. Did you find any moldering bodies?"

"Not a one. But I did talk to a few neighbors. No one remembers seeing him leave with suitcases, but one of his next-door neighbors remembered hearing a lot of noise in the middle of the night."

"When was this?"

"About ten days to two weeks ago. She didn't hear any confrontation or angry voices. Just a lot of heavy footsteps. It could have been that he was packing."

"Or he was being packed."

"You have a way with words, Daddy."

"I think in images."

"What's going on in New York?"

"We're making our way to Gerrard's apartment. I suspect if we talk to his roommates, we'll find out he just didn't show up one day."

"Let me know what you find out. I'm not opening up an MP file, by the way. It appears he left on his own accord. Just keep me posted. I'll see you next week."

"What's next week?"

"Grandparents' day." A pause. "Didn't we just talk about this three hours ago?"

Decker took the phone off speaker. "I've got it written down. No worries."

"Sure you do. I'll call Rina. She's good at keeping her appointments—and her promises."

418

"Another low blow."

"I love you. I'll see you next week."

"I love you, too—" But she had already disconnected the line. His cell buzzed again. This time it was Radar.

"This is one for the good guys. We found the bin. It was under a pseudonym but not a very good one. Jeffrey Morrow spelled M-o-r-r-o-w. Her last name Anglicized and his middle name. Doesn't take a rocket scientist to figure it out. It's crammed with stuff: stone statues, marble urns, silver urns, pottery, antique books that were stolen from libraries . . . the date stamps were still inside."

"Brilliant."

"What's brilliant?" McAdams said.

"They found the bin."

"The storage bin?" Excitement in the kid's voice.

"Are you there, Decker?" Radar said.

"Hold on, Mike, I'm putting you on speaker."

"Hi, Captain," McAdams said.

"How are you feeling, Tyler?"

"Coming along. You found the storage bin?"

"We did and it was filled with material that was probably taken from cemeteries or churches. We also found a half-dozen small paintings, and two file cabinets filled with art plates and maps. Plus . . . we found the two Tiffany panels along with boxes of stained glass. One case down and a bunch more to go."

"Ken Sobel will be thrilled."

"Good work on your first solve, McAdams. You give Sobel the good news."

"Okay. Thanks."

"What are you up to, Pete?"

"We're about to go look into an apartment that Victor Gerrard sublet. I don't suspect I'll find anything." He took

419

the phone off speaker and recapped his conversation with Cindy. "Looks like he's rabbited."

"Maybe he and Lance Terry are meeting up at Lance's aunt's house near Malibu. Didn't Terry say that Victor looked familiar?"

"He did," Decker said. "I have a friend in Ventura PD. I'll have her drive by the place and keep an eye out for one or both of them."

"Good."

"We should probably get someone to start cataloging the stolen items."

"I've already contacted Littleton. They're sending over several professors."

"I know you haven't gone through all of it, Mike, but did you find anything in there that looks really valuable?"

"Nothing worth killing over. At least not to my eye."

"What about the paintings? Did they swipe a Da Vinci or something?"

"Not unless Da Vinci painted New England landscapes."

"Are they signed?"

"If you hold on, I can tell you."

"Sure, I'll wait." He took the phone off speaker. "I'm on hold."

"Your first solve," Oliver said to McAdams. "Congratulations."

Decker looked at Tyler. "It's okay to smile, Harvard. You did do a good job. Go call up Ken Sobel and tell him the good news . . . although I suppose it would be better news if we found out who shot you."

"You know, Old Man, you'd make a terrible therapist." McAdams took out his phone. "And I should know. I've been to a thousand of them."

"Anything in the bin worth shooting people over?" Oliver asked.

"There are some landscape paintings. He's checking out the signatures now."

Radar came back on the line. "Okay. I've written down the names the best I can figure out. One was unsigned. The first is by a guy named H. Herz or Herg or something like that. It's faint. I'm looking for a magnifying glass."

"Can you spell it for me?"

Radar complied. "There's one by Jasper Pressley. There's a K. Kennedy, a T. Cole, an A. Durant or maybe it's Durand. There are two by a guy named Gifford and the last one is by H. Matusse."

"Matisse?"

"No, not Matisse. I know who he is and this is definitely not Matisse. It's H. Matusse." He spelled all the names. "Like I said they're all pretty landscapes of what looks like New England."

"Hold on. I'll give the list to Harvard and he'll look the artists up."

McAdams stowed his phone. "Ken Sobel's not in. I told him to call you."

"Could you look up these names," Decker said. "See if these artists are worth anything? I'll put the phone back on speaker."

McAdams regarded the names. "Captain, are the paintings landscapes?"

"Yes, they are. You know the artists?"

"I certainly know Thomas Cole and Asher Durand. They're well-known Hudson River Valley painters."

"Yeah, it does look like the Valley," Radar said. "What are the paintings worth?"

"How big are they?"

"Small. Eight by ten . . . a few a bit bigger."

"Okay, so probably not major works. They're still worth in the thousands. More like four figures rather than five although Thomas Cole can be pricey. But that's usually the big canvases. I've also heard of Gifford. Hold on . . ." He clicked. "Okay, he's Sanford Robinson Gifford. Also worth something. The H. Herz is probably Hermann Herzog."

"Where are you finding all this information?" Oliver asked.

"Ask Art. It's an art website that, among other things, has auction histories. And speaking of which, there are no auction histories for K. Kennedy or H. Matusse or Jasper Pressley." He looked up. "Too bad it wasn't Matisse. That could be worth killing over."

"If you like that kind of stuff," Radar said. "Thanks, Tyler. This helps. We'll be sorry to lose you in August."

"Not as sorry as I am to go. This detective stuff isn't half bad—aside from the bullet wounds."

Oliver saw a car pull out and abruptly swerved to get the parking space. The car bumped and jostled. He backed in amid an angry chorus of blaring horns.

McAdams said, "Done like a true New Yorker."

Decker said, "We're almost at Victor Gerrard's apartment. I'll keep you posted."

"Thanks." Radar paused. "Good work, everyone. And keep safe."

Oliver killed the motor. "Shall we?"

But McAdams was playing on his phone. "The Thomas Cole and the Asher Durand were stolen from the Auxiliary Ladies' Club in Joslyn, Rhode Island."

"Art Loss Register?"

"Yep. Let me look up the club. It's gonna take a minute."

"You got any more coffee in the box, Deck?" Oliver asked.

"I do. Black?"

"That's fine."

422

"Here we go," McAdams said. "The club was started in 1878 for care and support of a local orphanage. Now it organizes local charity functions and events and holds a ladies' luncheon once a month." He stowed his phone. "You know, these clubs were gifted a lot of early twentieth-century paintings. The artists were contemporary and weren't worth the big bucks that they are today. It was like me going to the local art fair and picking up a painting for five hundred dollars."

"Security on these old places isn't too tight," Oliver said. "Didn't something like that happen at the Scottish Rite Temple in L.A.?"

"I think it was the Wilshire Ebell," Decker said. "They had some old paintings and the secretary stole one of them."

"Hold on," McAdams said. "E-b-e-l-l?"

"Yep."

"Right you are, boss. It was a William Wendt and the secretary sold it to a gallery in Laguna Beach."

"Same pattern," Decker said. "Swiping valuables from unsuspecting places."

McAdams was still playing with his phone. "William Wendt is a California impressionist. Some of his big canvases are worth a lot of money." He looked up. "Lots of times these clubs don't even really know what they have. Although you'd think they'd be careful with a Cole or a Durand."

Decker said, "It would take Angeline too long to copy a painting. More than likely, she just replaced them with a cheap landscape. All that green . . . probably no one would notice at least for a while."

"Good point," McAdams said. "You know there are tens of thousands of period landscapes in period frames floating around. Most aren't worth that much."

"Breaking and entering into cemeteries is one thing," Oliver said. "But there's something really brazenly cocky about swiping a painting off the wall."

"I agree," Decker said. "They got cocky. And that's what got them killed."

CHAPTER THIRTY-SIX

They hit the road for Greenbury at ten in the morning, leaving the crush of hump day Manhattan traffic behind. It had been good to see the family, but the commute was getting cumbersome, especially with a carload of people. Decker was at the wheel with Greg Schultz sitting shotgun, peering out the window with steely eyes. In the back, Rina was seated between Oliver and McAdams. She wasn't grumpy, and that made her mood the best of the bunch.

"So Victor Gerrard is gone?" she asked.

"Appears that way," Decker answered.

"Is he a victim or a bad guy?" Her question was met with shrugs and grunts. "That he took off so quickly could indicate either one."

"Right," Decker answered. He was trying to be polite since no one else was talking.

Rina kept at it. "What do you think?"

McAdams blew out air. "I'm too tired to think."

Schultz continued to stare out the window. "Your grandmother is very nice. She wants to hire me as a bodyguard."

"You're *kidding* me." Tyler rolled his eyes. "Her place is a fortress."

"Exactly what I told her. She replied that her apartment couldn't accompany her down Madison Avenue." His eyes swept over the highway—front, back, and sides. "I declined, but I thanked her for her vote of confidence. I'm only telling you in case she says anything to you."

"Thanks for the heads-up," McAdams answered.

"Can we get back to Victor Gerrard?" Caffeine had kicked into Oliver's system. "The names were deleted from Jason Merritt's client list about two weeks before the murders."

"Yes," Decker said. "And it appears that Gerrard left the gallery right after our first visit."

Oliver said, "So could be that Gerrard deleted the names, executed the killings, and then stuck around to shoot you two before he packed up and ran."

Decker said, "I suppose he's as good a candidate as any since he's not around to offer an alibi."

"Curator by day, hit man by night," McAdams said. "Not as loony as it sounds. Art people are a foul bunch."

"I'm questioning Merritt's innocence in all this," Oliver said. "The guy's a sophisticated dealer and then he leaves his computer unprotected for anyone to hack into."

"Doesn't even sound like Gerrard had to hack into anything," McAdams said. "Just went inside Merritt's office and fiddled with the files."

"That's what I'm saying," Oliver remarked. "I think Merritt's involved."

"He's been cooperative with us," Decker said.

"So you don't think he's involved?"

"Reserving judgment. He could just be one of those academic types with his head in the clouds. I'm betting Gerrard ran the nuts and bolts of the gallery."

426

"Victor Gerrard," Rina said out loud. "The name has a foreign feel to it. Maybe German?"

McAdams took out his phone and called up his search engine. "Gerrard is English originally derived from the Old German name Gerhard meaning 'spear/brave.' And I can tell you without looking it up that Victor is Latin and it means victorious."

Rina was quiet. "How is Victor spelled? With a 'c' or with a 'k'?"

"Good question," Decker said. "I never bothered to ask."

"If he spells it with a 'k,' it could be Russian."

"Or German," McAdams said.

"Or German as in from *East* Germany," Rina said. "In which case, Viktor with a 'k' might speak Russian. And maybe that's why Merritt hired him. He was Russian speaking."

"You know, Rina, maybe Deck should have hired you instead of me," Oliver said.

"Why thank you, Scott."

"She's always been the brains in the family," Decker said. "Want to give Merritt a call, Tyler?"

"On it." McAdams waited. When his phone kicked in, he said, "Mr. Merritt, this is Detective McAdams from Greenbury . . . I know. I am sorry to bother you, but your gallery man, Victor Gerrard, is still missing and we're still working two murder cases . . . I'd just like to ask you a few questions about Victor Gerrard. Does he speak Russian by any chance? . . . he does. Is he Russian? . . . okay, okay . . . so he was born in East Berlin? So he speaks German as well? Okay. His first name Victor—is spelled with a 'k'? It is spelled with a 'k' . . . no, that's all for now, thank—" The kid looked at the phone. "He hung up on me."

"Rude little man," Rina said. "Although he did give me a free book."

"Speaking of books," Decker said, "what's going on with the codebook? Do you have Mordechai Gold's cell number?"

"Affirmative on that one as well."

"Ring him up."

"Right-o." A few moments later, McAdams left a message. "I could call his office number."

"I don't want to leave a message on a public machine." Decker tapped the wheel.

Tyler said, "Penny for your thoughts, Loo."

"Just trying to summarize things in my mind."

"Go on," Oliver said.

"First of all, what we know. Lance Terry stole a statue from a cemetery. Angeline Moreau sold it and decided that this was a business with a decent return since no investment capital was required. They did it together for a while but eventually Terry got nervous and stopped stealing—or so he says. But we'll take it on face value for the moment. Angeline wasn't ready to give up her life of crime. So she found another partner—John Latham.

"We know that Latham and Angeline hooked up but we don't know how they met. Maybe at a party, maybe they met through a common fence, or maybe she began to see his name on the date stamp in every book that she razored and made a logical connection that he was also doing funny stuff. However they met, they began thieving together, storing their take in a bin that was mutually rented: both of them had keys."

He paused.

"So that's Latham and Angeline. Now we have Gerrard to consider. We don't know if he's connected, but we do know that Viktor with a 'k' is missing and we know that three names were deleted from Merritt's client list—one American who sets up traveling exhibitions between top museums, one rich Russian, and one Finnish art dealer. It's possible that Gerrard deleted the names, but we don't know why."

"So actually you do know a lot," Rina said.

"Always a cheerleader," Decker said. "The sad truth is we don't know who killed Angeline and Latham. We don't know who tried to take down Harvard and me. We don't know if Gerrard is victim or perpetrator. And we don't know anything about Latham's codebook or if it's even relevant to the murders."

McAdams said, "If Gerrard was dead, we probably would have found his corpse by now. Whoever killed Latham and Angeline left the bodies in the open."

Decker said, "You're right, Harvard. The killer wanted to make a show of his handiwork. He was trying to impress someone."

"Which makes Gerrard more perpetrator than victim," Oliver said.

"Listening to all of you, I do have a question," Rina said.

"Let's hear it."

"Why go to all that trouble with a very complex codebook in a bunch of languages to hide things when it seems that Latham and Angeline weren't stealing items of major value?"

Decker said, "I think in the process of stealing minor items, Latham hit on something very big that he felt was worth hiding in code."

"Or," Rina said, "maybe Latham and Angeline didn't have anything worth hiding in code. Maybe the book belonged to someone else. Maybe Latham or Angeline stole it and then Lathem figured out the code and realized that he had hit on something big. Maybe Latham tried his hand at blackmail. And finally, since both of their

429

apartments were tossed, perhaps whoever murdered them was looking to get the codebook back. And maybe that someone was Viktor Gerrard. We know he spoke a few languages. Maybe he knew other languages as well."

The car fell silent. Then McAdams said, "You go, girl."

Rina beamed. "You live with a guy for nearly three decades, something rubs off."

Oliver said, "Gerrard also had access to Merritt's contacts. I'm liking him as the bad guy."

Decker gathered his thoughts. "The codebook was found behind a piece of paneling around the bathtub skirt where the Jacuzzi motor should have been. Mulrooney said the pipes were capped off and it was placed behind the pipes and well hidden. Latham's place had been trashed. All the logical spots to hide the codebook had already been checked out: the freezer was open, the toilet tank top was off, a few loose floorboards were ripped off, the walls had been pierced for hiding places—"

McAdams said, "So that's why the living room walls had those round holes punched into them?"

"Yep. They were checking for hollow spots or a safe that had been walled up."

"Aha!" Oliver said. "You're wondering why the killers didn't check the Jacuzzi motor area, which is a prime stashing spot for drug dealers and thieves."

Decker said, "They missed the Jacuzzi spot because they were *foreign*. They know about wall safes and floorboards and toilet tanks, but unlike we spoiled Americans, how many Russian goons have familiarity with Jacuzzis?"

McAdams said, "But Viktor Gerrard had lived in America for years."

"He lived in New York. How many regular Joes in Manhattan have a Jacuzzi?"

"I thought he lived in Philadelphia."

"Even if he was renting a weekend apartment in the heart of Philly, it probably wasn't high on luxury features. I'm just saying that everywhere I turn, I see the Brown Bear staring us down."

The car went silent.

Decker continued on. "Gerrard spoke Russian, Latham's field was Soviet art, and one of Angeline's last known thefts was plates from the Petroshkovich art book." He shook his head. "This case is dealing with a different set of rules. I think it's time we clue in Quantico. I usually don't like multiple agencies because communication is so poor, but . . ." He threw up his hands, and then he clutched the wheel. "Maybe you're right, Harvard. Maybe I am an Old Man or at the very least too old for this job."

"You don't mean that and neither do I," McAdams said. "If you think we need help, then we need help."

"Once it's dropped into Quantico's lap, we'll have to bow out. And viewing that someone had no qualms about shooting us, that may be a good thing."

"I agree," Oliver said. "Retirement is boring, but you're dead for a very long time. You took it as far as you could, Deck. I'm sure Radar will be happy to punt."

Rina said, "Nobody could have done any better with what you were given."

A band of cheerleaders. But it did little to calm Decker's sense of failure. "I'd still like to know what's in the codebook."

"If that's worth killing over, Peter, maybe it's better not to know."

"And what do I say to Angeline Moreau's parents? Whatever happened, she didn't deserve to die. And whatever happened, her parents deserve to know the truth."

Decker's phone buzzed. The call was from Radar and it

431

immediately went into Bluetooth. "Hi, Captain, we're two hours away."

"So that will put you into Greenbury around one?"

"That sounds right. When we see you, we'll update you with what's going on."

"Like what?"

"Some names had been deleted from Jason Merritt's client list. Viktor Gerrard spoke fluent Russian and German. We're thinking that maybe he was dealing art behind Jason Merritt's back. The whole case is feeling like a foreign entity is involved." Decker paused. "I hate to say this but I think we might have taken this as far as we can on our own."

"Interesting to hear you say that because I just got off the phone with our friends in Virginia."

Decker was stunned. "You called them?"

"Of course not. I'd let you know before I made a move like that."

"My bad. So who called them?"

"I don't know, but I suspect it was your contact at Harvard, McAdams."

"Mordechai Gold?"

"Didn't you say he was a former agent?"

"I did?"

"That's what he told me when I first spoke to him, Tyler," Decker said. "So what's our next move, Mike?"

"It's the CIA. What do you think happens next?"

"A meeting."

"Three o'clock at the police station."

"Will Gold be there?"

"Since he knows all about the codebook and called them in, I suspect he will be there. No need to feel defeated, Decker. The case would have been yanked from you anyway."

"I suppose that is some solace. Maybe we can get some answers."

"From the CIA?"

"Then again, maybe not."

"Wear a suit and tie and sunglasses and try to look very officious," Radar said. "That way, we'll blend in very nicely."

CHAPTER THIRTY-SEVEN

"Change of plans," Radar told Decker over the phone. "They want to meet at your house."

"My house?"

"Yes. They claim there are too many people to meet at the station and they'll draw too much attention. All that is true."

"How many?"

"Last count we're up to eight: Dr. Gold, some Russian, an American big shot, two agents, the mayor and the lieutenant governor of the state of New York, and Chris Mulrooney, who's already here. I don't know what you all hit on, but it's big."

"Meeting at my house . . . taking over my personal space. That's pure intimidation."

"It is. I suggested my house, but they seem bent upon making you uncomfortable."

"It's fine, Mike. I can deal. I'll see you in a bit."

"Pete, you and the kid and Oliver did good. Whatever happens, I want you to know that."

"Thank you." Decker hung up. To Rina he said, "The

phone isn't the right place, but I promise I'll let him know about all your input, honey."

"Oh, don't do that," Rina said.

"Credit where credit is due."

"I thank you, but I'm fine in the background," Rina said. "Besides, there are lots of advantages of being that pesky fly on the wall."

Rina was used to men. She had grown up the youngest behind two brothers. Her first two children were sons. She could usually speak their language and rarely had to use feminine wiles to get what she wanted. But in this instance, she knew she'd do anything to calm Peter down because he was seething. Men with suits and steely eyes had invaded his domain and while she knew he wouldn't do anything reckless, he wasn't going down easily.

Counting Mike, Scott, Tyler, Greg, and Peter, there were thirteen men crowded into a living room meant for six to eight adults. Dining room chairs had to be brought in. She had gone into the kitchen to make coffee and tea and to prepare a plate of whatever baked goods were in the freezer. While everything was brewing, she took the opportunity to size up the enemy.

The two CIA agents were easy to spot. Both of them were good-looking, tall men with broad shoulders and very short hair: one was fair haired, the other was brunette, and that was about the only way she could tell them apart. They could have been cast in the movies to play what they did in real life.

She knew the mayor, Logan Brettly. He was in his fifties with curly white hair, a stocky build, and a bulldog face. In the past, all her dealings with Brettly had been positive. He was a nice man who cared about his constituency. In this setting, he looked decidedly tense.

She supposed the professor with the scant, woolly gray hair was Mordechai Gold. His dress was more collegiate: corduroy jacket with patch pockets over a sweater over a shirt, and slacks with boots on his feet. He had perceptive eyes, taking in everything.

Of the other four men, she guessed that the blond man in his fifties with the perpetual tan was Alex Beckwith, the big-shot American. The suit with him was the lieutenant governor of the state of New York. Being a newcomer, Rina couldn't remember his name.

The most exotic in style and dress was a man in his fifties, built like a professional wrestler. He wore an expensive jacket with working buttons on the sleeves, and there was a gold Rolex on his wrist, a bejeweled stickpin that kept his tie in place, and a large diamond winked from his pinkie. She figured he had to be the Russian and most likely, he was one of the names that Gerrard had erased from Jason Merritt's client list. The remaining man looked like a cop: basic suit, tie, and rubber-soled shoes. Irish face, uncomfortable eyes and hands that he continually clasped and unclasped. Probably Chris Mulrooney from Summer Village.

Introductions had been made by the time she brought in the refreshments. She lowered the tray onto the coffee table. Then they thanked her, thinking that she'd make herself scarce.

They were wrong.

Rina sat on the arm of the couch next to Peter. "I'm Mrs. Decker. Depending how this conversation goes, perhaps by the end you can call me Rina."

McAdams clamped his mouth with his hands to keep from smiling. The mayor grimaced with displeasure.

"Mordy Gold." The professor stood up. "Please take my chair."

"I'm fine but thank you."

"Thank you for allowing us to invade your house. I'm actually the one who went to the officials. I felt that they had to be notified."

"And here we all are."

The man who looked like a cop stuck out his hand. "Chris Mulrooney."

Peter said, "He's the detective from Summer Village PD working on the Latham case."

"Good to meet you, Detective," Rina said.

"Chris, please. Sure you don't want a chair?"

"I'm okay."

It was the tall, tan man's turn to be polite. "Alex Beckwith. I insist you take my seat."

"All this chivalry is very heady," Rina said. "I'm fine next to my husband." She patted Peter's shoulder. "Actually, sitting on the arm of the sofa makes me feel taller."

The room went silent. Her presence was clearly not wanted. Rina stood and sighed. "I see no one is going to take anything unless I pour." She turned first to the wrestler, the one who hadn't introduced himself. "What can I get for you, sir?"

A long pause. Then he said, "Tea. Two sugars and a slice of lemon."

"Certainly. I didn't catch your name."

"I didn't give it to you."

Peter's eyes went dark, but Rina warded him off with a smile. The man's accent was thick. "And you are . . ."

The man smiled back with Machiavellian eyes. "Martin Kosovsky."

"That was two sugars and one lemon slice, Mr. Kosovsky?"

"It was."

She handed him his tea. "Here you go." It took another

five minutes to pour for the remaining group. Beckwith and the mayor also took tea. Radar and Greg took coffee. The rest of the clan including the spooks passed. She returned to her armrest. It was her house and with that ownership, she had the privilege of saying whatever she wanted. But with a soft voice and a smile.

"Since you called up the dogs, Dr. Gold, maybe you can explain what's going on. I assume it has to do with the codebook since that was your sole involvement with the case."

Decker laughed. He couldn't help it. "Lay it on the line, why don't you."

"Last I heard in America, you can speak your mind in your own house."

"I think that's still true."

Rina turned to Gold. "Professor?"

"Of course, you're right, Mrs. Decker. It has to do with the codebook. After breaking most of the code, I realized within the first couple of pages that the contents dealt with sensitive negotiations between our government and other countries. I called up Agent Marcus and Agent Grimm and explained to them what I had and at that point, I found out that the book had been stolen."

Beckwith interrupted. "These negotiations have been going on for quite some time. It is a very good thing that the book was found and returned to the proper authorities. And for this reason, we're actually here to thank all of you for your hard work."

Rina looked him straight in the eye. "If all you wanted to do was thank the Greenbury Police Department, you could have just sent a bottle of wine."

"Of course there's more to it." Beckwith sighed. "As I was pointing out to Captain Radar, further investigation into the current cases of Angeline Moreau and John

Latham might compromise some very long and hard government negotiations. We are asking Greenbury and Summer Village to consider the consequences."

"Consequences of solving two brutal murders?" Oliver asked.

"Of ruining delicate matters that have been going on for years."

"How can we consider anything when we don't know what you're referring to?"

"It's a government matter and that's all you have to know," said Agent Brunette.

Whether he was Grimm or Marcus, Rina didn't know or didn't care. She said, "The problem is, sir, we already know a great deal. And when there are holes, people fill them in, often with erroneous material. It's in your interest to correct any misconceptions."

Decker said, "She's absolutely right. Why pretend that the two murders are just going to disappear. It doesn't work that way. If you want help, we need answers—"

"Decker—" Radar said.

"Two people were slaughtered. My wife and I were shot at in my own bedroom. McAdams was injured; he's on crutches for God's sake. We deserve to know what's going on."

McAdams gave Decker a thumbs-up.

When Kosovsky talked, he had a condescending smile on his face. "It is terrible, what happened to you."

"Not as bad as what happened to Angeline Moreau or John Latham," Decker said.

Mayor Brettly's eyes beseeched Radar, who pretended not to see.

Mulrooney said, "You just can't call off this many people on two brutal murder cases without some explanation. I got my own men to consider."

"It is terrible," Kosovsky said again. "These brutal murders."

A slight smile on his face? Maybe Rina was imagining it. While Rina was pretty certain that Kosovsky wasn't the hit man, he seemed like the perfect candidate to order a massacre. Something cold and evil in his eyes. She said, "They were terrible murders."

Kosovsky said, "Yes, of course. But I can assure you that there wasn't any official government inwolwement in them."

Decker said, "It warms my heart that the United States and Russia weren't behind trying to assassinate my wife and me, but that begs the question of what happened."

Kosovsky sipped his tea. "Rogue agents are big problems, Meester Decker. Just ask your friends from your CIA."

"Who's the rogue agent?"

"Names are irrelewant. But the rogue has been dealt with, saving your gowernment a lengthy trial and many tax dollars. So for you, it is done. There is no one to hunt down because we have already done it."

"How do I explain that to Angeline's parents?"

"You tell them it is done," Kosovsky said. "It is a big shame about the young girl, but when you play with fire, you get the burn. To tell them about their daughter, they will find out about her inwolwement in unpleasant business. Perhaps it would be better to tell them what they want to hear rather than the truth."

No one spoke.

Kosovsky said, "Assure the girl's parents that her killer has been punished."

"Without prejudice," Decker said.

"Excuse me?"

"Just an old army term. While I'm assuring Angeline Moreau's parents that the rogue has been taken care of, what do I say to Detective McAdams who was shot three times?"

Kosovsky turned to McAdams. "My sincere apologies, Meester McAdams. If you are ewer in Moscow, I would be honored to host you . . . show you around my city."

"Thank you." McAdams raised an eyebrow.

"I think we're done here," said Agent Blond.

"Not by a long shot," Decker said. The room went quiet for a moment. "Let me take you on a theoretical walk and you can tell me how theoretical the walk actually is."

Silence.

"Go on," Kosovsky said.

"We know that the codebook was found in John Latham's apartment hidden in an out of the way place, but recovered brilliantly by my colleague, Detective Mulrooney. We also know that someone was desperately looking for it—in Latham's apartment and in Angeline's apartment because both places were tossed. I believe that Viktor Gerrard—who is missing—is our key player. He was born in East Germany and spoke Russian as well as German. He was also an art dealer working in a gallery that specialized in Russian art. I suspect that Viktor had a bad case of sticky fingers."

"I don't understand sticky fingers," Kosovsky said.

"He was a thief."

"Ah . . . go on."

Decker said, "Maybe Gerrard was the rogue agent you're referring to. Or maybe he's just a rogue, period. Whoever he really was, Gerrard had contacts in Russia, including you, Mr. Kosovsky. Could be he was trying to buy something from you. More likely, he was trying to *sell* you something. Because like Latham, Gerrard probably had a side business in stolen goods. I believe he accidentally came across the codebook in a client's house in Russia and he knew he had found something big. So he decided to take it back to America. How am I doing so far?"

"I hold judgment," the Russian said.

"Always a good thing to be open-minded," Oliver said.

Decker held back a smile. "The problem was that Gerrard couldn't break the code. So he enlisted help. Enter John Latham who was clever enough to figure out enough of the code and realize what he was dealing with. But instead of cluing Viktor in on what he had, he embarked upon his own blackmail scheme against you, Mr. Kosovsky." Decker turned to Beckwith. "And possibly against you."

"Me?" Beckwith's cheeks had pinkened. "What do I have to do with any of this?"

"Obviously something because you're here," Rina said.

Smiling, Decker wagged a finger at her. "I have no idea what's in the codebook other than meaningless foreign words that transliterated into cliché Latin phrases. But . . . I suspect it was all about art negotiations between the U.S. and Russia. For the last six years, Mr. Beckwith has been trying to curate the foremost traveling exhibit of art by Leonardo Da Vinci. Because Da Vincis are so few and far between and so rare and priceless, they never travel. What's the payoff for you, Mr. Beckwith, if you succeed in this coup? You not only get a pat on the back, you probably get a percentage of the exhibit ticket price, which, if you could pull it off, could amount to a fortune. But there was a chink along the way. No one is lending the United States valuable art, especially Russia, because the Russian government is involved in a messy lawsuit with Chabad where the U.S. judge has already sided with the Jewish organization. So you, Mr. Beckwith, were stuck, unless you had something remarkable to give Russia in return for the loan of a Da Vinci. How am I doing so far, Mr. Beckwith?"

Silence. Then Beckwith said, "For the record, we refer to the paintings as Leonardos."

"I stand corrected."

Kosovsky said, "And what does that haff to do with me, I wonder?"

"You, Mr. Kosovsky, were negotiating with the Hermitage to get one of their two Da Vin—excuse me—Leonardos. What are the titles, Tyler?"

McAdams had them in his notes. "*Madonna Litta* and *Madonna Benois*."

"Thank you," Decker said. "But you knew, Mr. Kosovsky, that the Hermitage would never, ever release such masterpieces unless the government got a truly one-of-a-kind in return."

"Which would be?"

"I'll get to that," Decker said. "The point is you had negotiating powers, but Latham was getting in the way. So someone told Viktor Gerrard to solve the problem. I can't swear to it but I suspect that someone in this room knew that Latham and Gerrard were in cahoots. What I suspect is that Gerrard was scared enough of you, Mr. Kosovsky, to solve any problem you might have. Angeline was a by-product because she had gotten too close to John Latham and no one knew exactly how much Latham told her."

"Your theories are very interesting, I must admit," Kosovsky said. "But alas . . ." He threw up his hands. "They are just theories."

"You're right," Decker said. "But given enough time, I know I could substantiate them. Not that it would matter to you, Mr. Kosovsky, but it might matter to those of us here who reside in America."

The lieutenant governor finally piped up. "Detective Decker, the perpetrator of these horrible murders is not in the country. And as Mr. Kosovsky has pointed out, he has been dealt with. It's not in anyone's interest to continue on."

"You mean it's not in the interest of New York to continue because the first museum to get a Leonardo exhibit would be the Met. And that would be quite a coup for you, wouldn't it?"

"Decker, what's the point?" Radar said. "It's over. You're not going to get anyone's cooperation. So unless you want to go rogue, just put a fork in it."

"He's not going rogue," Rina said.

"Ah, the little lady seems to have a grasp on the situation," Kosovsky said.

Decker started to boil, but Rina held him back with the palm of her hand. "I can't control what my husband might do. What woman can? But maybe if you do me a favor, Mr. Kosovsky, I'm betting that Detective Decker might think twice before going to the press."

"That wouldn't be wise," said Agent Blond.

Decker said, "I'm not wise, sir, just practical. And I'm not asking for money or anything illegal, God forbid."

"Ho-kay," Kosovsky said. "Let us hear what the little lady wants."

"It is always wise to let the little lady speak," Rina said. "I do believe that my husband is right. That you, Mr. Beckwith, must have some great bargaining tool that Russia really wants."

"And what might that be?"

"Maybe like . . . the original Amber Room. That's what Detective Decker and Detective McAdams have thought all along."

Kosovsky tried to hide it, but he looked stunned. When no one answered, she said, "Well, maybe not all twenty-seven cartons. Maybe just a couple of them were magically 'found' in America in some unknown warehouse." Rina made quotes with her fingers. "And as a gesture of goodwill, perhaps the U.S. government has agreed to return a carton or two to Russia in exchange for the willingness of the Hermitage to loan out a Da Vi . . . a Leonardo."

The room was absolutely silent.

"But that's just a theory," Rina said.

Beckwith spoke first. "Mrs. Decker, you can hardly compare the value of a Leonardo with a box of amber from the original Amber Room."

"Of course there is no comparison in rarity and value. Any Leonardo is priceless and even amber from the original Amber Room isn't anywhere in that league. But I happen to know that your fearless leader, Mr. Kosovsky, was once the deputy mayor of St. Petersburg. To bring home part of a historical treasure would no doubt endear him to his people. The PR would be enormous."

"You have still not told us what you want," Kosovsky said.

"I'm getting to that," Rina said. "The Marylebone Police have been working on a case of missing icons by the famous Russian artist Nikolai Petroshkovich. They were taken from the local church. It would be nice if they could be recovered before the poor detectives passed. They're elderly and it would be grand to give them some closure."

Kosovsky was stoic.

"Perhaps you know what I'm talking about?" Rina asked.

"Perhaps."

"And perhaps you can help?"

"Perhaps . . . with one."

"Or two."

Kosovsky's eyes narrowed. "At the most."

"That would be lovely."

446

Kosovsky looked at his Rolex. "I have a plane—"

"I'm not done." Rina smiled. "Just another minute, please."

"What now?"

It came out with anger. Rina spoke quickly. "The Russian Library still holds a vast amount of books and papers from Rav Schneerson's collection. And while I know that your fearless leader has given the Jewish Museum around five hundred books and articles, there are still many items in dispute. Perhaps you can arrange for another batch of items from the collection to be donated to the Jewish Museum or to the Museum of Tolerance. Think of all the wonderful PR it would generate, Mr. Kosovsky."

Again, the room went quiet. Rina simply waited him out.

"I can do my best, but that is all I can do," Kosovsky said. "I am not the fearless leader as you call him."

"I'm sure your best is better than almost anyone, Mr. Kosovsky."

"You are a clever woman, Madame Decker. I admire that."

"Thank you, Mr. Kosovsky." Rina turned to the CIA agents. "Now you are done."

The Russian stood up. "I extend the same invitation to you, Madame Decker, and your husband that I do to Detective McAdams. If you ever find yourself in Moscow, please allow me to host you. I think you would learn a lot about Russia from me."

"I'm sure that would be true." A small arch of her eyebrow. "Thank you very much for the invitation."

The Russian again looked at his gold Rolex. "As I said, I do have a plane to catch. Good day."

As he headed for the door, Beckwith followed without a word. With Beckwith and Kosovsky on their ways, the lieutenant governor got up. He thanked Rina and then he hurried to catch up. The CIA agents and Mayor Brettly tailed him at a brisk pace.

As soon as they were all gone, Mordechai Gold said, "Check your place for bugs and not of the insect kind."

"That fast?" Rina said.

"Your house, your cars, your phones, laptops, tablets, ovens, dishwashers, refrigerator . . . and your Jacuzzi." Gold smiled. "I used to sweep my house and office every few months after I left the CIA. I found bugs all the time. In the last ten years, they've given up although I'm sure that will change after this afternoon."

"How close were we in our theories, Professor?" Decker asked.

"That Kosovsky was willing to negotiate with you should tell you how close you were." Gold smiled. "Please feel free to call me if you're concerned about anything. I know these guys and they can be a bit intimidating." He looked at Rina. "For most people, that is."

"Never let them see you sweat," Rina said.

Gold smiled. "I do have to get back to school. Stop by if you're ever in Cambridge. I'll show you around."

"That's an offer I can take you up on," Rina said. "I don't see Russia in my future."

"No, that trip has been deleted from the bucket list," Decker said.

"Glad I saw it when I did," McAdams said.

"I couldn't afford it anyway," Mulrooney added.

"You and me both," Radar said. "Besides I don't see a lot of vacation time in my future. Brettly's pissed."

"Sorry about that," Decker said.

"Screw him. You, Oliver, McAdams, and Mulrooney did good." A pause. "Not as good as Mrs. Decker I have to say."

"I blush," Rina said.

Decker shook his head. "I have to call Angeline's parents." To Mulrooney, he said, "You'll take care of Latham's parents?"

"Of course. The news won't make any of them whole again, but at least we can say the guy was . . . dealt with. Maybe it is better . . . sparing everyone an emotional trial where bad things can come out."

"Pleasure working with you, Chris."

"Same here, Pete." He smiled at Rina. "Nice meeting you, Mrs. Decker."

"You're earned the right to call me Rina."

"Thank you." Mulrooney waved and left.

With the locals remaining behind, Rina said, "How come it feels like midnight when it's only five o'clock?"

"Did you know about the Amber Room or was that just a lucky guess?" Radar asked.

"I did happen to know that the fearless leader was the deputy mayor of St. Petersburg. So since I couldn't think of anything else, I went with what Peter and Tyler have always said." Rina picked up the kettle. "Tea, anyone?"

"Are you sure Kosovsky didn't slip a Mickey in it?" Decker asked.

Rina laughed. But then she looked inside. "I don't see any powder or anything." She felt the pot. "It's a little cold. Maybe I'll just put a fresh kettle on—after I wash it out with soap and water . . . very, very hot water."

Decker said, "Throw it away, Rina."

"It's pure copper."

"I'll get you another pure copper kettle. For your contribution to the mess, it probably should be gold plated . . . and studded with diamonds."

"A copper pot is fine," Rina said. "No diamonds necessary unless you want to take a trip to Maxwell Stewart's gallery."

449

Oliver said, "This is gonna cost you, Deck."

"Big time," McAdams said.

Decker said, "Do you think Maxwell Stewart will give me a discount?"

"After what happened, I think he'd do just about anything to get rid of all of us," Rina said. "That is only if you're inclined to prey on the weak, God forbid."

CHAPTER THIRTY-EIGHT

Winter snows melted into a very wet spring, flooding streets and highways. But that was okay with Decker. He and Rina decided to stay put for a while. By the time June rolled around, Greenbury had turned positively bucolic: sylvan woods and clean air filled with warm days, and balmy nights hosting twinkling stars and darting fireflies. There were free concerts and community fairs almost every weekend, the events held in the numerous park grounds that surrounded the town. The Fourth of July fireworks were particularly spectacular. The local theater was gearing up for another season, the performers cast with summer stock from the local colleges and even some New York stage actors in the mood for a change of scenery.

As the weather turned mild, Decker and Rina ventured out again, taking road trips to visit the children and the grandchildren, enjoying their time alone in the car as much as their time with their large family. They took up Professor Gold's offer to visit Cambridge and Harvard University. They ended their day in Boston with drinks in Summer Village at Chris Mulrooney's favorite bar.

Chase Goddard continued his antique store up in Boston

and with the influx of summer tourists enjoying New England, Decker supposed he was doing fine. Jason Merritt's gallery certainly did a brisk business especially with the return of two Petroshkovich icons. It was a great day of celebration for Marylebone, Rhode Island, and a great day for Allan Sugar and his partner, Douglas Arrenz. There were some murmurings of more of the Schneerson documents coming to the United States, but nothing had materialized so far. And there were no news items or articles about any traveling Leonardos, same with the Amber Room.

But these kinds of sensitive negotiations took time.

On midsummer's day, Decker followed Gold's advice and swept the house for hidden bugs. There were three of them—one in his car, one in the dishwasher, and one in the bedroom. At first Decker was incensed at the invasion of privacy. After cooler minds prevailed, he found humor in it. Maybe the recipients on the other end would learn a thing or two from them.

He still thought about the case, mostly when he was relaxed and alone. He knew things were irrevocably changed for Angeline's parents and for the Lathams. But thirty years of police work had taught him to compartmentalize in order to stay sane.

With the dog days of summer passing quickly, McAdams began folding up shop. By mid-August, he was ready to roll. His injuries had healed and he felt better than ever, spending more time in the local gym. He still retained his Upper East Side superior attitude, but it was tempered with humor. The week before he started law school, he decided to go to the Hamptons to visit his father and mother—separate houses—for a few days.

On McAdams's last day in Greenbury, he went to say good-bye to the Deckers. It was on a Saturday afternoon and the Loo and his wife were in the backyard on the patio, lazing in a couple of lounge chairs. Decker was in shorts and a T-shirt, Rina was in a polo shirt and a denim skort with her hair tied up and covered with a kerchief. On the tabletop were lemonade and beer, potato chips and crackers, and of course, Rina's homemade cookies. McAdams pulled up a chair, popped a cold one, and nibbled on a cracker.

Decker was swigging from a longneck. "Are you sure you don't want to wait until tomorrow? We'd be happy to drive you down . . . we just can't do it on Shabbos."

"No, I think I'd rather take the train," McAdams said. "Unless you want to visit the Hamptons. But it comes with my crazy relatives."

Rina said, "I like Nina."

"She's in Florence, Italy, for the summer."

"Well, then I'll pass." Rina took a potato chip. "Are you excited about law school, Tyler?"

"I am resigned about law school."

"It won't be so bad."

"I'm sure it'll be better than getting shot."

Decker said, "You'll sail through it, Harvard."

"I'm not worried . . . more like annoyed. But there are worse positions to be in. So I won't complain . . . unless I feel like it . . . which is often." He turned to Decker. "How happy will you be not to hear my bitching?"

"Very happy."

"You'll miss him," Rina said.

"No, I won't," Decker said. "But I might miss your iPad."

"I'll send you one."

"It's not the iPad, it's the brain," Rina said.

"I will concede that you had promise," Decker said. "But it would probably all go to waste anyway. Not much has happened in the last four months other than a lot of drunk and disorderlies around graduation time."

453

"And the OD at Kennedy's Pub," Rina said. "That was pretty exciting."

"Not so much," McAdams said. "The kid made it."

Rina laughed. "You're terrible."

McAdams smiled. He set the empty beer bottle down on the tabletop. "I spoke to Radar this morning. He said I can come back anytime. Unusually nice of him. Maybe he's hoping for a donation."

"Maybe he means it as a sincere offer," Rina said.

"Technically I do have summers off."

"Even cops go on vacation and you know the ropes," Decker said. "Not a bad idea."

"You think?"

"It's easier than training a temp, although you'll have to bone up on your shooting skills. I'm not working with anyone who can't use a firearm."

"That can be arranged," McAdams said.

"What do you mean technically you have summers off?"

"Summer is traditionally the time where lawyers-to-be grab coveted legal internships. So being the contrarian that I am, I'm figuring that while most of my classmates will be slaving away with long hours and great food allowances at white shoe firms, I'd like to be back here in Greenbury, rescuing cats from trees, bitching about mankind's stupidity, and working on my screenplay."

"You're like shingles," Decker said. "I can't get rid of you."

"There is a vaccine for that," McAdams said. "But you've got to be old to take it."

Decker threw a potato chip at him. "So I'll see you next summer?"

"That would be a definite yes."

"About your screenplay, Tyler," Rina said. "What about making the protagonist a woman?"

"It's a possibility. I do have some good role models for it. But I don't think I could write it as good as the real thing."

Rina grinned. "So make it a man. You've got a lot to choose from there."

"I do."

"What's that I hear?" Decker cupped his ear. "Is that Hollywood calling your name?"

Tyler laughed. "I don't know about that. But you know what they say. Write what you know. And I know some pretty gutsy people." He stood up and grabbed a handful of cookies. "For the train."

"Help yourself," Rina said.

Decker stood up. "I'll walk you out."

"Stay where you are, Old Man," McAdams said. "I can see myself out." He hugged them both. "Thanks."

"For getting you shot? You're welcome."

"No, I could have done without that. But at least I'm walking on my own two feet. More than that, Old Man, thanks to you, I've learned how to stand on my own two feet." A genuine smile crinkled the corners of his hazel green eyes. "I'll see you and the rest of Greenbury's finest next summer and that's a promise."

After he left, Decker sat back down and took a swig from the long neck. "I think I'll miss him . . . maybe."

"You'll miss him. Admit it."

He thought a long, long time about that. Then he turned to Rina and smiled. "Maybe."